"...a marvelous seam of gold...the Epoch of decline..." Isabelle Allende

✱   ✱   ✱

✱   ✱   ✱

Spectacular. The next great American novel! —Ivor Thompson: The New York Review

Few novels have such breadth of scope and quality of detail. Pastore is a great author of the first magnitude —Charles Hymes: New York

I think good books can be slotted, characterized, explained; great books often cannot. I believe Stephen R. Pastore's novel Guilt is a very great book. I believe it breathes new life into the historical fiction genre, the borrowing-a-character-from-the-deep-past phenomenon, the old I-shall-tell-you-a-story-through-letters tradition. I believe it honors the best of the imagination. I give it a hero's welcome. Clarity of vision, fine, meticulous pros, the unexpected historical detail, a life-sized protagonist caught inside an unimaginably huge history. Guilt shows the same seamless marriage of research and imagination. Pastore's version of the human condition is both harrowing and moving. Guilt is an altogether successful book, casting a spell that lasts much longer than the reading of it. —Magdalene Albright: Washington Bookman

GUI∤T

A NOVEL

by

STEPHEN R. PASTORE

Cohort Press
New York

Cohort Press
420 East 64th Street W9H
New York, NY 10019

ISBN 978-0977719655

Library of Congress Cataloging-in-Publication Data
Pastore, Stephen R.
    GUILT/ Stephen R. Pastore
        p.   cm.

First Edition

For Heather

The author would like to acknowledge the invaluable help of Ryan C. Thomas, Arthur Walsh, Glenna Suits and Steve Porpora. And a special thanks to Karen and Albert Silvestri for their love and support. And to Dr. Octavius J. Pastore, for his erudite encouragement

Guilt: a Novel

We are all of us a little bit guilty——

Albert Camus

One

My father having attained the venerable age of ninety-four years had outlived three of his four children and his wife of seventy-four years. He had spoken often of his honeymoon in Italy and in particular of his and my mother's visit to the Villa Franca, a taciturn medieval monastery hatched in one of the innumerable niches in the Apennine Mountains, two hours by automobile north of Rome. The Apennines, he said, were like the vertebral column of some titan of the pre-classical age that had died when Italy was the home of dinosaurs and that time and wind and rain had uncovered. This chain of bone ran much of the length of the Italian peninsula. On his deathbed, not three weeks from his ninety-fourth birthday, he told me a part of the story of his visit to Villa Franca, he had not divulged to anyone, except my beloved mother, his much-cherished wife. The two of them visiting the Villa, which had been turned into a sort of museum, had wandered off the proscribed route for tourists and found themselves in a dusty bedroom that looked like it had not been occupied since the Quatrocento. The dust was so thick and the mouse and rat droppings so profuse that the room resembled the remains of the outlying abodes near Vesuvius that received only a smattering of the ash that had immolated poor Herculaneum and Pompeii. Ever the rascal in trying to impress his wife of only two weeks with his audacity, my father opened a single drawer of a bureau plat that nestled cozily in a niche which surrounded a picture window that overlooked the stone walls and skeletal remains of a once abundant vineyard.

He had been an orphan there from birth to the age of five when the monastery was converted to an orphanage for boys. He had no memory of the place except vague ones, as you might expect, which he often confused with dreams, the blurring of fantasy and reality indecipherable. He was fortunate enough to be adopted by an American couple visiting Rome who were looking for a "cute Italian baby boy to call their own" and he was selected. He never learned his true name nor the whereabouts of his birth mother. But, his adoptive parents were loving and kind and he put any notions of discovering his true identity in a box along with other vestigial remnants of his youth such as an old teddy bear and his first book. But he did know the story of his adoption from the orphanage of St. Ubaldo, now called the Villa Franca. His past called to him often like a siren to Odysseus.

In the drawer, there were a few scraps of desiccated paper and a beautiful fountain pen with a coat of arms engraved on its thick barrel. This, in a fit of larcenous courage, he placed in his pocket as a memento of his visit and of his hormonal rush to prove his manhood to my easily impressed mother.

He told me the tale within a scant three hours of his last breath and bid me retrieve the pen from the armoire in his bedroom, an imposing Victorian mass of wooden scrolls and gargoyle heads. I did as I was told, and he informed me that in addition to being the sole heir of his modest estate, I should treasure the pen as a symbol of his long life with my dear mother and, further, that if I were so inclined, that I should write his eulogy with it being certain it was neither too long that the mourners might get bored or too short that they might think his life unimportant.

That night after my tears of remorse had dried, I sat down with the pen at my dining room table and began to write my father's eulogy. The pen, mysteriously full of ink, became warm in my hand and sought the pad of paper beneath it as a man dying of thirst might dive headlong into a murky pond in the desert not knowing whether the water was pure or fetid. The pen possessed me fourteen hours a day for many weeks. The following story is what emerged from its golden nib.

Two

2 The Villa Franca was neither a villa in the strictest sense of the word, it was really a late medieval castle turned into a monastery that was eventually deserted by the church under suspicious circumstances, nor was it French, as it was located high in the Apennines in Italy and purchased in 1888 or ë89 by an Englishman who claimed to be a Duke and the second cousin of King Emmanuel himself. Even on the brightest days the Villa Franca sat like a huge loaf of gray moldering bread at the end of a long serpentine road overgrown with wind-twisted cypress trees that shut out all daylight as if they were the infinitely fringed hands of a mythological Hindu serpent that slithered its way up the mountain road. The road itself, built in Roman times, was deeply rutted and but six feet wide often getting so close to the precipitous edges of the rock-filled canyons on both its sides that drivers and passengers alike looking out the windows of their rambling conveyances felt that they were airborne on the edge of a limitless abyss.

The building itself was three stories high and from the air, had anyone flown over it, appeared to be a large, thick, orange-tiled H. It seemed windowless at first but upon closer inspection one might notice narrow slits here and there as in medieval fortresses used by archers to peep out and fire their arrows at invading interlopers. Indeed, the light let in by these tall, thin apertures when the sun was low in the winter sky looked like slash marks on the gray oaken floors, the surrounding gloom all the denser by comparison to the concentrated white light piercing through.

There were large cisterns at the corners of the structure that collected rain water from the vast roof and even after a dry spell, the dripping noise of residual moisture magnified by the large cisterns sounded like the spirits of dead workers that constructed the building who had been buried within its walls. A monk in the building's day as a monastery said the dripping sounded like rats swimming in the darkness after having fallen in, thinking the rain sluices were cozy and protective burrows.

Duke Phillip Montrose, if that was his real name, purchased the Villa Franca as a winter house. Like most Englishmen, he adored Italy or at least the idea of Italy with its sun-drenched lushness, its unprepossessive people and its low prices. It was a Briton's dream mainly because it was everything England was not. He had arrived with his beautiful wife, twenty-five years his junior, and two bright-eyed daughters aged six and seven who had already adopted their mother's haughty ways and overly-mannered British disposition. In a matter of months, extensive renovations were underway to bring the thirteenth century castle into the late nineteenth century. Ancient and moth-eaten tapestries were torn down, stiff backed chairs and oak-seated settles were consigned to the servants' quarters and ornate and over-upholstered furniture from the far corners of the covetous Victorian British Empire arrived by carts drawn by stout warm-bloods over the difficult ruts of the roadway, sometimes as many as six transports in a day. Indeed, so many draft horses were employed by the impatient Duke that many of the local farms and vineyards allowed a good portion of their crops to be delayed and their harvest ignored to the point of near total loss. Of course, this was not altruism but the craving for British pounds sterling which the rental of pack animals earned. The prospect of the Duke and his glamorous family requiring the services of innumerable maids, butlers, gardeners, gamekeepers and the like to keep the family and the busy idleness of the British nobility was considered a boon to the local economy. Whereas the Villa Franca as a monastery was a constant drain on the poor resources of the local citizenry, the Duke's funds would flow outward as a winter freshet precedes the floods of spring. At least, this was the hope that glistened in the eyes of all the contadinos for miles around.

It was an unfortunate and unforeseen fact that unlike the Duke's lovely home in London, in the evening, after the workers left, the surrounding area went quiet as the tomb. Nightlife and suitable visitors were non-existent and the soirees that filled winter evenings in London and its surrounds with beautiful people in diaphanous gowns and silk-lapelled tuxedos were not to be known in these rural parts. On one memorable evening with an hour or two of daylight still left, the Duke loaded his wife and lovely daughters in a two-horse fly and went down the road toward the town of Saltura.

It must be understood that Saltura was a town only in its narrowest sense. It was a collection of buildings at a crossroad near a navigable river. But its primary purpose was as a market town on Saturday mornings only, and the rest of the week it was simply a way station for the deposit of agricultural items in warehouses to await the barges that floated down the river to Rome. Sundays were commandeered by the church and by 2:00 p.m., the town looked much like one that could be imagined at the height of the Black Death which is to say it was deserted in its entirety and what merchants or laborers lived within its boundaries were safely holed up behind closed shutters enjoying wine, the favors of their wives or in some instances, their neighbors' wives.

Needless to say, the ride of the Duke's family was at best a waste of time. At worst, it caused a major rift between the Duke and his wife when they had the misfortune of passing a pasture where one cow had mounted another in pantomime of the sex act and the farmer and his son were keeping time with claps and raucous laughter.

"Oh look, Mam·, they're playing piggyback," said one daughter as the other stared in amazement.

Their mother pulled them from the window of the carriage and tried her best to cover their innocent eyes.

"Mam·, whatever is the matter?" asked the older daughter.

"Never mind. This is a dreadful place for us. We should return home…and I don't mean the Villa. I mean London."

"Oh come now, my dear," said the Duke in his most patronizing and usually effective tone. ìThis is a land of nature and natural impulses and surely…"

"Enough. We have our home amidst a rural abomination. Why these people barely speak our language and they are peasants, all peasants and I shan't spend another day among them."

"You'll feel better in the morning, my darling. Think of the rain, the sleet and the dreadful damp of London. Would you trade all this for that?" he said, sweeping his arm in a panoramic display of the arid countryside.

"In an instant. If London were in the Arctic Circle I should inhabit a cottage made of ice there before spending another day here."

"Please, not in front of the children, the children..."

"They need to learn that one cannot and will not mingle with these people in this primitive place. I'm sorry I should have spoken sooner but I was hoping against hope that it would be different or perhaps some of our friends would come to visit. But I see now that this is impossible."

It should be said in the Duchess's defense that it was not just the importune sighting of the ridiculous cows. This feeling of agrarian remoteness had burdened her from the first time she and the Duke laid eyes on the monastery. Women often have the notion, among hundreds of others, that a timely concession to their spouse will result in some sort of future benefit without realizing that what might seem a minor surrender today will give birth to a hideous brood of regrets tomorrow. A silent, agreeable woman has an ovary full of future disagreements just waiting to be fertilized by anger and matured into all sorts of domestic disharmony.

As the Duke headed back to the Villa Franca in silence, the sky, which had been rose and purple with the setting sun became overcast and dark with clouds crowding in from the sea and night falling from the east. A heavy rain started and soon the narrow roadway was reduced to twin rain gutters where thousands of carriage wheels had carved two ruts the full length of the road.

Rumors had it that the Duke was quiet but deeply enraged and lashed his horses the way he wanted to lash his wife. In the turmoil of the storm that rapidly intensified and the jittery horses, it was a suicidal certainty that the carriage and its occupants would careen off the road and fall into the boulder-strewn valley beneath. While the wreck was inevitable perhaps, the rumors were, as usual, wrong. In fact, had he been angry and racing home, the history of Villa Franca might have been very different.

The truth is that the Duke was a restrained and loving man who felt it best to deal with his wife's frequent outbursts as a passive force. He was a cliff by the sea and he would permit the salty waves of his wife's emotions to beat themselves out against his craggy but immovable stoniness. Even the most violent storms eventually peter out and calm seas are only so far away as the next sunrise.

The bruised and lumpy sky bled its rain on the Duke and his family and the narrow mountain road. The carriage ambled slowly and carefully home, the Duke reassuring the skittish horses in soft tones that they would soon be safe and dry in the snug stalls of the Villa Franca stable where Arce, the stable boy, would towel them dry and give them clean straw to bed down on.

What the Duke could not have foreseen was that a pack of Apennine wolves was crossing the road just around a blind turn, not five hundred meters from the gates to Villa Franca, in search of deer that dusk and rain would normally force out of the deep woods in search of grazing. The wolves were as startled as the horses by the sudden meeting but the wolves, ever the opportunists, recovered their composure and attacked the horses which reared in a defensive posture and turned abruptly to the left in a vain effort to escape, forgetting that they were tethered to the Duke's carriage. The turning forced the vehicle to topple to the right, the door popping open from the torsion. The Duke's wife and daughters were flung out by the force and slid down the graveled and stony sides of the precipice, stopped only by the rigid branches of thorny barberry hedges that were the only flora to inhabit the inhospitable slopes of the gorge. The Duke meantime, with the reins and whip still in his hands, landed on the roadway as the carriage rolled over on him pinning his torso, head and one leg beneath its weight. With the other leg free he kicked wildly and futilely trying to free himself. He could see out from under the carriage the precarious situation his family was in and called out to them to remain calm and not try to free themselves from the rescuing arms of the barberry hedge.

As he attempted to use the whip handle as a lever of sorts to relieve some of the weight of the carriage off his body, he heard the first shrieks. He turned and saw that the wolves had descended the slopes to where his family lay prostrate on the ground. The wolves, unaccustomed to such creatures circled cautiously. The Duke, in a wild effort to scare them off, yelled at the top of his compressed lungs, but to no avail. In a matter of minutes that seemed like hours, the wolves pounced on the three helpless female forms tearing at their throats and abdomens to a chorus of unimaginable screams from the victims that echoed throughout the canyon. It did not take long for the shouting to cease and for the snarling and growling to take its place. The Duke in a fit of uncontrollable desperation shrieked until his voice rasped like a frog's. A young male wolf, low on the pecking order waiting for his turn to feed, cautiously approached the trapped Duke. Seeing the one outstretched leg, he fell upon it, tearing the Duke's wool trousers, his skin and muscles to the bone. The Duke found refuge in unconsciousness.

The next morning, a team of masons on the way up to renovate the grand hall at Villa Franca found the hideous remains of the tragedy that unfolded ten hours earlier. The Duke, they thought, had had a terrible accident and his leg had been mutilated. He had bled out what appeared to be most of his blood. As they lifted the carriage off his still breathing body, the son of one of the masons saw the carnage only thirty feet away. All that remained of the beautiful wife of Duke Montrose was a pile of bloody clothing. Next to her were two similar small piles that had been shredded and scattered like dolls clothing in a child's playroom. Under one of the barberry hedges was the head of one of the Duke's daughters, its blond curls and blue ribbons plastered in dry blood and sand, one eye open, the other closed in a devilish wink that haunted the masons until their dying days.

The hapless horses were found about a half-mile from the road well into the woods near the western end of the estate. Having freed themselves from the burden of the carriage but still tethered to the reins and each other, they had gotten entangled in a stand of elm saplings. Scratched in a thousand small places, frothing and exhausted from the ordeal and vain effort of untying themselves, they were found by the orchard-master and his son. Their heads were covered with flour sacks and they were led back to the stables. The Duke ordered them both shot and so they were as Arce, the stable boy, wept uncontrollably.

The Duke had been hurried back to the Villa Franca and the doctors were called. It is pointless to discuss what the treatment was but suffice it to say that the Duke recovered his physical health after the amputation of his leg and a local carpenter of some considerable skill fashioned a wooden leg for him modeled after the legs of the marionettes he was famous for crafting for the children of Saltura.

Maria, the housekeeper, sent the stouter-hearted field workers out to collect the remains of the Montrose family. A few hours later they returned with the head, the clothing and three sets of intact intestines, it being common knowledge that no self-respecting predator will devour the fecal entrails of its victims no matter how driven by the blood-lust or hunger. The faces of the men were ashen and one of them had the residue of a vomited breakfast clinging to his scraggly beard. Maria cleaned it off with a damp cloth and bid the men sort the three piles of clothing and remains into three laundry baskets she had placed on the huge kitchen table in anticipation of their return.

Three coffins were fashioned in the town by the local undertaker and the three female members of the Montrose family were buried on the grounds of the Villa Franca high on a wind-swept hill that offered a view of the river to the north and the roof and gardens of the villa to the south. The Duke attended the funeral on a stretcher and only a few of his employees were present along with the local parish priest. It was a bright cold day and while the breeze always blew at the hilltop, that day it seemed to have lost its interest in buffeting tree limbs and tossing peoples' hats.

Whether it was the laudanum, the tragedy or both that worked upon the mind of the Duke, he refused to speak to anyone, sending notes via Maria's eight-year-old son Ernesto, from the guestroom he occupied to various servants. All construction stopped, of course, and if a roof was incomplete or awaiting repair nothing was done and the rain found an unimpeded entrance into the Villa Franca.

Three

3 The Duke sold all his properties in England including all the furniture, pictures, and valuable heirlooms his family had accumulated over the years. He was, by monetary standards, the richest man in the region. He refused visitors no matter who they were and the servants could hear the thunking of his wooden leg at all hours of the day and night as he paced from his bedroom to the former master suite to the children's rooms and back again.

He made it known that there would be a five pound reward for the head of every wolf killed and brought to him. This sum was more than most of the contadinos made in half a year so that virtually every able-bodied man and boy armed with musket, pistol, rifle or bow spent endless hours scouring the surrounding mountains for the lupine trophies the Duke sought in a hollow attempt at revenge. The hunters were instructed to leave the heads, and the heads only, of the slaughtered wolves on the lawn outside and just below the Duke's window. In a few months' time, there were hundreds of skulls in varying degrees of decay lined up like fieldstones being readied for the erection of a wall. Flies and maggots swarmed but the Duke forbade any interference with their work at devouring the flesh of the wolves' heads. Eventually, there was not a wolf to be found for miles around and several townspeople had notified the local police chief that their shepherd dogs and Alsatians had gone missing. In any event, within a year, no more trophies appeared on the Duke's lawn and the empty eye sockets of nearly a thousand animals looked up blankly into the chaste sky over the Villa Franca.

Maria's sixteen-year-old daughter, Costanza, was the only servant permitted to bring the Duke his meals and while he ate she read him in her native tongue the finest works of Dante, Boccaccio and some crude translations of Shakespeare. For meals, he refused anything fancy or over-prepared and subsisted on polenta, pork and zucchini all done simply by cooking with little or no seasoning. When Costanza was not reading to him he would sleep or wander the second storey bedrooms.

After the first year of his confinement, packages started arriving at the Villa Franca, some in wooden crates, some in brown paper boxes securely tied and addressed to the Duke with return addresses of various people or companies mostly from Eastern Europe, particularly Hungary, Poland and White Russia. The Duke ordered these brought to the grand hall and at night, after everyone had gone to sleep, he would hobble down the huge stairway and stay in the grand hall into the small hours of the morning. When Maria arrived to start the house up, there would be a pile of empty boxes, string and wrapping paper strewn outside its locked doors.

For several years this went on until one day when Maria arrived, there was no rubbish and the doors had been left wide open. Inside, she found an astonishing sight, one that left her dumbstruck and terrified but one she could not help but look upon.

On every shelf, sideboard, table and flat surface were jars, cylindrical and rectangular, containing specimens in formaldehyde. Human embryos at every stage of development of all races, stillborn infants with grotesque deformities, Siamese twins, fish, snakes and embryonic mammals with two heads, no heads, odd numbers of limbs, no limbs, birds without eyes, cats without mouths, monkeys half covered in fur and half naked with pink humanoid skin.

Maria threw her apron over her face and ran from the room screaming, slamming the doors behind her. For the first time in three years, she heard the Duke's voice from the second story in a bellowing echoing laugh. Needless to say, the terrified housekeeper, the Duke's most loyal servant, resigned that very day and vowed never to return. But fate has a way of proving that vows are made to be broken and within a month and a half she returned, informing the Duke that her daughter Costanza was pregnant with his child. Not only did he not deny it as she or anyone else would have expected, but he offered to rehire Maria at twice her former salary and he insisted that Costanza move into the house with her mother or, at the very least, to occupy the vacated chauffeur's quarters just off the rear garden. Maria and her daughter agreed to this and with Ernesto in tow they moved into the small stone cottage a mere twenty meters from the Duke's main residence.

In time, Costanza went into labor and the doctor was called. By the time he arrived, however, she was shouting obscenities and cursing every saint known to the Catholic calendar and a few no one had ever heard of. It was a breach birth with the feet protruding from her birth canal and it took four hours for her son to be born. That night, while the babe suckled at his mother's breast, Costanza died from internal hemorrhaging.

The Duke retained the services of a wet nurse, immediately discharged Maria and Ernesto and within a few days, had his lawyers publish papers as was required in those times, claiming his fatherhood and announcing that the name of his son was Edmond Montrose.

One might expect that the Duke would shower young Edmond from the reserves of love that he had been unable to give his dead wife and daughters. But one's expectations rarely if ever coincide with reality. The Duke provided a surrogate mother in the form of a nanny that was hired from an agency in France, one Mademoiselle Montesquieu. She was full-figured, about forty years of age and had a back as straight as the handle of a pick-axe.

As Edmond grew, the third story of Villa Franca was renovated to provide him with a bedroom, playroom and classroom along with a large cast-iron bathtub with a newly invented water heater. Tutors for music, art and science were brought in and Edmond was schooled in all the classic disciplines. On Friday evenings he was permitted to push his father around the circular drive of Villa Franca in his wheelchair in exchange for which the Duke questioned him about the topics of his week's studies.

The boy was served all three daily meals in his quarters and a doctor from the town was brought in for annual physicals. If he became sick, he was nursed back to health. He was exercised by a local soccer player and was taught to ride by Arce, but he was never permitted to leave the confines of the tall wrought-iron fence surrounding the front garden and drive nor the brick wall of the rear garden except to ride his pony in the paddock the Duke had built for him at the foot of the hill above which the Montrose family plot lay, as most graves, naked to the weather.

After a time, on Saturday evenings, Edmond would perch in one of the many attic storeroom windows and watch the arrival of guests that the Duke had invited from Rome, Milan, Venice and other towns and cities from all over Italy. One particular Saturday, Edmond counted two hundred guests, the driveway and road a veritable cavalcade of horses, carriages and automobiles.

He thought it quite grand that his father the Duke had begun to come out of the shadows of the tragedy he had heard the servants whisper about. Music and laughter drifted out from the grand hall and wafted up through the floor and open windows to Edmond's quarters where he lay in bed with his eyes closed imagining gentlemen and ladies dancing endlessly to Viennese waltzes and the latest rondos from Paris.

The truth was quite different from the boy's dreams and it should surprise no one that if one thing is a certainty for a young boy or girl, dreams tend to remain dreams and the reality of adulthood is but an endless road to those dreams which never materialize except in sleep or insanity. In fact, the Duke had turned the grand hall of Villa Franca into a sort of brothel where women of all ages and young men were at the disposal of the guests. His collection of grotesqueries were lit from behind with large candles casting the revelers is a murky yellow and shadowy glow. The Duke particularly enjoyed having women present who were deformed in some fashion with limbs amputated, some lacking their wits, some blind, some deaf, some both blind and deaf, some Asian, some black, some from the Indian subcontinent. Wine flowed like water, as they say, as the debaucheries slithered through the night into the early hours of the next day when, by noon, the last of the guests were transported by their sleepy chauffeurs down the narrow road to Saltura and beyond.

Four

In January of 1920 it all ended when Edmond was sixteen years old. Mademoiselle Montesquieu walked calmly into Edmond's room when he was studying astronomy and, in a calm tone, as if asking what he wanted for lunch, told him his father the Duke was dead, apparently from a heart attack.

The Duke, marionette leg and all, was buried on the hilltop with the other Montrose family members and, as per his instructions in his will, had neither guests nor clergy. The gardeners dug his grave and placed the oak coffin in it as if they were planting a tree with a large root ball. Not a prayer or farewell was said. In the will, the Duke left everything to Edmond who now inherited the title of Duke Montrose. There was one proviso, however. Edmond had only a life estate in the Villa Franca and all his father's considerable wealth. He would not get full ownership unless and until Edmond became a physician, in no event later than his thirtieth birthday. Failing that, the estate was to revert to the Duke's cousin Mortimer, a fop residing in Dorchester, Dorset.

One might hypothesize that once Edmond did in fact become a physician, thus satisfying the condition of his father's will, that upon obtaining all the Duke's wealth, he could simply abandon the notion of an actual medical practice. The Duke knew his son much better than you do, for he had observed the boy at play and at his studies. He carefully remarked to himself the look of total absorption upon Edmond's face as he collected his stamps, then his coins, then his butterflies, then his rare books. Indeed, Edmond had a streak of obsession far wider than the narrow roadway to Villa Franca, wider even than Hitler's new autobahn and it ran through his very soul. The Duke would watch from his window as Edmond carefully examined the carcass of a dead squirrel, or hedgehog or fox that the Duke had furtively placed in the rear garden the night before. Edmond inquisitively searched the innards of the dead animals to discover just what made them "tick." Yes, the Duke thought over the course of a decade, once this boy has opened the ribcage of a cadaver in the school of medicine in Bologna, he will be hooked.

What our Duke did not realize was that while the mind of a child is like a sponge, his heart is like a well. Deep waters run there, born in underground aquifers, cold and pure. But a well without a drinker soon becomes polluted with unresolved desires, wild fantasies and subterranean urges that seep up from some dark place in the earth.

The whole time the Duke had been alive, no one ever saw him touch Edmond or Edmond touch him, neither hugs, nor caresses, nor handshakes, nor slaps. One must also remember that Edmond lost his mother at birth and that only the rarest of wet nurses or maids could even approximate a mother's touch and none of these were employed at the Villa Franca. While young Edmond craved the physical affection that normal children are nurtured with, he was unaware of its absence as a person blind from birth is unaware of color. Lacking awareness of something, however, does not mean it does not exist.

Around the time of Edmond's twelfth birthday, the chambermaid reported to the Duke that she had noticed the tell-tale signs of staining on Edmond's bed sheets. Mademoiselle Montesquieu was summoned that afternoon and after a brief talk and a small raise in her salary she commenced to read Edmond some bedtime stories. She had not done this since he was six or seven years old but not knowing what normality was, Edmond was never surprised by anything that occurred at Villa Franca.

Mademoiselle Montesquieu's favorite story was the Morte D'Arthur, particularly the part where Launcelot finally beds Guinevere out in the forest by a sylvan brook. In the original perhaps three or four lines are all the author spends on the lovers' passion, but Mademoiselle Montesquieu felt that this needed elaboration. She read, at least from pages in her own repressed mind, how Launcelot's probing fingers found Guinevere's breast, buttocks and secret parts, how she kissed every inch of Launcelot from his lips to his toes and particularly his "staff of manhood," as Mademoiselle called it. Intricate details of their passion filled the darkened bedroom as

Mademoiselle read by the light of a single candle, a task her eyes were certainly not fit for had she actually been reading. At usually the same point each evening in the tale of Lancelot and Guinevere, just as the two are to revel in the elusive lust and joy of mutual orgasm, Mademoiselle with rubber glove on one hand well lubricated with mineral oil or heavy cream as the mood struck her, would stroke Edmond's "staff of manhood," aroused to the breaking point by the salacious rendition of King Arthur's legend and skillfully catch his seed in a dinner napkin she always carried in her pocket. As he afterwards would fall blissfully asleep, she would blow out the candle, silently leave his room, discard the napkin and glove and return triumphantly to her own quarters, exhausted from a job well done. Edmond would dream of Arthur, the Knights of the Round Table and all the damsels they rescued, all, knights and the king included, with bare buttocks, heaving bosoms and buckets of mineral oil and heavy cream everywhere.

Edmond barely noticed that his father was dead and gone, so absorbed was he in the task of being admitted to the University of Bologna, the oldest university in Europe. Bologna was a smattering of a city, provincial in its ethics and morals, devoid of glamour and weary in the way only northern Italian industrial cities can be. But remember that Edmond had never been off the grounds of Villa Franca and even though he could come and go as he wished now, he did not wish it and, if the truth be told (which is all that this tale can tell) he feared whatever lay beyond the confines of the Villa. His imagination, however, soared and Bologna was as a mirage, the heavenly city, paradise on earth not because it was actually so. No, it was any place not the Villa Franca that to Edmond seemed special.

Five

About a week before his eighteenth birthday and two weeks before he was to depart to Bologna, tragedy revisited the Villa Franca. As the story was told and retold among the wagging tongues of the servants to the contadinos of Saltura and the surrounding countryside, a sparrow had flown into Edmond's study on the third floor and it proceeded to defecate on his collection of rare maps and atlases that were carefully arranged for easy perusal on an ornately carved library table in the middle of the room which sat under a large wrought-iron chandelier. The unfortunate bird, perhaps thinking the fixture was a sort of indoor tree, perched on it and let lose its bowels on the treasures below.

Edmond looking up from a book, indicated with a nod to Mademoiselle Montesquieu that the bird needed to be ejected. In anticipation of her shooing the bird out the upper sash of the tall window, she stood up on the ledge and in attempting to push the sash down, she used such force that the entire window along with Mademoiselle Montesquieu emerged from the third story and dropped like a cannonball to the ground below, the window shattering into a million shards of glass and wood fragments and Mademoiselle's head smashing on a large stone statue of a lion. Her skull opened like a melon being slammed by a sledge hammer.

Edmond spent half an hour examining the innards of her head while awaiting the police and the undertaker both of whom arrived after they had finished their noon meal. It was easily determined to be an accidental death and only the carpenter's observation that the windows of Villa Franca were stronger than prison bars made anyone think differently. Quite frankly, though, without a family or friends and only her haughty quiet disposition for company, no one cared to raise these observations to the police and so Mademoiselle Montesquieu's embalmed body was donated to the medical school in Bologna as the first of many gifts that Duke Edmond Montrose would bestow upon his alma mater. The window was quickly replaced and the wayward sparrow allowed to nest in the study on an upper bookshelf, Edmond providing an abundance of seeds and crumbs with instructions that the bird should be maintained after his departure for so long as it lived which by everyone's best recollection was three years.

Edmond purchased a Mercedes-Benz automobile and loaded it with his trunks and some of his favorite books, including the Morte D'Arthur. His chauffeur drove him through the iron gates of the Villa Franca which to Edmond was a more strenuous and emotionally charged event than Caesar crossing the Rubicon with his forbidden legions. A gamekeeper standing by the roadway as the enormous, shiny black automobile made its way down the road spitting gravel and dust in the air like a herd of bulls, reported back to all the staff that he could see tears streaming down Edmond's face. Everyone loved the strange Duke Edmond all the more, if they ever thought of loving him. In fact, Edmond had experienced an attack of anxiety so severe that despite the cool weather and the breeze blowing through the open windows of the car, his face was flushed and sweaty and it was the perspiration not tears that was pouring down his face. Once on the road to Saltura, he had not a single thought of the Villa Franca and if he had searched his mind for a month, he could not have remembered the name of even a single servant.

It would be futile to discuss Edmond's successes at the university where he was virtually every professor's pet and where he threw several lavish parties a year leasing out a posh local bistro for the evening. Whenever classes were out for more than a week, he would travel to all the capitals of Europe and indulge his every whim in multiple doses. Whether in Berlin, Prague, Brussels or Warsaw, he caroused with the best of them, bedding hundreds, all of whom remarked in their diaries if they kept them how this unusual handsome young Duke had made them pretend to be Guinevere or Lancelot and what a romantic at heart they had made passionate love to. Had King Arthur known how his legend would be employed a thousand years later by Duke Edmond Montrose, he likely would never have drawn the sword from the stone and would have spent his days happily in the hairy arms of a scullery maid.

In the summer between his fourth and fifth year of study, Edmond traveled to Vienna in the company of another student, Carmine Corea, a Neapolitan with little polish but a quick mind and an easy purse. The Corea family had made their money exporting cheese and olive oil to America but Carmine, with a full bottle of Chianti in him one day, revealed that the cheese and olive oil were really a front for the heroine trade, his family's warehouses in Sicily and Naples being a collection point between the Middle East and the United States. Edmond was oblivious to the moral implications and simply saw Carmine as a friend and sometime lover that did not need to be supported financially. Carmine, on the other hand, tall with dark southern Italian features, deep-set small eyes and a thick head of ebony black hair, was infatuated with Edmond and followed him like a lap-dog, running errands, arranging liaisons with married women and acting in every way much as a private secretary. In any event, they always occupied separate rooms with the tacit understanding that they would indulge their separate tastes as they saw fit, it being understood that on those occasions when Edmond desired Carmine that he, Edmond, would always have priority.

One evening in the lobby of the Victoire Hotel on the Strasser Taunhausser, the two medical students were exchanging niceties with a number of overly dressed, overly proportioned young ladies from a place called Chicago, noted for its railroads, its slaughter houses and its stench. Edmond, gazing at the pale white abundant bosom of a Miss Nelly Schwartz whose father owned several slaughterhouses, and trying to imagine her rotund features as this evening's Guinevere, caught the eye of a young Viennese woman of statuesque proportions entering the lobby from the street in a blue silk gown, her blond hair tossed by the wind and her maid fussing with her satin shawl and hairbrush. Edmond was stricken as they say and he left Carmine with the two heifers as he called them in his best Italian while he brazenly pursued the lovely Antoinette Von Schiller as he soon learned her name to be.

There was nothing extraordinary to report about the wooing, courtship and seduction of Fraulein Von Schiller and Edmond thought for several days at least that he had found his true love without ever realizing that he might be seeking one out. Antoinette, on the other hand, was impassioned by Edmond who she reluctantly had yielded her virginity to and imagined her life with the young Duke Montrose as an endless round of soirees, trips and indulgences. Within a week or two of his first seduction, Edmond tired of Antoinette whose education consisted mainly of crocheting flowers, small dogs and, in one instance, a large grotesque parrot, upon which she devoted nearly three months of her life. While she was certainly one of the most ornamental creatures he had ever known, her lack of anything interesting or provocative to say left him wanting. One evening, after a particularly strenuous exercise of physical delights, he informed her that large breasts were no long-term substitute for brains nor a perfect rump a replacement for a well-conceived idea. He bid her farewell and she cried herself to sleep.

Edmond returned to Carmine's room, told him to rid himself of the two street urchins he was romping with and they hurriedly left Vienna for a premature return to Bologna. Rumors circulated as far south as Milan that Fraulein Antoinette attempted suicide by jumping off a bridge into a shallow tributary of the Danube but was saved almost immediately by two fishermen in a small rowboat who had stopped under the bridge to eat lunch. The splash she made wearing a bright yellow and gold gown startled them so much they thought it was a heavenly visitation. After the shock wore off, they fished her out and received a suitable reward from her father, Herr Von Schiller, when they brought her to the local hospital soaked and shivering, but very much alive. Her father vowed revenge, but it is well known that Austrians have short memories and after a time Antoinette was happily engaged and then married to the son of a Polish baron, a young man who adored model trains and assumed that the daughter his wife gave birth to, was three months premature. Meanwhile, Edmond vowed to Carmine and the world in the train from Vienna to Milan that he would never love again, a promise that would be easier for him to keep than one might expect.

By the time Duke Edmond reached his twenty-fifth birthday, he was a licensed physician and after contemplating a practice in Venice, after all, even to Edmond, it was the most beautiful city in all the world, he decided on Rome, the center of gravity for everything he thought important in life. He maintained the Villa Franca and visited there often but his large apartment in Rome and his beautiful office near the new Ospedale Nazionale was an ideal combination for him to ascend the social ladder and to hob-nob on intimate terms with the power elite of Italy. Ever on the prowl, it was simply a matter of time until Edmond was one of the most successful doctors in the capital, it being a well-known but unpublished fact that he was the personal physician to Il Duce himself.

Seven

7

Daria Berenson was born in America to parents that had met on one of the numerous ships carrying the hopeful from the Old World to the New. Jan Berenson had arranged to meet his brothers in Boston who had emigrated five years earlier and had established a thriving business in the saloon trade. Jan was the youngest of the four brothers and the expansion of the business finally required his presence, it being axiomatic that only family members could be trusted as business partners. Mildred Bosch was a chambermaid on the ship, young, shapely with a large bosom and a shock of reddish hair that many said could be seen through the thickest fog of the North Atlantic. She had a winning smile of sound peasant teeth—she could and did crush walnuts with them—and enjoyed simple pleasures especially when she did not have to worry about where her next meal was coming from. Some said later that it was fate that brought them together, but the truth is more likely that Jan saw her one evening coming out of his room on board ship after making up the bed. Having had a few scotches and being stoked up by the low-cut bodices of the dancers in the ship's cabaret, it was simply a matter of timing that allowed him to ogle Mildred, her arms full of cleaning supplies, and to convince her that she should help him find something, a cufflink he thought he had dropped in his stateroom.

As seaboard romances are encouraged by the rhythmic beating of the waves upon the hull, the dramatic sunrises and romantic sunsets, the forced mixing of the classes, the inability to escape and limitless alcohol, nature took its course and by the time the ship docked in Boston Harbor, Jan and Mildred were engaged to be married.

Jan's brothers were not particularly approving, but Mildred's female charms worked some magic on them as well and her willingness to serve drinks to avid patrons in one of their saloons convinced them she was an ideal mate for Jan.

Within a year of the marriage, Daria was born. Sadly, she would be the only child the Jan Berensons would have as the difficulty of her birth, exacerbated perhaps by Mildred's love of drinking the products her husband's family sold, made future pregnancies impossible. Meanwhile, as Daria grew up, the Berenson family fortunes grew as well and before long, certainly by her eighteenth birthday, they were one of the richest families in Massachusetts where Jan's older brother, Frederick, had become a U.S. Senator, no mean feat in a state known for the power of the Irish electorate. But few Irishmen could withstand the power of the Berensons' money, nor their influence in getting Irishmen hired to important non-electoral positions in state and municipal governments.

Daria had her father's good looks and her mother's limited view of the universe. She was charming and indulged but could not formulate an original thought nor take a position on any topic excepting the fashion habits of her friends or the moral behavior of men and women in her now very elevated class. In her mother's homeland, southern Germany, she would have been someone's maid or perhaps an assistant cook. In Boston, she was a princess. In either place, she was the same person with the same intellect, emotions and looks but in Boston, she had her father's money and was living proof that notwithstanding the crime, poverty and filth that most American cities were submerged in, hard work, catering to human vice and a lack of scruples could make a princess out of an urchin. While the French are often quoted as saying one cannot make a silk purse out of a sow's ear, Daria was proof that a sow's ear could be transformed not only into a silk purse filled with the hog's money, but a silk dress, satin shoes, an ivory-handled parasol and a shiny Packard automobile with a chauffeur that could service the car, the housekeeper, the mistress of the house and even the princess herself. All of them were dismayed in their own way when the Nordic, blond, blue eyed Lars, only seventeen years of age, a wonderful chauffeur really, had been murdered in an alleyway in a thwarted robbery attempt. This tragic event convinced Daria that her father's insistence that she visit a particular doctor in the south side who could solve her "problem" for two hundred dollars was, under the circumstances, the right thing to do.

Now, before it is too late, it must be revealed that we were all caught up in a lie of sorts and rarely will it be more obvious that lies are often better than the truth than in this instance.

Jan Berenson did have another child, only not with his wife Mildred. Jan had taken up with a beautiful Swedish barmaid who had saved her pennies and made the voyage from Stockholm to Boston some few years after Jan and Mildred arrived. A true daughter of the north, Inga had pure white skin so fine that the thin blue lines of her veins could be seen as if she were made of the finest marble. Her golden hair, when it was not up in a discrete bun, fell the length of her back. Alone in the United States with only her wits and her strong will, she avoided the unfortunate paths that were so treacherous to such as she and secured a job in one of the Berensons' establishments. Jan was taken with her immediately and despite the reverence he felt for his marital vows and the love he had for his wife, the temptation, influenced by his naturally superior position as her employer, made him a victim of his own irrepressible urges. A year after his daughter Daria was born, Inga had a fine son by Jan.

Jan took quiet pride in his lover and her son and paid for such things that she could not earn by her own wages as a barmaid. To the best of his knowledge, no one, not even his own brothers knew of the liaison or the subsequent life he maintained with the exception of Inga's landlady who was so under Jan's thumb as the mortgage holder on her boarding home, that she was deaf and dumb to any questions concerning him.

In time, the boy looked so much like his mother that many thought they might be brother and sister, Inga being only seventeen when he was conceived. Jan felt it incumbent upon himself to provide employment for the lad. The simple boy never had reason to suspect the true nature of Jan's and Inga's relationship. Naïve by birth, more a physical specimen than an intellectual one, he knew Jan only as the kind "Mr. Berenson," his mother's helpful employer.

Jan had purchased a new Rolls-Royce and the boy was so taken with automobiles in general and this one in particular, that Jan instructed the regular chauffeur, Richard, to teach the boy to drive and on certain occasions when Richard was off or on vacation or driving Mr. Berenson on the rounds of the business, Inga's son would drive Mrs. Berenson, Daria or the housekeeper on their various domestic or social errands. The boy was named after his maternal grandfather, a corporal in the Swedish army who had died fighting the Russians of Czar Alexander Romanov. Inga's son by Jan was named Lars. Sometimes the most obvious of problems is the most difficult to ascertain. It would never have entered Jan's mind that his son would, to the eyes of most women, appear to be a Greek god. At seventeen he was six feet tall, had dark blue eyes and his mother's cascading hair. He had the chiseled features of the Aryan ideal that would dominate many of the political posters of Nazi Germany. Filled with the hot blood of his pagan peasant ancestors and of his true father, Jan Berenson, even the kitchen maid could see that it was only a matter of time before Lars bedded the Berenson housekeeper, Mrs. Wilkinson, a widow, Jan's wife, Mildred, and ultimately and tragically his own half sister, Daria.

Yes, it was an abomination, but it should not go unnoticed that these two young people did not in any way know of their true filial relationship. How could they? Daria, it is true, recognized something in him that was familiar, even comforting. But women, ever seemingly at a tender age, are drawn to a man for the strength of his character, for the condition of his soul, for his good heart. Lars had all of these and a handsome face and body to keep it all enclosed.

Some psychologists, practicing the most inexact of all the sciences, have made the observation that all love is founded in a human being's sense of narcissism. Some have elaborated on this philosophy by saying that one cannot love another if one does not love one's self. Perhaps the virginal Daria saw in Lars much of herself, never knowing that it was not a figment of her imagination or infatuation, but a genuine attraction to what she saw every day in the mirror. Such ironies are the stuff of tragedy and these two were about to learn the meaning of truly being star-crossed.

Eight

8 Lars had forsaken all others in favor of Daria and likewise she could think of no one but Lars. They had discovered that the Berenson gardener, Mr. Brown, would spend weekends away with his family in Providence, Rhode Island, thus leaving the cozy gardener's cottage on the large Nob Hill estate of Jan Berenson deserted. At varying times on Saturdays or late in the afternoon after church on Sundays, they would meet there and exercise their youthful passions upon one another. On one particular afternoon, as a light rain drifted down onto the gardens and the cedar roof of the cottage, the two fell asleep in each others' arms, cuddled naked on a thick blanket in front of the fireplace. Mrs. Berenson looking out at the wan afternoon weather noticed gentle curlicues of smoke weaving their way toward the clouds from what was supposed to be the unoccupied gardener's cottage. She ordered Mrs. Wilkinson, the housekeeper, to accompany her to the cottage to see why a fire was burning there in the hope that the gardener had returned early from Providence in anticipation of an upcoming party she was throwing which required innumerable cuttings from the abundant greenhouse stock that was maintained on the grounds for just such a purpose.

One can only imagine the look on the faces of the housekeeper, Mrs. Berenson, Daria and Lars when they were all together in the small cramped cottage. Mrs. Berenson immediately discharged Lars from the Berenson employ and told him never to return. Daria was confined to her room until further notice and Mrs. Wilkinson wept bitter tears into her pillow that night before she dozed off and snored like a buzz saw. When Mildred informed Mr. Berenson of what she had discovered in the gardener's cottage he could feel the blood drain from his head and he had to grab the back of a chair to keep from falling to the floor. The blood soon rushed back to his deprived brain and he became more enraged than anyone had ever known him to be. Had he ascertained the entire truth of Lars wide-flung adventures in the Berenson household, he would likely have murdered the boy himself, but years in the political minefield of Boston taught him that cool analysis of a problem was infinitely superior to a hot-blooded headlong dash into a situation which, if revealed, could ruin not only him but his entire family.

He sent a messenger to Inga's home that he would be away on business for several months and he sent some cash to tide her over as was his habit, including some money for Lars whom, he said, had been fired for reasons unknown to him by Mrs. Berenson. He assured her he would find the boy a job somewhere else upon his return.

Having barely imagined the faces of the four people in the gardener's cottage, it would be impossible to describe the look on Jan Berenson's face when Lars showed up the immediately following Monday morning to plead with Mr. Berenson to allow him to marry Daria. A dialogue better suited for the first circle of Dante's inferno ensued with recriminations, disappointments, betrayals and a vapid sociological discourse on marriage between the classes. None of the talk was about incest, a word which would have been a bomb dropped, its reverberations and destruction more far-flung than anyone would have dared to approximate.

Eventually, Jan's manipulative nature prevailed and he told Lars that he would think about it and under no circumstance was he to tell anyone of the lovers' activities or of the current conversation, or the marriage would be strictly forbidden. Lars took great hope in this and was more than excited and anxious when he received word from Mr. Berenson to meet him at one of the saloons at 10:00 p.m. on some forsaken Tuesday night in a dreary week to discuss his decision.

Lars was filled with youthful anticipation of his future union with the powerful Berenson family. He foresaw his purchase of a fine automobile that he could flaunt to his former friends, all of whom he would in the future ignore because of their low status in the community. He even thought of Daria fulfilling his every need and quite a few he would take great lengths to think of. Unfortunately, on his way to that meeting, three men waiting in the alley not far from Lars' home pounced upon him, cutting his neck with a butcher knife so deeply, it sliced halfway through his spinal cord. He lay there twitching a few seconds, making guttural gurgling sounds to the beat of the killers' running footsteps down one of the innumerable dark streets in that poorest section of the city.

Everyone of the people that knew Lars cried for a different reason at his funeral for each had known him in a different way that best suited their own needs. Mr. Berenson spared no expense in making it a fitting tribute to the son of his faithful employee. Tears abounded. Even Daria's unborn child, conceived out of incest, would have wept had he known that had he been born, it would have been into a world of retribution, condemnation and ostracism from which the abortionist's dull blade had saved him.

Daria subconsciously knew, although she had no proof other than her instinct, that her father was responsible for Lars' death. Her love of her father mutated into fear and her fear into hate, but she was her father's daughter and disguised her emotions under a thin veneer of civility. She found comfort in alcohol, starting with wine and then graduating to gin. When in her cups, she would fantasize about slipping into her father's bedroom and, as he slept, jamming a knitting needle into his ear and through his brain, pinning him as a naturalist might skewer a rare beetle or butterfly to a velvet-covered board. But fantasies are not realities except in novels and on psychiatrists' couches. One day, therefore, feeling that to live one more hour under the roof that sheltered her father would be worse than death, she packed a small bag with some cash she had saved and the jewels her father had given her on various occasions since she was ten years old and ran off into the metallic aura of the city streets.

$\mathcal{N}ine$

Hemonides was the first human by any expert's opinion to have drawn a map of the Italian Peninsula, what we like to call the boot of Italy because of its obvious shape. Hemonides working mainly from Greek and Phoenician reports of the rugged coastline drew it somewhat differently twenty-five centuries ago and he had called it the great cock of Europe noting in a diary found in the charred wreckage of the library at Alexandria how Italy was Europe's penis and Greece its testes, hypothesizing that Greece was the wellspring of intellect that was ejaculated into the world by the Italians.

Whether anyone agreed with him or not, the Italian Peninsula was isolated on three sides, west, east and south, by the green waters of the Mare Mediterraneo and, in the north by a spiked craggy fringe of titanic pubic hair now known as the Alps. Thus, in the times before hairy ape-like men found their way through the snow of the frigid north through the Alpine passes, fleeing from their cousins with less hair, larger crania, and better weapons, the peninsula became inhabited. Italy was isolated from the migratory travels of the gargantuan lizards we now call dinosaurs and nature's second preposterous act, the great mammals such as mammoths, treesloths and saber-tooth cats. Many have postulated, particularly in the confines of the gilded walls of the Vatican, that Italy may have been the very sight of the Garden of Eden so empty is its fossil record, so inviting its climate, so pure its air and so close its proximity to the Pope. Whether this is true or not matters little to the story as it unfolds for it is almost urgent to focus on one small area perhaps a thousand acres by modern measure, approximately twenty miles north of where Romulus murdered his brother Remus shortly after being suckled by the she-wolf and settled in a green pasture by the Tiber calling the place Rome in honor of the fratricide. By the time all this transpired the earth, if we can believe the scientists, was already a very, very old man circling around his even older but still hot-tempered wife, the sun. Mythology and our own foolish sense of sexual order invariably reverses these roles and so we call our planet Mother Earth and the sun is depicted as a flaming masculine face. Whoever started this clearly had no realistic knowledge of the marital relationship for rarely do we see a cool old woman seeking out a hot-blooded old man. Old men are always looking for women half their age with half their blood pressure and half their brains. If they are married, they cling to their healthier wives like grim death for nothing so terrifies an old man as the prospect of being alone, except perhaps having a failing erection.

This one thousand acres is in the middle ground between the subtle peaks of the Apennines and their rolling foothills. The peaks are barren and time worn, victims of countless eons of exposure to the elements. The foothills are fertile, having received the runoff like beggars in a wealthy neighborhood from the stony peaks and the millennial flurries of volcanic ash. This combination provided the perfect breeding ground for vines and other less important crops and ultimately for the greatest civilization of all time if we measure such things by the size of buildings, the territory of empires and the numbers of the slaughtered.

In the narrow mezzanine of the Apennines there is a vista that from a distance appears to be two large cupped hands reaching down as if to scoop up water from a brook and cutoff at the elbows —a river runs conveniently some three hundred feet below — which are the twin peaks of local legend called the Monte Fumo and the Monte Blanco. These cupped hands through the miracle of geography held some very fertile soil, indeed, and would have been a perfect locale for a productive farm or vineyard. Unfortunately, beneath those supplicating upturned palms a spring of sulfurous water bubbled for more years than stars in the sky and rendered the land a dismal swamp, a wasteland of desolation with a blanket of poisonous air. The gases emitted by the steamy cauldron would asphyxiate passing animals whose dead and rotting corpses filled the air with the odor of putrefaction that attracted other animals which, while feeding on the carcasses of their brethren, would in turn become carcasses themselves. Easy access to these lands was created by nature in one of its perverser moments.

The lush foothills were connected to it by a spit of land, more a spine really, that meandered through the arid highlands that surrounded it much as a python asleep in the sun might be found on the edges of the Gobi. Not ten meters thick but several miles long, the spine of sand and rock made access not only easy but inviting as even the most simple-minded of God's creatures is endowed with a lethal dose of curiosity.

Over time, the sulfur springs died down to a few fetid pools and by the time the Romans found the pathway and made the journey, the carcasses of animals and birds had dissolved into the soil and the pools were announced to be curative of all diseases from gout to gonorrhea. A beautiful bath was established by a Roman general named Nero Septimus Franca who ingeniously devised a series of aqueducts to draw the river water to the marble bath where it was conveniently heated and salinated by the weakened sulfur springs. He built a lovely villa there and with his wife, his daughter and his three sons added to his considerable fortune by selling admission to the curative baths at the renowned Villa Franca.

If the Romans adored anything more than excess, it was slaves, the more exotic, the better. General Franca had a special penchant for Nubians and Ethiopes. He relished their black skins and would often excuse them from their household duties to allow them to lie in the sun and thereby get darker still. He owned five male and one female black Africans and he took every opportunity that arose to bed the female usually when his wife was in Rome, Ostia or Capri. What the General did not know was that the female slave, known as Luana, was not only in love with one of the males by the name of Basolo but was actually married to him in a secret ceremony that took place in the early hours of the day when the General and his family were sleeping off the previous nights indulgences. Basolo, a tall handsome Nubian with eyes the color of pitch and skin as glossy and black as a Steinway Grand Piano, despised the general for the sexual abuses he heaped upon the defenseless Luana. But he could neither protest nor dissuade. As a slave, he had no more rights than a fly might have in protesting the conditions of a web to the spider. So, he plotted revenge, not a dish that is best when served cold, as some fool has postulated, but a feverishly demonic ceremony of retribution full of fire and brimstone.

ᒣen

The General's favorite child, the apple of his watery eyes, was his daughter Agrippina, a fulsome nineteen-year-old of unexceptional looks and personality. When Basolo would notice that she was resting by the bath or supping alone, he would bribe the other servants to allow him to wait upon her. With a short tunic and no undergarments he would bow before her, lean farther over than was necessary and carry himself in such a way that his blue-black manhood, scented with amboyna oil, would swing in the open air in front of Agrippina's gaping eyes. Boredom, ennui and a fallow brain coupled with a libido which rarely hibernated, made Agrippina an easy victim for Eros, god of lust and in short order, Basolo was plowing with the general's young heifer.

Fate, ever the trickster, found its way to the Villa Franca up the rock-strewn road. Luana discovered Basolo's amorous liaisons with Agrippina, something not even Basolo could have imagined although had he not been driven by the lust for revenge and kept his cool about him, he would have realized was the one result that had to be avoided at all costs. Revenge, though, knows no master and is ever the blindfold of he who seeks it.

Luana was enraged, as might be expected, and thoughtlessly informed General Franca of the lascivious habits of his daughter. Foolishly, she thought the General would be angry with his daughter and would simply whip Basolo for his transgressions. There was precedent for this and Luana was not a fool without a memory. However, the mind of the general was as far from Luana's comprehension as the mind of a lion is from a gnat. Indulged and beloved children are punished by minor deprivations and Agrippina's penance was to be confined to the Villa for a month and to see none of her friends. This caused her to weep salty tears into the ample shoulder of the general's wife, her mother. The general reserved his true anger for Basolo. He was stripped naked and tied to a winch with heavy ropes and chains. The winch was suspended over one of the boiling sulfur pits a few hundred meters from the baths and slowly, over the course of three days, he was lowered into it. The smell of his roasting flesh, the sulfur and the cacophonous guttural screeches that emerged from his tortured body pleased General Franca to no end. Luana was driven insane knowing her plan had backfired and, with vultures circling her beloved Basolo's roasted carcass, she flung herself off the precipitous edge of the eastern boundary of the estate falling into the boulder-cluttered chasm below to an ignominious death, the funeral attended by only twenty or thirty ragged vultures.

Had this been the end of the story, we would have no story. But two months after the deaths of Basolo and Luana, the general noticed his daughter's increased girth and overheard her complain of morning sickness. The court physician from Rome confirmed that she was pregnant and that it was most likely the child of Basolo. So fate had overstayed its welcome and Basolo's revenge unfurled like Satan's flag over Pandemonium.

There is no word in their language or in General Franca's, or likely any language of any race on this planet that could describe the fury of General Franca. He had all his African slaves decapitated as unwilling witnesses to his family's shame. He instructed his sons to go to Rome and wait for his word there, which they did forthwith. He locked Agrippina in her room and nailed the door and windows shut allowing only a small portal for the passage of bread and gruel to minimally maintain her existence. She was allowed no intercourse with anyone even her mother, denied clean laundry or even the most basic of her sanitary needs. The general placed his couch at the door and sat and listened daily to her shouts and screams and her pleas for mercy which ultimately dissolved into hoarse groans. His wife, grief-stricken, pled for Agrippina but all she received for her efforts was a lashing. The baths were closed and the Villa Franca, once a happy spa and gathering place for Rome's privileged class, became a prison with but three prisoners. All the other servants had been sent to Rome with the General's three sons and his wife had to cook and clean or risk his further wrath and she dare not leave for fear of deserting Agrippina.

How this miserable threesome survived the next half year would escape even the most stouthearted, but they did. One night, in the midst of a terrible rain storm, Agrippina's screams reached an almost supernatural pitch as she went into labor and gave birth to Basolo's son. The general outside her door spent the night pulling his hair as his wife wept uncontrollably. By morning, the screaming stopped and no infant's cry filled the void. The general called to her, but there was no response. He pulled the spikes from the doorframe and entered the room. There, on the floor, lay Agrippina in a pool of blood, urine and feces. Her child, a young mixed-race boy, half white, half black, purpled with suffocation, lay between her legs still connected by the umbilicus and covered in clotted blood. Both were dead. The general's wife ran to the kitchen and returned with a large bread knife and rushed at the stunned general who struck her full in the face with his fist, knocking her unconscious.

As fate was about to depart, it decided on one last day's stay. The Emperor had heard talk at court of the peculiar goings-on at the Villa Franca. As governments tend to move quite slowly today, they did then as well and by the time the Emperor dispatched a cohort of soldiers to the Villa Franca to verify the truth of the rumors, it was too late. The general was arrested and summarily executed for the murder of his daughter, a practice even the Romans frowned upon. The general's wife as an accomplice was sold to a brothel where she was forced to service Roman sailors who were less selective about the age of the women their lust sought than the aristocracy. The general's three sons were sent to Palestine, Egypt and Carthage where they served as foot soldiers. Whether they survived or not, history will not divulge. The Emperor, covetous of the baths and empowered by the Senate to personally confiscate the property of criminals, had the Villa Franca leveled in preparation for building his own villa on the site, three times the size of the original. After its demolition but before construction started, the Emperor was assassinated as emperors are wont to be. Three years of civil war following the assassination eradicated the memory of the baths but not its name. The site of the Villa Franca, a disarrayed pile of marble, granite and faded memories was absorbed back into the Apennines like a prodigal child.

Eleven

More than a thousand years later, well after the empire had adopted Christianity and fell into ruin, after the barbarian hordes had had their way with Rome, and Europe had fallen into fragments, each fearful, paranoid, self-contained and ruled as much by superstition as by Mother Church, a group of monks charged with founding a monastery journeyed north by mule-driven carts. While the history of Villa Franca never expanded to legend, rumors, like the discarded skins of molting snakes, blew through the streets of Rome and snippets were picked up here and there of a spa fit for the emperors that had vanished. Many said the Goths or Huns had demolished it, others, an earthquake. The monks, lead by Monsignor Furano journeyed up the serpentine road and found the ruins or what was left of them, anyway. The sun perched on the twin peaks and doves flew down into the valley toward the river, their enlarged shadows making patterns on the ruins like angels floating through Heaven. The monks fell to their knees seeing this as a sign from heaven that this was to be the site of the new monastery dedicated to Saint Ubaldo. Had they been more observant, they might have seen the she-eagle which had frightened the birds into flight with a dove in her talons, squirming as it was devoured alive, perhaps wondering why it, of the many that nested in the mountain, should be the one chosen to die.

Fate will move mountains, they say, but an edict from the Pope will move it faster and at a lower cost. Peasants from miles around were summoned to the chore at hand and the same power that made Notre Dame climb to the clouds did its magic here: the power of fear, sweat, tears and suffering. It took six years for the monastery of Saint Ubaldo to be built. Within another five years nearly one hundred Franconian monks occupied it and had planted apple and pear orchards and a fine vineyard of

Montepulciano grapes. One small sulfur pool was found at the base of Monte Fumo and the yellowish water that percolated up from it and dribbled down the side of the chasm into the river below was bottled and sold in Rome for it curative properties.

The Franconians were an austere group founded on vows of silence, meditation, physical labor and self-flagellation, although how the last could have pleased God is a mystery to all but the most devout. Monsignor Furano, the founding father, lived to see the monastery flourish, if that word could ever be used to describe so silent and morbid a place. Not all deprivation, the monks produced some of the most beautiful illuminated manuscripts in all Italy— many of them adorned the Pope's personal library. The tempera paint they employed was infused with the sulfurous water of the spring which increased its sheen and durability beyond even that of the best mixed oil paints of the Far East. If there was a secret that the monks held tight to their bosoms, it was the secret of sulfur. Anyone perusing one of the manuscripts, could not help but notice the slight sour egg smell given off by every book produced at the monastery, but this was attributed to either the tanning process of the velum used as pages or the general sulfurous odor that lightly permeated everything on the plateau.

In every book produced during Monsignor Furano's rule he inserted on the rear endpaper in perfect script a coded message in a language of his own inventing, an anagram based on some long-forgotten language which no one could decipher until many years later when it was decodified by a collector of rare books and incunables who had also been a cryptographer by avocation to the Emperor Napoleon. The message was, "When Saint Peter inquires of my desire to enter through the Gates, I shall remain true to my creed that I prefer Heaven for the weather, but Hell for the company." An American writer of limited ability who purchased one of the monastery's tomes adopted this motto as his own, but everyone knows Americans are pickpockets of ideas and covet them as Midas did his bullion.

Over the course of time, the monastery became the refuge of punished priests and little boys whose parents had died or had deserted them on the steps of one of the many churches in Rome or had been sent to prison. Many came to believe that the boys would have fared better had they fended for themselves in the gutters of the Eternal City. But they would not have been entirely correct.

Twelve

12 The centuries passed like tidal waves, great mountains of time that pummeled the shores of St. Ubaldo's, the rocks and empty seashells tossed on wayward currents. Such were the young boys interned at the monastery which had evolved into an orphanage by edict of one of the Medici Popes, a scoundrel by anyone's reckoning but deified over time to saint-hood the way Caligula, human blood on his lips, had become a god.

The children's' whimperings in the night after the candles' flames were extinguished with a gust of garlic-laden breath, their punishment for imaginary misdemeanors, their confused eyes, their bullying of each other in the psychology of mutual victims and the near-perfect isolation, endured for many years, the only residue, a sinuous string of small unmarked graves time-clustered at the river's edge down in the eastern chasm below the monastery. Their ephemeral voices were the muffled echoes of sand, something between a whisper and a rasp that follows receding waves on a beach. From the shore, people look at the sea, marvel at its grandness and beauty, the cradle of life, never for a moment picturing what creatures teem in its murky unknowable depths. Had the voices of the children arisen in a chorus from their graves, the sea would have run red as it did for Moses. But his adventure was writ large in the Book of Life and the boys of St. Ubaldo's, not one of their names could be remembered.

Sometime in the decade that began in 1650, a courtesan name Fanucci in a powdered wig and satin waistcoat reclined on a sofa in Rome. He was neither a count nor a duke, but considered a number of counts and dukes as friends. He was an entertaining fellow in a number of ways that are unimportant now. As he reclined, a small flea had found its way up the silk stocking of his thin leg and made an innocuous puncture into his pale pink skin. This was a common occurrence everywhere, even at court. Fanucci reached down and scratched the little creature away. Without malice, however, this flea, which was known as a Cheops bug named after the great early king of Egypt, had, only a few days before, hitched a ride on one of the many rats that traveled the Mediterranean like English tourists. In less than a week, Fanucci was covered in black buboes and died a hideous puss-gorged death on a bed imported from France at great expense. He had many friends that visited him and a large number of house servants. Within a year, a third of the population of Rome had followed him as if to some marvelous soiree held at the bottom of a trench dug outside the city walls and filled with the decaying revelers as the plague romped through the streets of Rome, its lush countryside and the luxurious villas of the elite.

The monks of St. Ubaldo's had locked their gates and for the next three years, as the plague enjoyed its visit in Rome, the orphans and their wardens were safe within, many people thinking in later times that the sulfur-soaked earth that the monastery and its gardens were built upon had cleansed the air they breathed. Looking back three hundred years, one might be tempted to say that the orphanage was not, therefore, all bad. In fact, nothing is all bad. Goodness sprouts here and there like flowers on desert plants. Several monks took their vows quite seriously and led virtuous, if not altogether useful lives. Many of the boys grew to be adults and left the gates of St. Ubaldo's headed for the army or the navy or the jails or the graveyards of places as far off as Moscow.

One boy in particular made his way down the sinuous road from St. Ubaldo's to Saltura with his head full of notions. He was called Marco Fontana by the Monsignor that ruled St. Ubaldo's from the time Garibaldi united the Italian peninsula into one sovereign nation, until his remains were buried at the end of the Franco-Prussian War. Marco was sixteen years of age by the monks' reckonings and some sensed he would be more trouble than he was worth if retained to the age of eighteen as the boys usually were. They made him pack a small burlap sack and sent him into the world. No one knew his real name or where he had come from. Like all the boys, he was named by the monks after a classical hero of mythology, the Bible or history. So Marco was named for Marc Anthony. The surname of Fontana came sometime later when the cook saw the five year old playing near the fountain in the center of the courtyard. The lad had reached in to touch the bottom, misjudged its depth and fell in. The cook laughed himself silly and, were it not for another older boy sitting nearby, Marco would have drowned. He was pulled out by his feet like a bear would catch a seal. Soaked and unconscious, he recuperated in a few hours and awoke to his new name, Marco Fontana.

It was the day after Christmas when a large wagon with six new boys pulled up at the door of the orphanage. It was the inevitable delivery which the monks called the Saint Stephen's Day Exile. Christmas, normally a time of familial good will if not good will towards men, was not always the cheerful season of carols, novels and other frivolities of the well-to-do. The church steps would often be littered with deserted infants on Christmas Eve and particularly Christmas day. Not only infants felt the impact of financial deprivation, but young children of all ages would be left to fend for themselves on street corners in towns they had never visited or left in church while mamma went to "meet someone" and never returned. It was a miserable day for most of the world despite rumors to the contrary, for, after all, the baby Jesus had two loving parents, a roof over his head despite a lack of room at the inn and the means to pay for such a room had it been available. Then there were the visitors, poor and wealthy, leaving the first Christmas gifts. The children of the street of the cities of Europe were not even aware of the notion of Christmas gifts and in a way they suffered less disappointment than those who received what they did not want. The children on the wagon had expectations of nothing except deprivation, cold and hunger, all they had ever known. In short, they had no where to go but sideways.

The boys of the St. Stephen's Day Exile were a typical lot except for one child of four years of age who said his name was Giulio. There was already a boy called Giulio named by the monks after Julius Caesar, so they renamed him Stephen after the day of his second birth, the day of his arrival at St. Ubaldo's.

Marco took a liking to him and soon they were fast friends, Stephen following Marco about like a lost puppy and Marco defending him against the predatory nature of the other boys who would ordinarily have tormented him because of his youth and diminutive stature. Marco taught him checkers and hide-and-go-seek and never called him Stephen, but

always Giulio, Marco subconsciously feeling that the last possession anyone had on Earth was his name, the only possession to survive death,
appearing on one's headstone; to steal a name was evil. The monks always
reprimanded Marco for calling Stephen "Giulio" but they had other fish
to fry and made their reprimands haphazardly and more a matter of prin-
ciple than anything of consequence.

One day, in August of the year following Stephen's arrival at the
orphanage, the two boys were playing hide and seek. Stephen hid behind
a large boulder perched on the eastern chasm taking advantage of its shade
and his small size to pick a spot inaccessible to a larger boy like Marco.
Packs of wild dogs were known to frequent the environs of St. Ubaldo's
usually at night feeding off the refuse that the monks dumped into the
chasm below. These dogs were neither coyotes nor wolves but packs of
domestic dogs that had been turned out by their owners to fend for themselves or were lost or simply had gotten born into the pack. It was a ratty,
mangy bunch of pathetic outcasts eking out a living in the arid Apennine
terrain with no god to watch over them and biological skills severely limited by eons of dependence on intemperate humans.

A large yellow dog, solitary and straying in the heat of an August afternoon, found poor Stephen behind this rock and bit him on the leg as his
shouts brought Marco who beat the dog off with a tree limb. Marco carried Stephen, so small for his age, to the monks who washed the wound
and treated it with sulfur and vinegar to Stephen's tears and cries. Marco
never left the little boy's side and fed him and brought him water, staying
by him asleep on the floor.

In three days, the symptoms of rabies appeared and Stephen was tied
to his bed as he struggled against the torturous, fatal illness. Marco took a
crucifix off the wall of one of the confessionals and placed it by him, praying everyday for his friend's survival, the first time he ever prayed for anything. In another three days, ravaged by the disease, dehydrated and starving, the small defenseless body of Stephen could fight no longer and he
died early in the morning, Marco caressing his head and crying tears that
flowed inward not from his eyes but from a secret place within him that
watered an unnamed flower.

Complaining of the heat, a monk said a cursory prayer over the small
grave by the river, one of many, as the other boys paid scant attention and

skimmed pebbles into the shallow slow moving river. A little wooden marker with the name Stephen scratched into it was all that remained of Marco's little friend. That night, Marco sneaked out of the orphanage and made his way to the grave. He scratched out the name Stephen and wrote Giulio in his best handwriting using the sharp edge of the crucifix. He folded up his checker board and checkers and placed them on the grave, then he placed a great many stones on top of the grave to keep the cursed wild dogs away from his friend's body. Each stone seemed a bit of happiness that he had experienced with Giulio and like Giulio they were to be buried forever beside the indifferent river.

When he finished and saw that the rocks were neatly piled and the small wooden marker perfectly straight, he took the crucifix and placed it on the ground, smashing it under his foot. He took the pieces and, one by one that none would inadvertently lie by the grave, tossed them into the river where each made a pleasing plopping sound, a fitting thank you, as Marco saw it, for one of a million, million unanswered prayers.

Thirteen

13 The reader must forgive the ink on the following pages for those errant marks hereafter are intended to rouse nothing but a search for the truth and while some among you may find them wicked or salacious or worse, so often is the truth and, really, who are we that hold ourselves above it all, but seekers of the truth, that often we are fooled or disappointed by it? Lowly dogs have no sense of the tomorrows or of the yesterdays as we do, their roads have no ending or beginning, but ours? Their truths are in front of them, minute by minute, accepting of whatever may come. We learn of the truth of things far too early and are all aware of our own destinies which are to become food for the worms. Perhaps that is why dogs do not attend Mass nor take any sacrament more seriously than a good defecation in the woods.

Marco arrived in Saltura as the sun sank into the sea and lazy, roseate clouds drifted aimlessly in the sky like vagrants in the piazza. The friendly face of a woman standing in an open doorway with a warm, yellow light outlining her rotund silhouette, beckoned Marco to her. She was Ismelda, the only whore in Saltura, a dark- complexioned Sicilian who owned her small adobe cottage indirectly paid for by the merchants and laborers of the town. Marco's youth and fine features attracted her. When business was finally discussed, he naively revealed that he had only a few lira, the severance allowance begrudgingly given all the orphans of St. Ubaldo's upon their departure. Ismelda was in a magnanimous mood and scanning the roadway to see if any of her regulars might be seeking her out, she realized that the evening would not be profitable otherwise and a few lira were better than none as her mother always taught her.

We have been instructed by experience that we must take people as we find them and little thought and less philosophy are devoted to the unassailable fact that people are the sum total of their experiences and only in the fewest of instances do faces match personal history. Rarely has this fact been more easily provable than in the handsome Marco Fontana, as Ismelda would soon discover.

After Marco had been at the orphanage for some years, at the age of eleven, he experienced his first nocturnal emission, an event every normal male endures with a mix of trepidation, anxiety and, sometimes, joy. With no father or uncle to confide this newly discovered mysterious event in, he sought out Brother Xavier Zeugma, a plump forty year old monk from Budapest more adamant about slathering butter on his bread than slapping his own pink-skinned back with the lash of the Franconians.

Brother Xavier immediately informed Marco that only punishment would cure this illness of the flesh and that to prevent Marco from pursuing a path of carnal sin he must cleanse his soul in one of the small cubicles off the main chapel employed by the monks for the application of a curative salve to the soul.

After the dinner meal, Brother Xavier led Marco to the chapel chamber. It was small, only eight or nine feet on a side with a narrow window of red stained glass and a high ceiling. There was a backless bench in the middle of the room and a single icon on the ocher stucco walls, a picture after Giotto of the Blessed Virgin Mary kneeling in prayer in her blue robes sadly looking up at heaven as if waiting for some answer. The only lighting in the room were two candles, one each on either side of the small image of Mary, their flickering light giving her clothing the illusion of rustling in some beatific breeze.

It must be understood that knowledge of the female anatomy to any of the boys at St. Ubaldo's was a far deeper mystery then anything St. Thomas Aquinas could have postulated to them. Most of the boys had come to the orphanage while still in swaddling clothes and the Franconian Order forbade any forms of intercourse with females even if it was as narrow as a woman making a delivery of salt pork from a provender in the town. So, much of what lay between the legs of women was a matter of conjecture and an endless source of discussion among the boys. Then there was the matter of the Blessed Virgin and her womb, the topic of one of their most important prayers. No other saint or blessed figure had quite so much attention paid to the space between her legs. The Virgin Mary did that. The Virgin Mary did this. Seek the Blessed Virgin for succor in your time of need. In short, Mary's virginal secret parts were inextricably linked to her divinity in the minds of the orphans.

Some of the boys enjoyed discussing women's secret parts and attempted crude drawings in the halls of the dormitory and the outhouse where their imaginations ran wild. There were anatomically absurd visions of sex organs carefully sketched with bits of charcoal from the cook's fire pit. Marco studied these drawings with some scrutiny but the topic was simply too abstract for him. Several of the older boys took to experimenting on themselves having concluded that the rear end of a boy must be similar to the secret parts of a woman. These boys, if caught, were lashed to the point of collapse and many bore the scars of these enthusiastic beatings to the end of their days.

Brother Xavier sat on the bench with the hood of his thick, brown moleskin robe over his head like an executioner. He told Marco to disrobe which he reluctantly did. Marco was pulled face down across the monk's lap with his buttocks skyward in preparation for a beating. This was common in the orphanage but it was the first time he was naked and this was the first time it was not in front of the other boys as an exemplar of what could happen to them.

Marco was instructed to look upon the icon of the Virgin and pray for her aid in conquering sin. As Brother Xavier ministered an unusually gentle slapping to his exposed rear, Marco faced the icon and prayed. He was certain, however, as he realized, that far from being guided from the precipice of sin, he was falling into its open maw. His pubescent manhood was erect and was being massaged by the thick folds of Brother Xavier's robe. He imagined the Virgin, not much older than he in the painting, without her robes and instead with the peculiar orifices he had seen scrolled on the walls of the latrine. He sweat profusely as he tried to control his loins with his mind and had begun to win this inner war when the tide turned and the battle was lost; he ejaculated as silently as he could into the monk's garment, hoping that the punishment had preoccupied the monk as he imagined most holy duties did.

Marco's mind was confused to the point of delirium as all the next day he was a model resident of the orphanage, cleaning more than he was required and saying extra prayers, long after the other boys had risen from their knees and gone to chores or playtime. Brother Xavier was particularly lenient with Marco and often skipped over him for unpleasant duties such as cleaning the kitchen, the latrine or scrubbing the floors. A week later, Marco again went to Brother Xavier to confess that another wet dream had occurred and Brother Xavier dutifully administered the same penance. In a short period of time, Marco was confessing to sins he never committed and punishment became as much a part of his life as the evening meal. Thus, as the hatchlings of Northern geese are imprinted with the facial features of their parents, and mimic the adult goose in the ways of migration and survival, so Marco was imprinted with the aberrant behavior of Brother Xavier who, when Marco was fifteen, mysteriously fell to his death into the western chasm. Several younger boys had nightmares where they imagined three older boys leading the monk to something they had apparently discovered and then collectively shoving him off the cliff to a brutal stony death. While justice is not one of the seven Heavenly Virtues, at least in the minds of the boys, it should have been.

Behind Marco's beautiful sad eyes, Ismelda could not see, nor had she seen could she have understood that the years in St. Ubaldo's were like the leaden wires of the espalier, tightly twisted around the branches of boxwoods and fruit trees, distorting their natural form into some phantasmagorical image in the mind of a perverse gardener.

$\mathcal{F}ourteen$

14 Ismelda led Marco into the anteroom which was furnished much like the inside of a gypsy caravan with bright colors, mostly scarlet with garish splashes of yellow and green. Cheap plaster statues of saints adorned tabletops and a primitively carved crucifix hung over the bed, which Marco could see from where he stood. She brought him a cup of spiced wine which he downed in a gulp. She brought him another and warned him that there would be an extra charge for any further refreshments. She left him on the divan and went into the bedroom.

His head was spinning either from the long walk in the town or the two glasses of wine or both. She called to him. He rose unsteadily to his feet and walked to the bedroom. Opening the door on its slow hinges, Ismelda lay nude upon the bed, her large floppy breasts sagging to left and right along her ribs practically into her armpits. Several rolls of fat girdled her mid-drift covered in skin pocked and crinkled as the skin of an orange. Beneath the rolls, there was a large triangle of dark, matted hair, much like his own, but more profuse, absent his male organs. He looked but could discern no orifice. Perhaps, it was mythological, the daydream of idle boys confined to the company of other idle boys and holy men. Actually, he was somewhat relieved for had he found it, the last thing he would have thought of doing was putting his member into such a lump of unwholesome flesh.

She told him to undress and robotically he did so, but his parts were limp and uninspired. She beckoned him to the bed and dutifully he did what he had been used to doing and lay across her lap as if waiting for the lash. He looked about for the familiar beautiful face of the Virgin. She was nowhere to be found. On the wall, he saw only the miserable countenance of St. Sebastian with a score of arrows piercing his semi-clothed body in the ecstatic throes of martyrdom.

She began to laugh at him as she pushed him off her generous thighs with such force that he fell to the floor. Her laughter was as loud as thunder in his ears as he rose and stood in front of her, blushing and ashamed, feeling his anger rising in him from his crotch to his throat. To anyone with the least bit of sense or perhaps knowledge of the frescos of San Domenico in Florence, Marco looked much like Michael the Archangel, eyes full of fire, chiseled muscles firm and taught with youth and righteousness. He held not a sword in his upward arm, but an iron candlestick from the bed stand. Before she could raise her arm in defense, he had leaped on the bed, straddling her torso with his thighs and brought the weapon down on the top of her head. The first blow stopped the laughing and the subsequent strokes from high above her stopped her breathing and then her heart. The rhythmic beating of his arms caused his thighs to rub her belly and by the last blow, many more than was needed to kill her, he had ejaculated.

He climbed off her and looked down at his handiwork. Shame rose in him with the wine and he vomited on the ragged carpet beside her bed. He dropped the candlestick, picked up his clothes and went back to the anteroom where he sat on the divan and pondered what to do next. He was exhausted and it was late. He dressed and lay down and, in a moment, was sleeping soundly. He awoke before daybreak and remembered his dream of Brother Xavier, realizing that the demonic monk had turned him into a murderer. The monk was dead but, as they often said in St. Ubaldo's in speaking of the sins of the father befalling the heads of the children, the nut did not fall too far from the tree. He would escape under cover of darkness and travel to Budapest to find the parents of Brother Xavier Zeugma. They had created their child and their child had created him. He must excoriate his pain at the source and, perhaps, cure it.

Before leaving, he searched the cottage methodically. Marco found Ismelda's money box, emptied it into his sack, got a loaf of bread off the table and silently slipped out the door into the deserted streets of Saltura. A tomcat stared at him from the top of a wall, a small pile of feathers at its feet.

Marco traveled north walking confidently along the main road to avoid arousing suspicion. He analyzed correctly that Ismelda was a night creature and no one would likely notice her missing until the next evening, if then. Therefore, he had at least fifteen or sixteen hours to get distance between him and her and perhaps another twenty-four on top of that.

The trees and the scattered buildings were like ghosts in the darkness. The moon was near full, lopsided but bright, the eye of the Cyclops high overhead. When he had been in St. Ubaldo's, sometimes when his dreams made him wake in the middle of the night, he would look out the small window near his bed. In moonlight, all the color he could see was black or white and the notches of gray in-between. He often thought of the moon as the thief of color, its own pocked and blistered face the color of …what, he could not say. But tonight, the air was as still as the water in a swamp. Tonight he could see blues of every shade and hue; the furrowed needles of cypress trees, the roof of a chicken coop, the grass-filled rut by the side of the road. Even his own hands glowed blue, he thought, as he looked up to see why the moon had decided to regurgitate blue. He saw the halo around the moon, the blue of the Virgin's robe, a perfect circle, a blessing just for him. This was the blue of shadows on the snow, that mysterious color that emerges from pure white on the dark side of mountaintops. Icy, frigid, the perfect blue of understanding. The blue of being chosen by God, not to suffer, nothing so simple as that, but to stand by and witness suffering and to endure. The blue, frozen peaks of the Alps stood by unchanging and witnessed stranded climbers, lost sheep, the army of Hannibal dead from the creeping, lethal frost. Mary's robe was no arbitrary color. The low moans of cattle in a distant pasture were like the voices of saints in the stars. The Blessed Virgin had not deserted him; she watched his every move, forgave him and sent the blue of heaven's dreams as a sign. For the first time in his life, he had purpose. What it was, he did not exactly know.

Marco had no knowledge whatsoever of the geography of this area other than from a large wall map in the classroom back at St. Ubaldo's. He did know that Milan was an important railing town and from there he could travel anywhere. At midday, he stopped at a local farm and for a few lira he received a solid peasant's meal. Energized, he walked on after discovering from his hostess that the next town, a small agricultural marketing center called Estradura was some twenty kilometers away, at least a day's walk. Such facts cannot be argued with and while men for a thousand years debated whether the sun revolved around the earth or vice versa, Marco would in a second, have taken whatever position best suited his needs at the moment. Truths such as those, put no money in your pocket nor food in your stomach. They were the realm of idle minds, of philosophers and of drunkards. The distance to the next town was more important to him than the Ten Commandments.

He walked until the stars began to rise and wandered off the road a short distance when he found a barn. The farmhouse was a stone hovel with no light shinning in its windows. Farmers were slaves to the sunlight and worked "from can to cannot;" that is, from when they can see to when they cannot. Marco stood for a moment or two and watched to see if someone might be about. A movement off to the left caught his eye, but it was a sow, teats dragging the ground and grunting under her breath as she shifted positions in the light of the moon.

Assuring himself that all was safe, Marco entered the barn and moved some of the sour-smelling hay into a mound. He sat upon it, opened his sack and ate the crust of bread he had taken. It was dry and tasteless but it killed the pangs in his belly. He lay down and drifted off to sleep. A gentle rustling near the door woke him a few hours later. It was neither the farmer's wife nor the farmer's daughter. The farmer had neither. It was his old cat sidling around in the dark hoping to find a careless rat that would not require too much effort to kill.

The next day, with the aid of a wine merchant's van loaded with barrels, Marco arrived at the town of Estradura. The train station was a few blocks walk, but by the time he arrived, the last train had already departed. He walked to a café with a few tables on the plaza and had a sandwich of tomatoes and sardines and a large glass of the house wine that had an aftertaste of kerosene. The breeze from the south invited him to find a safe place in a hayfield under a stand of cypress trees. He slept well and by 9:00 a.m. had boarded the train to Milan.

Fifteen

At a little after three in the afternoon the train arrived in Milan. The station was crowded with people, baggage carts, porters, finely dressed women and men, all the like of which Marco could never have imagined. He walked as if in a daze through the throngs, echoes of whistles and hissing of steam. Venders of food and fine items of clothing and bibelots. Children ran at their returning parents, lovers wept as they parted, wept as they were reunited. Father's proudly saw off sons in military dress. Nuns in groups, priests with bishops, and above it all the three story high canopied roof with flocks of pigeons flying between buildings, platforms and clouds of white steam. Marco felt as if he had been transported to another realm of existence. He was frightened, than elated, then anxious; emotions he did not know he had flooded through him, ebbed and flowed like currents in a tidal stream. Carabinieri patrolled in twos and civil guards stood at ticket counters and the entryways to the departure platforms. He knew he had to purchase tickets for the train to Budapest, so he sought out the ticket counter, signs indicating that it was located in the main hall.

Marco soon discovered that he did not have enough money to get to Budapest. In fact, he barely had enough to get to Prague but he boarded the train anyway with the hope that he might prevail upon the conductor to perhaps ride on at no extra cost or perhaps something else might present itself. He was certain divine providence would guide him in his journey. No, it was a quest, perhaps even a quest he was born for. He had never been told his purpose in life for his parents were dead and the monks, well they had their own reasons for doing the things they did. But now he knew what it all meant.

He boarded the last car of the train remarking to himself how beautiful the railroad cars were with their maroon and green lacquer, so glossy he could see the swirling crowds reflected in them, doubling an already huge number of people, more people than he had ever seen. He walked slowly up the central corridor starting in the rear and moving toward the front carefully but surreptitiously looking into each compartment to see who was sitting where and, if the truth be told, what sign he might receive from heaven as to who might help him. He threw in a little prayer.

Anyone who prays, especially if it is for divine intervention, can relate the fickle nature of the results. Hospitals and infirmaries everywhere always set aside a small room as a chapel so that there is a convenient and quiet place to sit while asking. There is always a cross on the wall lest anyone forget the nature of their faith and perhaps a few scented candles to dramatize the event. Clearly, some prayers were answered and some were not. The nots filled the cemeteries of the world and the prisons of great civilizations. The litter of the nots fills the coral reefs of the ocean, the leper colonies and the orphanages. Answered prayers can be seen everywhere especially in palaces, castles, chateaus and mansions, cathedrals, museums, theatres and opera houses and especially in the halls of government offices. Marco was told once by Brother Lambrusco that God had so many requests and petitions that he needed an army of saints to help handle the load and, when that was not enough, he rewarded many of the nots with that job, which had many benefits, and so martyrs could be prayed to as well in the hope that with all those spirits available for supplication, one of them might hear a prayer from a small, insignificant chapel and decide to answer it in the positive. It was a matter of timing, Marco realized, and therefore he came to believe that the best time for getting one's prayers heard was in the very small hours of the morning or during the lunch and dinner hours when the rest of the world was asleep or too busy to take the time to pray and he might then be heard as one voice in a much smaller crowd.

It was in the third car from the rear that Marco saw a promising passenger that might provide him with some guidance in his quest to reach Budapest with a purse sufficient only for Prague. A man was sitting alone with what appeared to be a small Bible and he could have been a twin of Brother Xavier. Conclusions should not be drawn and in point of fact, Marco, without realizing it in a conscious sense, bore no ill will toward

Brother Xavier anymore than one could bear ill will against the bullet that enters one's shoulder. It is not the bullet that is the villain, it is the demon who holds the gun and pulls the trigger. In fact, Marco had grown quite fond of Brother Xavier and if he had been the type to weep at bad news, he might have shed half a tear upon hearing the news of Brother Xavier's death. But when it was announced, there were too many other boys around and if even one of them had seen Marco weeping, then there would have been no end to the ridicule and he might have been forced to do some of things similar "sissy boys" had to endure in the latrines at night. While he was not certain what that was, he did not want to find out.

He opened the door to the compartment and took a seat opposite the portly passenger and said, "Good day." The man looked up briefly from his reading and acknowledged with a nod, and continued staring at the page. Marco looked out the window and watched the varied countryside unfold before him and it would be tempting to define it in his eyes and describe the rolling hills, the crossed rivers and streams, the rows of trees, the grazing cattle, the small multicolored towns and all the usual verbiage most people feel is better suited for travel books and romance novels written for young girls or people with the minds of young girls. But Marco saw it only as a proof of his motion and he imagined a giant hand and arm with a fine layer of golden hair rippling over well-defined muscles attached to a shoulder enveloped and invisible in a thick layer of pink and purple clouds, pulling the train on its twin rails of stretched steel to the place of retribution, to Budapest.

Marco attempted to engage the man in small talk and told him in his most naïve tone of voice how this was his first train trip, how fine the weather was, how large the world was and how surprising it must have been to people to discover the earth was round because it looked so very flat especially from a train window and he even asked if people in Budapest could speak Italian. The man nodded to every query or observation politely but annoyedly until the last when he laughed and said that Budapest was in Hungary and in Hungary they spoke Hungarian but that Italian might be understood in hotels, restaurants and places frequented by tourists. He added that he was Hungarian and could understand and speak Italian because his business brought him to Italy three times a year.

Marco asked him what his business was. The man suddenly had a glow to his face and he put his Bible down and started to explain how his company had been started by his grandfather in the days of Napoleon III. It manufactured holy statues, statues of all the saints and martyrs made from a unique type of clay that was light as a feather and could be painted with the same magical patina as the famous iridescent glazes of the Zsolnay factory that was his competition, only his were half the price. He then stood up and reached into the overhead bin for a large square suitcase which he carefully brought down and put on his lap. He had put the small Bible on the seat next to him and when Marco looked at it he saw that it was printed in a language unfamiliar to him, probably Hungarian and there was a small etched drawing of two men doing something quite odd to a woman. It was likely some imaginative Old Testament tale he thought. There were so many, no one except the Pope could keep them all straight and even he may have had his difficulties.

The man opened the box as if it were the Ark of the Covenant and brought out a small statue of the Blessed Virgin, only three inches high. She was kneeling and her flaxen hair flowed down from under her blue cloak as her azure eyes and powder puff pink cheeks looked upward at the heavens. As he turned it in the light, the iridescence was magical as if the prism of the rainbow had been captured within the colors. Here is the sign Marco had been seeking as he noticed the shadow of the small statue was enlarged to life size in silhouette against the door of the compartment by the sunlight. Before he could say anything, the conductor entered and asked for tickets. The man reached into his wallet which was filled with bank notes and produced his ticket to Budapest. Marco, who had not purchased his ticket at the station, told the conductor he wanted to travel to Budapest but he had only enough money to get to Prague and might the conductor see his way clear to helping an orphan get home. The conductor made a comment about wishing he had been an orphan and both he and the man laughed. When the conductor asked again, Marco asked again and the conductor seemed to take offense at being asked to betray his employer by selling a Budapest ticket for a Prague price even though everyone knew that the train was going to Budapest with or without Marco. This was Marco's first encounter with the brain of a bureaucrat and when the conductor threatened to throw him off the train, Marco handed over his liras for the ticket to Prague. The conductor intentionally dropped the ticket on the floor and snickered as Marco bent to pick it up, winking at the man who nodded and smiled in appreciation of Marco's humiliation. Leave it to a wop, the conductor observed, to try to get something for nothing. On his last tour of duty on a train from Berlin to Milan, a young German woman, a little fat in the rump perhaps, but pleasing none-the-less, offered oral sex for a free ticket. This was a quid pro quo the conductor could understand, but Marco had nothing of interest to him and he had to pay not only with money but with the further embarrassment at having to retrieve his ticket from the floor. Marco made a mental note to himself to research the term "wop" and to seek out other conductors for retribution, for they must all be alike, much as clergymen are. The conductor departed nodding his head and the man replaced the statute in its case and continued to read as if Marco had fallen through the floor and disappeared.

The train slowed as it entered one of the very long tunnels that snaked its subterranean path through or rather under the Alps. The train rocked back and forth as it was thrown into total darkness and the squeals of metal wheels on metal tracks and the lightening bursts of sparks which cast a strobe light eerie glow into the compartment seemed to touch some part of Marco's brain that he thought he had left in Saltura at the home of Ismelda. He unbuckled his belt and slid it out from his pants loops, stood upright in front of the man who had only the briefest vision of Marco in one of the sparking cascades of the grinding train wheels. Had he not known better, Marco thus illuminated was like a vision from the ceiling of the Sistine Chapel and as the compartment went into absolute darkness with the thundering echoing roar of the train and its massive engine magnified in the tunnel, the man could not utter a word as Marco tightened the belt around his neck like a garrote and choked him so hard the fat folds of his neck bled and soaked his shirt as he futilely struggled against his invisible murderer.

The light within the tunnel had begun to increase as the exit approached. Marco reached into the dead man's pocket and took the bill-fold, emptied it into his sack and opened the window. As the train picked up speed making its way into the clear alpine air of the Austrian frontier, Marco shoved the body out of the window and it fell and rolled on the stone bed of the tracks like a sack of mail. The man's shoes had fallen off in the compartment and Marco tossed them out as well. There was not a trace of the man left except his book which Marco put in his own pocket and the case with the sample statue which Marco placed his open palm on and said a quick prayer of thanks with his eyes closed as he used to do in chapel at the orphanage. He took his sack and made his way forward to the dining car where he ate the first good meal of his life and de-boarded the train at the Austrian City of Linz. He spent the night there at a small inn and the next day he boarded a train for Budapest.

Sixteen

16 Thirty-six hours later Marco found himself in the Hungarian twin cities of Buda and Pest and thought to himself how silly such a name was. He spent several weeks wandering the twin cities and crossed the river that divided them many times inquiring after the Zeugma family whether in cafés, bars or on street corners. No matter how helpful the questioned citizens tried to be, no one had heard of the Zeugmas. He had begun to lose hope but he knew that God had not provided the means to get him there if the search was to be futile, nor had he held on to the fleeting thought that Brother Xavier seemed ancient to him as most forty-year-olds look to young people and perhaps his parents were dead. No, he was here for a purpose.

Two policemen were standing on the sidewalk smoking cigarettes and talking. Marco approached and asked politely and reverentially. Much to his joy, they spoke passable Italian. One said he knew of such a family and thought they lived on Pedruzki Street in the Saint Cecile of Crete section of Buda. In fact, he said, he was certain because he recalled there being a robbery there and that old man Zeugma had died of a heart attack during the commission of the crime and the intruder had left without a thing leaving poor Mrs. Zeugma holding her dead husband's head in her lap as he lay in a widening pool of urine. The police rounded up a number of known thieves in the area but she could identify none of them which surprised no one because her eyeglasses were thicker than the heels of a shoe. The policeman did not remember the number of the house but did remember that it was painted blue with a brown door which was below the level of the street. When Marco was asked why he was interested in the Zeugmas, he responded that he was a friend of their son, Brother Xavier.

That seemed to satisfy everyone's curiosity and after a brief set of thank-yous that followed a complete set of directions to the street the Zeugma's lived on, Marco said his farewell.

He remembered the directions only vaguely for he was not trained to or experienced in the need to pay attention. His education at Saint Ubaldo's was sporadic and cursory and there were no examinations to test the progress of the boys because no one cared enough. There were no parents or relatives to send reports home to and if one of the orphans was a genius, another a moron, it made no difference to the monks so long as they obeyed the rules and no trouble was created. Whatever they were destined to be once out of the orphanage was in the hands of God and while the monks were proficient and well versed on what God expected within the walls of Saint Ubaldo's, outside, well, that was another matter.

Marco wandered in the general direction the policeman had indicated and he was confident that God would guide him to the exact location. He ended up walking through an area where women of all ages, young and old, thin and fat, average and striking were leaning out of windows or standing in open doorways in all phases of undress from fully clothed with a few buttons undone to nearly naked in a transparent nightshift and high top boots. One house in particular drew his attention because there were three young women perched at the front door smoking cigarettes and talking and laughing among themselves as casually as they might be at a church social but they were scantily clad in a parody of schoolgirl's uniforms, which is to say that they had very short, pleated skirts, knee high white stockings and white starched blouses unbuttoned to the waist which revealed thin nubile bodies beneath in a pleasant peek-a-boo style so that onlookers would get only the briefest glimpse as they turned this way or that.

Marco went over to them and they all greeted him in a warm and friendly fashion as was the trademark of their profession, to make the humblest, poorest, or most decrepit man feel as if he were a young and handsome prince, for the right price. In Marco's case, however, each of the three girls beheld him for what he was which was truly young and handsome and although he might not be a prince, these women were unconcerned for the moment. He tarried for a while and made innocent small talk about his status as a newly arrived tourist. They invited him in for a glass of wine and he was almost tempted but these women, while not quite as young as they appeared from a distance in their schoolgirl costumes, were pleasant to him in an earnest way. In particular, one by the name of Sonya seemed to touch him somewhere in his insides in a place he did not know he owned. He told them he was on important business, at which they laughed in a friendly but not mocking way and with a smile he assured them that he really did have to go on his way but that he would return perhaps for dinner and he paid them three sovereigns with which to purchase vittles and wine and offered to pay for an empty bed if they had one for him. He departed toward Pedruzki Street which Sonya informed him was but not a half-mile distant.

He found the blue house with the brown door as the sun was setting behind the tall spires of Saint Sophia's Cathedral and the ripples of the river looked like the autumn leaves of sugar maples half red, half gold and every shade between. It was a well-kept house with blue Belgian ceramic pots filled with geraniums. Around the street, parishioners of the church lined up for Evensong. Marco knocked on the door and after half a minute, a short old woman with white hair done in twin braids answered the door. She inquired what he wanted and he answered that he was a friend of her son, Xavier. A smile appeared on her thin lips and then her eyes filled with tears as she reached out and hugged Marco. This was the first time he had ever been held physically close to anyone in friendship and his body shuddered. She invited him in and he crossed the threshold as she closed the door behind him. She showed him into the parlor and bid him to sit and tell her about her son whom she had loved so much as her only child and who had died so tragically in the service of Mother Church. With this she crossed herself and waited for Marco to speak. He was surprised at the news of Brother Xavier's death, but was careful to conceal his emotions.

He told her how kind her son was and that he was the favorite of all the boys who looked upon him as the father they never had. He added a few more lies to flesh out the story and watched her eyes fill with tears and brim over down her deeply wrinkled cheeks. As she wept, he looked about and saw a letter opener on a small table, pewter with a carved wooden handle like a medieval dagger. He stood and went over to her, patting her on the shoulder and simultaneously picking up the letter opener. He was about to stick it into her neck when she put her hand on his and leaned her face upon it letting her warm tears drop on his skin. She began to tell him what a good boy her Xavier was and how cruelly her husband, his father treated him. Her husband had been a deacon of the church and he treated the boy as a stranger because Xavier was more interested in art and poetry and music than in sport, fighting and drinking, declaring that this sissy of a boy could not be his son and that he was an abomination in the eyes of the church after he discovered Xavier and another boy kissing in the wine cellar under the house. Xavier was whipped with his father's belt that night and when his mother tried to intervene, he beat her in front of the boy leaving them both huddled and bruised holding each other in a heap on the floor.

When she awoke the next morning with her husband snoring in a drunken stupor beside her, Xavier was gone. She received a letter six months later telling her he would make amends for his actions which brought so much pain and suffering to her. She did not understand the enigma the letter propounded but another six months later she received a letter saying he had joined the Franconian Order in Florence and would dedicate his life to God as atonement for the shame he had brought upon their family name. The boy whom he had kissed in the cellar came to visit, asking after Xavier and she told him that he had left for parts unknown. As he was about to leave with tears in his eyes, her husband returned and in a rage, a scuffle ensued. But the years and the wine had taken their toll on Mr. Zeugma and he collapsed on the floor and died of a heart attack in the midst of attempting to trounce the lad. She told the boy to leave and to summon the police on the street which he did and soon they arrived. She told them it was a burglar that Mr. Zeugma had encountered and so on and so forth. She never heard from Xavier or the boy again until the monastery sent her a letter informing her of his untimely death only yesterday.

Marco placed the letter opener back on the table where he found it and without another word let himself out the front door.

As Marco emerged from the doorway, the setting sun illuminated Saint Sophia's Cathedral across the street full in the face with a blood red light, the gargoyles and elongated emaciated saints that covered its infinitely detailed façade seemed more a vision of hell. A priest in a full length tunic emerged from a side door holding a little boy by the hand, walking toward the plaza as a thousand pigeons took off in an unnatural shower of feathers and flapping wings. It was then that Marco realized the source of his pain, indeed, the source of the world's pain. It was the Church, Holy Mother Church. It was the Church that ordered mass burnings of countless Protestants and Jews, the church that ordered the Crusaders' onslaught. He knew that behind every war lurked the shadow of the Pope, his cardinals and his bishops all organized like a vast military machine that ate souls as a whale eats plankton. The church fed a steady diet of guilt to its members, endless sermons on sin and the wickedness of man's most basic instincts. Sex was a sin. Thinking about sex was a sin. Eating was a sin. Eating the wrong thing on the wrong day was a sin. Arguing was a sin. Anger was a sin. A litany of human activities from the simplest to the most grotesque were to be rewarded by an eternity, a forever, of punishment unless, unless, unless one stayed close to the church, feeding it reverence and servitude and, above all, alms. It was Eve, he was taught, who started it all. The first emotion after love that shown from her face was guilt as the bitten fruit in her hand bled its sweet nectar. Beautiful, shapely, a naive female, designed for an hour's pleasure on the grass. Eve. Had he the power to travel in time, Marco would have been by her side and slit her throat himself. Adam with no patch of hair to chase after, would have wept himself to sleep and in the morning Marco would be there to comfort him. But this was the dream of the impossible. There was no going back, only forward.

As the pigeons made ambiguous undulations around the bell towers, Marco thought back to Saint Ubaldo's. Perhaps he was seven or eight years old. It was dark and the dinner bell had not yet rung. He had spent some time, his private time, fashioning a sling shot from a small yew branch. While he hid behind a row of junipers, a covey of quail chittered across the gravel of the drive pecking randomly at invisible food. He took aim and the rock he launched hit one of the birds which keeled over in a small flutter. The other birds, seeing and hearing nothing, looked at their fallen comrade a second or two and then continued their wobbling walk onto the lawn and then down into the valley below leaving their fallen comrade behind. Marco emerged from his hiding place and examined the small mound of feathers gently twitching in the air currents. Birds were very much like him. Death was irrelevant, an abstraction too profound to ponder. Eating, sleeping, surviving until tomorrow was all that mattered. No other humans cared about him and if he was struck down in the street by some unknown hand and fell to the ground, no one would come to him. Everyone would just walk on, too concerned about their own lives to help.

As the hydra sprouts a head when one is severed, Marco knew that killing the men of the church, even the Pope himself was a fruitless exercise in bloodlust; in a matter of days or weeks, each severed piece would be replaced. The Church was an organism with an infinite reach from its brain in the Vatican, through its tentacles, to the minds of people all over the world. Killing any single part was fruitless. It could only be destroyed from within by a virus, the minutest of assassins, which once inside the body of its victim cannot be resisted. Marco knew that he was to be that virus, that once inside the body of the beast, nothing could prevent its eventual death and once it was dead, he could be free from the nightmares, the blood and the empty hole in his chest.

Marco, with a clarity and lucidity in his head that he had never experienced before made his way back to the house of the three young women. They were not waiting outside but instead had donned near normal attire and were preparing a small feast. He knocked and Sonya answered with a broad smile and a light in her eyes.

Seventeen

The dining table was set with all manner of wonderful Hungarian dishes and two gallon jugs of Transylvanian wine of dubious international reputation but a favorite of the locals. They ate and drank and talked the night away, Marco learning that Tanya and Eva, as he learned the others' names to be, both had been orphans like himself, their families killed at their farm near the Polish border by marauding Poles intent on killing Jews but actually enjoying the hunt for human prey so much that anyone even in the neighborhood of a Jew in a rural outlying area suffered the same fate. Eva had been only six when the Poles arrived and they raped her mother and older sister in front of her father and then put out his eyes, kicked him into the street and took turns punching him and beating him with their rifle butts as he staggered sightless with his arms outstretched. Eventually they threw him alive down the village well and his shouts for help echoed up the megaphone of the shaft until the Poles got so irritated they dropped stones on him. Eventually his shouting stopped. In the meantime, her mother and sister had been raped and re-raped by all the men until one of them found Eva hiding under her bed, brought her downstairs and on the dining table raped her young innocent body as well. For reasons unknown to her, she was not murdered as were her sister and mother and she was taken in by another family that had the good fortune to be out of town attending the funeral of a relative in Janskya. They made her into a servant girl although they themselves were poor as blackbirds. When the father, an old man with only one tooth in his head came down to the kitchen one night and began to fondle her as she lay on her mat on the floor by the stove, she pushed him off, kicked him in the face knocking out his one tooth and ran out the door, never to return. She made her way to Budapest and met Sonya and Tanya on the street living by their wits which was a nice way of saying that they picked pockets, robbed rich children and rolled drunks. Eventually, an old lady that owned the house they now sat in taught them the ways of the whore. Eva and Tanya became lovers and were as devoted to each other as husband and wife while Sonya, quiet and introspective, simply did her part to establish and maintain the house especially after the old woman died. It was Sonya who disposed of the cadaver in the river and before long, everyone assumed that the three girls were the daughters of her body and had every right to the home without ever ascertaining or caring whether or not the old lady was still alive or had ever had children.

They were all three happy that Marco had accepted their invitation to stay the night and he sat and told a completely fictional account of his life as the son of an Italian count from Calabria that had opposed Garibaldi and had been executed by firing squad. He and his mother had fled north to Rome with a small fortune in gold coins in a small trunk. When they arrived at the Eternal City, there was a cholera epidemic and his mother succumbed but he had the good fortune to love anise root and apparently his ingestion of the bitter-sweet herb in candy, vegetables and pork made him immune, or so he said. He lived in a fine hotel and finally when he tired of city life, traveled the countryside and had met a rich man on the train to Budapest who offered him a partnership in a copper mine in the Carpathian Mountains. It was with that man, at his home in Budapest, that was where he had had his pre-dinner appointment that afternoon. The story came out like a piece of string being unrolled from a spool but there were several irregular knots in it that did not go unnoticed by the three women. When he finished, they all looked at each other with the knowing eyes of women of the world who had heard it all. But they liked Marco and said nothing. Eventually the wine had its soporific effect and Tanya and Eva went to bed. Sonya prepared the sofa for Marco with a large comforter and a well-worn down pillow, kissed him good night on the cheek and went to her own room. None of the women noticed that the carving knife was missing from the cutting block.

The reader might assume that a few hours later either Sonya crept into the sofa with Marco or Marco crept into her bedroom. In fact, it took Sonya three days to decide to awaken at 2:00 a.m. and go to Marco whose soft, youthful breathing as he slept was as a beacon to her in the dark shadows of the house. She lay next to him naked and caressed his face and neck with the back of her hand until he awoke. So in a world of his own, he had to ask who it was and when Sonya whispered her name, he was quite pleased because he felt protective of her and the others as well, although it turned out that they were protecting him. She took his hand and placed it on her breast and he immediately pulled it away because it felt like a man's chest. Sonya had such small breasts that she was, indeed, more like a young man and had taken to wearing what they called in those days, "falsies" which were really, in her case, a carefully folded woolen sock inserted in each bra cup. Many of her customers were at first disappointed, but by the time they had reached the point of discovery, their passions were too inflamed to stop, their money had been paid and her secret parts were what they were after anyway. Some clients actually were happy with the boy-like chest and her small rump, perhaps, was a good substitute for what they really desired, a small boy, but which would have been unacceptable if discovered not only to his wife and children but to the authorities as well, who looked down at homosexual pederasts as if they were Satan's minions. Those types of men did not fair any better in prisons than they do now.

Marco took the opportunity of having an attractive woman in his bed to explore her crotch and he reached down feeling the hair and assuming that that was all there was. But Sonya's adept movements encouraged him to search further and eventually he found the labia and the moist area between as she began to moan more out of the habit of feigned ecstasy than its elusive reality. He put his index finger in her and quickly removed it, rubbing his fingers against his thumb to ascertain the texture of the moisture, then putting his fingers to his nose expecting the odor of urine but much surprised to discover its own unique scent which was like nothing else he had ever smelled, despite foolish and ignorant reports by male slobs to the contrary.

She reached down and firmly grabbed his flaccid member and it came only partially to life. Her experience indicated it needed some coercion, a common procedure in her trade and when she lowered her head to place it in her mouth, Marco jumped and reached for the carving knife secreted under the sofa cushion for fear she would bite his penis off. Fortunately, before she went any further, she sensed his tension which she attributed to shyness and youth and reassured him that he needed to relax and let nature take its course without her realizing that his nature had been so twisted and malformed by his years at the orphanage that her task was doomed from the start. Without relaxing his grip on the knife handle he lay back as rigid as a corpse as she proceeded to the task at hand. In a few minutes, despite his anxiety, he was fully erect. Analyzing that the sofa did not provide the space he needed for the rest of the sex act as he thought it to be, he suggested they go to her room, to which she assented. She drew back the bed clothes, lay down and he immediately lay crosswise on top of her, his buttocks in the air expecting her to commence the slapping. Sonya had more clients that expected this than she dared to count and was going to proceed apace when she realized that she was not going to be Marco's prostitute but wanted to be his true lover. She spoke comforting adoring words to him as she tried to maneuver her body under his so that their parts would line up as nature had intended them to. But no matter how she shifted, he managed to remain perpendicular to her and not parallel as she wanted. Women, ever the wiser and more tolerant of the peculiarities of the human animal, have an intuitive sense of problems and solutions and Sonya, despite appearing to be a boy with a girl's face, was certainly a woman. She gently told him what she wanted him to do which was simply the act of intercourse but she soon realized as Marco's member went flaccid again that there had to be an intermediate step and she suggested that he lie down face up on the bed. She then convinced him that for his own good as well as hers, she would tie him to the bed, ankle and wrist, and that she would handle all the rest, that he could learn the pleasures of the body without having to work at it and could therefore dismiss the insecurities so common to men that they would not properly perform. Seeing her silhouette in the light of the moon which shown through the window and wanting and needing very much to trust someone, he decided to allow her to teach him. She tied him with some soft satin ropes she had used on a few customers at their insistence and aroused him again with her mouth. She mounted him and in a matter of fifteen minutes had initiated him into the rarified world of sexual union. She untied him and they fell asleep in each others arms, she feeling that she might have fallen in love and he developing a knot of poison in his guts which he later learned was jealousy, not only of Sonya's future clients which he could stop but all her past liaisons as well, which he could not. As she snored lightly in the waning hours of the night, he thought that perhaps by killing her he might keep the memory of this night intact forever. But he wanted more. To kill her was to kill something he loved. And why was she a whore? Because of the woman who took her in. Then, a parade of whores crossed his mind as he came to think that they were all victims as she was and he was, victims of pimps and that to rid the world of pimps was a task he would gladly take on, not forgetting that the Church needed a lesson as well. All in due time, he thought. He was a young man and had his whole life in front of him and, at last, he saw it stretch out toward an infinitely far, but defined, horizon.

Eighteen

18 Marco, Sonya, Tanya and Eva lived in the home as a family. Tanya and Eva continued their work as prostitutes, but Marco forbade Sonya from engaging in her profession. As a bargain with Tanya and Eva, she agreed to do all the cooking and cleaning and Marco would contribute some money. Unfortunately, his funds were running low and he knew that once he was penniless, he would be back on the street and, worse, Sonya would have to resume her work or leave and she had nowhere to go. Eventually, he changed the story of his life to his running away from home because of an abusive father and that settled the issue of why his funds seemed to be diminishing and he was not having them replenished.

A month after he moved in, he left the house at about 11:00 p.m. while Tanya and Eva were busy with two brothers from Warsaw. Sonya stayed in her room after serving wine to the guests and cleaning up after them and she agreed to answer a small bell each of the other girls had in her room to fetch them further refreshments or to show the customers out. She also kept a close ear for the sounds of trouble and would have been quick to respond with a long saber one of the patrons had left behind several years earlier when the old woman was alive. Marco returned at about two in the morning as the last customer was leaving, tipsy, wearing one shoe and carrying the other. He told Marco he had warmed up the short blond for him but to go easy that he had just about burned her out.

Sonya was up waiting and doing some final straightening out and he took her by the hand putting his finger to his lips to silently tell her to make no noise; he had news for her ears only. He made her sit on the bed and lock the door. He took out three hundred forints and poured them on the bed with a great smile on his face. She asked where he got them and he replied it was all in a night's work, that he did not have to sell any part of his body for it and that if she did not ask any more questions, she could have half. She was beside herself with glee, although she sensed something much amiss.

The following Sunday night, he went out again and returned again and every Sunday thereafter he did the same, returning at 2:00 or 3:00 a.m. with sometimes as much as five hundred forints, sometimes as little as twenty. One night he returned empty-handed with his face scratched so badly it appeared as though an alley cat had attacked him. In fact, he said that that is exactly what had happened and he had had to choke it to death with his bare hands for it would not back down from attacking him. Sonya tenderly cared for his wounds and kissed each one. If it had been Marco's last night on Earth, he could not have been happier.

Marco had used some of his money to purchase books mainly on religion and philosophy and a few on science. He spent all week reading and re-reading as if studying for a university degree. The women were much impressed, particularly Sonya to whom he tried to explain his studies not only to educate her but by way of testing himself as to how much he had retained. One particular weekend, he did not leave the house but instead sat in the small chair by the bed and read the Bible almost from cover to cover. Sonya brought him food and drink as he read. The following weekend he repeated the process.

The next Monday, he entered a large building in Pest near the Cathedral of Saint Otis. It was a Dominican seminary and Marco had applied for admission to the priesthood. While he appeared to the committee who met with him as well-intentioned and well-spoken and he certainly had educated himself, his lack of any provable formal pedagogy was a severe hindrance. When he told them he had been raised in a Franconian orphanage in Italy, the priests looked at each other out of the corner of their eyes, smiled and informed him that he could not enter the Seminary of Saint Otis. Marco was peculiarly accepting of this and he made no vows to return or to work harder, to alter his true history and substitute a better one, whatever that might be, or to attempt another frontal assault on the high walls outside Mother Church. He walked back to the house taking a longer way than usual so that he might mull over what choices lay in front of him. Marco, of course, had anticipated the rebuff but he felt that it was good to try with little to lose.

He stopped by the river and watched the barges make their slow way through the city, trucks and automobiles, horse-drawn carriages all clogging the bridges, crossing it as the workday came to a close. He got home in time to help Sonya put dinner on the table and she remarked to him that his face had a wonderful glow to it, the same glow she had imagined a saint to have. He turned to her and in front of Tanya and Eva he knelt in front of her and proposed marriage. Tears filled her eyes and she hugged him saying yes, yes, a thousand times yes and her two friends hugged each other and cried and they all drank and drank that night, locking the front door and pulling down the shades, irritating at least four regulars who knocked and knocked and then left grumbling as they returned to their wives.

The following Sunday they were married at a small chapel and they left for a honeymoon in a rented car at the Bosnian port city of Gadiah which nestled serenely on the Adriatic where the meek eastern waves of the green Mediterranian kiss the cool, white quartz sand. Marco rented a room in a small pale stucco inn with blue awnings and a private terrace that overlooked the sea. It was a perfect week; it never rained, and the only spat they had was resolved amicably. Sonya had tried to make love to Marco without the satin ties, but she failed, or he did, rather and in his frustration, he dressed hastily and stormed out, sitting on the beach by himself until she came out later and begged his forgiveness which he obligingly gave.

Nineteen

19 When they returned to Budapest, they fell back into their routine which continued like the water in the river, to run slowly but predictably, seemingly without beginning or end. News of the Archduke Ferdinand's assassination in Sarajevo only a short way from their honeymoon spot had little effect on their lives but when war broke out, business momentarily dropped off. Tanya began to buy the daily newspaper to follow events as an investor might whose fortune was in the stockmarket. At dinner, she had related how a series of murders and robberies of pimps across the river in Pest had mysteriously ceased while they were on their honeymoon, but that police were still searching for the killer or killers. A few pages later, she read a short article out loud how three train conductors had had their throats slit from ear to ear as they walked home from work, one a day for three days, for no apparent reason, the series of homicides being attributed to anarchists although Eva postulated that it could have been a disgruntled passenger. Laughter ensued, but everyone at the table agreed that it was time to stop buying the newspaper. Eva suggested lowering the price for their services to encourage business and Tanya turned to her and said, "this is a whorehouse, not a poultry market." With that Marco and Sonya returned to their bedroom like an old married couple and Eva and Tanya put on their tried and true schoolgirl's clothing and waited in the doorway for customers which never arrived. That evening the rain was falling in buckets and even the most lecherous of husbands had to be content with their fat wives because not a one of them could concoct a plausible excuse which would fesibly require them to go out in such a downpour with war looming on the horizon and anarchists murdering train conductors and pimps in the streets.

A brisk Sunday night in November, Marco left the house. The city had fallen back into its routine which now consisted of young men enlisting in the army, draft dodgers hiding in the countryside and anarchists putting small bombs in trash bins around the various city squares. While people were angry and uneasy and more than a little anxious about the future, the rent still needed to be paid. Business for Tanya and Eva eventually resumed its former pace; it even seemed to increase, Eva remarking that in times of social upheaval, forms of entertainment that took people's minds off their troubles became more in demand. And as most of their customers were well beyond the military draft age, the enlistments had no effect whatsoever.

When Sonya awoke on Monday morning, Marco was not in bed nor did it appear that he had been and arisen early. Nonetheless, she hurridly donned her robe and went through the house looking for him. She woke Eva and Tanya and the three of them worried through breakfast and came up with all manner of possibilities, none of which seemed probable. All that Sonya could do was sit and wait which she did for three days and nights worrying herself into losing weight and getting, as Eva put it, pekid. There was no sign of Marco and she feared the worst. Even Tanya and Eva, ordinarily taciturn and sarcastic, were concerned and Eva finally suggested that Sonya should go to the police. Eva would accompany her and Tanya would remain home in the off-chance that Marco might return.

They were told to wait once they arrived at the massive police headquarters, an overly ornate and garrish formal palace built by a deposed Duke nearly five hundred years earlier. They sat in a crowded waiting room for four hours where they witnessed tearful women, crying babies and men in and out of shackles being led here and there in a snake-pit of confusion and chaos. Finally, a sergeant beckoned Sonya over to him and Eva followed holding her hand. He gave her a green cardboard pass and told her to take the elevator to the third basement level and to hand the card to the officer on duty. This they did and when the officer read the card he lead them to a small room that was so cold it could have been a meat locker. He wheeled in a gurney with a corpse covered in a sheet on it and he informed Sonya that the body had been found in the street Monday morning and that a piece of paper in the pocket indicated it was the body of Marco Fontana, but that there was no address or any indication of how the police could notify the next of kin. Sonya and Eva held onto each other and trembled, tears running down their cheeks. The officer unceremoniously removed the sheet as if he was unveiling a new statute of the Archduke in the cathedral square at Pest. There, on the gurney, was the body of Marco Fontana, in the clothes Sonya herself had bought him for their honeymoon, his Italian shoes of which he was so proud and the small gold wedding ring. His face was so battered and bloodied that there was no recognizable feature, not a one, and his hair had been scalped revealing a bloody yellow-white skull. Sonya collapsed and she did not awaken until an hour later when the police gave her a small bundle containing Marco's clothes, shoes, the ring and a ticket to retrieve the body when an undertaker had been retained.

Sonya and Eva returned home in a daze and another bout of weeping and sobbing followed their disclosure to Tanya. Sonya went to the bedroom and cried herself to sleep. When she awoke at three or four in the morning, she held Marco's books to her breast then arranged them on his side of the bed as if he were under the covers. The other girls refused visitors for the next week and the three of them never spoke again of the loss, none of them having adequate words for such a morose turn of events.

On Friday, Tanya went to Sonya's room and nearly collapsed in terror when she saw the shape of Marco in the bed under the covers. Sonya ran up to comfort her saying it was only his books and they cried again that evening till their eyes were as puffy as if they had been boxing.

Sonya retired early, locked the bedroom door and prised up the floor boards. Within a space between the joists was Marco's and her money box. Sonya counted out nearly two thousand forints, enough to live on for a few years as they had planned to do, to return to Marco's homeland and perhaps open a shop. Marco even debated going into the book trade. She wept over the thought of their scattered dreams and how when all seemed certain, the winds of fate had sent a tornado to dislodge the paving stones of the road to their future and drop them in front of her like the wreck of a collapsed castle. They would never have had children, she knew, because she had had so many bouts of venereal disease that the doctors told her she had been rendered barren. She accepted this fact then as a natural, even a convenient side effect of her profession, but today, she cursed the old woman, all the whores of history, Mary Magdelene and Saint Frederica, the patron saint of fallen women. At least, she might have borne Marco's child, someone to comfort and to love as the years stretched before her in disarray, but it was not to be.

Of necessity, the routine of the house was restored over the next two months. Christmas came and went without a mention and the three women planned a little trip to the mountains for Easter but the war was droning on and the news of the dead cast a pall over the city thicker than the worst London fog. At the last minute, on Good Friday, Eva and Tanya decided they should make the trip after all, but Sonya had resolved to stay and attend mass each of the holy days. They argued and cajoled but to no avail and they kissed her good-bye and said they would return on the following Tuesday.

Sonya made a spare dinner in keeping with the solemnity of the day and she read Marco's Bible, particulary the tragic events of the scourging and crucifixion of Jesus. She imagined how touched Marco must have been and she shed more tears, went to her room and opened the night-stand drawer where she kept the satin ties. She picked them up and cried into them rubbing their smooth coolness against her blotchy, heated cheeks. She lay down and fell asleep dreaming of Marco and she on their honeymoon and how they watched the sea and talked of their future.

She was awakened at midnight by the sound of footsteps coming up the stairs. She must have forgotten to latch the door and one of the pre-sumptuous customers looking for Tanya or Eva must have simply come in even though there were no lights on. Perhaps, the girls had returned early. She called out, but there was no reply. She shouted with trepidation in her voice that they were closed for business and that whomever it was should leave or she would call the police. It was Good Friday, she yelled and even a whore should have that day off. To her horror, the door to her room creaked open and in the murky dark a man stood in a long tight robe. Trembling, she was certain Satan had decided to take her there and then as a Pascal sacrifice. Summoning courage from the bin of her grief, she shouted at him to leave, that she had a gun aimed at his heart and that if he did not immediately go, she would shoot him, little analyzing that Satan, of all things, had no heart.

"Would you make me rise again?" the man said. The voice. Could it be? "Woman, would you make me rise again?" he said a second time, this one unmistakably the voice of Marco. She reached over and turned on the nightstand lamp. In its sudden glare she could see Marco standing in the doorway in the garb of a priest, a long black tunic, the high collar, the rosary glinting on his chest and the red sash of a Monsignore. Sonya collapsed as he rushed to her, catching her as she fell and kissing her face until she recovered.

"Do not ask questions," he said. "Pack your things and do not forget the money box," he added with a warm smile. We leave tomorrow for Rome. I brought you some new clothes. Please do as I ask. We have world enough and time for me to explain everything." She hugged him until her arms went numb.

"Oh my love, my husband, you are not dead. My prayers have been answered. Oh, Marco."

"And mine as well, beloved. But you must never call me Marco Fontana again. Never. Marco Fontana is dead. Do you understand? Now tell me he is dead."

She did not respond for the words were trapped in her mouth. "If you do not tell me, I shall leave and you will never see me or hear of me again. Now, tell me, Marco Fontana is dead."

She fought back tears that could fill a tea cup but finally she said with a quivering voice, "He is dead."

"Who is dead?"

"Marco, Marco Fontana is dead."

"Never forget it, but know that I am reborn and I am now Father Paolo, Paolo Sabatinni. Do you understand?"

She did not respond but over the coming months it all became clear to her, as clear as the night sky when the frigid air from the Arctic creeps over the face of Europe and allows the million stars to perform for any who inhabit the gutter that might for a moment, perhaps, look up.

Twenty

20 Father Paolo arrived in Rome on a chilly, rainy day but with a renewed vigor for life and to him, his mission was his life. He gave Sonya sufficient funds to rent a decent furnished flat in the north end of the city about three miles from the Vatican. With all his papers in order he reported to the administration and was assigned to the Financial Office of the Church of Santa Maria Della Croce, the third largest church in Rome, which serviced the poorer sections of the city in the west where the Tiber turns before entering the city from its source in the Apennines. Here its water ran clear and blue as it reflected the Italian sky, but with each turn through the city it had more and more waste dumped into it and by the time it left Rome on its way to the sea it was a murky cesspool where dead animals floated here and there, raw sewage and even an occasional corpse, usually one of the Polveras, a teen gang member or a prostitute, people of the street that became souls of the river, as they were called by the Romans.

Father Paolo arrived at the rectory office and met Monsignor Ricci, a man of about sixty years, tall and wiry with rimless glasses and gray eyes that seemed to focus ten yards behind one's head as he spoke. Paolo saw him as able to read minds or sense auras but after twenty minutes of conversation regarding the parishioners and their relationship to the Holy See while being shown to his quarters, he knew that Ricci was simply a small cog in the huge mechanism that was Mother Church. In addition to Monsignor Paolo, there were three priests assigned to various tasks in the office and six novitiates that served as staff.

The Church of Santa Croce had been built in 1650, designed by Bernini Della Robbia who was overly fond of a marble quarried on Corsica that was white and filled with purplish veins and golden chips of mica. In small quantities it had a jewel-like quality. But the entire nave and altar with six serpentine columns was constructed of it and the deep violet veins gave the appearance to the structure of the innards of a behemoth, the large, round stained-glass window over the crucifix, the look of a gapping maw as if the worshipers had been swallowed and were looking back toward the mouth that had engulfed them, a view that Jonah in the gullet of the whale might have understood.. Bernini himself had died during the construction and was buried beneath a large slab of the marble in the apse. When the earthquake of 1782 had struck, a baptismal font had fallen over on the slab and cracked it. When the slab was removed to effectuate repairs, no human remains were found beneath, but the two workers who were delegated to lift the marble fragments swore that there were three skeletons of dogs or wolves within. This was never confirmed by anyone that would speak about it, but a new slab was in place within twenty-four hours and the stone cutter had to carve Bernini's name in the stone in place on the floor instead of upright as he would have preferred in his own studio. After he had finished, the slab was anchored with four bronze bolts and then the heads removed so that the vault could never be re-opened. This only stoked rumors even more and no matter how crowded the church became on High Holy Days, no one sat within twenty feet of it. If someone inadvertently stepped on it, they crossed themselves three times and slept with a horn over their bed and a cross made of holly bows. What these amulets signified was known only to the locals and when questioned by a priest, they denied any knowledge of the custom. In 1824, a priest named Father Rodolfo in an effort to disprove the mystery surrounding the Bernini vault did a little jig upon it in front of twenty catechism students. Within a week, he was dead from a stroke and buried unceremoniously in a churchyard outside the city limits. Old women said they could see Rodolfo's ghost still dancing on the slab as nipping, snarling jaws snapped at his feet from below. Frequent splashing with holy water did little to alleviate the fear the space engendered, although it became a place for cures when a parishioner who had been bitten by a rabid dog was brought to the tomb in a stroke of superstitious good fortune and was miraculously cured. Anyone who thinks that there is a connection between the mysterious remains in Bernini Della Robbia's vault and the bizarre stories related about them over the centuries will be at a loss to explain Father

Paolo's behavior. A week after arriving at the rectory, he awoke at 2:00 a.m., went into the church when the corners and ceiling were as dark as a forest at night and the weak flickering flames of almost extinguished votive candles cast dancing shadows on the walls, and urinated upon the stone having drunk just before retiring two large glasses of communal wine from a jug blessed by the Pope himself. Had one approached the stone after he departed, one might have seen the crude script he drafted with the flow of his water which said, before it soaked in as an indecipherable stain, "Marco."

Twenty~One

21 Father Paolo did admirably well at his new position although had he not, it was not likely anyone would have discovered it, for it was as true then as now that any singular malfeasance in a large organization will go unnoticed until it is too late or until it reaches the ears of someone who cares. What else could explain the rapes, sodomies and the abuse of children by the clergy of a church, when one would think all churches are meant to be safe and should have the welfare of people everywhere foremost. One might wonder how Marco Fontana could so adroitly slip into the identity of Paolo Sabatinni without so much as a sideways glance. The fact is that no one in Rome knew Father Paolo personally, so that any glance directed at Marco would have seen nothing unusual except perhaps too youthful a countenance, too thoughtful a look as he furrowed his brow, too pleasant a smile. The real Paolo, murdered and mutilated in the street by the real Marco, was referred by the Archbishop of Budapest for a position in the Vatican City theoretically at his request as was the custom. What leverage Paolo had over so powerful a personage is not known, but whatever it was, and it could have been nothing other than a single, simple request, it was honored. It might even have been expeditious for the Archbishop to rid himself of Father Paolo for some indiscretion. But Marco fit in very well, avoiding unnecessary intimacies, speaking only when spoken to and never posing a threat which is a surefire method for blending in and making influential friends.

Marco, or rather Father Paolo, as he would be referred to hereafter, had responsibilities that included the accounting for donations received from parishioners. This was a simple but important job that precluded him from having to perform Mass which he might have been able to accomplish had there been no experienced altar boys or other clergy present. Fortunately, he was in an administrative position and, if the regular priest was sick or disabled or detained, Father Paolo would be reached to assign the duty to someone else. On occasion, he performed the sacrament of Extreme Unction, especially if it was for a wealthy parishioner. He would be certain of his being the only clergy present, as was the tradition and could safely muddle through Usually such last rites would be attended to by a Monsignor or on occasion, a Bishop but, if either was unavailable, Father Paolo jumped at the chance.

In one instance, perhaps six months after his arrival, a businessman who owned a company that manufactured the shirts for Mussolini's Black Shirts was dying from pneumonia. It fell upon Father Paolo to administer extreme unction and he arrived with a solemn expression and in full regalia. Ordinarily, an altar boy would have attended, but Father Paolo simply left the rectory alone. In his best Latin, which was not very good, he administered to the dying man and heard his final confession which included the names of several of the Pope's closest advisors who had been bribed and, more importantly, a Count Corcini, a friend of Il Duce who received kickbacks for the awarding of the contract. Father Paolo absolved him of all his sins as the man rasped his last words into his ear, the smell of death on his breath like the moist stench of the Etrurian Swamp. As the man's family wept and his widow nearly collapsed from grief at the foot of the ornate bed in which he lay on satin sheets embroidered with his family crest, Father Paolo anointed his head with oil. He swung his small incense burner in the air, waved his hands in the sign of the cross over the man's prostrate body and, as he breathed his last, he whispered in his ear, "Rot in hell you Fascist piece of shit." Whether he heard it or not at least on this plain, Father Paolo could not determine, but his family was thankful for the kind words they could not hear and for guiding their friend, husband and father to heaven like Chiron taking him across the River Styx.

When Father Paolo returned to his quarters, he jotted down the information he had thus acquired and over the next three years his notebooks became full.

Father Paolo sat at his desk feeling that a time had come for him. The only person who stood in the way between himself and Il Duce was Cardinal Rodolfo Biozzi. He leafed through his notebook, the jottings of various confessions and the leads they provided. Biozzi's name was everywhere, not because he was looking for it, but because Biozzi was shoulder-deep in every aspect of the Fascist regime. In fact, he had been admitted to the College of Cardinals only because of Mussolini's influence and very few of the Pope's inner circle trusted him except insofar as they were protected by his connection to Mussolini. Biozzi was the necessary evil spoken of so much in the political world of 1935. It is a wonder that no one with any real gumption realized there were more necessary evils than any of the goods that were supposed to be derived from them. Father Paolo knew that Biozzi was in cement as far as Mussolini was concerned and that to undo him and take his place would be difficult, if not impossible. But Father Paolo knew that everyone ever born from Adam on down had a weak spot and it was only the worst of men and the best that it was the most difficult spot. It was just a matter of tireless effort and Father Paolo focused on Biozzi's life as if it were his own.

Rodolfo Biozzi had emigrated to America in 1893 with his parents and siblings but in 1913 at the age of 30 he returned to Italy with a mastery of English and a sound grasp of American values and the American approach to world politics. There were rumors that he had murdered two Irish police officers in New York City as a contract killer for the Maranzano crime family, but Father Paolo thought it unlikely that he would follow orders from an ignorant Sicilian like Maranzano. While he believed that Biozzi had killed the two policemen, it was likely for his own ends. He renounced his American citizenship and enlisted in the Italian army. Because of his knowledge of English and his pedigreed education he was assigned to desk work and had the good fortune of becoming the secretary to Bishop Potenza, the head chaplain. He endeared himself to the Bishop through various means and by the time of the Peace Treaty of Versailles in 1918, Biozzi was a chaplain himself with a title of Monsignor for even the clergy was rewarded for battlefield successes and Biozzi in the tunic of a chaplain lead a charge that destroyed two German machinegun nests and captured a German colonel. He was the first chaplain to do such a task and to anyone's best recollection including the ill-informed writer of the history books, the only one.

Twenty~Two

After the war, Biozzi decided to stay with the power base he had created and with Bishop Potenza moved into the Vittoriano, a huge wedding cake of a building dedicated to King Victor Emmanuel II, who with typical Italian mathematics, was the first king of Italy. In front of the Vittoriano was the Piazza Venezia, the grandest square in Rome. On the other side of the square was the Palazzo Venezia where Mussolini held court over as many as one million cheering Italians dutifully standing in the piazza, his famous strutting and near absurd facial contortions made renowned by his appearance on the balcony. Rodolfo Biozzi would look out the window of his office over the throngs and with the aid of his binoculars get a good look at Il Duce as he mesmerized the Italian people. He could imagine himself saying things in boisterous tones from that balcony and vicariously sense the waves of fear and admiration that would emanate from the crowd and wash over him. But he knew that with fame and power came enemies and it was always better to be a few steps removed as Bishop Potenza was. When a large tree falls, some small ones are sure to get crushed, so keep a distance.

One night Rodolfo couldn't sleep. Actually, it was the third consecutive week that he would awaken and see the clock telling him it was 2:00 or 3:00 a.m. He would lie awake in the dark and let his mind wander which only made things worse. Tonight, though, he arose and sat in the dark in his chair. He heard footsteps in the rooms over his, the ones occupied by Bishop Potenza. Then he heard the Bishop's door unlatch and relatch as he walked out. The clock said 3:00 a.m. He resolved to be awake the following night to see if this was a regular pattern or some unusual behavior as a result of there being more than one insomniac in the Vittoriano.

The next night, fully clothed, Rodolfo waited in his chair counting the hours. At 2:30 he heard the footsteps and at 3:00 A.M,.the door opening and closing. He crept out into the darkened corridor and headed to the stairwell to surreptitiously intercept the Bishop. He could hear the rustling of his cassock and see the shadow descend the stairs. He followed. It was early June and the night air still had a slight chill to it as he walked behind the Bishop, ducking into doorways and alleys like a rat looking for dropped garbage. The Bishop made his way down the Via Del Impero and then disappeared down a small side street. Visions of prostitutes filled Rodolfo's head. Perhaps a small naked boy purchased at a pittance from a dark Sicilian pimp. He would soon discover the Bishop's secret vice, the pull of sin that extricated him from his bed and drew him into the world of the creatures of the night by its invisible but taut thread.

When Rodolfo got to the corner where the Bishop had turned, he stopped and peered around the edge of the building. He saw the Bishop enter a thick wooden door with a small lantern over it. Rodolfo scurried down the narrow street staying close to the building so that he could duck for the cover of the shadows should someone appear. When he got to the door, he read a small plaque attached to the wall "Chapel of San Domenico." Was it possible that this ancient chapel built in 1100 was being used as a whorehouse? The thought thrilled him, for it proved he was correct. Every man has a rotten piece of flesh within him that must be tended to. It is just a matter of finding it.

He checked the door to see if it was unbolted. It was. He carefully opened it and saw that it led down a corridor lit with only one small lantern at the end. He went in and followed the stone pavement to an archway. He stopped and saw the flicker of candles, turned in that direction and saw that this was a humble chapel, perhaps forty feet square with a low vaulted ceiling and a simple crucifix and a statue of San Domenico behind a row of blue and red glass jars with votive candles flickering, their gentle paraffin smoke and odor filling the air. In front of the crucifix, carved from wood from the Holy Land, lay the Bishop prostrate, like a novitiate at a robing ceremony. Other than Rodolfo and the Bishop the chapel was empty. He could not believe his eyes. Surely, there was a secret room off the chapel with a bed and chains where some street person waited to receive the Bishop but, no, the Bishop lay there praying flat against the floor, the bottoms of his sandals the only thing looking upward.

The next three nights Rodolfo Biozzi followed the Bishop to the chapel and each night the result was the same. As Rodolfo pondered at his desk in the afternoon over a small lunch and three cups of dark coffee, he realized that the Bishop's weakness was piety and like any other vulnerability, it could be exploited.

That night, Rodolfo left ahead of the Bishop by an hour at least. He got to the chapel and waited behind the confessional in the darkest shadow where no candle's weak light illuminated him or his purpose. As the Bishop entered and lay upon the stones and Rodolfo could hear the bass whisper of Bishop Potenza's prayers, he crept out on bare feet and stood over and slightly behind him, the face of the crucified Jesus flickering in the irregular light of the votives, small glints of blue and red light dancing on the dun walls. Holding his breath, and leaning over the Bishop, with a quick thrust, he pushed with all his might the pointed blade of a dagger deep into the back of the Bishop's skull, making a slight cracking sound and then a thick slurp as the blade entered his brain. Blood and cranial fluid squirted then seeped as the air trapped inside the Bishop's lungs escaped in a death rattle and his prayers ceased forever.

Rodolfo stripped the Bishop's body and spread it on the floor face up in the shape of a cross, as if he had been crucified. He cut holes in the hands and feet and in his side, like stigmata. Then he gouged out the eyes and placed them one each on the side of his head. He removed the Bishop's tongue and placed it over his private parts. Deliberately, as if at a drafting table, he carved a large pentagram on the Bishop's white chest with the point of the knife in an imitation of a satanic ritual. He lifted out thirteen of the votive candles and placed them in a circle around the body. Kneeling down he whispered into the Bishop's ear, "I do not believe in God, but I am afraid of him." Then he stood back and admired his handiwork imagining the gasps of the first people that would enter the chapel in the morning. Yes, he thought, piety had its drawbacks.

That evening, La Prensa reported the ritual slaying of Bishop Potenza, a revered friend and a loyal follower of Il Duce who vowed to track down the satanic Communists who perpetrated the dastardly crime. It was a well-known fact that Communists worshiped the devil and this was a message to the people of Italy that it should not be ignored.

A month later, Rodolfo Biozzi, with a Bishop's miter on his head, sat a large table with Benito Mussolini and pledged his undying support. He proved himself to Il Duce by arresting three known Communists, two men and a woman who had confessed under torture to Bishop Biozzi personally that they were responsible for Potenza's death. They were hanged in the basement of the Vittoriano and their bodies cremated, their ashes scattered in the streets. A year later, after weeding out and personally overseeing the execution of nearly one thousand Communists, Bishop Biozzi became Cardinal.

Now you see how the ink on these pages has convinced you of its veracity but look carefully and see if it can be determined what actually transpired as there were only two men who knew, one dead and the other as mysterious as all men are who show a gentle smile, carry a Bible, wear red garments neatly pressed and who never have been known to utter even the tamest curse. Everyone who needs a truth, constructs a truth and what is actually true, even God would be at a loss to determine.

Twenty~Three

23 Father Paolo was suspicious of Cardinal Potenza's death, but it worked to his advantage by bringing him one step closer to genuine power and authority. He never doubted for a moment that Biozzi was involved, but who was he to criticize? It was a masterstroke of planning and, pardon the pun, execution. There was much he could learn from Biozzi. He opened his desk drawer and placed his daily accounting books in, locking it with a small key he kept in a silver plate on the desk. It was well past midnight as he bolted the door to his quarters from the outside and made his way to Geraldo's room.

Three months later Father Paolo received a memorandum from Cardinal Biozzi concerning an International Red Cross mission. When he met with the Cardinal in his massive office, Paolo was informed that under the orders of Il Duce himself, a delegation from the Vatican was to meet with the Red Cross in Geneva where, with two Americans and two British legates they were to fly to Berlin and then by motorcade to a small town in eastern Germany called Buchenwald to settle international rumors that the Germans were committing atrocities upon political prisoners among them, a number of priests of the Catholic faith.

Mussolini's private plane touched down in Geneva with Father Paolo, Cardinal Biozzi and two pilots. They were greeted by a Swiss member of the Red Cross, a tall silver-haired man named Kriller. In the terminal, were the two Americans, one a woman with a too serious expression on her flabby face and two Britons both aristocratic and in their forties. A more unlikely group of investigators would have been difficult to assemble, Father Paolo thought. They couldn't find a fly in their own bowl of broth had it been doing the back stroke. Such appointments were never merit-based but they were made on the basis of political affiliations and other amorphous criteria. One decent police detective would have gotten to the truth of the Nazi's dirty business in less than half an hour. These people charged with the same task would be so busy dressing, primping, preparing reports and making dinner reservations, that if anything was discovered at all it would have to occur right in their hotel room, perhaps an old Jew strung up by an SS guard from the chandelier and even then they would raise questions and seek a humanitarian explanation. The guard would explain that the Jew had raped Eva Braun and then committed suicide in the hotel room and he was trying to save him for questioning. They would believe it because people of that class, like all diplomats, cannot understand the workings of a mind that cherishes violence and mayhem over justice and humanitarianism. While the British delegate would be concerned about the proper diet for his favorite fox hound, the SS guard had just manufactured a paper weight form a nine year old Jewish girl's skull. It was not a matter of degree that separated them, it was a matter of species differentiation. The Germans were a breed apart from the Italians, the French, the British and the Americans. The French had poodles, the Germans, Dobermans. The British wrote great novels, the Germans made great tanks. It was often questioned how a nation that produced Beethoven and Brahms could produce the Holocaust. Anyone genuinely puzzled by the query would be a fool. German sensibilities and priorities were very different from the rest of Western Europe and to expect an American, for example, and a woman no less, to understand or even question that a German officer would throw a Jewish infant alive into an oven would be like asking a mule to explain a Picasso: impossible is the only word that applies.

Father Paolo was by chance a perfect person for the task at hand at least at arriving at the real truth as opposed to the truth that would appear in the press. His diaried confessions had already been splattered here and there with tales and details from meetings between high-ranking Nazis and high-ranking Mussolini Fascists. Paolo didn't need a visit to know what was going on. He had it from the mouths of penitents, from his own knowledge of the human animal and a familiarity with his own soul to know exactly what the Nazi Horde was up to. He did not judge them, it is important to note, as one might be tempted to do. Rather, he understood their motives and methods and only thought, if anything, they were sloppy about it and illogical. It did not take a genius to see that the little dictator from the land of the Huns with the paintbrush mustache was insane beyond insanity. Only a lunatic would spare the life of a beer-swilling, sausage- gobbling ignoramus of a German peasant and execute a Jewish scientist on the verge of unlocking the secrets of the atom. Discard the baby and keep the shit-filled diaper. If Hitler had any struggle to relate in Mein Kampf it was convincing an otherwise average population of shopkeepers that this made sense. Of course, he did, in spades.

From Geneva, the plane flew to Berlin where it was greeted by four members of the German Red Cross, all hand-picked no doubt for their loyalty to the Twisted Cross. The entire party was to spend the night as guests of the Reich and in the morning they would be driven by limousine to the "Rehabilitation Center" as the Germans called it. In one document that was given to each delegate clumsily translated into their native tongue, it stated that the Furher had decided to remove political dissidents from the general population to protect them from the potential anger of the mob. Tolerance for dissent was a time-honored tradition in Germany according to the documents, but it was only Paolo who could say to himself that if anyone did not believe it, they could ask the dissenters themselves. Unfortunately, they had all met with unpredictable accidents, one way or another.

The ride to Buchenwald was uneventful, the gray and drab towns along the way, forlorn farm animal, taciturn farmers, endless railroad crossings, so many that it seemed Germany must have more rails than roads. Eventually, after the first hour of small talk had exhausted all that could be said, the three limousines pulled up at the gates. As allies of the Germans, Cardinal Biozzi and Father Paolo had the privacy of their own car. They had a driver that could not speak one word of Italian, a thoughtful touch that kept the occupants and the chauffeur from discussing too much about each other or their work. The entourage climbed out of the cars and stretched, maintaining as much dignity as possible, the Cardinal in his shiny black, moire cassock with the red sash, his small skullcap askew. The Commandant and three adjutants appeared as if from nowhere, very obviously awaiting the arrival although everyone but Paolo had thought it was to be a surprise visit, as if the Huns could be surprised by anything. It was Attila who invented surprise.

The facility was only six months old and made of freshly cut pine from the adjacent forest which had been cleared, a railroad spur led through the front gate and the narrow roadway that the cars arrived on led through a double row of fences to the front of the Commandant's house which was a quaint timber and stucco affair so popular with the German bourgeoisie and the inadvertent model of many homes that would, in twenty years time, dot the landscape of suburban America.

The Commandant introduced himself as Claus Brochmeier. He had a narrow face with a long aristocratic nose, narrow-shouldered and trim, looking more an equestrian in his black jodhpurs than a German SS Colonel. He politely invited everyone in for refreshments after the long journey whom all accepted enthusiastically more like an invitation to a garden party or the home of a new neighbor than an investigation into reported atrocities. Erase from your memories the endless runs and reruns of newsreel footage of Buchenwald taken after the war. When Father Paolo and company arrived, the camp was indeed a collection point for dissidents, but genocide was still only in the planning stages on the desks of Himmler and Heydrich. That is not to say that there were not tortures and murders occurring every day at Buchenwald but they were haphazard and experimental as the Germans, ever the perfectionists absorbed in details, sought the most economical and efficient way to kill large numbers of humans.

After tea, the irony of pleasantries exchanged in such a place escaped everyone but Paolo who could see through the smile and the clear blue eyes of Commandant Brochmeier to observe the dispassionate, merciless, fiendish robotic arm of the homicidal German Reich. The entire entourage was escorted to a waiting wagon fitted with seats and pulled by a tractor. It had all the guilty face of a hayride and the green and white striped awning on the wagon made it seem all the more that everyone was going on a picnic. They all boarded and made small talk about the sunshine and the yellow dandelions that profusely sprouted along the dusty road.

Not far from the house, there were twenty long, narrow wooden barracks that held two hundred prisoners each with neat bunk beds fitted with drab woolen blankets carefully arranged along the walls. The "detainees" as they were called, wore khaki uniforms and all had short hair, men, women and children, the sexes being separated in different barracks. There was a soccer field and playground for the children and when random inmates were questioned, always in the presence of the Commandant or one of his adjutants, they all had a stock response, that they missed their homes and relatives and looked forward to a return, that they were well-fed and that their medical needs were attended to regularly and efficiently.

The delegates all smiled after hearing the answers they all hoped for and their original stern and serious demeanor as befitting their rank as delegates of the great nations of the world soon evolved into an easy camaraderie with the Germans, speaking to the inmates as if at an elementary school on parents' day. Paolo could sense behind the skin of the prisoners, their fear and abject desolation, very much akin to what he saw in newcomers to the orphanage, a sense of hopelessness, desertion and above all, isolation and vulnerability. While the Americans shook hands with the inmates and the Britons commented on the weather and the gardens, Paolo told Cardinal Biozzi that if they were going to make an accurate accounting to Il Duce, they had best not be mislead by these barbarians and shown only what they wanted them to see. The Cardinal agreed and it gave him an opportunity of pointing out to the Commandant that he was a personal representative of Mussolini and wanted to view the camp unescorted by the guards. Surely, he said, as allies of the Reich, there could be no objection. The Commandant became shifty-eyed with this unexpected request. After a warning not to get too isolated in too large a group of inmates, after all, he said, it was a detainment camp, he gave his reluctant permission.

As hoped for, the tea at the Commandant's made its way through Cardinal Biozzi's kidneys. As they entered a barracks on the end of a long row of similar buildings, he informed Father Paolo that he needed to use the latrine. Father Paolo disingenuously suggested waiting to use the facility at the Commandant's house, but the Cardinal's bladder had a will of its own and it was not to be denied. Father Paolo quickly selected an inmate and asked in Italian where the latrine was. When no answer was forthcoming, he asked another and finally a third who managed to understand, being a southern German Jew who lived formerly in a town close to, and sometimes over, the shifting Italian-German border. Each time, although no one could have noticed, Father Paolo asked an inmate that looked just like the previous one and had anyone been suspicious or observant or both, everyone he asked looked very much like Cardinal Biozzi.

Paolo requested that the inmate accompany them which he did, leading them out the back door to a small, squat cinderblock latrine, the smell of which was overwhelming. Paolo pretended to have difficulty with the door and again asked the inmate for help which he gave, putting a shoulder against it and having it fly open because in fact it was not jammed at all. Paolo silently imprecated the inmate to stand at the door as if to guard his and the Cardinal's privacy while they relieved themselves. As the Cardinal stood urinating over an open trench complaining about the smell, that he should tell the Commandant that the facilities were sub-par, as he put it, Father Paolo came up from behind and with both fists clenched and raised over his head, came down with such force on the back of the Cardinal's neck that he lost consciousness and collapsed, Father Paolo having to grab the red sash from behind to keep him from falling feet first into the urine and feces-filled trench.

The inmate was shocked and about to call out when Father Paolo told him to shut the door if he wanted to live. In such a place, the threat of death was taken much more seriously than at other locales and certainly created a far more instantaneous peril in its vocalization than, say, in a bar between two inebriated patrons fighting over a whore who may have been the wife of one of them.

He ordered the prisoner to undress as he started to disrobe the Cardinal. At first, the inmate stood stock still but as Paolo stripped Biozzi down to his underwear, he spoke in level tones that he was to switch places with him, that the Cardinal was a baby-killer and most assuredly if the inmate ever expected to breathe the air of freedom again, he was to obey every word that Father Paolo spoke. In short order, the clothes were switched and as the Cardinal began to stir, Father Paolo picked up a loose brick that lay in the corner and brought it down on his skull.

After surveying the area around the latrine, they dragged the Cardinal behind it and propped him up as if he were sitting. As a finishing touch to his plot, Father Paolo reached in his pocket and took out a leather necklace with a Star of David on it and hung it around the Cardinal's neck. The prisoner by the name of Misha Roth, now in the garb of a Cardinal of Mother Church, advisor to Il Duce, in the companionship of Father Paolo Sabatinni made his way deliberately back to the Commandant's house where the entire entourage waited and chatted.

It was three in the afternoon and a light rain began to fall as the limousines traveled back to Berlin. By 8:00 p.m. the plane touched down in Geneva and Misha Roth and Father Paolo alighted in Switzerland. Father Paolo gave his suitcase to Roth and told him to change clothes in the men's room and to make his way to a safe house in the city. While the Swiss, he said, were indifferent, greedy bastards, he had heard that Jewish bankers had established certain havens for Jewish refugees and in no time he might be reunited with his family or in the alternative, transported to a safe country. Misha's eyes filled with tears and he told Father Paolo that he would never forget him, that he owed him his life and was certain God would protect him wherever he went. Paolo smiled and said nothing although he could not agree more.

That night, two SS guards found a prisoner at the back of the latrine, someone who had obviously been thrashed senseless by the other inmates. When he protested in an indecipherable language, they beat him with their rifle buts, knocking out his front teeth and lacerating his face so badly that his cheeked flapped open revealing the inside of his mouth where his tongue lolled like a rat trying to escape down a burrow. They roughly picked him up to a standing position and the necklace popped out of his prisoner's jacket. This enraged the guards further and they slapped him, saying he had a lot of gall to wear such an obscenity, the Chosen People, indeed. With eleven other prisoners selected at random but all Jewish, as the one behind the latrine, he was loaded into the back of a military van that had been modified so that the exhaust fumes were pumped into the van. As it rambled around the camp for twenty minutes, the choking fumes exterminated the dozen riders. The back door of the van was opened and the bodies pushed out by inmates assigned to that task. The corpses were stripped down and carried one by one by two inmates one holding the feet, the other the hands. A Jew from Bonn noticed that one of the dead men had an uncircumcised penis. He gestured with his chin to the other Jew, a young Communist from Berlin, who smirked in response as if to say, "I wonder what he did, the poor bastard." The SS Sergeant who drove the van reported that it took two gallons of diesel fuel to kill twelve prisoners at a cost of twelve pfennigs per man, twenty-five percent less than a bullet but twenty minutes longer. Commandant Brochmeier wrote it all down, had Helga his secretary type it up and had it forwarded to Reinhardt Heydrich, Aryan protégé of the Final Solution, for his perusal.

In the morning, Father Paolo reported to the Pope's liaison that Cardinal Rodolfo Biozzi deserted his post in Geneva, having run off with a young woman that he had obviously known for some time, telling Father Paolo that he intended to marry her and emigrate to America. Within a week, an all points bulletin was out for the Cardinal's arrest and Father Paolo, formerly known as Marco Fontana, replaced him as Vatican Liaison to Il Duce

Twenty~Four

24 Gauls, Romans, Merovingians, Carolingians, a platoon of imbecile Pippins, degenerate Louis's, profligate Charles's, and spiritually and physically deformed Richards came and went while the chalk, sand, and volcanic ash of Burgundy became the most fertile soil for the vines of the Fontenot family. This family was older even than the Roman occupation of Gaul under Julius Caesar. Originally, the Frontanagorax Clan painted their faces blue, wore animal pelts, procreated like bears in the woods and were wild enough to secure thirty-three thousand hectares in the valley and surrounding foothills of the Lorax River, today called the Loir, by being slavishly devoted to every Frankish barbarian king that could secure them the wealth they coveted in exchange for fealty.

Like all of the Gauls, the family softened under the organization and tutelage of the perversely sophisticated and addictively decadent rule of the Romans. The face paint was discarded in favor of rouge made from rose petals and the pelts of bear and fox became Egyptian linen, togas and tunics. Their penchant for roaming and living off the spoils of conquest and pillage was abandoned down to their chromosomes and they became fat and happy agrarians who abused their slaves and serfs as well as any Roman patrician, with enough leisure time to visit their own scaled-down coliseum and watch atrocities for amusement and titillation. And so the guttural and brutal name of Frontangorax, as wild as a Pyrenean boar became Fontenot, as tame as a drop of snot seeping from the nose of weeping whore.

A visiting Roman procurator charged by one of the emperors with increasing tax revenues, convinced with little difficulty the second or third Fontenot patriarch that wheat and cotton would not fair as well in the dry, chalky soil as the scraggly, paper-barked vines that grew so abundantly in Umbria, a place known for soil so poor that even the ants had to subsist on stealing from one another's colonies. In exchange for fifty of the grapevines, which the procurator by no mere coincidence had in his caravan, he received some gold, a Frankish ivory-handled scimitar and three nights with the patriarch's only daughter, Lavinia. From this union sprang the master's sole heir, a bastard son named Julius Borax Fontenot whose marble portrait bust can still be found in the cellar of the Fontenot mansion and who was the founder of the Fontenot winery, the finest in all Burgundy. He was as wily as a dragonfly and as quick-witted with gold coins as the best croupier in Monte Carlo. But by the time of our story or at least the roots of it, his seed had been so debased by the sometimes insane, often lazy and generally simple-minded semen of the successful suitors of the Fontenot women, that it is a miracle that one of their offspring did not uproot the ancient vines and replant wheat and cotton. Somewhere in the chaotic history of the family, the original thirty-three thousand hectares were reduced by parceled sales to three thousand.

We must digress if we are ever to truly understand the characters of this tale, into a licentious purview of Europe from the vantage point we occupy today, arrogant and self-important as every generation that proceeds. The English are noted for their passion under the lash, spankings and punishments a substitute for supple lips, firm breasts and even, white teeth; the Italians for their promiscuity, some bedding as many as a thousand in a lifetime and these delivery boys, bakers and mule skinners; the Italian aristocracy, well, it is no coincidence that Casanova was an Italian. The Germans prefer domesticated animals, sheep, sows, heifers on the hoof which end up minced, rammed into their own intestines, then boiled and spread with noxious mustardy condiments accompanied by flatulent brews. The Russians, the world knew, had little luck with the seduction of Russian women and far preferred the less discerning taste of the rape victim. The Irish, flaccid from alcohol, the Spanish, quick as dogs and like dogs asleep in a minute for the better part of the afternoon. And the French? They make love with their mouths, placing their tongues and lips in places most other races are reluctant even to touch. When a tongue is a substitute for a penis, lips concealing teeth, a replacement for lips with no teeth but a fringe of inviting hair, it is easy to surmise why the French are masters of the culinary arts and the taste buds of French vintners are the envy of heaven itself. A race with kings that look like women with powdered pink wigs, layers of satin, thick silk undergarments, high-heeled shoes and the brains of a Burmese baboon, it is no wonder that they had no conquests, could win no war and retain no empire until a short Corsican, more Italian than the Pope and despising the French more than the English, by the name of Bonaparte provided France with its only glories outside the wine cellar and the kitchen.

While peasants fret themselves to a face full of wrinkles and warts about whether there will be food to last the winter and enough profit to pay the rent, rarely looking beyond the next harvest season, the nobility never ponder the availability of food, rent money or the weather. In exchange for the certainties of daily necessaries, they must, on occasion, ponder a fork in the road without guideposts, one path to continued idle prosperity, the other to ostracism, bankruptcy and even death. Such a divergence in the road presented itself to Baron George Fontenot as the 1700s began to wither in the winter of the century while the spring buds of the 1800s waited to bloom.

Twenty~Five

25 The Baron was on intimate terms with Louis XIV, visiting Versailles and entertaining the king and his Austrian wife Marie Antoinette at the Chateau Fontenot, now one of the most beautiful houses in all of France. The grapes of the Fontenot vineyard produced the royal family's favorite wines and it had been recorded in some newly discovered secret diaries that the queen would visit the baron with her entourage and engage in sexual acts with him under the vines, both dressed as harvesting laborers in one of Marie's frequent attempts at imitating the lower classes without even remotely understanding them. Not that it made any difference. The mob, sweaty, unwashed, smelling of onions, pickles and greasy hair, wanted blood, especially the blood of the educated, the rich and the privileged. What other chance would it get to avenge the status quo? There is no proof whatsoever, nor is there likely to be, that the death of the king and queen of France put one sou in the ragged pocket of any of the riff-raff that toothlessly cheered as the rusty blade of Madame La Guillotine ignorantly dropped in a thronged square in the City of Lights on the most pampered and privileged necks in all Christendom.

The Baron, being a Baron, appeared on many lists of the enemies of the government, but he was small potatoes in the scheme of things and, being a country man known more for producing great wines than decisions of state, little time was wasted on him by the new regime.

The Fontenot vineyard master was Pierre DeLuge, a rough man who substituted his love of the fruit of ancient vines to the fruit of his loins, for he had no children. At fifty he thought he was content with his plump wife and the comfortable stone cottage on the grounds of the chateau. But the new egalitarian dogma that swept over France like a plague put thoughts in his simplistic mind. After all, he did all the work, while the Fontenots reaped all the benefits. Is there a man or woman alive who while sweeping the floor in his employer's shop does not indulge the same thought?

The Baron and his wife had three children. There was Michel, the oldest son at twenty-five, Philippe at twenty-three and Rosalyn at twenty. The two boys looked forward to the ownership of the chateau and were, as they say, dyed the rich burgundy of the grapes to their shoulders. For years, Pierre eyed Rosalyn who cut a fine figure with pert breasts, a narrow waist and a behind that was as round as a pumpkin. Even the most faithful servants and employees have eyes and sex glands and the battle between loyalty and animal instincts rages in everyone. Ask any clergyman, if you doubt.

It was a simple matter for Pierre to inform on the Baron, especially seasoned with the tale of his doings with Marie Antoinette. Ultimately, Robespierre, the monster of the revolution received word that the Chateau Fontenot was still unjustly owned by a nobleman and that the vineyard master, Pierre DeLuge would gladly take over the operation and contribute fifty percent of the revenues to the revolution, more specifically to the secret Swiss accounts of Robespierre himself. Of course, Pierre did not want harm to come to Rosalyn, at least not at the hands of the Directoire. And then there was Madame DeLuge, Pierre's wife who loved the Fontenots, particularly the children whom she knew all their lives. She frequently had reactionary thoughts and was opposed to the revolutionary "cleansing" of the nation. In short, she was a threat as well, or so Pierre informed. While Roslyn went on one of her daily outings to the river edge with her maid, Lucille, Pierre arranged for two of his loyal men to kidnap her. She was kept tied up in a deserted forester's cottage while the men received the maid as a plaything for several hours as payment for their services. Lucille's body was, after they had finished with her, put in a shallow grave under the apple trees in a remote corner of the grounds.

That day, the men of Robespierre revolutionary guard arrived regaled in their tri-colored buttons and three-cornered hats. They arrested the Baron and his wife and in a scuffle the two sons were killed defending their parents along with Madame DeLuge as an accessory. As an example of the futility and moral turpitude of resisting the righteous cause of the revolution, their bodies were dumped in the large oak winepress and their juices along with half a ton of grapes were squeezed out. Nearly thirty cases of the 1799 vintage Chateau Fontenot were produced during that pressing and the few surviving bottles are prized today above all the vintages of France. One bottle recently sold for forty thousand francs.

Pierre retrieved Rosalyn from where she was bound and blindfolded the next day, she thinking he had rescued her. Hungry, thirsty and disoriented, she accepted the facts of her family's demise with an ocean of tears, thanking Pierre for saving her from the clutches of the kidnappers, never realizing they were her father's own workers directed by the duplicitous Pierre. To her eyes they were both alone in the world as the waves of the revolution had swept away all who were near and dear to them and in a matter of months, with the liberal application of laudanum to Rosalyn's drink, Pierre married her in a civil ceremony under an arbor on the grounds of Chateau Fontenot. He cherished her, at least as far as a simple agricultural heart allowed. He purchased special sheets made in Italy and dyed black for their honeymoon bed, not out of a morbid urge—this was beyond him, but because the image of her milk-white body on the black linens made her appear to him as a rare flower, his own Fleur-de-Lis, forbidden emblem of the monarchy. His coarse, dark-skinned hands callused from decades of wrestling with the vines, ran over her body like crabs scuttling over a corpse thrown off a bridge into the Seine. He devoured her and her spirit withered five years for every year of her life at the Chateau. He changed his name to Fontenot and became, along with the two sons and two daughters he produced with Rosalyn, one of the most ardent supporters of Napoleon, Emperor of France and ruler of all Europe.

The daughters were married off and one of the two sons was killed at Waterloo at the age of fifteen, a drummer boy that perhaps had beaten his drum a little too hard in the face of Wellington's enraged troops. The other named Victor returned home to discover that his father Pierre had died of blood poisoning from a gash he received while trimming one of the vines. Rosalyn, his mother, had lost her wits and was confined to a mental hospital in Lyons where she committed suicide or fell by accident out of a third story window, depending on whose version one listened to, a short time later. She was thirty-eight years old but even the attending physician thought she was sixty, if she was a day.

Do not get your calendar out or your ciphering pencils and pads nor your fingers to count upon. If the years and the dates seem confused either they are or you are. Time telescopes in and out and if mathematical accuracy is important to you or the dates of elections, assignations and battles, then you should be a journalist where such things can be twisted and bent to suit your purposes and matters of the human heart which are all that is writ here, are as far from your understanding as the north star is from the bottom of the ocean. Return this and buy an almanac.

Twenty~Six

26 The combination of the peasant stock of Pierre and the watery, noble blood of Rosalyn produced a handsome strain of children, particularly Victor, but the dedication to the vines, a genetic predisposition in agrarian workers, was lost. Victor's children were more interested in drinking the product than perfecting it and by the time Victor's grandson Drouet was born, the reputation of Chateau Fontenot was, as they say, lost in the dustbin of history.

Drouet was six feet, four inches tall, of medium build and a submissive personality. He inherited Chateau Fontenot and saw his future there. He read books on wine-making and talked to the field hands, the wine-master his father had hired and tried to absorb all he could which was not very much. He had dedication without ambition and lacked the intellect to see how the Chateau's product was a continuum from ancient times and a connection to the future. He saw the random, neglected vineyard as a thing needing to be fixed, very much the way he might have repaired a broken wagon wheel. He wanted to do it all himself, a combination of a narrow vision of reality and an overbroad vision of his own talents. If he did not after twenty years of work at the Chateau recapture its former glories, he at least stopped its decline. At the age of thirty-five, he could stand on the roadway looking back at the sweeping hills of the Chateau covered in spidery vines content knowing they produced a passably good product and a newly painted house. For Drouet, this was an accomplishment of which he was proud. The bills were paid, his broken bones and injuries from the years of doing work his ancestors would have hired better qualified men to do were healed. The smile on his face was genuine; his bed was empty except when he was in it.

In the nearby town of St. Laurent there was a grape growers' co-operative. Small vineyards that did not produce enough fruit to justify the equipment needed for the fermenting process pooled their crops together and the profit from the table wine thus produced was divided up according to the percentage of the total crop each member of the group contributed. This was the brainchild of a vineyard owner by the name of Etienne Melot, a wild snipe of a man who relished sadistically teasing his children—he had two daughters—and psychologically tormenting his enduring wife, Rochelle. He was thought a daredevil of sorts, often racing his carriage on narrow roads through the spiney chalk mountains and even attempted climbing the shear eastern face of Mont Ste. Victoire. Some said he had a death wish, but it seemed not even death wanted to keep company with him. When he finally contracted pneumonia and was gasping out his last, he made amends with his wife and daughters none of whom shed a tear. Sorrys are a lonesome group, mementos of hurts that are best forgotten. In any event, Etienne was buried in a modest grave that only deer visited in the evenings to graze on the untrimmed grass near the dull gray headstone.

The two daughters, Flavia and Jeanne, inherited the vineyard and the co-operative and were adept as any females can be at operating a business that should really be the province of men. What they lacked in force of personality they made up for in physical beauty. Many in St. Laurent would have bet twenty years in purgatory that Etienne could not have been the father. Many others would have bet an even greater wager that Madame Melot could not have been the mother. Between the two groups, Flavia and Jeanne were seen as sister Aphrodites, born on the half shell amid foaming waves instead of from the womb, so surreal was their beauty.

Flavia fell in love with and married a captain in the French infantry, a handsome, tall dark-haired man with a large mustache named Andre Casteau. He treasured her above all things and together they moved into his family's chateau in Normandy near the town of Vertemont. There was a rose garden where she spent long hours, radiant in the sun and he would watch her in front of every rose bush or tree as she stooped to smell the velvet blooms and her skin would change to the color of the rose. He told her in the softest tones how this was their Eden. She smiled and said how much she loved him. On their first anniversary he gave her his deceased mother's gold necklace, a rope of gold, thin and fine for a lady's neck and from it hung a small golden apple. His mother had received it from his father who said she was the apple of his eye. Andre repeated the benediction when he gave Flavia the necklace.

The winter was severe that year. Snow fell for three days and Flavia who loved the out-of-doors was getting cabin fever. Andre was content to read in front of the fire but he sensed his wife's restlessness.

The snow stopped. She told him that she wanted to go to Vertemont to buy some things. He knew it was just her way to get outside under the pretext of a useful purpose. The trip was about six miles and she was better than he at handling a horse-drawn sleigh. She wanted no company and told old Wolfgang, the Prussian man of all work, who would normally accompany her, to stay behind. Wolfgang's daughter, Hilda was the chambermaid.

The wind blew snow ghosts all about the garden and as the sun cast its weak red- orange glow onto the glistening snow, Flavia had not returned. Andre, deeply worried, had Wolfgang saddle up their two horses and together made their way to Vertemont. It was a moonless night and stars, as beautiful as they are to dreamers, lovers and philosophers, looked down indifferently at the two men making their way through the cold night. The wind had obliterated any trace of anyone having traveled and Andre assumed, hoped really, that Flavia had shopped and visited in town longer than she realized and decided to stay the night rather than travel alone in the woods after dark.

When the two arrived in town, they went to the hotel and asked after Madame Casteau. No one had seen her. They knocked on closed shop doors waking the merchants who lived above. No one had seen her that day, not just one grumbling to his wife after Andre had left, hinted that she must have run off. Other peoples' pain is no excuse for inconveniencing others and the petty minds of the bourgeoisie will assemble all the pettiness of their caste into well-modeled rumors.

Andre finally went to the police, but he was told it was too late, too dark and too cold to organize a search party. It would have to wait until morning. Andre muttered a curse concerning the sergeant's mother and departed the police station, intentionally leaving the door wide open behind him. It was 2:00 a.m. when he and Wolfgang made their way back home. They rode quietly and steadily scanning the barren woods on both sides of the roadway for telltale signs but the wind and the snow had erased everything. A stag trotted out of the woods in front of them and stopped in the middle of the road, startling even the torpid, exhausted horses. Its antlers rose like arteries above its head, its steamy breath catching the wan starlight glowing like the white of its eyes. It moved on with a snort of indifference.

Less than a mile from the chateau something skittered across the snow from right to left in front of them. Andre's horse took several steps backward and was about to rear but Andre regained control immediately. Wolfgang handed the reins of his horse to Andre and jumped down to see what it was. He picked it up and brought it to Andre. It was Flavia's cape.

They tied up the horses and walked in the direction from which the cape had blown. The moon had risen and a dull light cast obsidian shadows across the blue snow. In less than thirty minutes of searching, Andre found his beloved. Her face and her naked breasts were all that shown in the snow, like tropical islands breaking through a calm sea. Her skin was as blue as the snow. Her eyes the color of black pearls, glazed iridescently over, crystallized by freezing, stared up at the innocent stars. Had anyone been awake in the town, they would have thought the wolves had gone crazy so shrill were Andre's cries.

He dug furiously at the snow until her body was revealed, naked, her throat slashed, her groin bloody, she lifeless as stone. Wolfgang wept silently as he trailed behind his master who carried the corpse of his beloved wife to the waiting horses.

Twenty~Seven

27 Andre was in a trance as he carried Flavia up the stairs of the chateau and dressed her in a white sleeping gown that covered the gash in her throat. He lay her in their bed and sat in a chair beside her as one might keep watch over a feverish child. The next morning, Wolfgang rode to town to tell the police and the undertaker. Both told him they would be there the next day; there was no longer any urgency. The culprit or culprits had probably been passing through and Madame had been at the wrong place at the wrong time. What with the wind and the snow, any clues would have been lost and God would have to judge her murderers although the police would send word to neighboring towns to be on the lookout for "suspicious strangers."

That night, Andre sat by the fire in his bedroom, the flickering light dancing on Flavia's ashen cheeks. Snow was falling outside again. A knock at the front door echoed through the empty house like gunshots. Wolfgang came up to the master suite and informed Andre that a man and a young boy were seeking shelter from the storm and might he invite them to stay in the stable. Andre nodded in ascent.

Echoes of Flavia's weeping caromed in Andre's brain. He went down to the kitchen and made himself some tea. He looked through the frosted window at the stable, put on his coat, took a lantern and went out into the swirling snow. Someone standing in the rose garden seeing this silhouette cross the lawn with the lantern would have thought they had seen the Grim Reaper himself. His two guests were asleep in one of the stalls, snoring like bulls. He raised the lantern to get a better view of the two wanderers to whom he was host. The man wore a jacket of sheepskin, the boy tattered cloth. Their faces were grimy, but innocent in the mellow features of sleep. As he turned to leave, a glitter caught his eye. He turned again and lowered the lantern to the face of the man. Around his neck was Flavia's necklace, the golden apple Andre had given her, tangled in the filthy beard of this vagrant.

As if possessed by Satan himself, Andre walked back to the house and awakened Wolfgang. He told him to get dressed, to get the blunderbuss and to lock the back door of the stable. He was ordered to shoot anyone who might leave. He made Wolfgang swear on the life of his child that he would obey. He swore. Andre went to his dressing room and donned his brilliant blue and red army uniform, his boots shiny in the firelight, his sword polished as glass.

Wolfgang did as he was told and Andre entered the stable slamming the door behind him to awaken the two guests and bolting it. The man bleary-eyed bid Andre good morning and thanked him for his hospitality. The boy sat saucer-eyed in the presence of Andre in his uniform. The man saw that night still covered the world like a shroud. He asked if perhaps Andre would need the help of two stout workers who would gladly trade employment for food and lodging at least until spring planting time. Andre did not respond. After a time, he said, "Perhaps." And then, "That is a fine necklace. Where did you get it?" The man responded that it was the only thing of value he owned now, that it was a gift from his mother long dead and he would never part with it, not for a million francs. The boy was silent but something in Andre's face made him begin to tremble.

Andre seemed to turn as if to leave but with a sudden, silent whip-like motion his sword was unsheathed and like a bolt of lightning struck the man at both ankles severing both feet. The man inhaled with a gasp and commenced to shouting, floundering about in the straw like a stranded seal. Unable to rise on his stumps and run, he cowered in the corner. Wolfgang, hearing the shouts, unbolted the stable door and stuck his head in asking if his master was all right. Andre told him to go back and wait if he valued his child's life. He obeyed.

Andre grabbed a rope and trussed up the boy. He tied a rope to the lad's ankles, tossed the end of the rope over a rafter and pulling on it, hung him upside down. The boy whimpered and cried, tears streaking the grim off his cheeks and forehead like spring rain on a muddy hillside. The man begged for mercy, astonished at the hideousness of their predicament.

Andre turned to him and said, "The sins of the father are visited upon the heads of the children." And with that the sword made a slow arch and fondled the boy's throat. He wriggled and gurgled in a slow pendulum arc as his blood watered the dry straw and dusty earth beneath. In a few minutes, he was dead, rocking slowly in the air casting a dark shadow swinging on the oak walls of the stable.

"Remove the necklace," Andre said softly to the man who, weak from blood loss and abject fear was turning blue in the face. He obeyed. "It was my wife you killed in the forest, pig." The man understood and as Andre leaned over to take the necklace from his outstretched hand, he leaped out from the corner of the stall to tackle Andre. But he was too weak and vengeance, sitting on the rafter like a vulture, alerted Andre. The sword danced one more waltz in the air and coming down in a delicate dip, cleaved the man's skull in two.

Andre summoned Wolfgang who sheepishly opened the rear door again and entered, the blunderbuss at the ready. Together they dismembered the bodies and carried them to the compost pit where Flavia tossed garden debris, autumn leaves and table scraps to create fertilizer for her roses.

The next morning, the police sergeant arrived and viewed Flavia's body. He asked a few questions of the somber Andre, ruled it a homicide and turned over the proceedings to the undertaker who said the ground was too frozen for a burial. He suggested embalming Flavia, waiting until the next thaw. Andre told him to leave. He then instructed Wolfgang to clear the snow, build a fire in the garden and maintain it for eight hours. This Wolfgang did and while the soil thawed, the two of them constructed a coffin of pine planks which Andre lined with their bed linens gently placing Flavia within. He kissed her goodbye, placing the apple necklace on her bosom. Flavia was buried near her roses. Andre sent word to her sister Jeanne. He could not know the devastation his missive wrought upon her.

That spring, Andre went to the compost heap. The body parts had not dissolved into fertilizer as he thought, but had become mummified, the skin wrinkled, leathery and brownish black. He lay them out in the sun and, with a pruning axe, chopped them into bits. Mixed with the rich loam of the compost, he carted the mixture to the rose garden, spread it generously around the bushes and worked it tenderly into the soil.

He saved the heads of the man and the boy and packed them in a box with camphor and wood shavings. Wolfgang carted the box to a town some fifty miles to the south where no one knew him and had them delivered from there by post to the police sergeant in Vertemont who received it just after a solid meal of lamb stew and tomatoes. He opened the box, saw the two heads and vomited his lunch all over his desk.

Twenty~Eight

28 Jeanne Melot was looking forward to seeing her sister soon, so that it was with some considerable joy and anticipation that she opened the letter with the Vertemont post mark. It was late in the afternoon and she sat in the dining room at the large oaken table that had been there for generations, scuffs and stains, scratches and dents that were the reminders of previous members of the Melot family. The letter was short and to the point. Andre had been out of his mind with grief, drunk with suffering and what little emotion he had left for a thirsty world, he poured for Jeanne.

She read the letter three times before it had sunk in. In truth, it never really penetrated but lay upon the tracks of her life as a boulder might fall from a cliff onto the railway. Her soul collided with it and her mind became jarred, derailed. She neither wept nor screamed nor shook her fists at the heavens, nor looked inward at memories unrolling as string from a ball. Her brain simply tilted ever so slightly off its normal axis giving an imperceptible wobble to her thoughts that would remain there for the rest of her life. The sister that attended the funeral of Flavia was not the sister that Flavia knew. The damage was permanent and irreparable but hidden deep within the emotional foundations of her spirit. Life went on at the co-operative as it had for years and no one could see the changes although some of the more intuitive people coming in contact with Jeanne came away sensing something very much amiss.

Late in the autumn of the next year, Jeanne now the sole owner of the co-operative, met a tall, gentle, nice-looking vintner by the name of Drouet Fontenot. He was polite and patient and a year later they were married at the Chateau Fontenot, the bride's blond hair more golden than the August wheat cascading down the sides of the distant foothills. Drouet was more proud of his new wife than even of his chateau and the wine it produced. Each label from his wedding day forward had the name "Jeanne" printed on it just above the vintage year. The blood of his vines, the blood of his ancestors and the blood of his wife all mixed in a single ceremony. In less than a year, Isabelle Fontenot was born, the blood of all three coursing through her veins.

The birth was difficult but the mother and daughter survived. Future pregnancies were out of the question, the attending physician told Drouet. Jeanne felt that the death of her sister and the loss of her ability to bear any more children were a judgment upon her. She sought the counsel of the parish priest, Father Jacinto, a Spaniard, who heard her out and tried to explain the mysteries of God's will. The vagaries of his explanation did not soothe Jeanne but only added to her sense of loss and confusion. She began to weep into the priest's shoulder and he comforted her as best he could. She looked up at him and apologized for her tears. He responded by kissing her full on the mouth and grabbing her breast. She pushed him away and cursed him as he grinned. From that point on she renounced her Catholicism. Sometimes, any excuse will do to vent anger, the easiest of all human emotions.

In a few months of soul searching, she became a Lutheran joining a small congregation in a town twenty miles away led by a German minister named Gerhardt. She was entranced by him and in a short time had transformed her grief and sorrow into a profound love of her new faith. All vestiges of Catholicism were removed from the chateau; statues of saints, the Virgin Mary and crucifixes were carefully packed into a crate and burned. A small wooden cross over the bed replaced them all along with her new, somewhat repressed joy for life. Because she could not get pregnant, all sex relations between her and Drouet ceased as Reverend Gerhardt instructed her that marital relations not for procreation were sinful. She cut her blond hair short and always wore a bonnet and all her fancy dresses were packed in mothballs and stored in the attic. The wine of the chateau would never pass her lips. A Lutheran Bible was by her bed, in the sitting room and in the kitchen and she never failed to read from it. Prints of Bougereau nudes, women in gardens, women holding grapes, men dancing were all taken down and the walls of the chateau were as bare as the head of a bald man. Only nail holes and the faint shadow of the removed artwork remained, all unnecessary or frivolous details of the décor, expressions of a material joy in life and pride in one's home were discarded with the trash. In a matter of days, the chateau's formerly inviting interior resembled a monastery. Some visitors thought it looked like a prison.

Drouet became somber and silent, doing his work as if in a trance. He now had separate quarters from Jeanne and they rarely spoke. One day he walked up one of the surrounding foothills and sat upon a rock gazing back at the Chateau Fontenot, gold in the light of midday, the thermal currents rising up the slopes caressing the vines. Nikolai had followed him and after a time so as not to intrude, he sat down near Drouet and began to speak. This was the tale he told:

"As you know, Drouet, I am Russian. I was winemaker to the Czar who rewarded me with a beautiful dacha in the Crimea and three hundred hectares of the finest land for the vines. There was nothing I needed, for he saw after all my wants and my wants were simple and few. After all, I had met the love of my life, Katya, in Moscow. She had hair the color of midnight—no darker, so black it was blue in the light, with gypsy eyes and a fine pointed nose. I don't know what she saw in me but I've been told I cut a fine figure as a young man and everyone knew I was a sharp-shooter by avocation which impressed the women for miles around. That wolf gun was a gift from the Czar and I could shoot a tick off the ear of a wolf at one hundred paces; at fifty I could shoot its little ugly head off.

"Katya and I were happier than the law should allow. We loved one another like you read about in novels. We made a beautiful little girl whom we named Vera which Katya said was Latin for truth, which I think it is. I would call my little baby girl Verashinka and hold her to me as much as I could, she looked so much like her mother that I could not help but love her, my little gypsy daughter, the light of my life.

"At the vineyard we had a foreman to oversee all the workers. His name was Zhukov, a short unpleasant man with a thick neck and a face like a weasel punctured by tiny dark eyes that never looked into your own. I used to think he was overly respectful and would look at the floor when addressing me or Katya but I came to realize too late that it was not respect but secrecy for he did not want me to see what lurked behind his eyes in his sick brain. When he thought I was busy tying up the vines or examining a leak in one of the barrels, I could see him eyeing my Katya, the way a wolfhound will watch a poodle on the divan, as if waiting for no one to see and pounce upon it as a midday snack. I would have discharged him but his work was impeccable. All the hatefulness about him caused the workers to fear him and while I was sappy with love and affection in my life…they would have taken advantage of me, you know how shiftless laborers are if given any leeway…but Zhukov was feared if not respected and so without him I would have been lost. He was like your asshole: you preferred not to see it, you wanted to wash every time you touched it.

"My cousin Vanya lived with us, an old man who was not as selective about who he kept company with as most. He was lonely and rarely left his room but he was quick-witted and a master of chess. Each Thursday, Zhukov would challenge Vanya to a match and they would play in his quarters at the other side of the hall from my study. Here I would read when I was not working on the accounts, waiting to be summoned by my lovely Katya for whom I would have counted all the souls in hell.

"There came a time when Russia had got a cancer, a terrible cancer that ate her from within. The Bolsheviks, whom we now call the Communists were rampaging through the countryside, stirring up the peasants, the serfs, the workers, and the army. They had ridiculous notions of equality as if anyone with any sense could think a beggar was the equal of a prince. But the poor are lazy at heart and where their souls should be is a knot of green mucus called envy. Now Zhukov was a smart man, a survivor. He would never let anything so useless as a soul or loyalty or honor stand in the way of surviving, maybe even getting ahead, and so with a band of good-for-nothings from the town they formed a sort of militia. More like a gang, really. Of course, when the Czar's troops were about or the Cossacks, these men dug ditches and cleared latrines, the ass-pickers, but when it was only the civilian folks scratching out their daily lives, they would raid and do terrible things especially to the Jews and the women. Terrible. So Zhukov became feared even more. I should have shot him when I had the chance but I didn't, fool that I was…am. Then word came that the Czar was killed by a bunch of ruffians with dirty balls and toothless whore-wives and Russia was a great bear without a head, the White armies of the old regime fighting the Red armies of the new, each passing through villages like storms leaving destruction behind. Eventually, the soldiers revolted and killed all the officers and everyone was a Bolshevik—

comrade this and comrade that. But it was all bullshit. The poor stayed poor and the degenerates got rich.

"While it was up for grabs as to who would rule Russia, Zhukov put his eggs in the Bolshevik basket and took to wearing a distinctive red hat with a tassel on one side, strutting about like a Mongol prince. He looked the clown, but no one laughed.

"One evening Katya went to bed with a terrible head cold, poor dear, and I stayed up late, finished the account books and read some Pushkin, dear old Pushkin, a relic of another age. It was a Friday and I heard footsteps down the hall near Vanya's room. I looked out the door thinking it was he up and about at midnight; perhaps he was ill. But no, it was Zhukov leaving Vanya's room. He was carrying a small bundle; they must have played chess, I thought. At least he kept old Vanya company, the prick. I finished reading and took my candle with me to light the way. I checked on Vanya and he was asleep. I checked on little Vera but her crib was empty. I looked under it, behind it, all over. I woke Vanya and asked if she was with him. He answered, no. I ran to Katya and woke her. Vera was not there either. Poor Katya, sleepy-eyed, started her frantic search but to no avail. Where could our infant daughter be? Then I remembered Zhukov and asked Vanya why Zhukov had visited him on a Friday. Vanya said he had not been there. The truth washed over me like ice water from the Garutzki Falls of the Volga. The package he carried was no package. It was my Vera. Zhukov had stolen her. The rumors of the Bolsheviks trading girl-children for food or worse for eating children in these times of starvation must be true. I ran downstairs, got my wolf gun and my horse and made my way out into the snow. The moon was up. Zhukov's tracks were clear like black splotches in the snow. His old nag of a horse was lame and it was easy to see the crooked tracks, even in the weak moonlight. His horse was wobbling while mine cantered. I followed him to the woods at the crest of the hill that rose to cover the feet of Mt. Skalnikov. There, the land dropped down hundreds of feet. He must have gone to meet his men holed up in a campsite in the valley below. My horse, blessed animal, confidently went down through the brambles and drifted snow and then I caught sight of him. I could see that infernal red cap with the tassel at one hundred paces even at night so fired up were my senses—like the scent of a wounded stag to a wolf. On the back of his horse was the package, my darling Vera, tied like a bedroll.

"He was stopped at the edge of a narrow rock-filled stream and paused to cross. I dismounted quietly and took aim. The first shot knocked him to the ground. His horse stood still, shocked from the noise that echoed like thunder and the sight of her master lying in the streambed. He crawled through the water and started to make his way up the hill on the other side. I aimed and shot again. He stopped moving. I waited fifteen minutes to see if his men had heard the commotion and was prepared to shoot his nag if she decided to bolt. But the horse was old and tired and stood there, head hung low as if at the end of a very long trail. I wanted to run to my Vera but if Zhukov's men were about, attracted by the shots, we would both be killed. So I waited.

"When no one appeared and I could wait no longer, I walked to where the horse was. I untied the bundle and was shocked to see it filled with only a rag doll. I waded through the stream and found Zhukov's body. I turned him over, but it was not he. It was someone dressed like Zhukov. I didn't know who he was but he must have been some patsy Zhukov offered a few kopecks to.

"Then, as if the Lord Jesus Himself had reached down from heaven and touched my brain, did I realize that Zhukov had lured me out here—I had been gone over an hour and my lovely Katya was home in bed at the dacha unprotected except by old cousin Vanya.

"I remember no details of how I scrambled up the hillside back to my horse. My face was covered with hundreds of scratches, my eyes tearing from being lashed by a thousand small branches. I raced back to the house and saw many horse tracks in the snow leading in and departing. My heart turned to coal and dropped into the empty furnace of my stomach.

"The front door was wide open and I ran in yelling her name 'Katya, Katya.' But, no answer. I ran upstairs and found Vanya on the floor, a knife buried in his back up to the hilt, the handle broken off as the murderer tried to remove it. Muddy footprints covered the rug toward our bedroom. I entered fearful of what I might see, but the room was empty. I called out her name. No answer. They would never have taken her. She must have hid. I ran through the dacha calling her name, opening the attic door, the cellar door, the pantries, then, I thought of the stable, she must have slipped out the back, hearing the commotion of the thieves in the night.

She ran to the stable. It had to be.

"I charged out the kitchen door and ran to the stable. It was quiet. I opened the door and beheld my Katya naked across a bunch of hay bales. She had been stabbed in her breasts innumerable times. Her private parts were bloody and the precious triangle of pubic hair had been scalped off as a souvenir. Her teeth had been knocked out and her eyes blinded. This was Zhukov's vengeance for my success and my happiness. This was the calling card of the New Order. The old ways were dead with my beloved Katya. And barbarians had raped the world.

"I knelt before her body and wept, more tears than I thought my aching head could hold. I cursed God and told him that should I encounter his son Jesus, I would personally crucify him again. I carried what remained of my Katya up into the hayloft to keep the wolves from finding her. The scent of blood must have floated for miles. I covered her with my cloak and made my way back to the house in a haze of fear and loathing. I searched everywhere for Vera, in every nook and cranny of the house and all the outbuildings. I went to Vanya's body and started to lift him to take him to his room where my grief overcame me. I simply knelt again and wept, collapsing like a mother at her child's funeral in a faint.

"I was awakened by Petruska, the housekeeper arriving with her daughter Anna. I told them what had happened, having to slap poor Petty to get her to listen to me through her tears. They helped me carry Vanya to his room and I readied for my tracking of Zhukov. I had a skinning knife and my wolf gun, a day's rations and enough fury to make Satan blush.

"Hatred is like a virus, my friend, it made my senses keener than the animals. The tracks in the snow were as lighted beacons to me. You might only have seen the confused clutter of horseback travelers. I saw Zhukov in the lead and three men with him. They were not in a hurry to escape thinking, perhaps, that my grief would turn to fear and self-protection. They did not know, nor could they have, that I had traded my soul for venom. Had St. Peter himself tried to stop me, I would have slit his throat.

"They were heading north to Moscow. I calculated that at my rate of speed, I was traveling two to three times as fast as they. In the village of Masanka, I saw four horses outside a tavern and hid myself and waited to see who would emerge to mount them. There was no sign of Vera and I had to put my darling child out of my thoughts because to ponder the possibilities of what terrible things they could have done to her would have cost me my mind which I needed today. Tomorrow, I would gladly throw it in God's face and tell him to make me into a cockroach, that I might dwell in darkness forever and eat garbage as if it were a feast, anything so as not to think of my lost family. I was impervious to the cold and stood in the shadow of a doorway like a statute. I don't think I even blinked my eyes.

"In an hour's time, Zhukov and his three comrades emerged from the tavern, drunken and shouting foolish obscenities and greasy laughter. I did not recognize the other three but one looked like Fyodor, one of the field workers at the vineyard, but I could not be sure. And, what difference would it make?

"They traveled several hours on the narrow road and I followed through the woods to the right of them keeping back one hundred yards. My eyes like telescopes saw every nuance of their behavior. They stopped and one man dismounted to relieve himself in the woods. Shy as a girl he walked deep into the woods to take a shit. I tied my horse and as he walked, so did I as an iceberg floats silently hidden beneath the waves toward a ship. He dropped his drawers and squatted, humming a tune. I could see the steam of his breath and his turds. I came up behind him, grabbed his hair and with the skinning knife severed his vocal chords and his arteries. He struggled like a hen as I twisted him by his hair and forced his face into his own feces. His death was too good for him.

"After a short time, the men on the road called out his name, Petrov! again, they shouted Petrov? They dismounted and followed his tracks to where they saw their friend, his ass facing them and the stench of his shit in the air. They crouched low like trapped animals but it was too late. The first bullet of the wolf gun found the second man's forehead and pieces of his brain and the back of his skull flew out like slop for the hogs. The two remaining men turned to where they thought I was hiding and raised their weapons, firing into the pine tree which still had the smoke of the wolf gun's breath. They fired into it but to no avail because I had sidled to the left behind a large boney- skinned elm. My second shot tore into the other man, hitting him full in the chest, and sending him sprawling like a rag doll thrown by a petulant child. He was gasping and writhing on the ground, his ribs protruding from his torso like a crown of lamb. But Zhukov looked only at the elm. His first shot hit the stout tree as did his second. The third never left its home, as his gun, neglected by a crass and careless owner jammed with a loud but vacant click. I stepped out from behind the elm and took aim. He saw my face as a man sees his own ghost. Mr. Nikolaievich, please, sir, please have mercy, dropping his gun and falling to his knees in the bloody snow. Where is my daughter? I asked with a steady voice. I don't know, sir. How could I? I aimed the gun and fired, clipping off his left ear which flew into the air like a wood chip from a woodman's ax. He fell to the right and shrieked as a woman in labor shrieks, putting his hands to where his ear had been. Back on your knees, I commanded. He obeyed. You can still hear out of your other filthy ear, swine. I asked again, where is my Vera? He saw that the aim of the wolf gun was at his right ear. We traded her for food and drink. She's at the tavern back in the town of Maranska. The tavern owner's wife was barren and she wanted a child. It was a kindness. I fired and lopped off his right ear and three fingers of the hand that was holding it to protect it. Traded for food? I asked. But I remember nothing of his answer if he even had one.

"I ordered him to stand up which he did and with his hands on his bleeding ear-holes I lead him down into the valley. The sun which had begun to shine brightly thought better of it and hid fearfully behind a blanket of anonymous clouds. I found a stout tree and tied him to it in a kneeling position, his arms and legs tied behind him, his belly protruding outward. I chose the spot more carefully than you might guess. My brain, not so quick when I am content, was now as a razor. Napoleon himself would have feared me. Near the tree was a burrow, perhaps three feet in diameter, with freshly scraped snow and gravel at its mouth. This I knew to be a wolverine's den. Wolverines, animals that would never have been allowed on the ark. These were vermin designed in Hell, the animals that even bears and wolves would run from. Larger than foxes, teeth like a crocodile's, and the souls of fallen angels, assassins of the wild, proof that man is not the only accursed sadist on this planet.

"I exposed Zhukov's belly and smeared it with the blood dripping from his ear holes. I threw a rock into the den and retreated twenty paces to wait. Zhukov may have been pleading or praying or cursing his mother's womb or repenting or some such waste of breath but it all turned to shrieking as four wolverines emerged to see what the ruckus was about. They circled cautiously, perhaps remembering the Trojan Horse and thinking this meal was too good to be true. But the leader of the pack cared less for Homer than I do and he approached the squirming Zhukov's belly and sniffed it. Then he licked it. Undaunted by Zhukov's screams and made brave by the salty smell and taste of his blood, the others came near, licking the fresh blood from his ear holes and face as he squirmed and frantically wriggled. The leader of the pack took the first bite and in a matter of minutes Zhukov's liver was hanging out of his belly like the tongue of some insane monster. They gnawed hungrily and leisurely on it to the background music of his wails.

"I made my way out of the hiding place and told them to enjoy their feast, that they now owed me a favor. They looked over their shoulders and sensing that I might be more ferocious than they, returned to their eating. As I got to my horse and then to the four horses tied at the roadside, I could still hear his muffled weakened shouts.

"I made it back to the village and was reunited with my infant daughter Vera, whom I hugged so hard I had to release her for fear of smothering her. I gave the four horses to the tavern owner. The presence of my blood stained clothing and the wolf gun paved the way for he and his wife to surrender Vera without objection. When one meets Lucifer's brother, it is wise not to argue. I buried Katya and Vanya in the graveyard at the St. Boris Chapel in Chiozhny, the priest's words were like tamed doves released at a coronation, food for hawks, crows and alley cats, empty words muttered without feeling or sense repeated ritually a thousand times over a thousand graves.

"Soon rumors from Moscow were worse than bad. There were stories of strikes and battles, starvation and murder, atrocity and pain, the weakly throbbing heart of the Czar's dying empire. A million Zhukovs were born in those years while Europe stupidly slaughtered a generation in trenches in France over some misperceived effrontery. The world is shit, my friend, but some shit can be used as fertilizer and if you can plant a flower somewhere and stay near it, it is a way of getting through. My flower was Vera. Yours is Isabelle. I left Russia and returned to the home of my sister, here in France for I knew that eventually the Bolsheviks would get my Vera one way or the other. Yes, friend, my sister, your mother's sister. I am your uncle and what love I do not pour into Vera, is yours. Forgive me my not telling you but I needed my anonymity and the curses I heaped on God I did not want it to land on your head. Remember, Isabelle is your flower. Do not let your wife kill her. She is poisoned with hate and poison sees no difference between friend and enemy, stranger and daughter; it kills all without discernment, sorrow, or regret. Now, hug your Uncle Nikolai who loves you more than you know."

Drouet rose as did Nikolai and they embraced for many minutes, shedding tears onto each other that had been stored in the deepest recesses of their hearts. Shadows of passing clouds floated lazily like ghosts or memories over the green and purple vines of the Chateau Fontenot.

Twenty~Nine

Drouet insisted that his Uncle Nikolai move into the chateau with Vera immediately. Nikolai at first resisted the idea, initially out of politeness then from the subliminal suspicion that such close-quartered living arrangements would create problems which hitherto did not exist. The Russian maxim that circled Nikolai's head was "familiarity is the father of contempt" and he did not want anything to jeopardize his position at Chateau Fontenot. Russians, it seemed, had insightful sayings and mottos for many occasions which may seem somewhat surprising for a culture so inhumane, so quick to violence and so primitive in its spirit. While the Czars worshiped everything French from food to Faberge and paraded before the world in a false costume of civility, the peasants delighted in raiding Jewish settlements and torturing and killing the inhabitants for the sheer amusement of it all. While Russians take pride in Dostoyevsky Tolstoy, Tchaikovsky and Stravinsky, the truth is that these are the crown jewels on the head of a beast, cloaked in a peculiar brand of Christianity which gives an excuse for murder, mayhem and cruelty. Inherently paranoid and innately distrustful, Drouet and Nikolai were suspect of the other for different reasons and neither were mistaken for his suspicions. Nonetheless, Nikolai and Vera moved into the chateau and Jeanne made no objections although she forbade any iconic Christian images. Nikolai saw this as the tip of a problematic iceberg, but he was wise in acceding to Jeanne's wishes because he clearly knew she was, as he had warned Drouet, the devil in disguise, although he never openly criticized her to anyone. He knew well that taking sides in a battle between spouses was a sure way of becoming the enemy of both. Husbands and wives will reconcile and the friend or relative that criticizes the one to the other, will be scorned by both.

Nikolai kept his traditional crucifix in his nightstand drawer. His silver and painted icon of Saint Basil, the patron saint of Mother Russia, he kept in a small velvet-lined box in Vera's dresser in a drawer with a small lock. When Jeanne was out of the house or they were in their private moments he would tell Vera of the life of Jesus and show her the crucifix. When he related the journey of Saint Basil and his martyrdom he would take out the icon as if it were a treasure. He encouraged her to kiss both of them after a prayer. Of course, she could understand nothing of the religious significance of these mute objects but they were imbued with a sense of magic that appealed to her child's mind and she would think of them in much the same way as Nikolai thought of the rabbit's foot he always had in his pocket, as an amulet of good luck and the best thing to touch if she needed something good to happen like not being punished for sneaking into the kitchen and eating an extra piece of cake when no one was looking.

Vera was ten years older than Isabelle and when she was twelve and Isabelle was two, she would carefully play with her as if she were a doll. When Vera was fifteen and Isabelle five, they continued to play, their favorite game being tutor and student and Vera would make Isabelle sit at a table as if it were a school desk and write on a chalk board teaching her about all sorts of things most of which were factually incorrect but interesting both in the telling and the hearing. Eventually, of course, Vera decided to teach sex to young Isabelle not out of a prurient or malicious motive, but because she was consumed with the curiosity of it, her own hormones racing through her body like a band of Mongols laying waste to the steppes, the true innocence of youth and filling her with all manner of wants and desires she herself was only vaguely aware of. Vera had no friends to share her thoughts and problems with, Nikolai deciding that she needed no education other than the ways of the housewife which would naturally best be taught at home. He paid Paulette, the wife of one of the vineyard workers, to teach her darning and crocheting and he hired a music tutor to give her lessons on the violin. At various times of the day when her lessons first began and she was left to practice in the parlor or out on the veranda on warm days, the workers would look up in unison as the screeching cacophony of her thick-fingered playing echoed through the valley like tomcats in a fight to the death over a wayward female feline in heat. Eventually everyone but Jeanne got used to it, but one day she could stand it no more. She stole into Vera's room, pulled out the vile instrument from under her bed and hid it in the attic under boxes so thick with dust they seemed grey-haired. In her strictly religious mind, she was not stealing but helping the girl avoid the pitfalls that musical instruments and music in general led young women to. Music encouraged listening and listening encouraged toe-tapping and toe-tapping encouraged dancing and dancing encouraged — well, she didn't even want to contemplate it. The fact was, that in sparing Vera a life of sin by taking and hiding the violin, she also spared her own sanity and many of the Chateau Fontenot's employees who said silent prayers of thanks for the restoration of quiet even if they were directed at a god very different from Jeanne's.

In any event, Isabelle asked Jeanne one day, after one of her playtime lessons from Vera, whether or not a penis would hurt when it was placed "where the pee pee comes out of a girl." If Jeanne had been the fainting type, she would have collapsed right there, but it is a well-known fact that people most averse to sin are never surprised by it and any offense they may take when encountering it is much like the confrontation one might have with an old friend that he has not seen since a falling out. No people are so familiar with sin as those who are the most pious. Before placing a bar of homemade soap in Isabelle's mouth, she coerced the source of the question out of her. That very day, tempers boiled over as Nikolai and Vera were forced to vacate the chateau and resume their lodging in their former residence, the small stone cottage of the vineyard-master. In so doing, the current occupant and his family had to move and so on down the line in a human domino chain that eventually left Claude DeBoeff and his wife and son out on the roadway without a job or a place to live.

Claude was an ordinarily quiet man, some might say taciturn, but he was a devoted father and husband and had a real sense of propriety about the way people were to treat one another. In a matter of days, he discovered the true cause of his dismissal and while he and his family trudged up the road in search of housing and new employment, he plotted his revenge against Jeanne, although fate or a force so similar as to be indiscernible from it, had similar plans.

Thirty

30 Isabelle was a bright endearing child with an avid curiosity and a natural penchant, as all children have, for disobeying her parents. As Drouet was indulgent, lackadaisical and rarely, if ever told her to do anything, Jeanne became the law-giver and, as is so often the case, mother and daughter found themselves at odds frequently as if Isabelle enjoyed the game of dodging her mother's regulations and Jeanne enjoyed their fashioning, which would have surprised no one for everyone who knew Jeanne from the chamber maid to the village butcher saw in her a person that had an opinion on every subject, a way of doing everything she thought the only way , and a terrible inclination to attribute to God even the most minute joys, such as being able to easily open a new pickle jar, to the most common mishap, such as a mosquito bite on a difficult body part to scratch.

Jeanne subconsciously assumed that she was a major preoccupation for the Almighty and that He kept His divine eye on every cell of her body. If asked, she might have responded that God did this with everyone but she would have been lying. While some might be Methodists, others Episcopalians, some Catholic, some Jewish, Jeanne was a Jeannist, the high priestess of the cult of her imagined virtues. No matter what house of worship she entered, she could tell immediately the quality and depth of pastor and parishioners, the truth of the sermon and the earnestness and piety of those listening. Had she been born two hundred years earlier, she would have been a witch hunter, torturing and executing souls that disagreed with her and her god. A hundred years earlier still and she would have put Torquemada to shame. Passionate theology and a wide sadistic streak would have made her a perfect tool of the old God, but in the twentieth century she was simply considered a bitch from hell, albeit a beautiful one.

One day, shortly after Isabelle's twelfth birthday, her tutor arrived. His name was Monsieur D'Orsay and he was hired by Drouet to teach Isabelle Italian and English. D'Orsay was an amiable man of forty with a pleasant wife and two sons. He lived at Verly about three miles from the chateau and came highly recommended, although by whom, Drouet could not remember.

Of course, Jeanne was suspicious of any man and every man because it was a tenet of her belief that men had only one motive in life after the accumulation of money and that was sex. She had analyzed it all very carefully so there was no doubt about it. While many might agree with Jeanne on this point, she was wrong about D'Orsay. Yes, he was typically masculine and, yes, he rarely passed a pretty woman on the street without imagining her naked, but he took pride in his profession and as a father, even of sons, he did not for a minute entertain the remotest notion of Isabelle as a sex object or even as a female. In fact, the thought would have been repugnant to him. Of course, Jeanne thought she knew better and after losing the battle with Drouet to discharge him, she settled down to catching him in the act, much the way a disgruntled man in the fifteenth century would wait for his neighbor to do something "satanic" and then turn him over to the Inquisition. Accusations did not have to be true, only convincing, which is a very different thing.

Isabelle's lessons went well. Monsieur D'Orsay was a patient tutor and a good man and he came to appreciate her earnest endeavor at learning which he thought unusual in a girl so young and, although he would not have stated it, from parents so inept, one, Drouet, simple as bread, the other, Jeanne, unhinged in a most unpleasant way like a door blown partly off in a gale. D'Orsay had not been born last Tuesday and while he was a studious man, a lover of knowledge and books more than people, he could recognize the wild woman behind Jeanne's attractive exterior. As a student of Voltaire, he new beautiful women were creatures of disaster and Jeanne was beautiful indeed. In fact, he appreciated Isabelle all the more, even having a protective inclination toward her knowing that her mother lurked so nearby. Of course, it is easy to avoid stepping on a cobra if it is seen; the one that hides under a rock or in tall grass, well, that is another matter.

Jeanne had taken to using a small hole in the wall between a storeroom and Isabelle's study to watch D'Orsay instruct her daughter in languages. She devoted a great deal of time to this vocation and although she heard every lecture, every practice session, she never picked up a word of either Italian or English so narrow was her focus. Nor was she fatigable. She sat at her peephole for almost six months, two times per week for three hours without ever missing a syllable of the lesson, going so far as to urinate in advance so that she would not have to take a "potty break" and miss some untoward act of the wicked Monsieur D'Orsay. Lesser women would have abandoned their posts months earlier much the way watchers on the icy shores of Scotland gave up their scanning of the North Sea for Vikings who long before had chosen the southern fattened calf of England over sparse Caledonia. But Jeanne was adamant in her task, as she was in all her beliefs and not the most skilled of medieval torturers could have dissuaded her.

There came a time, as one might have anticipated, that Monsieur D'Orsay brought over his son, Leon to the lesson. Why he did this is unimportant. It may have been that Madame D'Orsay was ill or visiting relatives or just to alleviate the boy's boredom during a school holiday. He was ten years old and rather ordinary, but he was made like his father, patient and serious and as Monsieur D'Orsay taught his lesson, the boy read a book or drew pictures or simply watched Isabelle exchange niceties in English or Italian with his father. The boy attended his father for two weeks or there about until finally he spoke to Isabelle and she to him after Monsieur D'Orsay left the room for the latrine or wrote in his notebook about Isabelle's progress. In short order, they became friends especially important for Isabelle who was isolated and beginning to feel the subliminal tides of her female hormones, chemicals that course through the body sometimes making fanatics out of bookworms and ranters out of the most sedate. On days when Monsieur D'Orsay did not appear, Leon began to show up on his bicycle at the chateau inquiring after her and while Jeanne might have objected, she saw this as an opportunity to show the apathetic Drouet that she was right after all for nothing pleases a lunatic so much as the opportunity to empirically prove the correctness of a preposterous theory which explains, for example, the millions of hours which might have been spent in useful pursuits seeking such phantasms as the remains of Noah's Ark or the Holy Grail. Imagine the hospitals that could have been built or the schools erected on the time and money expended on searching the barren and frozen wasteland of Ararat looking for the hull of that most famous conundrum in all the biblical Old Testament world. But that is another matter.

Isabelle would entertain Leon with lemonade and biscuits while they played checkers in her study. On occasion, they would draw together or speak English or Italian with their quaint French accents. This annoyed Jeanne all the more, playing on her paranoia about what the little boy was up to, what he was really saying, as if she didn't know. On the Wednesday before Easter, Leon appeared with a lovely bouquet of calla lilies and, just as Jeanne was going to lecture him on the impropriety of little boys giving little girls gifts, he handed them to her and said that the flowers from his father's garden were a gift of thanks for her hospitality. Most women would have melted at the sight of Leon, ten years old with deep brown eyes and the serious expression women find so enchanting in boys and so attractive in men. Jeanne, however, was cut from the cloth her mother had woven and her mother before that and the warp and weave were a twisted amalgam of suspicion, fear, abuse and superstition that when mixed with a lively intelligence and deprived of a useful education yielded up a garment of exquisite despicability. Jeanne thanked him, put the flowers in a cut glass vase and raced to the peephole to see what Leon was actually up to after so obvious a bribe.

Isabelle was speaking Italian and Leon was responding in English, a game that required considerable linguistic dexterity and often the children found themselves laughing as they fumbled between the two tongues with humorous results. After a time, they sat together next to each other and opened an Atlas pointing at faraway places and wondering out loud of what the people looked like or what their daily problems were. Isabelle dreamed, she said of visiting Ceylon and Leon said he should like to go there too but only with Isabelle. Jeanne's one open eye opened wide and she stopped breathing for a moment so that the sound of her own breath would not interfere with the already poor acoustics of listening through a thick plaster wall. Isabelle responded it would be nice to have him as company. Then she leaned over and kissed him on the cheek. Leon blushed and then made small talk about Tasmania probably being an interesting place to visit as well, it being on the way to Ceylon. At this point, Jeanne had already left the storeroom having seen enough and rushed through the door of the study, tripping over a pile of books on the floor and landing flat out in the middle of the rug. Isabelle stifled a laugh but Leon was terrified, but not as much as he was when Jeanne regained a perpendicular posture, grabbed him by the shoulder and led him to the front door, pushing him out and slamming it shut behind.

While Leon pedaled his way back home with tears in his eyes and the first lesson in his short life of the unpredictability and marginal insanity of women, he could just make out in the distance the rants of Jeanne chastising Isabelle for encouraging the boy to rape her. Isabelle had no idea what rape was but she had a distant recollection that it had something to do with pregnancy, although exactly what she, as yet, did not know.

It was only a matter of time before Monsieur D'Orsay was discharged and a wiry, old lady by the name of Lynette Defarge was retained over Drouet's weak objections, to replace him. Madame Defarge thought foreign languages a waste of time. Everyone with an education or polish spoke French as everyone knew and she felt that a young woman of Isabelle's background should learn geometry and perhaps a little physics which she admitted would be useless to a woman but might make her attractive to a professional man, especially a physician. Isabelle stared in space as Madame Defarge spoke of isosceles triangles, nanograms, cosigns and tangents and the use of a lever to raise a great weight.

In no time, Isabelle had gotten a note to Leon and they were meeting on a beautiful deserted lea owned by an elderly neighbor that overlooked the LeNoir tributary, a graceful small river that wiggled its way through the countryside like the trail of gold dust behind a fairy. By the time Isabelle was fourteen and Leon twelve they were as much in love as young people that age can be which is very much if you ask them but not much at all if you ask people older and wiser who have had the tender nerves in their brains severed from their hearts by years of experience.

Thirty~One

31 It was a rainy Monday when Jeanne was sitting in the parlor instead of being out in the stable with her horses as usual, when she noticed that Isabelle was going out for a walk. Now, she had been taking art excursions, it is true, usually up to the orchard or deep into the vines but the rain was falling steadily and no one would believe that anyone except the mad Vincent, would go for a walk and attempt a painting or sketch in the rain. Such are lies that the liar creates which seem so true on the surface but which escape reasonable analysis as the circumstances of reality render them false. Isabelle knew, of course, that she was going to meet Leon. Thus, the rain did not matter. She forgot the fable she had created about her drawing. Had it been true, she would have stayed home, perhaps producing a fine still life under a dry roof. Also, her mother at this time of the day should have been in the stable. Again the world of the lie betrayed Isabelle because she did not even notice Jeanne sitting quietly in the thick sofa, like an anaconda sunning on a rock, its rich scales blending into its surroundings.

With pad and pastel case, Isabelle opened the door, pulled her shawl over her head and departed for the rendezvous point not realizing that Jeanne was following her, wearing a large worker's straw hat, a poncho and carrying a vineyard bag. Had Isabelle turned about and saw the figure of her mother some one hundred yards distant she would have assumed it was a field hand, for Jeanne, from habit, was wearing her riding pants. She looked every inch the worker on an errand.

The two young lovers planned on meeting in a small thicket of silver birch that fringed the lea over the LeNoir. Isabelle had noted many times to Leon how she loved the changes the wind wrought on the trees turning them from a hazy sea-green to bright silver that shown in the sun like coins or the scales of a magical dragon, that if you stared long enough as waves of air pulsed in from the sea, one could see the shape of God's hand as it brushed the trees and made them bow before Him.

Leon brought a tent with him, the same one he used when hunting geese with his father in the fall. It was waterproof and perfect for the two of them to sit in and watch the weather unfold as if they were going to see the Folies Bergére at the Moulin Rouge. Such was their delight in each other's company. When Isabelle started off the road through the waving grass of the lea, Jeanne continued on the road so as not to be noticed but walked slowly to ascertain where Isabelle was heading. When it was clear that it was the stand of birches, Jeanne circled round and crouched low so that she would not be seen. It was but ten minutes or so until Isabelle found Leon and his tent. She entered it and the two young lovers kissed and hugged and then sat looking out the open flap at the trees, the rain and the sea beyond the glassy grass of the meadow. Thick gray clouds scudded in herds across the sky but the two of them were as happy as if they were on a beach at Cannes in the middle of August. It was their practice after being in love for so long to strip down to their underpants and hug and squirm and touch each other intimately but they had mutually decided that they would not consummate their passion until they were married to each other.

Jeanne gave them enough time to be together to catch them in the act and she waited for what she thought was a half an hour but which was, in fact, only fifteen minutes, just enough time for Isabelle to have removed her jacket and blouse and camisole exposing her breasts as Leon hugged and kissed her in the fire of his youth.

Jeanne approached the tent like a cat. When she could discern their silence and heavy breathing, she reached under with both her hands and lifted the tarpaulin up in a quick jerk, pulling up the tent and stakes like a sailor releasing the mizzen in a gale. Just as she had suspected, Leon had seduced her daughter for there she was bare-chested, a look of panic on her face and his, as the rain suddenly increased and drenched them. Jeanne struck Leon in the face so hard he toppled off balance and fell into the side of the tent that was still tethered, making it collapse. She yanked Isabelle up by the arm and shouted obscenities at her as a demon possessed.

Isabelle slapped her mother full in the face, regal as an Amazon warrior. Instead of bringing Jeanne to her senses, which admittedly were in short supply, the slap infuriated her and worse, convinced her that her theory was correct all along about Isabelle, that she was possessed by some infernal demon sent to derail Jeanne's mission in the world. Of course, what that mission was, was not yet evident to Jeanne but she knew that God paid too much attention to her for Him not to have a grand purpose for His most devout servant.

Jeanne looking every inch a harpy, screaming at Leon and threatening that if he ever came near her daughter again, she would kill him. Leon did not doubt the earnestness of this threat but made eye contact with Isabelle who looked all the more a goddess, soaked and shining, naked to the waste like Athena on Mount Parnassus. Jeanne retrieved Isabelle's blouse and made her put it on, then yanked her by the arm, holding her tightly all the way back to the Chateau Fontenot.

It would be difficult if not impossible to explain Jeanne's fanatic behavior toward her daughter because even she knew that by Isabelle's age, Jeanne had done much the same thing with many more boys. Actually, it could be hypothesized that Jeanne was possessive not out of a protective streak, the way a lioness will defend her cubs, but from a compulsion to control everything within her reach. She controlled the household by ordering the servants about and instructing them in the minutiae of their duties, all of which were already known to any servant worth his or her salt. She controlled Drouet by denying him intimacy and gave him days of petulant behavior which made him exceed to her every whim. She even controlled her God by her prayers and expectations never allowing in her dogmatic way that perhaps there might have been two Arks, one for Noah and one for some other fortunate man and his family, perhaps in China, or simply because God had wanted two Arks. After all, the Flood was His idea. The Bible said one Ark and God was stuck with that whether he liked it or not. So it is no wonder at all that her own child had to be controlled, but it is known throughout the world, if not the universe, that children will defy the most loving of parents and the more controlling they are, the more the restraints imposed are resisted.

By the time Jeanne had gotten Isabelle at home into the parlor, she had had enough and Isabelle attacked her mother like it was a wrestling match.

They rolled around the floor, thumping into tables and knocking lamps and vases to the floor shattering them or cracking them in a melée of shouts, thuds and slaps. Two house servants rushed to the room but when they saw who was fighting they thought it might be best to leave them alone. After all, if Madame wanted to beat her daughter, it was her business and they secretly hoped that Isabelle might land a lucky blow and put Madame in the hospital for a few weeks so that life at the chateau would be pleasant even if only for that short hiatus.

Both Jeanne and Isabelle managed to get to their feet and faced each other, bruised and scratched, their clothing torn and their hair looking like birds' nests that had only barely survived a cyclone. When Jeanne called Isabelle a tramp and a whore, something snapped in Isabelle and she laughed, momentarily frightening Jeanne who was expecting tears and apologies. Isabelle had a madness about her that was disconcerting as the toad of control secreted its mucous and slipped out of Jeanne's hands. Isabelle leaped at Jeanne, pushing her against Drouet's bookcase. On the top shelf, out of reach, Drouet kept a loaded revolver in a black lacquer box for "emergencies," as he would have called it, if anyone had asked. The impact of the two women into the bookcase brought the box tumbling to the floor where it broke open. The revolver discharged with a thunder-like crack, made all the louder by it's being fired indoors. The bullet went through the ceiling, hit the bottom of a table in the second storey study, ricocheted through the wall and into Jeanne's bedroom, striking her simple wooden cross over her bed and shattering it into thirteen pieces.

The pistol's report brought everyone running and put an immediate halt to the brawl. Drouet shouted at both of them for perhaps the first time in his life and told both of them to go their rooms immediately or he would summon the police and charge them both with attempted homicide. It was a ludicrous threat but the women were frazzled way past the point of logic and did what they were told. The servants crossed themselves several times saying silent prayers of thanks that none of them were hit but secretly wishing Jeanne had been less lucky.

When Jeanne got to her room and saw the cross shattered into the ominous number of pieces, she knew that it was a demon's work and she had already glimpsed his hideous countenance looking out from Isabelle's otherwise innocent eyes. What else could explain her lascivious trysts with

Leon? The fight? The pistol firing and shattering the holy rood of her Savior? A demon was inside the Chateau Fontenot hiding in the young bud that was her daughter and Jeanne would not rest until it was exorcised and control had been restored. She prayed that night for two hours until an answer came in a dream.

Thirty~Two

32 Jeanne Fontenot awoke the next morning with a perfect clarity of purpose. She would seek an exorcist that would rid Isabelle of the demon that possessed her. She had her tea and croissants sent up to her room and Fanny, the maid, cast a cautious look at her bruised mistress who sat in bed with a black eye and a fountain pen and paper jotting down, God knew what. In fact, she was making a list of potential candidates for the rights of exorcism. She knew her former priest in the town, Father Denoyer but she could not bring herself to seek a Catholic solution to her problem, as her desertion of that faith was well-known and the priest would not help her unless she returned to the Church which she most definitely would not. There was a Lutheran minister in town, a German by the name of Rheiner, but she knew nothing of him or whether he was qualified, nor could she take the chance in asking, being turned down and then everyone in the region knowing that she was seeking an exorcism for her only daughter.

Eventually, she settled on a gypsy woman by the name of Matilda, the widow of three husbands, who owned a small hut near town and received a few francs here and there for telling fortunes, curing animals of diseases brought on by curses and other such folk medicine as earned her a solid reputation as both a good Christian and a creditable medium between the benign forces of nature and humans with a record of three exorcisms, one of a young boy of six who had pushed his father down a well to his death and two women who were visited nightly by incubi, one being impregnated and spontaneously aborting a deformed fetus which was buried in the hollow of an oak wrapped in linens upon which the mother had urinated. The other was stillborn with six fingers on each hand. Both women recovered from their battles with Satan's minions and Matilda was credited with their victories. The young boy was sentenced to hang but after the exorcism, the judge advocate released him to the custody of his mother and the boy grew up to be a sergeant in the army fighting the Germans at Verdûn where he lost his right leg, then his life. He was awarded a posthumous Croix du Guerre.

Jeanne wrote her request in a lengthy note and sent Fanny to Matilda's hut. That afternoon, Matilda showed up with Fanny and explained that she was illiterate and could not read the missive, so Jeanne had to explain the situation in person. At first, Matilda was going to tell Jeanne that it wasn't an exorcism that was needed but a mental doctor and that Jeanne needed it much more than Isabelle whom, she felt, was just an average teenager trapped in a rural area with a mother with too much time on her hands and a warped mind. But when Jeanne offered her a thousand francs for the service, she quickly assented having no more scruples than any other gypsy that ever lived, which is to say, none at all.

It would be intriguing to relay the details of the exorcism which was scheduled for the second Thursday of the following month when the moon was new, how they drugged Isabelle with a small dose of yellow belladonna, just enough to make her woozy so they could tie her naked and spread-eagled on her bed which had been stripped to the mattress, covered with a rubber sheet, how holy water was sprinkled on everything in the room from an ancient Roman jug owned by Saint Benedict, how a long vial of the water was inserted carefully into Isabelle's private parts so that she could be cleansed from within and how she was force fed galaba root and green anise seed mixed with three knots of wool from an Easter lamb and how Isabelle evacuated her intestines in the bed, the putrid smell filling the house, proof of the demon within, how her eyes rolled back as a cross heated on the stove left a small scorch mark on her forehead that vanished when rubbed with a piece of cloth said to be from the tunic of Jeanne D'Arc and how after three hours of similar tactics and skirmishes with Satan's evil imp, the battle was won and Isabelle awoke the next morning as if she were her mother's child of only ten years, innocent as the day she was born and hugged her mother for fifteen minutes without letting go and promised to behave better than Saint Veronica, blind to the advance of any man until her mother approved in writing.

But the fact is, no exorcism ever occurred. Matilda, with the one thousand francs paid in advance in her handbag which smelled like feet when opened, got caught in a drenching downpour on her way home from her meeting with Jeanne. She caught a cold, then a fever and then pneumonia. By the time the doctor arrived, she was delirious and dehydrated and after sipping a glass of water he offered her with a tincture of iodine for her infection, she expired, Jeanne never discovering that the exorcism would not occur until after Matilda's death, a sad old woman appeared at the back door of the Chateau Fontenot with a note for Isabelle which she would only deliver to her hand, which she did. In it Isabelle read of the day her mother tore open Leon's tent, how he was distraught with the idea of never seeing his beloved again and how he threw himself off the edge of the lea and fell the three hundred feet of its height to his death on the rocky shore below, like Icarus, joyful in the morning of his youth, soaring to glorious heights, then having his dream melted by the twisted curses of Jeanne Fontenot. The next day, while Matilda suffered in bed and Jeanne plotted another exorcism, Isabelle slipped out the back door with the thought of running away to Paris. Five miles from home, she realized she could never survive. Frightened, downtrodden and more alone than a hermit on a rock in the Aegean, she returned to the chateau just in time for dinner. After a time, with no other exorcists available, Jeanne abandoned the idea, but never let her guard down, watching Isabelle's every movement and reading her every thought.

Thirty~Three

33 Jeanne would attend church every Sunday in the town of La Tour, as has been said, some twenty miles distant. This would require her leaving early Saturday morning or sometimes Friday afternoon and she did not return until after sundown on Monday. Drouet, who had drifted so far from her emotionally, did not care. In fact, he welcomed her absence when everyone both in and out of the house might readily partake of drink, an occasional obscene outburst or playful banter about the relative size of the women's breasts or the men's penises. In short, the vineyard had all the attributes of most such vineyards when Jeanne Fontenot was off to her worshiping of her severe and unsmiling god.

When she arrived in La Tour, she stayed with the Reverend Gerhardt and his wife, after helping them around the house because Mrs. Gerhardt had developed terrible phlebitis which left her legs unusable, often emitting a noxious odor due to weeping sores. While she was confined to her bed or wheelchair, the Reverend did most of the housework in addition to caring for her and the emotional and spiritual needs of his parishioners which were not many but more in need of his succor than the usual.

Gerhardt welcomed Jeanne as a bright, beautiful face in the gray landscape of his world and he would count the days and then the hours to her return. Passion can assume many forms. One can be passionate about a hobby, about caring for animals, about horticulture, about a lover, about a spouse or about faith. All true passions, though, share the same characteristics and all of those can be reduced to one, obsession. The outward signs of passion are all the same regardless of the subject. Gerhardt saw Jeanne's passion for her faith as a yearning look in her eyes, an avidity for finding the truth and a way of breathing that reminded him of the many women he had bedded as a youth. Where Jeanne was seeking a god that would shield her from her overwhelming but hidden fear of the world, Gerhardt saw a woman who would respond to his slightest touch. To him, her beseeching eyes looking skyward were no different than the look she would give him as he lay on top of her. Perhaps, and he never analyzed this for a minute, the appeal of the calling was not so much to serve God but to be the focal point of so many peoples' passion, particularly the women. His sermons full of sulfur and methane echoed off the walls of the ancient chapel and everyone was left being made doubly aware of how wicked humanity was and the gates of heaven were but a tantalizing goal that they could reach only by deprivation, self-denial and the rapid application of punishment to any transgressors within arm's reach.

After one particularly ferocious sermon which left everyone inspired and simultaneously fearful of what demon might descend upon them from the tree tops as they made their way home with shoulders hunched fearfully looking above them, Jeanne waited in the chapel for Gerhardt, her eyes full of tears because she had had an epiphany of sorts, especially of how sinful she had been with Drouet insofar as her enjoyment of the sex act. She confessed this to Gerhardt not the way a Catholic divulges sins to his priest in the sanctity of the confessional but by way of thanking him for showing her the evil of her former ways. As she spoke of her carnal transgressions, he looked at her fine features, how carefully she combed her golden hair, the earnestness of her deep blue eyes and the gentle determined rises and fall of her breasts as she breathed and spoke as they walked uphill to the reverend's modest home. He told her that sex for procreation was a good thing and that pleasure was simply the devil's way of encouraging the young to engage in sinful activity and that, in fact, with prayer and practice, copulation could be achieved with no pleasure whatsoever and in so discovering this he had managed to outwit Lucifer and deprive him of his most powerful weapons against the spirit of man. Gerhardt also reminded Jeanne that she had vowed before God to love, honor and obey and that she had a duty to obey her husband and if her husband ordered her to have sexual relations with him within the confines of the marriage she was duty-bound to comply although she was also duty-bound as a Christian not to enjoy it. This made perfect sense to Jeanne, the way the tale of Noah's Ark made sense, the parting of the Red Sea, the fishes and the loaves and the age of the Earth as six thousand years. What did not make sense to her was how she was to avoid any pleasure because, although she did not admit it, even the thought of the young Drouet mounting her made her sex throb with anticipation like a Pavlovian dog's salivary glands, as if the space below her naval and between her thighs had a mind of its own which most men will tell you it does.

They went into the Reverend's home and made a simple supper for the three of them. Mrs. Gerhardt, however, had no appetite and chose to rest. The weather being warm and sunny, the Reverend Gerhardt and Jeanne thought it delightful on the Sabbath to eat at a small table in the yard in the rear of the house. There were rows of apple trees from a neighboring orchard that were filled with blossoms and the sweet smell drifted on the air. They ate and talked and again the subject of what the minister called "reverent relations" came up. He begged her forgiveness for discussing it but said it was his duty as a man of the cloth to help her find her way if she was lost. He told her how he could have sexual union with his wife and feel nothing any more than a man exercising and that he had even been able to control of the flow of his fluids that would preserve them and make them the most potent when his wife was most likely to conceive. In effect, he had mastered his own body and would not be a slave to it or to Satan.

After they ate, Jeanne suggested they take a walk through the orchard. Large billowing clouds floated slowly over the hills. As they walked, the shadows of those clouds put them intermittently into cooling shade and vibrant sunshine. Jeanne, after a short time, said she would like to sit under the trees and she did so with the Reverend next to her. She lay down and remarked how this cloud looked like a house or that like a Spanish galleon. While she went on about the clouds the Reverend unbuttoned her chemise and fondled her breasts. She remarked how two clouds very close together might be the twins Romulus and Remus. He lifted her skirt up and removed her undergarments as she noticed how a cloud looked so much like the silhouette of Rousseau that it might well be his spirit enjoying nature from heaven. The Reverend mounted her and as he pumped rhythmically away at her he told her that he could feel nothing and that she should teach Drouet the same process and that the seed he was about to pour into her was but an impotent fluid that would prepare her for procreation when the time was right. She writhed beneath him in a feverish sweat and in the passion of the moment which she denied ever feeling, she forgot to mention that she could not bear any children as the doctor had warned her of the dangers after the birth of Isabelle. When they had finished their spiritual lesson, they both fell asleep though less than half an hour later, she awoke to a second lesson which took only slightly longer than the first.

When they returned to the house, Mrs. Gerhardt had fallen out of bed and, as the Reverend and Jeanne helped her back in, she slapped Jeanne across the face leaving four red finger marks. Jeanne reeled back in shock and the Reverend demanded an explanation. But Mrs. Gerhardt was not in an explaining mood and the Reverend apologized for his wife and as he changed the bandages on her legs which had come loose as she struggled on the floor and filled the room with a peculiar sweet smell akin to rotting meat, Jeanne bid them both farewell and headed home after some difficulty catching the horse which was nibbling at the apple blossoms, finally hitching him to the carriage. She was good with horses, actually much better than she was with people. Most of the way back she could think of nothing but the Reverend's ministrations and how she would return the next weekend for further tutoring in the service of his holy mission on Earth, but would make every effort to avoid his wife who was clearly possessed by demonic forces.

Because she had left late in the day and had departed in a sort of daze, she was oblivious for many miles that the sun was setting behind her seeking to hide its aged face. The long shadow of the trees on the roadside and her own shadow elongated and triangular on the road ahead of her all pointed in the direction of home, signposts of her renewed faith. Doves flew in circular patterns and spiraled down into a shallow vale, cooing as they landed, inspiring the crickets and cicadas to commence their nervous amorous clicking and clacking. Low clouds ahead over the distant hills were soft orange and pink against the violet sky catching the weakening rays and the vines on the hillside seemed like rows of young gypsy girls kneeling with their arms outstretched holding each others hands as their long and rapturously flowing hair cascaded down hiding their faces in disingenuous modesty.

She thought of stopping and perhaps napping awhile in the carriage but her blood was still flowing quickly as she saw the signs all about her of a new life, that by serving Reverend Gerhardt she was serving her god. He had taught her that God is everywhere and sees everything and surely he smiled on her love of the Reverend. Perhaps it was not love — she thought she might actually still love Drouet — but devotion to his cause to the word of God. Drouet would have to understand. She might even tell him of her experiences with Gerhardt.

The road ahead dipped into shadow and as the horse sped up because it was walking downhill, she could feel a presence, a shadow in the back of her mind. She sensed it was an angel sent by God to guide her home and to tell her she had done the right thing and that any doubt she might have should be put to rest. As the road began to rise before her, the moon in crescent appeared and she pulled on the reins and stopped a moment. This was a sign, she knew it, so she pulled off onto the grassy berm of the road and got down and stood worshipfully. She could feel the presence of the angel in the woods, the soft rustle of silver birch with its leaves fluttering like the wings of a million swallows on a summer breeze. She hitched the horse to a small tree and let it graze as she walked into the woods, a carpet of columbine and bluebells under her feet, the air sweet with the smell of her angel's breath.

Everything went suddenly dark as a burlap sack was thrust over her head, her arms held tightly to her sides and her legs swept out from under her as if she weighed but twenty pounds. When she let out her reflexive scream, she was hit on the side of the head so hard she nearly fainted. She could feel a small trickle of blood emerge from her ear and run down the side of her face. She was being carried somewhere but she could not tell where. In the delirious panic of the moment she started to pray and her mind saw her angel descending from heaven, sword in hand, fiery blue eyes, flowing red hair swirling slowly in an unearthly wind and chiseled muscles. As he got near, he faded into the dark of her blindfold. She was on the ground in a bed of leaves, the pungent odor filling the sack over her head and the deep crunching noise of the leaves mixing with the heavy breathing of her captors who said nothing as they stripped her naked, biting her breasts and entering her so ferociously she lost her breath and then her consciousness as she searched in vain through the dark fog of her mind for her angel to no avail.

When Jeanne awoke she opened her eyes and could see the filtered sun weakly coming through the loose weave of the burlap on her face. The sun warmed her naked body. As she arose, she could feel shooting pains in her arms and legs and she struggled to sit up. She removed the sack from her head and found herself in a small clearing in the wood where autumn leaves had accumulated having been tossed about by the winds finding refuge in the swale. She was badly bruised and blood had dried on her pubic hair. Her clothes were in a heap about six feet away. She rose unsteadily and touched the side of her face where she had been struck. Dried blood made a thick reddish brown line from her ear to her cheek to her jaw line and as she rubbed it off with her fingers and nails she realized she could not hear out of her left ear.

Jeanne Fontenot put on her clothes shakily then stood for a moment in the clearing as the sun warmed her and birdsong filled the air. She looked everywhere for the signs that her angel had been there to help, but she came to realize that he had not. When she needed him most, he had deserted her. As she followed the footprints out of the clearing, intuitively knowing they would lead back to her horse, she knew from deep within her mind that she had been punished for her transgression with Gerhardt, that whoever abducted her had done so with the permission of her god who saw it all as retribution for breaking her vows to Drouet, that even aiding one of God's messengers on Earth was no excuse for breaking the vow she had made the day she was married. She realized that God was just and loving but was never to be toyed with or second guessed. It even occurred to her that it was her angel himself who so brutally attacked her and why not, she had transgressed and transgressors were to be punished. The Bible was brimming with similar stories. She vowed to love, honor and obey Drouet and as she found her bewildered horse standing asleep in the morning sunshine right where she had tethered him the evening before, she made a promise to God to be His faithful servant and further, to make certain that Isabelle never wandered off the straight and narrow, as she had done. In fact, she would dedicate her life to teaching Isabelle the ways of righteousness or die trying.

She rode home with a renewed sense of purpose recognizing that she had only about five miles left of her journey. She saw the pink stucco of the Chateau Sur Mer on her right where Claude Deboeff had found employment. Poor man, it was because of her that he had to leave his position at Chateau Fontenot. She might write him a letter of apology for indirectly forcing Drouet to discharge him, but at second thought, it would do no good and besides, he was a decent man likely to have already forgiven her. After all, God worked in mysterious ways.

Jeanne arrived at the chateau a little past two in the afternoon. The field hands were sitting at the large round table in the front courtyard with Nikolai and Drouet and as she approached up the gentle S of the drive, they saw her and arose and departed as if a bell had rung signaling their return to their chores. Drouet remained seated finishing his glass of wine and idly pushing breadcrumbs in a plate with his forefinger as if arranging them in a pattern. As she got nearer, he saw the terrible condition she was in and rising ran over to her inquiring. She told him she had taken a turn of the Savarin Road a little too quickly and she had fallen out of the carriage as its front wheel hit a stone. She was shaken and bruised, but she was all right except that she had hit her ear on a log and she thought she was deaf on that side. She spoke robotically and stoically as if relating a tale of someone else's misfortunes. But Drouet, innately gullible and always taking people at their word, never realizing the secret power of lies, accepted what she said and tenderly ministered to her, drawing a bath and leaving her to cleanse herself, knowing that she would not permit him to see her nude for fear of rousing his dormant passion. Frankly, he knew it was not dormant but deceased and he never discovered the truth of her injuries even after the sun had risen and set another four thousand times, nor could he have realized that the Jeanne that he had married was long ago dead and buried and the beautiful woman with the flaxen hair and azure eyes he so deeply loved in his youth had been reborn a zombie to passion and a slave to a mysterious god only she knew.

Thirty~Four

For Isabelle's sixteenth birthday Jeanne and Drouet took her to the seaside town of Gascoigne on the rocky Atlantic coast. Leaving Nikolai who was eighty in the care of his daughter Vera and her husband Renee Deboeff, they loaded their luggage into Drouet's new Citroen Deux Chevaux and with the top down and the dust swirling, made their way toward the pebbly beach at Gascoigne.

They arrived that night and checked into a rambling rustic inn that hugged the chalk cliffs overlooking the beach and they all slept soundly lulled by the waves, the warm humid breeze and the gentle rattle of the pebbles on the strand whispering to one another as the withdrawing waves rearranged them for the ten millionth time. They awoke to a thick fog and sat on a veranda on the cliff top, the chairs and tables covered with sea dew, the long grasses growing in clumps in the sand bowed down by the serene weight of the droplets accumulated from the fog as it wove its way along the coast painting everything with a soft gray tint.

As the fog lifted and crawled back to sea by the gaze of the sun, the ocean spread to the horizon in shades of slate, green and blue the color of Tunisian granite. Long rows of whitecaps meandered toward the beach as small folds of water caressed the coastline as it arched northward to a cluster of chalk cliffs mantled with green grass. A row of rust orange rocks protruded above the waves in a sinuous line much like the scaly spine of a sea serpent's back where white water lapped anxiously around each frill as if trying to pull the beast back into the depths.

Drouet and Jeanne decided to walk the path along the crest of the down while Isabelle decided to descend a narrow primitive set of stairs carved from rock that led from the lawn to the beach below. There were already people strolling the beach and Jeanne felt none of the usual trepidation she had when Isabelle was not in her purview.

With her parents on their way toward the chalk cliffs, Isabelle descended the stairs and reached the beach which she discovered on closer inspection was not sand but rounded stones the color of wrens' eggs no more than a half inch in diameter made round or ovate by millennia of rubbing against each other the way friends and spouses lose their rough edges by close contact over the years, the brilliant plumage of youth reduced to the even stubble and baldness of middle age. She walked southward in the opposite direction of her parents and stopped to watch pelicans sitting on the waves rising up and down on the incoming swells, occasionally opening the mosaic of their scraggly wings to regain their balance.

A voice called to her from behind. She turned and saw a man of about twenty-three or so sitting on a small stool with a tripod easel in front of him painting the scene she now stood in the middle of. She didn't know what he said, but she quietly realized he was asking her to move out of the way. When she did, he asked if she could stay there for a few minutes that she was the perfect focal point for his painting. She thought better of it and started to walk again but he pleaded for just a few minutes of her time. She relented and stood gazing out to sea, feeling his eyes on her back and the blood rushing to her face.

After a time, she asked if it was all right to move and when he said yes he also asked her to come round to view his work. She hesitated and then gave in, unfamiliar with how to deal with a stranger because she had never been alone with one. She walked around the easel and saw her own image on the canvas, the blue horizon, the jutting rocks and the pelicans. She was delighted. They made small talk after she complimented the work and he thanked her more profusely than she thought she deserved. He asked her name which she gave and he introduced himself as Briand Neumann, a Dutch art student on holiday in France.

It would be facile and downright predictable to relate that they fell in love in those few moments, but it would be a lie. He admired her lithe and youthful beauty. She was captured by the adventure of it all for he was certainly not the vision of her juvenile feminine dreams but an average man his age, wiry with a nose a bit too large, eyes a little too small and some uneven teeth which some might have considered sexy but she thought peculiarly skeletal as if she had discovered the calcified structure of his body beneath his youthful smile, his strong arms and his long pale hair.

Briand asked her if he might see her again, perhaps that evening after dinner they might go for a stroll, or play some cards or listen to music together at the inn she told him she was staying at. As he spoke and the ocean breeze rustled his hair, his strong hands spotted with rubbed splotches of oil paint, his eyes so earnest, she said yes, that would be nice and they agreed that 8:00 p.m. would be good. He was staying at an inexpensive hostel inland a few miles and he looked forward to seeing her and perhaps meeting her family. As he said this, she realized her mother was now not simply Jeanne Fontenot who would be happy that her daughter had made an interesting acquaintance as all such girls her age were expected to do, but the cyclops of the Odyssey, Polyphemus, the twisted offspring of Poseidon standing watch over the cave of his treasure. There was no doubt whatsoever in Isabelle's mind that she was her mother's treasure, not treasured as a living child, but literally some form of congealed phantasm in preparation for sacrifice to her god, a god who was so covetous of his worshipers' devotion that not an hour could go by that Jeanne would not think of him or speak to him or ask him for something even if it was as minute a miracle as helping her to find the lost mate to a sock which had blown in the wind off the line into the field of poppies behind the chateau.

Thirty~Five

35

As it turned out, Briand was not staying at a hostel at all but was residing with a young girl named Diana, a mulatto, a beautiful mocha-colored twenty-year-old that worked as a maid in a large chateau owned by a wealthy Parisian merchant. Diana lived in an outbuilding, an apartment for the servants over the carriage house and the old merchant, a Monsieur Dupuis, never even thought of her or in fact any of the servants as anything but servants. He had lost two wives, one to invading Prussian soldiers and the other to an outbreak of typhus when he was with her on their honeymoon in Sardinia. The two deaths worked a poison on his brain and he vowed never to get involved with women again. As an inveterate gambler, he saw women as bad luck. The four house servants, three men and Diana lived in obscurity and harmony paying little attention to each other especially after Diana awoke one night shortly after arriving to find the gardener naked standing over her and grabbing her breasts. She reached under her pillow and retrieved a paring knife she kept there for protection, grabbed his erect penis and placed the blade against it. The man shivered and pleaded and she told him that if he made another move and if his penis did not deflate by the time she counted to twenty, she would cut it off like a sausage link. As any man could appreciate, the verbal threat was unnecessary and the reddened weapon of his nocturnal attack shrank to the size of a field mouse which in the light of day it much resembled except for the lack of fur.

Diana was in a long, ragged chain of women who had taken to Briand and had taken him in. While he studied art, it was without benefit of formal training and he used the easel and paint as a means to meet women in whom he was not really interested. What did concern him, however, was having a roof over his head and a bed to sleep in after a meal. His father was a preacher back in Amsterdam and both his father, mother and three of his four brothers did missionary work in the Belgian Congo and Rhodesia. He never did but had promised his father he would, a promise like many in his life that he did not keep. His fourth brother had run away from home to no one knew where, but Briand thought it likely that it was Paris. All of the religion in his household and his father's quick administration of the strap had essentially killed his sexual urges but it is likely that Briand was simply one of many who were born with no particular desire other than to live off of another. Sex was simply a task to be performed that could enable him to keep the roof over his head after his easel had gained him entry to a house. He was inept at love-making probably from lack of interest and most women who were attractive often tired of him quickly and on more than one occasion he returned to a locked door and an unanswered doorbell. When all else failed he had no problem seeking out sheltered areas out-of-doors or could manage a few coins in exchange for a space to sleep in a barn, a storeroom or any available location. The one thing he did not want to do was work at any kind of job, although sometimes when he could not dupe a woman he would work for a few days or even a week to avoid starving. On one occasion, he met an older man and for enough money to eat for a month and one night in a warm bed he allowed the man to do some things to him that he refused to talk or think about except when the man appeared to him in dreams and then nightmares. In short, Briand's First Commandment was not to work and any others varied as the need arose.

There was no question that Isabelle had grown into a fine specimen of womanhood even at the age of sixteen. She had inherited her father's tall stature and her maternal grandmother's large bosom, so large that she sometimes went to great lengths to wear clothing that underemphasized it simply to avoid the ogling and whistling that accompanied her every time she traveled off the grounds of the chateau and there were few vineyard workers in the region of Chateau Fontenot that did not at some point consider her naked among the vines even if it was in the fantasy world of their own bedrooms.

Ordinarily a boy or man of any age visiting the chateau after dark would have been rebuffed, but Briand used his charm on the impossible

Jeanne and while she refused to allow him entry. Keeping him for questioning at the front door much to Drouet's embarrassment. Briand had the good fortune to turn the conversation around to the missionary work his family did and that he had committed himself to do next year. Jeanne knew that a missionary of God who was not a Catholic was a godsend and it would have been sacrilege to deny him entry to her home. What better friend or future mate could Isabelle find than a Christian missionary, someone as dedicated to God's work as she was, perhaps even more so.

There were few things Briand could say to Jeanne that did not please her. Isabelle was simply enamored of her artist and his sensitive nature or at least what she saw as a sensitive nature. Nor did she mind watching Briand manipulate Jeanne because she knew it was because, in her fantasy, he loved her. To be taken out of the chateau and its rural boredom and taken to Montmarte as the wife of an artist — this was a dream she thought she could only experience in novels. The ghost of Leon who rambled in the shadows of her mind was suddenly released as if his mangled body had never been found off the rocky shore less than a mile from where she now stood looking at Briand.

Briand had finally found a long-term solution to his long-term problem. Isabelle, he knew, wanted to leave the rural valley and see the big, wide world but her mother was not ever going to allow it. The key to the mother was her religion and his religion was essential to bringing Jeanne around. Jeanne's intuition, as all mothers' intuitions, sensed a danger in Briand. Drouet simply thought him a goldbrick with no real future that he could ever foresee as suitable for his daughter. But he knew Uncle Nikolai was right all those years ago. Jeanne was poison and he could see in Isabelle the stunted emotional growth, the agrarian isolation coupled with a fanatic faith that after too long, and perhaps it was too long already, would render her a spinster — a zombie, dead and reborn under the powers of Jeanne's erratic god and the geography of ignorance that vineyards thrived in. It was a deadly concoction that Isabelle was watered with and Drouet knew that she was beyond his power to save. Perhaps the Dutchman with the penchant for art could be the cure. He seemed a likeable fellow from a reasonable family.

So it came to pass that Briand was a regular visitor at the Chateau Fontenot and never at any time did he not say the right thing as he wandered the minefield that Jeanne set out at one end of the house and the booby traps that Drouet had set at the other end. In the middle was Isabelle, the prize over which the three people circled in an orbit propelled by their own needs none of which coincided. Briand was in the hunt for the permanent meal ticket and within a few hours of talking to the Fontenots he knew Isabelle would always have a source of income, one that could more than support Briand as well. He wasn't getting any younger. Who knows, he might actually finish a painting and find someone to purchase it. After all he had received a good price for his bottom and he still owned it.

Thirty~Six

36 Briand managed to keep Isabelle and Diana separate and content for two years. He would never even have thought of having sex with Isabelle for fear of killing the goose he needed healthy to lay a lifetime of golden eggs. In that way, what little sexual interest he had, he retained for Diana. She was alone in the world, a former urchin brought into the house by the first Madame Dupuis to be saved from the horrors of the street and transformed into a first class chamber maid. In her own dependant way, she clung to Briand and saw his once a month excursion into the realm of carnality as proof that he was with her not for easy sex but because he needed and loved her. Somewhere in the course of human evolution, including the truncated version that appears in the Old Testament, women determined that if their man needed them it was a much more permanent emotion than love, perhaps because it was so easy for a man to say, "I love you" whether or not he means it. But it is a rare man who will confess, "I need you" which implies a dependency that men perceive universally as a weakness. Even the most submissive of men, the types who are the lap dogs of their overbearing wives, are reluctant to say, "I need you." But when a woman manages to coerce it from her man's mouth or she determines it one day on a stroll on her very own planet, it is a force that will sustain the universe of her fantasy and she will accept verbal abuse, beatings, a minutely short temper, drunkenness, a lack of even the most rudimentary personal hygiene and even infidelity, all of which she will explain away in favor of the fact that her man "needs her."

The fact is that Briand did need Diana. One day he asked if he could make the rounds with her as she cleaned and made the beds. She thought it delightful, but knew that Monsieur Dupuis would never permit a stranger in his house although he cared not a whit who was in the servants' quarters. But Briand had seen Monsieur leave with a portmanteau loaded into his large automobile and even an idiot would have realized he was going on some sort of holiday. Diana was told by the butler that indeed Monsieur would be away and so the path was clear for her true love to accompany her and see the intricacies of her work as she picked up socks from the floor and ran a feather duster over a bust of Julius Caesar and other nonsensical bric-a-brac.

While Diana was intently focused on making Monsieur's bed with the perfect tuck to impress Briand, he had noticed a small diamond ring in an open case on the dressing table. He easily pocketed it without her seeing it. She talked on and on how she had learned to make beds so that a ten franc piece would bounce on her tight sheets and how one could air out a smelly comforter by flapping it three times and then turning it adroitly in the air as it floated down to the bed. She discoursed on dusting places that her employer would typically check to see if the job was well done and sang a ditty while cleaning the toilet to distract her from the foul chore. Briand smiled broadly for her as if he were interested and she remarked how she loved his crooked teeth that gave his mouth such a masculine look. It was a glorious day for Briand who had set in motion a chain of events that would alter their lives.

Within a week's time, about eighteen months after Isabelle stood blocking his view of the pelicans on the beach, Briand proposed marriage to Isabelle. She accepted with glee. He placed the small, but elegant glittering diamond ring on her virginal finger the same as it had been on the finger of the first Mrs. Dupuis, raped and murdered by two Prussian officers in the small wood on the Fanteuil Road to Paris about fifty years earlier.

A week before he was to marry Isabelle, Briand told Diana that he had rented an apartment in Cherbourg on the English Channel in Normandy, that he had sold several paintings to a British collector who wanted all the paintings he could produce. He said in six days time he would be there waiting for her and that she should give her notice. He wrote the address on a piece of paper and pressed it into her hand together with a train ticket to Cherbourg. Tears of immeasurable joy streamed down her face. He left the next week, she thinking he was going to wait for her in the city. In fact, he had arranged quarters with a milkmaid living in a dairy barn about five miles away using the name "Luke." On the day of his wedding, the milkmaid awoke to find Luke packed and gone while Diana who had resigned her post, took the train, wandered the streets of Cherbourg looking for her beloved and their love nest, which, of course, she never found. In two weeks when desperation had faded and starvation followed her like a shadow, she met a man named Boudain who fed her, cleaned her and put her out on the streets where she sold her body for at first twenty francs, then ten, then five until one day two years later, they found her naked floating face down in the Puilly River.

With a substantial gift from the Fontenots, Isabelle and Briand rented a small flat in Montmartre in Paris with a chamber to sleep in and another for Briand to use as a studio.

Their honeymoon night spent in the new flat had neither a moon, it was raining buckets, nor honey, for nothing could have prepared Isabelle for the beast that hung between Briand's legs. Dutchman are known for their sixteenth century artists and their tulips and little else, but the fact is that it should be a wonder how Dutch women manage to spend the day in a pair of ridiculous, impliant wooden shoes, for it is a miracle that they can walk at all. Briand's private parts were like a baby's arm and lacking any empathy for his virginal wife or any amorous techniques whatsoever, he rammed it into her as only a Dutchman would. Needless to say, the neighbors heard the shriek and when a policeman knocked on the door, it took some explaining, several winks and a bevy of wry smiles to convince the officer that what had actually happened was no crime although many females would probably disagree. Pieter Van der Loden once asked, "Has anyone ever seen a beautiful Dutch girl?" While they may be born in large numbers like red tulips with yellow veins, the grimaces they inevitably make at night, night after night, soon turn them into rubber-faced, thick-featured trollish housewives bowleggedly stomping on cobble streets in their oaken shoes.

It is a heroic truth that Isabelle attempted to accommodate the clumsy giant that was her husband's member but it was beyond her ability and with all the inherent guile of women everywhere, it was simply a matter of time before she developed headaches, backaches and menstrual periods that lasted three weeks, sometimes longer. This suited Briand just fine and in fact he preferred what he used to call to himself. "the palm sisters" who were available at every hour of the day and night and neither expected nor received kisses, thanks, caresses or that most tiresome of all masculine burdens, foreplay.

Thirty~Seven

37 Over the next few years, Isabelle waited at first with fascination, then anxiety, and finally anger as Briand failed to finish even one painting, not even a portrait he started of her which perfectly depicted her more than ample bosom, but showed her nose longer than she thought it looked in the mirror and eyes perhaps a tad too close together. Briand was defensive about his lack of output in a passive way, rarely if ever defending himself and, if he responded at all, it was to laugh and walk out the door. Now anyone who has dealt with a woman, whether it is a mother, a sister, girlfriend, niece or any female of the species knows that a woman arguing with a brick wall will quickly evolve into a tigress intent on getting even. Everyone should be aware that women enjoy a good verbal battle probably with the innate hope that in reconciling afterwards, her position will be reinforced for the better, for it is a rare man indeed who will not swallow his foolish words to end a harangue. But Briand was different and would leave the flat as soon as the yelling reached a pitch that began to penetrate his self-absorption. When, at last, Isabelle threatened to move back in with the Fontenots, Briand thought better of it and explained he would give up his wandering of the Paris streets for just the right subject matter for his art in favor of taking a job. This was the equivalent to most men of promising to lop off their left foot with a golf club.

In a few days, he was a delivery boy for a flower shop, the oldest one they ever employed, the others being twelve or thirteen years of age and Briand already a man of twenty-five years. His salary was adequate for a young lad living with his parents, but it was paltry for a married man, especially when it was discovered by his employer that the tips he got from women, otherwise delighted to receive flora from their paramours or husbands, were sexual favors and Briand had developed a reputation among the neighborhood females for several blocks in every direction of the flower shop for the size of his manhood. Before long, older women, particularly those who had borne many children were sending flowers to themselves just to pay Briand his "gratuity."

Eventually his meager income forced Isabelle to seek employment and she became a hostess in a pleasant bistro, showing lovers to secluded tables where they would be less likely to be seen by their friends or spouses. One day a tall, elegant, distinctly effeminate gentleman named Monsieur Guimond with slicked-back gray hair, a razor thin mustache and a white rose in his lapel offered her a job at a local art gallery he owned catering to tourists mostly from Germany and America where he sold sappy, gauzy pictures of Paris cafés and the Eiffel Tower with little stick figures walking all about under parasols or umbrellas. Tired of moving strangers' hands off her rump as she walked between tables in the bistro, she accepted. Isabelle's bosomy good looks and the earnest expression in her eyes made her a natural, in his opinion, to appeal to foreigners and it turned out he was correct. She brought in a decent salary, nearly double what Briand earned until finally, one day, she had it out with him and demanded that he become the artist she thought she had married or she would leave him or, rather, she would throw him out.

To appease her and still not work, Briand applied to a small art school and was accepted as every applicant was, but he needed two thousand francs in tuition money. As this was half a year's combined salary, she wrote a supplicating letter to her father and received a bank draft in less than a week for the required sum. It all went well for the first six months as Briand produced some decent studies of wilted flowers, old shoes and a brazier hung over the back of a chair. Isabelle was ever the optimist for she still loved Briand in a way only a woman can love a lazy, leech of a man whom anyone with half an eyeball still functioning could see would amount to nothing had he lived to be a hundred.

One day she returned home early to retrieve some gallery documents she had left on the nightstand to find Briand and an Algerian named Sambala sitting crossed-legged on the floor playing Parchesi in a cloud of hashish smoke so thick Isabelle at first thought the flat was on fire. It turned out that Sambala was a notorious seller of the aromatic drug and had taken a liking to Briand calling him Sinbad, the perennially young boy of the 1001 Nights, who never grew old and longed to journey the earth on a magic carpet or a pink-sailed ghost clipper ship searching for the land of pomegranates, honey and bevies of lightly veiled swarthy Arab women to romp with. Sinbad had no visible means of support except as an opportunistic thief. Sambala knew Briand quite well for so brief an acquaintance.

As she stood in the doorway, mouth agape, Sambala offered Isabelle the rope end of his hookah but she was in no frame of mind to accept. She stormed out and returned to the gallery forgetting the papers she had gone home for, making up an excuse to Monsieur Guimond. That evening, she returned as usual from work prepared for domestic battle; she had rehearsed her lines and had practiced stomping her foot in a most aggressive manner. The Algerian was gone, but Briand was sound asleep in the murky apartment which reeked like old socks. As she was about to slam the door to awaken him, she noticed a letter from the art school that had been slipped under the door expressing their regrets that Briand Neumann had withdrawn the prior month but that the tuition he paid was nonrefundable. She hid the letter and permitted Briand the luxury of creating some story as to his whereabouts all the days she thought he had been attending classes. The rage she had felt earlier melted away and was replaced by a vacuum. Any love she had managed to maintain for him flew out the window like a trapped bird along with the stench as she raised every sash to let in the fresh air. When Briand awoke, she had no more to say to him than any stranger would, for her mind was made up, although he could never imagine what went on within the confines of her skull, or anyone else's for that matter, for he was concerned only with his own thoughts, his own comforts and the other people who occupied his world needed to comprehend that to Briand, Briand always came first.

Thirty~Eight

38

The next day Isabelle took a one week leave of absence from the Guimond Gallery and returned to the Chateau Fontenot to discover that Jeanne had run off with an itinerant preacher two months earlier and her father had not informed her, being at a loss to explain it and not really being particularly concerned although he wept when he told Isabelle the truth of it and confessed that he would always love Jeanne even if she was "deranged" as he called it. He also explained that he had wasted no time in seeking an annulment of his marriage to Jeanne based on her desertion of the Catholic faith. The Archbishop of Paris had granted it after receiving the required documents and a substantial cash contribution to the Diocese of Paris. Added to her bewilderment of life's sudden changes, Isabelle was shocked to find that Drouet was engaged to be married to a Madame Nanette D'Este, from Nancy, the town in the South of France renowned for art glass. She was a stout fireplug of a woman, a widow of six years with no children of her own but one who had inherited a considerable fortune from her late husband, the former owner of a prominent glass factory in Nancy, taken over by the famous Daum family. Everything about her appealed to Drouet's submissive nature and he seemed to love her in his own weak-willed way.

Isabelle, after absorbing the impact of the news of her mother's departure and her father's planned remarriage, explained everything to Drouet who in typical fashion told her he didn't doubt for a moment that Briand was a slothful idiot but that her mother had liked him and he knew better than to contradict her. Drouet offered to advance her some money over Nanette's quiet objection and she returned to Paris to work in the gallery, residing in a loft over a café only two blocks away with a co-worker named

Michelle, a wiry, dark-haired, dark-eyed slip of a woman who had been abused by her father and had taken to hating men in fruitless revenge.

Michelle owned a small dog, a black Pekinese bitch with a surly disposition that attempted to bite every man or boy it came into contact with. The postman had kicked out at her in self-defense knocking out two of the teeth in her lower, protruding jaw which gave her bark an odd whistling sound. The dog, named Francine, took an instant liking to Isabelle and Isabelle to her especially when Francine attacked Briand one day as he came to plead for Isabelle to return home to him or at least to pay the rent, which was now two months in arrears. His words fell on deaf ears. In fact, he returned the very next day to the gallery to report to Isabelle that he had been evicted while visiting her the previous night. She had less than no sympathy for him, turning her back in silence, going into the office of the gallery in much the same fashion he had left the flat when she was nagging him, in his words, to get a job. A few weeks later, Isabelle came home from work to find Michelle sitting on the divan perched like a featherless bird staring at the door waiting to tell her news. She immediately stood up and blurted out that she had seen Briand asleep in the doorway of an abandoned building with two copies of Le Figaro spread over him as a blanket. Isabelle thanked Michelle for the information and noted, as she went to the kitchen to prepare her evening meal, that she was happy for Briand for finally doing what he always wanted to do: nothing. As tears rolled down her face from chopping an onion, she added that Paris is the only city on Earth where starving is an art.

Thirty~Nine

39 The Village of Altamura rested in a niche in the foothills west of Bari and a third of the way across the ankle of the boot of Italy to Naples. The town was so old that no one's ancestors knew how long it had been there but it was likely an Etruscan settlement, the Etruscans a noble race that inhabited Italy before the Romans. They were very much like the Spartans, organized on masculine virtues of war, aggression, sport and ritualized homosexuality which had more to do with philosophical notions of comradeship than the gaudy dandyism associated with sodomites today.

The village was in a rocky, barren plane unsuitable for anything more than sheep herding and domestic brutality. Flowers fried in the streets. The dry wind turned everything into dust and then scattered it all into every small crevice and rabbit hole. When the rains came, the skies dumped water like Niagara, flooding latrines and causing them to overflow into the streets sending mud, urine and feces into alleyways and roads. It was a place of extremes where only the most truculent could survive. There had to have been a genetic predisposition to stay put because no one ever left or dreamed of leaving unless it was in a coffin. If the Earth around Altamura had ended and all human life ceased, the people of the high-walled village would never have known it and had they, they would not have cared. There was the obligatory small church, Santa Croce, ruled over by a frenetic priest who had too much energy for an urban parish: what other type of man would accept such an assignment? The townspeople were proud of their ignorant heritage, eked out a living off their wooly prisoners and were happy with a good loaf of bread, a jug of opaque home-made wine and the love of a good woman even if she invariably had the shadow of a mustache.

Altamura is Italian for "high wall" although there were virtually no walls anywhere other than those of the local stone and adobe structures and these were quite short. If there was a high wall, it was in the minds of the people who distrusted outsiders, especially if they were educated, northern Italians of any type, Sicilians and Calabrese that were considered more African than Italian. A peculiar mix of superstitious Catholicism and native witchcraft provided a lively spiritual life and so it was not odd, even to Father Rinaldi, to see a baby in his bassinet with a crucifix suspended above along with an ivory or bone horn. The cross was to be expected, the horn was to ward off the malocchio or evil eye, a belief that someone eyeing the innocent child in an evil way might influence his growth and safety. Most of the parents of Altamura, had they been forced to choose between the cross and the horn would likely have chosen the...well who can say?

The women of Altamura were revered in a way unique to the town. The only thing more precious than a wife was a mother. Whether this was a result of a deep spiritual devotion to the Virgin Mary or simply some newly evolved biological imperative has never been determined but it was universal in Altamura and similar villages that the only crimes that occurred were retaliations for effronteries to one's wife, daughter or mother. It was as if females were placed out as bait and death would be the price for the wrong sideways glance at someone else's wife or an inappropriate epithet for someone else's mother or daughter. The women of Altamura were no fonts of innocence, either, and were really no different had they lived in the streets of Barcelona, Balaclava or the Bronx. But, here, they were symbols of temptation, perhaps because they were the only soft and yielding places in a terrain where the rocks sprouted like weeds and the weeds made the crown of thorns look like a satin garland.

The men of Altamura considered the women to be without souls. It was a good explanation for why they outlived their husbands: God was not anxious to bring them home to heaven. They survived insults, beatings, the loss of children and accepted verbal and physical abuse without retaliation. They tolerated bad breath, smelly balls and crude handling. Only a being without a soul could tolerate their lot in life. But they could pass on souls much like someone can pass on typhoid fever without ever contracting it himself. Again, in view of the reverence paid the Blessed Virgin, all this had a certain indefinable logic to it. Mary could have a child with a perfect soul, in fact, a being the equivalent of God, without needing one of her own. After all, she was simply a human. It all made a logic-tight creed which controlled and explained all the interpersonal behavior in Altamura with the exception, perhaps, of buggering a ewe on a lonely night enshrouded hillside.

Saying that the people of Altamura led simple lives and had generally predictable behavior patterns is not to be taken as a criticism, nor should the smugness of modern people cause them to look down their pampered noses. The Altamurans had their million personal eccentricities, their head colds, their jealousies, their orgasms, their mid-life crises, their puberties, their menopauses, their feelings of inferiority, of superiority, their sadists, their masochists, their warmongers, their peaceniks, their dirty toes, their clean teeth, their ear wax, their pimples, their dying relatives, their new-born relatives, their weddings, funerals, parties and everything else that makes one think one is special. In short, they were as complex in the details of life as any generation before or since and volumes could be filled if each detail was repeated. So while temporal distances give present occupants of planet Earth a sense of looking not only back, but down, do not be self-deceived. It is a certainty that in years to come, when someone with a pen and paper or an infernal word processor writes of your town, he will be as facile and understated about your lives as this writer is being about the lives of Altamurans. Your furniture will end up in a second-hand furniture store, your favorite clothing in rag shops and your brains so full of memories and overblown notions of self-importance will be as forgotten as a cheese sandwich.

40 Nunzio Corona was a loving tyrannical husband to his wife, Antonia, and a cuddly monster to his five daughters, the youngest and oldest only seven years apart. He was illiterate like all the residents of Altamura and his knowledge of the world was gained at his mother's breast, his father's knee, his wife's private parts, rumors, experience and the Catholic Church as presented by Father Rinaldi. In effect, he had enough education to survive in Altamura, comment on the weather, the bad behavior of the young, the sins of his neighbors and to consider himself fortunate to be strong enough to father five daughters, although he preferred sons as everyone did, and to be able to beat most other men in the town to a pulp, especially if he was sober. He had a full mouth of hard white teeth, piercing blue eyes and fiercely red hair. Somewhat barrel-chested, he was of average height. He bathed regularly and took considerable pride in his appearance which made him attractive to men and women alike in a healthy sociable way.

He worked for Don Alfonso who owned most of the grazing land in and around Altamura. He was a property manager of sorts who made his rounds on a short stout horse named Lucinda and made certain that the tenant farmers on Don Alfonso's land did not abuse it. He also was proficient at calculating and collecting the rents. His counterpart in other villages were as despised as tax collectors but his charming smile, his clean appearance and his sense of fair play, while not endearing him to the farmers, made them tolerate him. Some even liked him. He never flirted with wives and daughters and always referred to people's mothers by the use of the title "Signora." He carried a Mannlicher forty caliber single shot pistol with him as protection against wild boar, wolves and desperados.

Antonia, was a deacon of the church. She provided flowers at the masses and was frequently called upon in times of need, more so even than Father Rinaldi, for it was widely thought that Antonia had healing hands and the ability to foretell outcomes. She was consulted on family matters and her blessing was always sought on perspective marriages. She genuinely seemed to accurately sense when a young man and a young woman were suited to one another. If she felt a proposed union would result in hardship and pain, the parents of the parties would call off the wedding. While infrequent, her power to cancel marriages gave many of the young men in Altamura the right to call her "mamma blue balls." Of course, this was always uttered under one's breath and never in earshot of Nunzio.

Their lives would have proceeded apace and they would have been buried next to each other in the graveyard of Santa Croce's had an incident in the neighboring town of Impretta not occurred. This was where Nunzio's widowed mother Margarita lived in a small apartment owned by a wealthy merchant named Giuseppe Gordi. She defrayed some of the rent by working as his housekeeper. In her sixties, she cut a fine figure still, trim and strong with long salt and pepper hair tied in an elegant bun. Nunzio visited her monthly and gave her some money to help with the expenses.

One fateful evening, Don Giuseppe had had one or two glasses of Chianti beyond his usual. His wife was in Naples with their daughter on a shopping spree and he decided, perhaps it was the full moon, that Margarita's backside was more attractive than he remembered. While she was clearing his dinner dishes, he came up from behind and reached around, cupping her breasts in his hands. She spun around and smacked him full in the face. Had it ended at that, there would be no need to spend this ink, but Don Giuseppe reacted violently and punched Margarita full in the face, knocking out one of her teeth. Blood dripped down her chin and tears flooded her cheeks. He apologized profusely and blamed the Chianti as he got a napkin and helped her blot the blood and tears. She accepted his apology and as much for her own reputation in the town and for her job, she vowed to tell no one.

Fate, in an idle moment, whispered in Nunzio's ear that it was the time of the month to visit his mother. Two days after the altercation, he appeared at his mother's door. In a matter of moments, he noticed her fat lip and the missing tooth despite her feeble efforts to conceal them. She pleaded with him not to ask questions, the answer to which could only result in trouble. She insisted she was fine but he would not desist and eventually she broke down and told him the story on the proviso that he not in any way retaliate or seek retribution. Getting a vow out of Nunzio for this would be like getting a vow from a lion that he would never eat a gazelle. This was a promise, much like a young girl's heart, that was made to be broken.

Rumors, the main source of entertainment after sex in the region, spread quickly—do they ever spread slowly?— of Margarita's injuries and it was obvious that something had happened in the Gordi household. What else could it have been? Did she trip and hit her tooth on a slop bucket? Walk into a wall in the middle of the night on the way to the latrine? While all of these might have been possible, even likely, the vicarious thrill of relating a sexual attack was far more intriguing and, only by the merest of coincidences, true.

Nunzio bit his tongue and bided his time. He calculated his alibi along with the method of retaliation. One might ponder the fact that there was no real loss of honor, "loss of face" they called it in Altamura, because only Don Giuseppe, Margarita and Nunzio knew of the incident. And the rumors would soon run out of steam, especially when it was discovered that one, Rocco Porcello had raped his own daughter and was hiding in Siracusa in Sicily. Or so it was said. The truth was never revealed and when the hapless girl was seen in town with a black eye and large belly, people looked away and crossed themselves because if they made eye contact with such a creature, she surely would have given them the most potent of all malocchios.

The fact is, though, that Nunzio knew of the effrontery and he could not bare Don Giuseppe's name or see his back without his stomach turning and his intestines twisting. Eventually, with great attention to planning every detail, Nunzio interrupted Don Giuseppe on the dirt road outside Impretta on his way to collect some debts. They greeted each other cordially as if the meeting was accidental but Don Giuseppe had the bird of guilt perched on his shoulder and he trembled ever so slightly around the mouth as he commented on the dryness of the weather. Nunzio pulled out his Mannlicher pistol and sidled his horse to within a yard of Don Giuseppe's carriage. Without being asked, Don Giuseppe offered every profusion of apology known to the martyrs but his fate was sealed. Nunzio aimed and pulled the trigger and the bullet blew out Don Giuseppe's teeth and exited his skull in the back, severing his spinal cord. His horse leaped forward with the shot and the body fell out on the road still twitching while the carriage tipped over and the horse insane with fear galloped a hundred yards with a broken leg and collapsed into a thickly clustered clump of sage brush, flailing and frothing until it died of shock.

Nunzio, meanwhile, had reloaded, dismounted and placed the gun barrel at Don Giovanni's crotch, pulled the trigger and blew his sex organs to oblivion. Not one citizen of either town, when they heard of the manner of death doubted its justification nor its perpetrator. But in the new Italian Republic, men's balls were only to blown off by the State under court order and vigilante justice would not be publicly condoned, even if justifiable. It took three days for someone to find Don Giuseppe's body and by that time, Nunzio was hiding in the hills with some friends who sympathized completely. Even if they hadn't, they would still have protected their friend from the grasp of some idiotic detective in a blue uniform from Rome asking stupid questions. Fortunately, no one had followed him to the port of Naples where he boarded a ship for America, nor had the police boarded at Gibraltar as he feared they might. In some conscious fashion, he realized how insignificant he was to the rest of the world especially out on the Atlantic where he stood on deck and looked down at the breaking foam that caressed the sides of the ship. But he would never understand why an Italian ship had stopped so close to its destination without reaching it, still out in the deepest water when the captain informed everyone, as he threw a wreath overboard, that they were a short distance away on the same latitude from where an English ship named Titanic had sunk only three weeks earlier. While others prayed and a few tears were shed, Nunzio looked at his pocket watch and the fins of dolphins making slow arches in the still water. He could not imagine that anyone on board this ship knew anyone on the British ship; to weep over strangers was an idle indulgence. Six weeks after seeing the silhouette of Vesuvius behind him, Nunzio stepped off the steamer Garibaldi at Ellis Island and smiled at the Statute of Liberty.

Forty~One

In a rooming house in "Little Italy" in New York City, Nunzio met Frank Fortezza, a short, brawny man from Bari who thought the two of them could pool their resources and purchase a livery wagon. With hundreds of immigrants arriving every day and the growth of New York exploding, people were always in need of strong backs and a good vehicle to transport goods of every sort. Nunzio agreed and in a matter of weeks he and Frank were busy twelve hours a day.

Nunzio bought postcards from a small stationery store on Mott Street in lower Manhattan that was owned by an attractive French woman named Amelie. He asked her to address them to his wife and she showed him how to sign his name. In this way Antonia knew her husband was well and that America was vast, as the postcards of New York City, the Grande Canyon, Yosemite, San Francisco and Coney Island arrived weekly. She recognized Nunzio's illiterate signature but could not understand the fluid feminine handwriting of the address. She was no more suspicious than most women in this situation which is to say she was beside herself with jealousy and only the monthly arrival of an envelope from Nunzio with an American five dollar bill in it prevented her from placing a curse on his private parts, for fear he might perish and the money would stop.

In a few months, Nunzio and Amelie were living together in the apartment above her shop. Nunzio was saving all his money to bring his family over and to rent a house of his own. With his own living expenses which included a fairly large sum for clothing, he managed to save enough money to rent a large attached house in a nice section of the Bronx, north of Manhattan and for six one way passages from Naples for his wife and five daughters. In the time it took him to accumulate the money, his son Julian was born to Nunzio and his "French Woman." When Julian was five, Amelie died from a cancer, Nunzio moved to his home in the Bronx and mailed the tickets to Antonia. It took them three months to arrive in New York, just enough time for Nunzio to concoct a story of the death of a dear friend and his wife in a terrible accident and his volunteering to adopt their child Julian, a tragic but simple way to have the son he always wanted.

Antonia, Nunzio, their five daughters and Julian settled into a regular routine in no time, Antonia accepting the story and pouring sympathy if not love onto Julian. Nunzio essentially ignored his daughters and focused all his love on Julian so there was a peculiar undercurrent in the home that no one could define but that everyone could feel, like swimming in the ocean at night, the moon glistening on the beautiful surface while the cold currents and empty-eyed predators lurking just beneath one's toes which could sense the gentle surge of water rising from the depths and pressing against the legs as the precursory swell of some giant gray and cold scaly body swam upwards and passed.

Over the ensuing years, Nunzio's daughters developed much as they would have in Altamura, except for the youngest who was the only one to attend school. They spoke only Italian and worked at menial piece jobs in factories owned by Jews and where all or most of the other workers spoke Italian. Nunzio's partner, Frank married the eldest daughter and all of them married good Italian husbands. Julian was bookish and thrived in school. If he did not do well in a course, it was because he was bored and would study topics of his own not on the public school curriculum. Antonia was not blind and could see in Julian little physical nuances of Nunzio. Too simple to think it might just be her heated imagination but too bright not to notice the real physical similarity, she harbored her resentment like a vile of acid in her abdomen. She refused sexual relations with Nunzio for a number of timeworn excuses until he had got the habit of not even trying. But his peasant background caused him not to understand Antonia's genuine hurt but instead take her refusals as insult. Remember, peasants live from day to day and each turn of misfortune can impact life quickly and tragically. Survival is a daily affair and so it was not uncommon to believe that everything that occurred centered on one's self. When hunger lurks around every corner, it is difficult, if not impossible to spend any time concerned with the thoughts or emotions of others. But Nunzio was cunning enough to know that he did not want to rock the boat of his marriage and so a daily routine of mutual disregard developed like weeds in an untended garden.

Nunzio would arise at four or five in the morning every morning, even though he did not leave for work until seven. He would dress in the dark while Antonia slept. She rarely rose before seven. He made only so much noise as he could to rouse her but not enough to make her think it was intentional and she would be awakened by the rustling of a stiff cotton shirt being donned or a fumbling for shoes, but pretend still to be asleep. Thus, both of them feigned to be someone they were not. One morning, Nunzio dropped his pocket watch and it clattered on the nightstand and fell to the floor with a small thunk, the chain rasping against the edge of the stand unraveling as it followed the watch. Antonia stirred and in the gray light said, "Is Julian your son?" Nunzio said nothing but simply left the house without his breakfast. He did not return that night but stayed with Frank and he sent word to Antonia that he would not return until she retracted the question. She refused and as he refused to answer, they stayed apart.

After two months, Nunzio returned to his home which he told her was his after all. He slept in one of the upstairs bedrooms and they lived together but apart for two years sharing only the bathroom in turns. One night, he sat on Antonia's bed, formerly their bed and waited for her to finish bathing. It had been a long and strenuous day and he had lain down only for a moment. He fell asleep. When she came into the room, she got into the bed on her side and shook him and told him to leave, that he was no longer welcome there. In the dark, he turned to her silhouette and said, "Yes, Julian is my son." She said nothing and from that moment on they slept in the same bed, never discussing it again.

Forty~Two

42 In a household of illiterate, uneducated people there was little encouragement for Julian. Neither of his parents could read his report cards and discussions were limited to local gossip, complaints about the five daughters' husbands, their countless disrespects which Antonia counted, and the church which loomed over everyone like a vampire draining the natural drives of the neighborhood's inhabitants and forcing them underground to ferment into phobias, perversion and guilt. In any event, Julian was made immune by the vaccine of his books which were stored in boxes under his bed despite Antonia's implication that they would one day spontaneously combust and burn the house down.

Nunzio and Antonio assumed that Julian would get a nice job after graduating from Bishop Manzana High School, perhaps in the shoe factory a few blocks west or waiting on tables at Fortuna's Italian Restaurant. They even thought the army was not a bad idea because he could learn a trade like laying bricks or plumbing. When he told them he wanted to go to college they simply looked at him and asked why he would waste all that money and time on so foolish an endeavor. When he said he wanted to become a doctor, pride welled up in Nunzio and Antonia imagined using the epithet, "my son, the doctor" at every opportunity, in church or out.

In that fashion, he convinced them of his monetary needs and he went off to a university north of the city while his sisters grumbled at his being their parents' favorite and not even being of their blood.

In a few years of study, Julian tired of poking around the entrails of animals, guessing the function of peculiar bones or the growth cycles of pole beans on final examinations. One fateful day he passed out when he witnessed an operation on a young boy to correct his crossed eyes. The surgeon forced his patient's tiny blue eyes open with forceps and when the scalpel slit the tender stringy muscles that forced his innocent blue eyes to perpetually stare at his own nose, Julian went down like the proverbial tree in the uninhabited forest bumping the surgeon's arm on the way to his appointment with the floor. No damage was done but Julian had several bruises to his back where the surgeon kicked him shouting, "Get this idiot out of here."

By the next semester, Julian switched his course of study from pre-med to English literature where he thrived as a flower in a drought that is suddenly receiving regular doses of rain. One of the most important aspects of his switch in studies from cat's gallbladders to the love poetry of John Donne was the easy access to sex. As a pre-med student he was considered one of a long string of scholars in the history of the university who would, it was rumored, use the excuse of cunnilingus as an opportunity to examine the working condition of a live vagina, an impetuous mixture of learning and pleasure unequaled in any other university department. But the female students quickly tired of being used for free anatomy lessons and discussions of labia, membranes mucosa and hemorrhoids made it become virtually impossible for a pre-med student to obtain the favors of any woman unless she was grossly overweight, covered in pimples, or both In addition, Julian, who seemed the romantic, had other ideas embodied by his father's advice on the day he packed his bags and left for college; "always keep your woman on a pedestal; it is easier to see under her dress."

In the English department, however, long discussions of the human spirit, man's lonely plight in the universe and the weepy sonnets of Shakespeare, Petrarch and the lovelorn creative writing students filled the hearts of the female undergraduates with a longing for the sensitive male who understood passion, love and a woman's innermost yearnings. In a matter of months, Julian's calendar was filled with homework assignments and with appointments to liaise with women to discuss their poetry and their aspirations and to be fulfilled in his small bed. Needless to say, Julian lost weight, had dark circles under his eyes, but always slept well with the hint of a meek smile on his face. Of course, compared to the male faculty of the department, Julian and his comrades were as crows in a November cornfield, pecking and finding scattered kernels while the professor farmers made off with the best part of the crop. Virtually every married instructor had developed the habit of pocketing his wedding band in his tweed coat pocket prior to class and the air of spiritual superiority and the words of the great poets of the world on their pontificating lips hypnotized the coeds into a miasmic euphoria of carnal passion which they, with their feminine wits, perceived as a quest for the joining of souls.

When Julian's long poem called "The Incunable of Love" was published in the university literary magazine, he was suddenly in even higher female demand than the professors who taught Keats and Shelley. But every silver cloud has a pitch lining and Julian contracted a most painful case of venereal disease which cured his naiveté about sex the way a bout with green nausea will cure a sea voyager with a desire to see distant shores. Fortunately, prescribed medicines worked and graduation day was only a month away.

Julian's parents, meantime, never discovered that their son was not to be a doctor, but had altered his course of study to literature and the humanities. He decided that to tell them of his change of plans would, firstly risk his being cast out without a dollar and secondly, force him into some type of manual labor or, worse, sales to support himself. So he told them he was going to study medicine in Paris. At this point, he could not surprise them and their pride in their son made them blind to the obvious, although Nunzio did ask why Julian did not want to enter an American medical school. Julian prevaricated with a series of confusing answers regarding the anti-Italian bias of large American universities, the excessively high cost and the longer course of study. These were all lies but they were lies that appealed to Nunzio's peasant sense of paranoia and thrift. It was settled that in September, Julian would start the study of medicine in Paris and that he would spend the summer in part-time work to accumulate some spending money and to study French, of which he already had a decent collegiate-style knowledge.

One languid July night that summer, two friends from the English department asked him to dinner. Dominic and Tim were homosexual lovers, bright, handsome and the life of every party they attended which was every party thrown because they were different in a substantially anti-establishment way and therefore in high demand. Despite the illegality of their sodomite behavior, they were safe among their liberal humanities-studying colleagues and while it might have disquieted one or two closet

Calvinist types, no one ever said anything even if, after a few drinks, they danced together or kissed. The possibility of these activities occurring made them the favorites as dinner guests, favorably implying that the host or hostess was open-minded and a vanguard of the new.

43 Dominic was a tall fair-skinned, blue-eyed Hun, born in Germany to a Prussian father and Low German mother. His father had disciplined him mercilessly especially as Dominic grew into the subtly feminine figure he cut when he was fourteen. He had light brown hair worn too long for his father's liking and had the face of a beautiful girl. His father, like most Germans, believed from the bottom of his Teutonic heart that corporal punishment was the path to manhood for Dominic. While it could be debated endlessly that Dominic was born a sissy, some might argue to a convincing degree that the harsh treatment he received from his father, Dominic interpreted as a lack of love, even loathing and for the rest of his life he would seek that love in the arms and groins of men. Suffice it to say that Dominic was queer as a three dollar bill and left his parents' home as soon as he had the courage which was at the age of sixteen when he escaped to America on a freighter and was every seaman's favorite passenger.

Tim, on the other hand, had the face of a movie star, chiseled and masculine with intense eyes that betrayed a quick wit and a lively intelligence. He was only five feet three inches tall which severely restricted his chances of good employment or most sorts of economic advancement in a country where everything big is good and to be respected and the small are to be ridiculed. Tim's father died when he was three so unlike Dominic he never experienced the dubious pleasure of having a live father. Instead, he was raised by his doting Irish mother, Maureen, who encouraged him to pursue his inner most thoughts and desires. Tim loved art and spent all his working hours sketching portraits of neighbors, neighbor's relatives, neighbor's dogs and eventually exclusively neighbor's sons, many of whom did not mind a quick excursion to a deserted part of the basement where they could experience Tim's particular form of friendship. They may have closed their eyes when he fellated them and imagined it was Shirley or Jenny at school but even the most imaginative had to open their eyes at some point and see that it was a boy named Tim. No one ever punched him or abused him and no one ever told tales for fear of being themselves exposed as "faggots" so Tim's childhood was filled with dreams of artistic heights and days of an endless supply of willing boys. His mother loved him too much to see any vice in him and wept for hours the day he moved into the dormitory at an art academy in Philadelphia, just a few blocks from where Dominic waited tables at a café. They met the way lovers usually meet and stayed together faithfully with only very rare excursions into the beds of other men, always returning to shouts of recrimination, tears and then forceful embraces much like married couples have done since Neanderthal times.

Julian, Dominic and Tim met at a downtown café enjoying a bottle of inexpensive wine at a sidewalk table. The air was thick with humidity and people walking by were the main topic of conversation after the new Modernist European poetry. Julian was running on and on how anxious he was to get to Paris, that he might carouse with the American ex-patriots. The idea that he could share a bottle of Beaujolais with Fitzgerald, Hemingway or Eliot gave him no end of joy, although he would have been hard-pressed to understand what theses great men would get out of such a meeting.

Sometime near midnight when the trio were scraping the bottom of their lint- filled pockets for enough change to pull together for a final bottle, a vibrant, blue eyed woman with a generous bounce in her step, a figure fit for Zigfeld and sex appeal that Julian could sense from across the street, caught Dominic's eye, and waved wildly at him as if he were a long-lost brother. She quick-stepped over, her perfect breasts swaying seductively and bra-less in a blue sequined flapper-style shift. She was Dominic and Tim's longtime friend Daria Berenson, out on the town after ditching her dinner date, a wealthy codger who paid her handsomely just to have her on his bony Cartier wrist- watched arm.

As true then as it is today, people are judged by the company they keep and Daria assumed that Julian was another fairy princess that Dominic and Tim knew from Greenwich Village. This made her more open and honest than she would otherwise have been, leaning unconsciously over the table and offering an unexpurgated view of her supple breasts to all at the table. In her mind, the three homosexuals at the table had no interest whatsoever in seeing her breasts or any other hidden part of her anatomy. As Tim had once joked to her when she provoked him by asking if he wanted to see her private parts he responded by saying that the last pussy he saw was his mother's when she gave birth to him and the very sight of it made him scream and cry for two hours, no thank you. She had also allowed Dominic to fondle her breasts one evening after a victory over a bottle of Polish Vodka and he was amazed at how soft and flabby they were compared to the firm muscled pectorals of men. He added that her nipples looked like they meant business and the nipples of men were clearly playthings that God had given them as a joke. He would no more nibble at her areolas than he would suck the teat of a goat. He paused and contemplated the idea of goat teats, got a sick serious look to his face and ran to the street to vomit his share of the fine Vodka, to everyone's dismay.

In Daria's mind, the attractive Julian was just another queen on the chess board of life and instead of acting distant, demur and reserved as she would have had she known he was heterosexual, she treated him the same way she treated the other two, as just another one of the girls. Disarmingly bright, attractive and in no way part of the pseudo- intellectual crowd that comprised the university's student body, he was immediately attracted to her in a fashion unfamiliar to him. Had he taken up selling shoes after high school instead of studying Chaucer, he would have thought it was love at first sight. But, as a graduate with honors in the study of English literature, he knew he was smitten. This was his Blessed Demoiselle Sans Merci, his Beatrice, his Juliet. She might have been more realistically appraised had it not been for the Beaujolais, the summer heat and the now-faded fear of venereal disease. She was no simple-minded coed. This was a real woman and he wanted her more than anything he had ever wanted.

Because Daria assumed that Julian was a sodomite, she did not make reference to her own situation by way of filling in potential paramours on background information the way playwrights must use unrealistic dialogue to provide information to an ignorant audience of important facts about the histories of the characters or action offstage. She never mentioned her four year old son Robert by her former lover, the alcoholic son of a man from a very wealthy family that traced their roots back to Betsy Ross. When Dominic had heard this years earlier, he remarked how Europeans bragged about being the descendants of Charlemagne, Richard the Lion-Hearted, the Duke of this and the Count of that, but that Americans boasted of being the descendants of the garbage of Europe, ignorant peasants and Puritans who fled for their lives because their beliefs were repugnant to civilized human beings. Indeed, it was the wonder of the Old World how a whole nation had been founded on the aspirations and primitive faith of the unwashed rejects of Europe. Daria looked at him after his diatribe as if he had snails climbing out of his nose, but loved him for his honesty and his effete Continental manner.

When Julian picked up Daria at her apartment for dinner, he met Robert for the first time and was struck by the four-year-old boy's physical similarity to Daria. He was a charming little blonde, blue-eyed replica who bounced around the furniture with delight and immediately took a liking to Julian. Whether this had been rehearsed or not, no one can say, but it certainly got Julian over the trepidation of falling in love with a woman with a child and within six months they were married, within eight months Robert was calling Julian "daddy" within twenty months Julian felt the first pangs of regret and within thirty-six months prayed for the day he could be divorced. Had he pondered it, he would gladly have boiled in oil, flayed and then ate the deep fried buttocks of the idiot who first propounded the maxim that "opposites attract." Julian discovered that they attract the way prize-fighters attract, the way angry mobs and politicians attract, the way opposing armies attract and the way God and the devil attract. Each seeks control of the other and, failing to achieve that, mutual destruction becomes the order of the day.

It must be understood that Julian had not discovered the identity of his true mother and Antonia never denied him that particular form of affection known as "motherly love." He always thought of his parents as rocks, faithful and true to each other and the neighbors' whispers when he was growing up about his father's various liaisons outside of his marriage vows were never taken seriously. One day, though, when Julian was eleven years old, a thirteen-year-old girl tried to kiss him and when he rejected her—not out of moral necessity but out of a young boy's instinctive dislike of the female of the species—she spewed out a new rumor: his mother had been having an affair with the family doctor. Every child that hears such things takes it differently and the age of the child is irrelevant, which is to say that older offspring, say forty or older, have experienced the vicissitudes of life where they may have been unfaithful or their spouses were unfaithful. Well, their children might react differently but everyone's mother is a Madonna and the sudden realization that she is very much human, driven by human needs and desires can jar the universe. Every person's world view has certain foundation stones upon which it is built—the role of parents, grandparents, and siblings are the stones and if, say, a father beats his son, that stone becomes part of the building of that son's life, crooked and distorted to the degree of the father's abuse and stones that are mortared above and around it as the years add them on, lean in precarious ways. When that son has his own child, the near-toppling wall with the crooked foundation stone falls upon that child and the son who was whipped for minor transgressions becomes the holder of the lash and in turn does the same or worse to his progeny. The lineal family is an apartment building, the distorted foundation stones will reach every storey and instead of rising straight and tall as the skyscrapers in New York City, these buildings are twisted, oblique, asymmetrical as termite mounds in the Kalahari. It takes a very strong, self-contained child to accept the faults of his parents without being twisted by them and Julian was such a child. He neither hated his mother for her transgressions nor adopted her immoral behavior as a justification for his own. More importantly, he did not doubt the rumors for he saw in Antonia a vibrant alive human being who might succumb naturally to a fear of the passage of time. And like a migrant worker on the back of a wagon, she might reach out and take hold of an orange on a passing tree, smell its perfect aroma and delve into its pulpy flesh for fear no other fruit will so present itself on the rest of the journey, never foreseeing that she might fall out of the wagon and be crushed by its passing wheels.

Of course, Julian did not ponder these issues. He was born with a sort of moral compass and had a facile ability to see the right and wrong of a situation without reference to dogma or rules. Once, in his second year at university, he wrote a paper about some moralistic French novel and made the observation that most of the Ten Commandments were rather obvious on their face. He asked, is it really necessary for God to tell everyone that it is wrong to kill someone, shouldn't that be obvious? As it turned out, he was only partially correct in his analysis because it is a certainty that a great many people are not aware of the evil of their transgressions and only upon further reflection many years later, when it was too late, did Julian realize that most people reflect on their behavior only after the fact and come up with all manner of excuses and rationalizations for breaking not only the Ten Commandments, but the other hundreds contained in the mysterious Torah. Julian, through no fault of his own, was simply not one of these people, yet. In short, Julian took his marriage vows quite seriously, as much as if he had made them to himself. He was that type of rare individual who would rather suffer through an imperfect marriage and take pride in the sanctity of his promise than forsake the promise for greener pastures and have regrets. The building of his life was erected on solid foundation stones and he had a self-confidence that permeated his activities, whether it was simply conversation or making love or doing business that instilled in others around him a sense of respect. It was not until his father told him that the French woman was really his mother, that the building developed major cracks as if damaged by an earthquake and only with the greatest of efforts could Julian keep it from toppling.

At first, Daria seemed quite content in her marriage to Julian and little Robert thrived in a precocious manner. She didn't even object to the move to Paris despite the obvious severing of ties that would result. In many ways, she looked forward to the new scenery, a new way of life and Julian's enthusiasm for their marriage filled her with a sense of security that she assumed would support her through any adversity.

Their apartment was on the Rue Auberge, a small dark street several blocks from the main thoroughfare. There were shuttered windows and empty balconies with Persian rugs draped over the railings. The limestone of the buildings was stained with the accretions of soot and water so that every crevice, cornice and gargoyle seemed to bleed a gray-black blood that ran down the façade almost to the narrow sidewalks. A romantic would have thought it a dark place where vampires dwelt or lost lovers committed suicide. A stoic would have been glad the buildings were sound and did not leak in the summer rain. A naturalist would have seen the stained buildings as a symbol of the humans that occupied them, fallen from grace and scarred with the outward sign of their sins. A realist would have seen the street that Daria and Julian were to live on as one of many such streets, ordinary and repetitious, the roots of the beautiful tree that was Paris. This was Julian's view. Daria saw it as an island of banishment. Within a few days, she was a stranger in a strange land with her vulnerable son. The windows had eyes. She longed for what she called "the good old USA," with its gregarious, friendly people, hustling and bustling on their way to bigger and better. As most people in foreign lands, even if that land is the future, the memory of the place is always superior to its reality. Memories favor the good, mute the bad. Daria was a firm believer in the superiority of her own country and Paris was to her the capital city of a former race of beings that could have conquered the world, but gave it all up for a good bottle of wine and a plate of tasty pâté.

Julian's study at the graduate school included a stipend and a position of teaching American literature to freshman students. This was an environment in which he thrived and his handsome face and confident demeanor made him the center of feverish amorous gossip among the female students, most of whom were far more open and blunt than their American counterparts. He unknowingly fed the imagination of the students with his easy charms and his insistence on keeping a formal distance between himself and them. In this way, he built a wall around himself that only he could see and the flirtation and amorous advances of the students made after class, on the campus grounds or in his small office cubical were unseen by him. His wedding band was truly a signal of his promise to himself and in a much smaller way to Daria, but to the students it was a beacon. An unmarried professor was just another licentious male using his superior position to obtain easy sex. But a teacher who did not hide his marital status nor in any way respond with so much as a double entendre at the overtures of the pretty Parisian coeds, this was a man to be wished for, a passion doubly forbidden.

Valerie Galle was a dark haired, green-eyed Jewish coed in Julian's class. She was of average height with a petite yet fulsome figure. She was one of those hallucinatory beauties that, with the application of liberal amounts of cosmetics are ravishing, but with a freshly washed face barely turn a head even on the most desperate of Paris's many avenues. Julian noticed her for he was not blind and she sat conspicuously in the front row of the lecture hall where typically few students excepting the most studious sat. Pretty girls, handsome boys, the popular and the notorious all sat as far back as possible sometimes leaving the first two rows of chairs empty as if distance from the source of knowledge was a form of protection from it. Perhaps his words, having to travel a few extra yards, would be more easily dodged or would be diluted by the auras of other students and fall harmlessly in heaps at the feet of those sitting in the rear. These were the thoughts that ran through Julian's mind, a mind livid with the world as he saw it, colored by endless hours of reading novels, plays, poems and other prismatic devices.

With an innate understanding that Julian would not have a personal relationship with a student, one of the many commandments of his life that he enshrined only to dodge and to weave around later, Valerie placed a note in her small blue booklet that contained the answers to her final examination in Julian's class. He noticed her do this and he saw her linger as the other students finished and placed their booklets on his desk and departed. When she was the last student in the room, she came up to him and handing him the booklet, said how much she enjoyed the class. They walked out together in the early summer light of Paris and he escorted her to the trolley on Boulevard Victor Hugo. The conversation was light and full of the clichés between teachers and students everywhere, but Julian was aware of the deep longing in her voice and looked at her as she walked and talked and sensed a woman within that was much older than the nineteen years her university records indicated. As they waited for the number 7 trolley to arrive, she asked if she might meet him to discuss her own future in literature. He accepted and they agreed to meet the following Friday at Café Tres Chats, a small literary hangout in the Carte Du Boulogne section of the city north of the university. Before the trolley arrived, Julian bid farewell and in so doing, not waiting with her, he established his superiority over her, that he would wait for no woman, that she would see his back as he departed, and that the question of whether he would turn around after twenty or thirty paces was always answered in the negative. Any woman who expected more would never interest him and those that expected less were to be the doormat upon which he would wipe the soles of his shoes. He firmly believed that women were the natural hunters. Look at the lions, he thought. It is the female that hides in ambush and brings down the prey. So with people, the woman must always be left to hunt but in his case, never be allowed to pounce. Julian's heart would be the allusive prey that no woman would be so furtive, so skillful, so beautiful that he would pause, even for a second, to allow her the triumph of the kill.

When they met at the café and had a few glasses of the Nouveau Beaujolais that had just arrived in the city from the vineyards in the south, he listened attentively to her questions about a career in teaching and a course of study. He answered in his professional manner which was genuine with him and not in any way a pretense. When he suggested they get a room at the Hotel Duchamp across the street, she agreed as if hypnotized. If the lioness needed a hotel bed as camouflage, then so be it. She assented silently by rising and waiting for him to leave the money on the table for the wine. She agreed only by the movement of her body and the limpid look in her green eyes. Verbal assent was too much like a business deal and lions in stealth do not growl. Theirs is the silence of necessity, the repression of passion, a subjugation of the natural intent to attack as just the right moment approaches.

They spent two hours in bed in a small room that overlooked a brick-walled alleyway, nothing so romantic as the reader would enjoy or expect. It could have been a twentieth-story view of Mount Olympus for all they cared. She was an orchestra which he conducted, moving her limbs and shifting her weight as he dictated. Her will was lost somewhere in the blue sky over Paris and try as she might over the following months, his heart never came close enough for her to pounce, no matter how her hunger increased even to the point of obsession.

Forty-Six

46 Martin Galle was Valerie's father. He was the son of an orthodox Jewish merchant of cloth in Paris. As a young man he worked in the store that his father owned and had a knack for dealing with the Parisians who frequented Galle's Fine Fabrics to obtain the latest silks, linens and brocades from Southern Italy and the Far East. One day shortly after his thirty-fifth birthday, a woman named Beatrice Montcalm came into the shop with her daughter Francoise, a beautiful girl of sixteen with Gaelic flaxen hair and eyes the color of Swiss chocolate. But for his awe at seeing Francoise, Martin might have noticed how beautiful the forty-something-year-old Beatrice was, but men are ever on the search for feminine youth, some even to a pathology. Twenty-year-olds ogle teenagers, thirty-year-olds ogle twenty-year-olds, forty-year-olds ogle twenty-five year- olds and older men ogle any female under thirty. Each man imagines himself as an Adonis, even the obese and the ugly, for the mirror is a friend that always lies and failing eyesight puts a soothing gauze on the lens of truth where yellow teeth, watery eyes and the wrinkles that are the scars of the lost war with gravity are gently erased. It should surprise no young woman that a man twice her age will seek her company, wear clothes a generation younger than he should, comb his thinning hair in the latest male fashion over his bald spot and smile seductively at her. She may see someone similar to her grandfather's friends but he presents himself as a man not only interested in the opposite sex but attractive to it. Fortunately, older men are often the wealthier because unless one is the heir to a fortune, fortunes take years, often decades, to accumulate and it is a rare woman who is not on intimate terms with the myopia of wealth, as if she sees the older man in the same image as he sees himself in his mirror. It is an acceptable conspiracy of lies that perpetuates the chase. No matter how great the distance may seem between man and the animal kingdom, females instinctively seek out the alpha male.

In this case, however, Beatrice was indulging not her instincts but her carnal desires. She had already married her alpha male, Cosimo Montcalm, some twenty-five years her senior and he had died five years ago after a protracted battle with some abdominal illness that left him emaciated and delusional but still quite wealthy. At the age of forty-eight, she was still attractive and looks and whistles, while not as numerous as when she was twenty-five, still echoed occasionally through the narrow streets of Paris as she walked by groups of laborers on the corners. Her husband's wealth was a great defense against the ravages of the life of the working class and sums that could feed a chambermaid's family for a week were spent on hairdressers, for a month on shoes, and for a year on dresses.

Most women would have seen Martin Galle as average with dark eyes and dark hair, a little tall and a little narrow in the shoulders perhaps, but he had the aura of the exotic to Beatrice because he was so obviously a Jew. Women tire easily of the familiar and of their husbands because their husbands tire of them. As the philosopher Maurice Dunand once said, "After three years of marriage, friend, how many positions do you still practice on your wife?" Fantasy will replace the extramarital liaison and the closed eyes of a woman in the sexual act are more likely a blank screen for her imagination than the throes of ecstasy and one of Beatrice's favorite fantasies was passion at the hands of a Jew. So, while Martin, as surreptitiously as possible, examined every curve and angle of Francoise, Beatrice wondered what realms of pleasure could be derived from Martin's circumcised member. Francoise, still an ingénue and a virgin could not help but notice her mother's sudden change in demeanor and the sultry look that occupied her face as she spoke to Martin about the qualities of this Cantonese silk or that Venetian satin. Each watched the other in a circle the center of which would be their future, as the survivors of a shipwreck, adrift in the storm, will circle the edge of a whirlpool slowly spiraling inward and downward, helpless against the current.

Francoise would no more have thought of Martin as a subject of her amorous desires than the man in the moon. In fact, she did not even see him in the sense of noticing him as an individual, as a man with eyes, ears, arms and legs, emotions, desires and a history, no more than the Matterhorne would notice a fat German tourist gazing in awe appreciatingly at its ice-capped escarpments. To Francoise, Martin was little different than the headless mannequin in the corner draped in two layers of yellow chiffon. He was a part of the store that could speak. Unwittingly as Beatrice protracted her perusal of the fabrics and bibelots that crammed Galle's Fine Fabrics from floor to ceiling, she gave him time for his interest in Francoise to take root. Beatrice's silly procrastinating banter allowed the rain of lust to moisten those roots and her inappropriately coquettish manner was the sunshine that warmed the sprouting seedling into a passion. Like mandrake, an abominable plant under any circumstances, once in the garden of one's life becomes a weed that no amount of pruning or uprooting can deter, so Martin became extricated in the lives of Beatrice and Francoise Montcalm. Had Cosimo been alive he might have taken an axe to Martin and gladly have died in prison for the crime of sparing his wife and daughter the fate that awaited them. But he was dead, moldering in his grave and impotent to alter the jest that fate was brewing in her battered copper teapot.

Within forty-five minutes and a sale of a few yards of green Syrian silk that Madame Montcalm was going to have turned into a summer shawl, Martin had become obsessed with Francoise. He watched her exit the shop like a man stranded in the desert, his voice gone from dehydration seeing a caravan in the distance but unable to shout loud enough to be saved. He knew he must posses her to live and at any means at his disposal. When Madame Montcalm returned alone to the shop the following day to order a silver clasp in the shape of a serpent she had seen on a woman on the Boulevard St. Germaine, Martin suddenly became aware of the path to Francois even if it was, in actuality, a secret tunnel under the walls of her indifference. In less than a year, Madame and Martin announced their engagement to be married and no amount of whispers, familial criticism or theological arguments could dissuade them from their respective quests, she seeking the fountain of youth in a much younger husband, he seeking intimate proximity to Francoise. If Martin could not induce Francoise to love him as an equal, she would be forced to respect him, at least, as her stepfather. And then who knew what could come of it? His mind spun like a whirling Dervish.

While Beatrice and Martin went through their courting ritual, Francoise met and fell in love with a twenty-one year old named Xander Chirac, the son of a minor nobleman. He had high cheekbones, a high forehead and high ideals and he was Francoise's best friend, a sure sign to anyone who has inhabited the earth for more than thirty years, that something was amiss. Xander delighted in delighting Francoise. He was attentive, immaculately groomed, wrote poetry, practiced the harpsichord and pianoforte endlessly, to little avail, and took Francoise everywhere, to every concert, opera and to the annual Salon exhibit where he always purchased at least one painting which he promised would one day adorn their little chateau in the foothills of the Loire. He adored Poussin and Gerome, particularly their heroic depiction of Greek and biblical heroes, with their dramatically shadowed muscles, chiseled faces and forceful poses overcoming demons, monsters and equally handsome enemy soldiers. He was always the gentleman, so much so that Francoise would often wonder for days on end why he always stopped with a kiss or a gentle squeeze of her budding breasts while she was amenable to much more. He was always restrained. She admired him for this and his promise of saving their passion for their honeymoon night encouraged her to love him more and when a formal proposal was made she said "yes" before he even finished asking and their families were overjoyed, hers with the prospect of a union with the nobility and his with the prospect of being able to pay the bills with her large dowry. It was a match made in French heaven, a unique paradise where, as it turns out, it is difficult to tell the male angels from the female.

Forty~Seven

47 Xander's closest friend was Maximilian, a dark brooding man who seemed much older than his twenty-one years perhaps because he always seemed to be thinking and laughed little, if at all. At soirees on the lawns of the chateau or in the bistros in Lyons or Paris, he always sat on the sidelines and observed like he was a student of human behavior brought to a zoo of homo sapiens where he could examine their inter-reactions, their feeding habits and their mating rituals. Young ladies, of course, were always attracted to him and it never failed that he would have two or three sitting close to him making silly banter and fluttering their eyelashes in every conceivable rhythm. But they might as well have been flirting with the Sphinx because other than an occasional response to a question even he could not avoid answering, he simply sat there like a handsome garden statue. No one so intrigued the women as Maximilian for it is well-known that females are ever in the mood to conquer men and the more difficult the man, the more dedicated the effort. When the fool asked the mountain climber why he wanted to climb Everest, he answered in the timeworn cliché, "Because it is there." If asked why young, beautiful rich girls would pursue Maximilian, they might have answered with the same silly farcical response, "Because he is there." But it was just as true. And so, while women often tired of their vain pursuit of his heart and did not last long, there was always a steady supply of new climbers who never made it past his enigmatic foothills.

When Maximilian's father was arrested in Greece for smuggling, some said diamonds, some hashish, some white slaves, it made women even more anxious to get close to him. His face, however, never shown on any of them and he was only slightly softened when he would walk with

Xander through the Tuilleries Gardens or on a carriage ride on the Champs Elysses. They seemed like brothers and depended on each other more so than on their own families. Francoise felt comfortable with Maximilian for she assumed that when she married Xander, she could always count on the support of his best friend; two for the trouble of one. While she may not have been wrong, her views certainly changed soon after her nuptial vows were solemnized in the church of Le Sacre Coeur in Paris. Two months after they moved into a small chateau twenty miles outside Paris, the same one occupied by his father's recently deceased bachelor brother, many truths became apparent about Xander to Francoise.

They had honeymooned in Venice and then the Amalfi Coast and everyday was a fantasy as one might expect between two young people with the good health, their handsome looks and their sound financial resources. The nights, however, were nothing less than lackluster, worse than disappointing, some might say unduly and unpleasantly mysterious. They would undress each other and caress every part of each others' bodies, but Xander would insist on the lights being off just as Francoise's passions were the most inflamed. He had an active mouth and his tongue explored her private parts to the point that she felt she would explode not just metaphorically but actually. When he finally mounted her, his manhood was only partially erect and no matter his heavy breathing and the tension she could feel in his muscles, he would climb off and lay exhausted next to her without achieving orgasm. He had subtle excuses whose effectiveness diminished over the weeks until one night in the middle of his efforts she noticed that he was fully erect while on top of her and actually orgasmed for the first time since their wedding. She felt that she had accomplished a difficult feat and as her own pleasure diminished as she endured his struggles, she became observant, as if watching from afar to see what the difficulty might be. So, while she might not have noticed a peculiarity in the early nights of their new love-making, she noticed every detail after two weeks and it did not escape her attention that his arousal was inspired only in part by her enthusiastic passion, the other part and apparently the one that enabled him to reach completion was the use of his hand on his own bottom, although exactly what he did there she could not ascertain as her view was obstructed by the darkness and his own torso on top of her. Her imagination, active as it was as most women's are, could not imagine what he actually did, but her musings were close enough to the truth to make her at first unhappy, then revolted, and then angry. She could not summon the courage to discuss the matter with Xander as in those days, even in the most liberal households, husbands and wives never discussed such matters, it being understood that nature would take its course and women would become satisfied with what was offered and the sexual act was of little importance to women anyway. Everyone knew this to be true and so it should be no wonder to modern people that there were so many unhappy, even suicidal women, out and about in the cities and countryside of Europe, while divorce courts were nonexistent.

Francoise always did her personal shopping with her maid Claudia on Thursdays, leaving at eleven in the morning, lunching in the city and returning before four or five, depending on what she was purchasing and on whom she ran into in the crowded streets of Montmartre. The sun was particularly hot one day and she developed a terrible headache and only a woman's headache will interfere with her ability to conduct any type of intercourse, social or sexual. She returned home by one thirty in the afternoon and immediately noticed that Maximilian's blue carriage with two white horses was outside the chateau, his driver asleep in his master's seat. Now, the reader will think the worst and envision the two friends in all manner of misconduct. But, Francoise assumed they would be playing chess in the study or dining in the garden. They were in neither place, so she guessed they had gone for a walk, the weather being so warm and bright. She went to her room to lie down and pray that her headache would disappear along with the nausea she developed on the trip home. She opened the door to the master suite to see Xander and Maximilian naked on her bed with Maximilian buggering her husband. So, you see, you were right after all and poor Francoise was wrong. She had heard of dandies and sodomites but like most women, she could not easily imagine a sex act between two men and her split second education on the subject in her own bedroom with her own beloved husband and his best friend as teachers was more than she could stand. She collapsed before they even had time to be embarrassed and by the time the servants discovered her lying in a swoon on the salon sofa, they assumed she had been caught by Xander making love to Maximilian. This rumor was as inaccurate as the advertised temperate climate of Greenland to potential visitors. It spread widely and easily, giving renewed hopes to women all over Paris that Maximilian might yet fall in love with one of them.

48 Francoise would say nothing of the truth and any idea of sleeping with Xander ever again vanished like the dew on a cactus in the Sahara. They both decided that it would be best for her to take a holiday and stay with her mother and her new husband Martin in his lovely townhouse in Paris. On Bastille Day, she arrived with her bags at the home of Martin Galle and he greeted her with open arms especially after losing her to Xander, a fop and a fool if there ever was one, in Martin's opinion, shortly after marrying her mother. On the limestone steps of the Galle home, her mother smiled broadly and told her how glad she was to have her daughter close again even if only for a few weeks.

Human beings are born many times after they emerge from their mothers' womb. Francoise was born again the day she fell in love with Xander, the day she fell out of love with him, and now back home with her mother and Martin, it was to happen again. Each birth changes the person immeasurably, rarely for the good and, if for the good, rarely for very long.

The Galles lived in a five story Beaux Arts row house in a very nice part of Paris, not the best neighborhood because there, no Jews were permitted to buy, but in the St. Germaine du Vollard section with broad sidewalks and tall elm trees planted in even spaces through breaks in the sidewalk. The top floor housed the servants quarters. There was a maid named Marie who had a husband and three teenage children that lived in a hovel in the Bonseur section of Paris. There was a Norwegian man-of-all-work named Peter who could also wait table. The staff was rounded out with a widowed cook, Madame Vemain, and a scullery spinster maid named Gertrude. Together with the owners, all resided there in the regular harmony of their class, which is to say they behaved amicably, for fear of losing their jobs and their references and then being condemned to a life of prostitution, beggary and crime on the cruel and indifferent streets.

The fourth story held three guest bedrooms and this was where Francoise was ensconced in the largest of the three. She had a view over two small gardens in the rear, one the Galles', the other the adjoining garden of the house behind. Little sunlight found its way there and a few locust trees and ferns and ivy made a living along with mosses and the occasional cluster of toadstools. The chamber that overlooked the street in the front was used by Martin as a library and study. He rarely read but no gentleman would be without such a room and he would take a nap there sometime or read Le Figaro while sipping a glass of sherry. The shelves were filled with cheap second-hand books for effect. Down the hall there was a small room used as a nursery by the prior owners and a tile-floored bathroom with a small zinc bathtub in the shape of a slipper very near a spartan coal fire place. The third floor held the master suit, one bedroom each for Madame and Monsieur and a large dressing room and bathroom with a porcelain tub and a fireplace with the face of the north wind blowing his hardest carved into the surround under the mantel.

The second story held two parlors, one large and formally furnished for entertaining which the Galles rarely did and a smaller, more casual family parlor to which they would retire to play checkers or to smoke small cigars after eating in the dining room on the first floor which also held a reception area and a small breakfast room which held an abundance of dusty ferns and which was the domain of a rather old white macaw in a large cage suspended from the ceiling in front of a window that overlooked the dreary rear garden. Macaws were thought to live to the age of sixty years and this one, more yellow than white, was the color of a middle aged woman's teeth. It had come with the house, it being said that it survived not only their occupancy but that of the prior owners and the ones before that. Each family that owned the bird over the decades called him something different. Martin christened him Robespierre after observing that one night a small gray mouse crept into the cage in search of uneaten seeds and by the morning, Madame had nearly fainted when she found the mouse dead in the cage with its head severed and covered with a generous amount of the bird's liquid feces. Martin laughed and said that if this bird was not the reincarnation of Robespierre, then there was no truth to any religion. From that day forward, the bird received better feed and care than at any other time in its long incarcerated life. Martin had cook boil the flesh off the tiny mouse skull and when it was dry he placed it on the top of Robespierre's cage. One day it disappeared and while Martin accused Beatrice of its removal, for she detested the very idea of it, she denied it so vehemently that he actually believed her and it simply became another miniscule mystery in the history of the house.

Once Francoise arrived, the atmosphere in the house completely changed. Before it was quiet, some might say funereal. The neighbors could barely tell if the house was occupied. But with the advent of Francoise's stay all of this changed. Martin had the cook stock up on all sorts of foodstuffs. Rooms were dusted and aired as Gertrude went from floor to floor loaded with dust mops, feather dusters, waxes, cloths and brooms. Freshly flowering plants filled the breakfast room and Peter even managed to bathe Robespierre although it did little to improve his appearance or his morose attitude. His cage was moved to a table near some African orchids and the yellowish plumage against the purple and magenta blooms gave such an air of exotica to the room that it resembled a small piece of the Amazon jungle, at least to the Galles and their servants.

Martin permitted, actually encouraged, Beatrice to indulge Francoise's every whim although she had few. Despite the shopping trips and the newly decorated bedroom—butterflies of every type in the world pinned to pink and black velvet under glass were everywhere—even the bedspread had embroidered butterflies all over it. Eventually, of course Francoise could resist her mother's incessant questioning no longer and she related the tale of Xander and Maximilian leaving out the details of their actual sexual contact and reinventing its history to finding them naked asleep in the same bed. Francoise firmly believed in the philosophy her mother taught her that it is important, even imperative, to leave a piece of doubt in every situation, for people always seek to fill in the blanks in a manner most favorable to their needs. Without some fuzzy areas in a story, there would be no room for forgiveness. As her mother told her on the eve of her wedding to Xander, "even if he finds you naked in bed with the gardener on top of you, never admit to your indiscretion for then he will know you to be a slut. Deny, deny, deny and eventually his brain will concoct some acceptable explanation—you fainted in the rose garden and the gardener, asleep for his siesta, rushed out, picked you up, took you to your room and removed your clothes so that you might better be able to breathe. Then he can blame the gardener, fire him and only suspect you are a slut. Suspicion, men can live with. Facts? A confession? Well that's another matter."

Martin insisted on knowing why Francoise was staying with the Galles and Beatrice told him again omitting details such as Maximilian altogether. Whatever disdain he had for Xander for stealing his prize away—after all, the only reason he married Beatrice was to be close to Françoise—faded into an inverse gratitude, which is to say he planned to undermine every effort Xander might make to reclaim his wife. Beatrice was impressed with Martin's devotion to her daughter and while she never truly loved him, his new approach to life endeared him to her. Had she had the intuition that women all over the world are said to possess—a larger myth never survived so long; ask the divorce courts and the coroner's offices—she would have suspected Martin's real intentions. Even his calling Beatrice "Françoise" in the middle of their honeymoon sex act did not light a lamp in her brain. She might have been forgiven her lack of understanding Martin for he was, indeed, as skillful a liar and as dedicated a pederast as there ever was, but not to notice how his eyes literally devoured Françoise whenever they all occupied the same room in the house, well, that is inexcusable even if Beatrice was a fading lily in the bouquet of life and realized it, which she did not.

Martin, too, occupied his own planet when it came to Françoise. He heard in her voice the silent voice of the coquette. If she asked him to pass the butter, he heard secret seductive tones and imagined they both thought of lubricating their private parts with the creamy condiment. If she spoke to Marie about the new sheets on her bed, he heard the double entendre of an invitation to share it with him. If she looked him in the eyes at any time in a conversation, he saw seduction, want and sexual craving, a duplicitous silent call for a burning passion within her. A mote in her eye became an excuse to dote over her and to brush her cheek with his hot breath as he worked the corner of his handkerchief on her inner eyelid which to him was the symbolic offering of her secret parts. He noticed with a certain pride in his astute observations that the small pink globe of flesh in the corner of her eye resembled that same small globe in her private parts that was the key to the lock of a woman's passion. All of this arousal netted Beatrice some active bouts in the master suite for Martin would vent his overweening passion on her. Again, she never connected the coincidence of his new nightly sexual advances on her despite the fact that for the year prior to Françoise's arrival, they had relations perhaps only twice a month. If she had written it down, she would have realized it was even more infrequent than that.

Forty~Nine

A letter arrived for Beatrice one day from her cousin Matilda who lived with her mother Auntie Fan in Devereaux, a small town on the Normandy coast. Auntie Fan was ill and was asking for Beatrice, her favorite niece to attend her. Indeed, Auntie Fan was more of a mother to Beatrice growing up than her own who was always too busy with socializing to spend much time raising her children. Beatrice asked Martin if it might be all right for her to leave, that she would be gone two weeks at the least. Martin protested in the quiet of their bed, how unfair it was for her to leave him, how he would miss her in a thousand small ways. He was expert in cunning and he sewed and crocheted a most wonderful blindfold for Madame Galle, so perfect its fit and so absolute its function in obliterating the truth that she almost said she would not go but would stay with her loving husband. Anticipating this path of her rationalization as a hunter aims his gun just in front of a running deer, just as she was about to cancel her trip, he said, yes, she must go, for he could not cause her the pain of making a choice and if her beloved aunt was in extremis he could never forgive himself for denying his wife the opportunity of so important a farewell. With that, the elastic band of the blindfold snapped against the back of Beatrice's head and within two days, on a sunny Friday morning, Martin, Françoise and the servants were the exclusive residents of the Galle household.

At first, the house ran as it normally did with Madame in residence. Martin ate his poached eggs and toast, two cups of strong coffee while reading LeFigaro and then he was off to work. He exchanged only the most perfunctory niceties with Françoise that he would put her at ease. She, of course, could not have cared less and sat most of the day in a depressed reverie over what to do with her marriage. She read novels by Flaubert and Balzac which only magnified her feelings of failure and isolation and she understood every pain that Madame Bovary experienced as a fellow female traveler through the austere land of males where acceptance of the status quo no matter how boring or terrible, was required of a wife and even the most insignificant complaints or dissatisfactions could lead to disaster. She contemplated suicide the way most women do, as if it were a drama or opera unfolding on a stage where her loved ones were the audience and she the star. Her death, protracted and painful would be a lesson to them all, a profound message of her importance to their lives and to the Earth in general. Weighed under by the burdens of living with a boorish husband and falling in love with a handsome footman beneath her class, it seemed only self-destruction could assuage the pain and if she had to be buried in unconsecrated ground as the church required, then that would show everyone the error of their ways and teach them a lesson they would never forget, preaching them a sermon even is she wasn't there to hear it.

Imagining suicide and doing it are two very different processes and it never failed that something would pick up her spirits or distract her at just the right moment. Francoise was particularly concerned with how her body might appear in death especially if she was in the tumultuous throes of poisoning like poor Emma Bovary, convulsed and vomiting. What if she breathed her last with her skirts up over head and the butler found her? Death was one thing, embarrassment another. One afternoon while debating with herself which new novel to read, she decided to go into the next town for a change of scenery and asked Peter to drive her to the apothecary, then a well-known purveyor of Bohemian bath salts, the finest available anywhere on the continent. She wanted to purchase the salts and take a hot soak to wash her troubles away and help her think. That morning she had received an especially plaintive missive from Xander begging her forgiveness and explaining it all as an error in judgment due to the overimbibing of brandy. It should have been long enough for the memory of her insult and hurt to fade, but the image of Maximilian pounding at Xander's buttocks would inhabit some portion of her brain forever. Interestingly, the idea that Xander was not entirely responsible served to cast a cloud over her anger and the idea that he was involuntarily engaging in sodomy due to inebriation was a palliative to her injured heart. She might have done the same under similar circumstances, possibly even with the same perpetrator who was, beyond any doubt, as fine and handsome a man as could be found in all of France. Only a liar would tell you that he never imagines foul behavior when in his cups.

So it became her plan that she, at some point, would forgive Xander and return to him when it best suited her and when she could extract concessions from him that would best increase her control over him and the household. This was not an intentional or even a conscious thought but it is widely known that there are few behaviors by women that do not in some way address this universally common goal. Eve did not bite the apple to taste it; it was the path for some sort of one-upmanship on Adam. At least until he bit it also, she was superior in her own way, albeit for a very short period of time.

Now it must be pointed out that Martin had gone to great lengths to intercept and review all the mail which was delivered through the brass slot in the front door of his house. Peter or Marie, whoever found it first, would place it on the silver tray on the round cherry table in the center of the front hall. They were supposed to notify Martin, if he was at home. If not, Peter was directed to bring the mail to the library and place it on his desk forthwith. In this fashion, Martin had intercepted three of Xander's letters and burned them unopened. But this day, Françoise found the letter on the floor as the postman delivered it, it being a new deliveryman running late on his rounds.

After spending nearly two hours in town with poor Peter baking in the sun in the carriage, Françoise had made her purchases and ordered him to take her home. The sun was low in the sky turning it the orange-rose of dusk and peeking out behind the tall cypresses that lined the roadway as the carriage rolled toward home. She noticed how the filtered light put a glow to Peter's handsome profile. In fact, she never noticed how handsome he really was, straight backed, dignified for a servant and quite masculine. She indulged herself in typical womanly fantasies as the gauzy countryside slipped into the purple half-dark of dusk and the sounds of the city ahead beckoned her to the refuge of her mother's and Martin's home. She felt so fortunate that her mother had selected Martin as a husband. He was kind, generous, a good provider and he treated Françoise as if she was his own daughter.

When they arrived at the front door, Peter held out his hand to help her out of the carriage and she held it a few moments longer than necessary, making an uncustomarily intimate eye contact with him that suddenly made him realize that she was indeed a very attractive woman even if she was in a class that he was by custom not permitted to even entertain the dream of a liaison with. And, had that dream come to fruition, he would most certainly lose his job and never be offered similar employ again. All of this shot through his brain in a few milliseconds. The possibility that he might have to work in the mines or the merchant marine if he ever made successful overtures to Françoise was tossed in his grey matter like radishes in a salad.. Everyone knows, however, that a man who argues with his penis will always lose and for the rest of the night he could think of nothing but how to bed Françoise, come what may.

Fifty

50 Hemonides the Greek once observed in his Treatise on Human Frailty that women are like the trees in a great forest. Some are pine, some cherry, some cedar, some oak. They all produce different foliage, different fruit, have varied barks and unique patterns of their limbs. Some are fond of the sun, some shun it. Some revel in the rain, others abhor it. When it comes to the flames of passion, each type burns at a different rate, some igniting at the approach of even a small match or spark, others resisting a roaring blaze. Françoise was ironwood, not by nature but by being inculcated to the ways of flesh by a homosexual husband. His flame was barely an ember and so, in many ways, some of them the most important, Françoise was that most unignitable timber, ironwood. She was, in effect, still a virgin, perhaps not in the physical sense, her hymen had been squandered on a sissy, but in her sense of desire. Women who do not know how hot the flame of sex can burn, do not ignite quickly and so are often immune, like ironwood, from the proximity of the flame with which all men approach. Nonetheless, her curiosity was piqued at least in part due to the peculiar love making with Xander. She responded to his letter in cool, some might say icy tones, as she noticed the firm buttocks of Peter as he took up her empty tea cup, deposited a letter from her mother which was just delivered and walked back to the house from where she sat in the garden for a moment's reflection on the state of her marriage and her life.

The letter from Beatrice informed her that Auntie Fan was suffering from consumption and was in quarantine along with everyone who visited and that Beatrice was forced to stay with her until the quarantine was lifted. She had also written to Martin, it said, and that Françoise was to do her best not to let Martin get too lonely because, poor dear, he would miss her so. Françoise resolved to pay a little more attention to her stepfather whom, she had to admit, she barely thought of even when he was opposite her at table.

At night in the privacy of her room when sleep would be resisted by a wandering mind and conflicting emotions in a war for dominance, she would throw the covers back, lift her shift and let her hands and fingers explore her body as the dark shadows of the armoire, the dresser, the cheval mirror and the escritoire watched in mute and impotent silence. Inevitably, it would be Xander who would appear in her mind's eye and, just as her breathing increased in her own ears to the volume of a Caribbean hurricane, Maximilian would make his entrance and mount Xander from the rear while he was on top of her. Her fantasia exploded into a hundred dollops of mud and the fire she herself had tried to ignite was reduced to a single lump of ash-coated red charcoal that burned in her abdomen like an ulcer. Sleep was elusive and she would awaken in the morning as if she had not slept a wink.

That morning, as usual, she put on her robe and went out to the garden to sit in a lounge chair and ponder what she should do next. Her marriage vows before God and her own sense of belonging at home helped her to resolve to return to Xander, especially if he promised never to drink again and, of course, to banish that pervert Maximilian from his life. As the prospect of re-establishing domestic bliss took shape in the fog of her mind, Peter without being asked or its being expected, brought a tray of croissants and a pot of Turkish coffee out to her. He placed it on the low table beside her and as she looked up at him as he stood over her, the morning sun was directly behind him, casting his face into dark shadow and igniting his hair like the aura of Gabriel, the angel she had seen in a painting by Velázquez in Madrid. Had he at that point asked her how her husband Xander was faring, she would likely have responded, "Xander who?" While Peter seemed to be waiting for any instructions she might have for him, he was in fact gazing at her as a martyr would at a visitation. Innocently, her robe had opened ever so slightly as her daydream stole off with her modesty and he could easily discern her pink nipples through the diaphanous silk of her nightshift. She said. "Thank you" and he turned away to resume his chores in the house.

The day passed uneventfully but the air was thick with unrealized dreams, pubescent fantasies and subliminal thoughts. Over dinner, Martin and Françoise spoke of Beatrice and Auntie Fan and Martin fabricated an excuse for his taking Françoise with him on a buying trip to Marseille. Remembering her mother's letter, she agreed but her mouth formed the words as if they were in someone else's for she was in a reverie occupied by Peter the Archangel and wondering at that very moment what fate befell a woman who dared have sexual relations with one of God's holy angels.

That night, while Martin lay in bed and dreamed of he and Françoise in Marseille as if it were a honeymoon, Peter put on three pairs of socks so that when he went down the creaking uncarpeted stairs from the fifth floor to the fourth he would be as silent as a shadow. He was at the Rubicon and if he did not cross it now and possess Françoise, he felt he would have to leap out the window to a certain death on the sidewalk. If she rebuffed him and woke the household with her screams he would say he was sleep- walking, apologize profusely and offer to stay in his room at night under lock and key at half his former wage. He was no Voltaire, but he knew Martin could not resist the savings and he could redeem his position of employment where, in other households on the Boulevard, he would not only be summarily fired but publicly prosecuted and jailed as an attempted rapist.

Fifty~One

51 Françoise was in bed, of course, and the phantasm of her own hands had banished Xander and Maximilian and openly welcomed Peter. As her passion climbed the long steep incline of the feminine mystique, her bedroom door slowly and silently opened and Peter entered more quietly than the most insubstantial ghost in his thickly padded feet and cotton nightshirt. He could hear her rapid breathing and the slight creaking of the mattress springs as she pressed hard into it in the throes of her imaginary liaison. He walked over to the bed and stood there beholding her naked against the blue-white sheets gently writhing to the rhythm of her own rapidly beating heart. Her eyes, only half closed, saw him and for a moment she thought it was her own private incubus made flesh. Instead of being startled, she knew in a millisecond it was Peter the Archangel in a visitation. She relaxed and spread her arms to welcome him. He disrobed and climbed on top of her, the three pair of socks still on his feet. They made love most of the night and never said a word to each other for fear of dispelling the magic that filled the room like a pink cloud off Olympus. In that one night, Françoise had transformed from ironwood to kindling and every man on the street as she walked by held a match. But her heart, the one that is connected to a woman's private parts, was the property of Peter and no one noticed how, over the ensuing weeks, dark circles formed under his eyes, he would fall asleep standing with the pruning sheers in his hands while a roseate glow flourished in Françoise's cheeks with a far away look in her eyes that only the witches of Macbeth could read as "Xander? Xander who?"

Normally Martin was an observant man because he took great pains to ascertain what other people were thinking in order to have some advantage over them. This was the key to his business successes but like most people successful at one area of experience, he thought he knew all areas. The opinions of rich people are always sought on all sorts of topics even if their fortunes were made from owning two hundred garbage trucks. His dreams were filled with Françoise and he plotted every detail of their trip to Marseille, the dinners, the drinks, the strolls along the quay, his observations about the stars which he memorized from some book along with a love poem by a woman whose name he forgot but which rhymed with "buttonhole." In his efforts not to tip his hand and put any warning sign in her mind of exactly what he intended to do, he avoided protracted conversations and acted quite indifferent to her. If he passed her something at breakfast, he took great pains to make sure that his hand did not touch hers and if he encountered her in a narrow space, he held his breath so that his paunch might not rub up against her. He always averted his eyes when he passed her boudoir and never looked up from his morning paper if she asked him a question. It was all a well-crafted act, a façade of lies so thick that even the most intuitive of women would never have detected his deeply lecherous intent. This suited her very well for only a blind person would not see the chemistry that percolated between her and Peter. Marie, the cook, knew and saw it, as did Gertrude, but Martin's dense layer of false indifference cut both ways and so deprived him of a clear view of her as she of him.

Martin left an envelope for Françoise with five hundred francs in it for shopping for her trip. He told her to spend it as she saw fit keeping in mind that Marseille was warm and humid at this time of the year. She was thrilled when she opened it and planned to spend only a little on something pleasant and comfortable to wear on the train, but she wanted to buy Peter a Swiss watch in the port as a present. This was how she knew she loved him so much, that she would rather spend her money on him than on herself, for what is true love, but an affection greater for someone else than for oneself. Françoise did not analyze this consciously but knew it deep within her, as if she had been born loving Peter. The more she loved him, the smaller Xander grew in her estimation and suddenly he seemed no more than a friend of her childhood like one met many years later; whom, after an hour's conversation, there is nothing left to say and all the old memories of comradeship and infatuation have faded like a photograph left in the sun where faces are as empty as the streets the hour before dawn.

Through no trick or artifice, Martin had sent Peter on an errand to Lyons and he was not due to return until well after Martin and Françoise had departed for Marseille. In a way, Françoise was pleased because she dreaded the idea of her leaving Peter behind but in her unselfish way she did not feel sad that he had to leave her. They kissed behind the large yew tree in the yard and then Peter got into a coach to go to the train station. It was just at that moment, as they kissed, that Martin had looked out the drawing room window to ascertain the weather to help him decide what type of coat to wear. His blood ran cold, colder than usual, and he immediately stepped back into the shadow of the house. It all made sense to him now. Not that his stepdaughter had fallen in love or was infatuated by a servant, but that the world had turned against him despite his plans, his oh-so-intricate machinations. He saw himself as a piece of driftwood floating in the tepid sea tossed by random currents, fickle winds and a god that despised him. All his life he had been subjected to ridicule both overt and covert because he was a Jew. Hardly anyone who is not Jewish himself always treated him as if he was something different, not like a Russian is different, or a Laplander, or even an African, but different in a subliminal way as if he were some sort of spy, that his evil was hidden behind a veneer of civility that others could easily see through. No matter how long his family had lived in France, he would never be considered a Frenchman. He was a stranger in his own homeland and he saw the frustration of his pursuit of Françoise as a divine punishment as if he was not fit to kiss her shoes, that even she, who owed him everything, her clothes, her food, the roof over head, even she preferred the kiss of a servant, his coarse unmannered hands on her body, to him.

He watched her in the garden as she looked up at the sky and imagined how her god had smiled upon her, given her so much. He felt neither pain nor loathing but only an emptiness and he resolved to cancel the trip to Marseille. It was going to be a charade at best but now, well, he was too empty inside for anything and he felt his true age for the first time in his life.

Françoise sat down in the garden and Martin imagined that she was already longing for her absent lover. The doorknocker's call echoed and he could hear Maria answer the door. In a moment, she brought him a letter. It was from Nanette, Beatrice's niece, telling Martin in her most sympathetic tone that Beatrice had succumbed to the consumption and had died, although her Auntie Fan had miraculously, if not ironically, survived. Enclosed with the letter was a death certificate. Martin sat for a moment in the blue velvet upholstered side chair with ornate gilded legs. He stared down at the rug and held the letter limply at his side as if waiting for the cat to come by that it might read it.

News which falls upon us from unexpected places at unforeseen times affects everyone differently, much like lightning striking people on a stroll. Some are immediately annihilated, others die of heart failure, some are partially paralyzed, some pass out and revive with speech impediments or blindness, some awake with mystical powers, others simply get up, go home and tell the wife and children how loud the thunder is close up. Martin was the last. No tears filled even one eye and there was not a single memory he called up about his life with Beatrice that could stir in him any emotion whatsoever, much like a man remembering his walk to work every day for twenty years. No memories had dates, there was nothing to separate one from the other. It was as if he had read about the death of the chief rabbi at the Grand Synagogue in Paris. He never saw the man nor the synagogue and quite simply, did not care.

As he mused in an introspective state unrelated to the contents of the letter, he stared at the oriental rug and with his finger in the air as if it were a writing instrument, outlined the complex and serpentine pattern of the weaving, as green melted into yellow into red and into a deep azure blue. How intricate it was, how many hours some filthy Arab man or sultry, coffee-skinned Persian wench had spent weaving it, the smell of her moisture infused in the wool so that on damp days it was brought to life as if she danced on the carpet for him and only for him. A cockroach crawled out from under the sofa and sensing that nothing was moving in the room, for Martin was as still as a stalactite in a cave, it had decided to risk the long journey in the light to the other side of the room in search of some rancid morsel. Like Zeus casting a thunderbolt, Martin's foot came crashing down and the poor, ugly despicable insect became a permanent part of the pattern of the rug. Even when its carcass would be swept up the next time Marie cleaned it, its juices, like the indigo of Samarkand and the crimson of far Caspia, were now part of the rug's history as intimately connected to its fibers as the chlorophyll of onion leaves. It would be the first stain of Martin's new life.

Martin arose, hid the letter in his desk and went into the hall shouting for Marie to find out if the coach was waiting for him and Françoise. It had only just arrived and when he saw Françoise waiting on the top step looking out into the street, he was filled with a new purpose and a new resolve.

Fifty~Two

52 On board the train as they looked out the smudgy windows at Paris, its rain slicked streets, its million souls scurrying everywhere as bad novelists and cheap painters have depicted for centuries, Martin began to read to Françoise from a little book he had brought with him. It was Troilus and Cressida, the doomed lovers and he selected the stanzas where Troilus dies in battle at the walls of Troy with only the thought of losing his beloved Cressida as a regret for leaving this miserable life. His spirit, the poet wrote, rose to the ninth crystalline sphere of heaven and from there he could see the earth as a sapphire surrounded by planets and stars, the moon and the angels. Troilus suddenly understood God, the universe and the intricate interconnectedness of it all. Martin closed the book and saw that Françoise had nodded off and could never have perceived the look in Martin's eye that said thanks to God for this gift which went a great distance in compensating him for all the wrongs he had been subject to all his life as one of the Chosen People.

When Martin and Françoise arrived at the Hotel Duchamps in Marseille he rented two rooms across the hall from each other and when they had unpacked, he suggested that she take a bath and perhaps a short a nap as he had to confirm his business appointments which might take an hour or so. She readily agreed. He went to the telegraph office and sent a message to his contact in Lyons that when his man Peter arrived he was to be told that he was discharged from Martin Galle's employ immediately, that his "indiscretions" were known. Martin was careful not to state the exact nature of the breach to avoid the rumor mill. Further, Martin had alerted the authorities that Peter had violated his immigration status and would be arrested on sight. He also instructed his contact to advance Peter the sum of two hundred francs which was an undeserved severance pay that would be sufficient to book passage immediately for Norway, his homeland.

After confirming that the telegraph had been sent and received, Martin found an apothecary in the Moroccan quarter of the city and purchased a sleeping powder, telling the druggist that it was for his obese wife who seemed, because of her large girth, to be immune to the thin, weak soporifics of French physicians. His wife, he told the apothecary, had not had a good night's sleep in a year and if the apothecary whose skin was the color of tobacco spit had nothing to help, he would join the French Foreign Legion and spend the rest of his life hunting down and killing the apothecary's entire family who still lived in French Morocco. The man looked at him with wide eyes the same way the very superstitious and ignorant always look upon mysteries: with awe and fear. He sold Martin a large packet of a sweet smelling powder with instructions on its use and would not hand it to Martin until he retracted his threat. Martin did, but the apothecary saw in his eyes that the devil resided there and that the promise was a false one as most, but not all, of the devil's promises are.

That night Martin took Françoise down to the quay and they boarded a barge that had been converted to a restaurant. She had read about it in Paris and it was one of the things that she most wanted to see. The barge steamed out with all the tables on board filled with reveling diners. It anchored about a mile or so offshore so that the lights of the port city glimmered in the humid night air and as the sky went from purple silk to black velvet another smaller boat further out in the sea let loose with fireworks. Lights and showers of sparks filled the sky and blotted out the weak stars. The faces of the diners were momentarily lit like portrait sitters when a flashbulb goes off as each display burst over the sea and the embers fell into the water like shooting stars, extinguished with a thousand small hisses.

It was an experience made for lovers. When the small orchestra struck up a romantic tune, most of the tables emptied and a small circular space set to the port side of the deck filled with couples dancing a smart waltz. Martin attempted to make idle conversation peppered with remarks about how pleasant it all was and how he should like to bring Beatrice here the next time business forced him to Marseille. Françoise nodded silently because she could only think of Peter and she imagined them dancing and how every woman would envy her in the arms of her tall Nordic lover. She was no more aware of Martin sitting opposite her than a dove in Paris is aware of a wolf in the Crimea.

They did manage to manufacture a conversation about purchasing a summer house on the coast. Martin mentioned that perhaps Peter could manage it while the family was in Paris. As he spoke, he watched her every movement, counted each blink of her eyes as he went on about what a good and loyal servant Peter was and that he had high hopes for him, perhaps even allowing him to take a position at the Galle shop. Françoise became nervous then relaxed as her stepfather discussed her beloved's fine attributes. Martin noticed it all and as the proverbial cat toys with its captured prey, he said that yes, he would promote Peter to some more responsible post and what did she think about it? As a glow filled her face and her lips parted to answer, he interrupted and, looking at his watch, said the barge was due to return to port, that he should like to stand by the rail and watch the city lights. As he stood and offered his hand, she was about to continue about Peter and he interrupted again much like when one starts to yawn but is interrupted and the yawn hides in one's chest waiting for the opportunity to escape. Before she could speak, he said that she probably never even noticed Peter and it was just as well. Martin continued with his philosophy that servants should never mingle with their employers and that such a breach of the rules of good social order had been the downfall of many a Parisian family. A society without castes and guiding principles that governed their behavior was anarchy and no such society could long survive. He apologized for ever discussing Peter with her and then started to point out to her how the lights of Marseille were like a diamond necklace on a whore. No matter how beautiful or perfect the stones, the whore was still a whore and depravity lurked in the dingy streets just beneath the skin upon which they glittered so brightly to the world. Of course, he never stopped watching her face and he saw the pain of his words creep up her neck and onto her cheeks like the flush of scarlet fever.

She was mostly silent the rest of the evening and when they returned to the hotel he insisted they stop in at the bar for a nightcap. He ordered two Brandy Alexanders hoping that the thick sweet cream and strong oaky flavor of the brandy would disguise the drug. At an opportune moment he deposited a sufficient quantity of the powder into her drink and when he proposed a toast, first to Beatrice, she drank and then to Peter's promotion, she drank even more. In short order, he could see the insidious effects of the potion and before she passed out at the table, he summoned the waiter, paid the bill and escorted her back to her room. She slurred a thank you and a good night and he was careful to pocket the key to her room which she had left in the lock. He returned to his room and disrobed staring at his watch and the sweep second hand as it rotated like a mower's scythe cutting down the seconds. When fifteen minutes had lapsed, he put on his robe turned out the lights, and crossed the hall gently knocking to see if she was awake. When she did not respond, he turned the key in the lock and entered. Françoise had undressed and gotten into bed and was breathing heavily and rhythmically. He called her name and nudged her shoulder even as he trembled with anticipation. She did not respond. He lifted her eyelid and touched her naked eye with his index finger and still she did not respond. Clearly the drug had worked even better than he had hoped and he said a small prayer of thanks to Allah for the handiwork of the Arab apothecary.

Fifty~Three

53 Now I must ask for your forgiveness as I implore you not to read the following words over which I have no control for, as I have said, I can tell only the truth for it is the very essence of this ink which flows from me that it, like the blood of a martyr, tells of passion and pain, of the sacred and the profane. Those of you who think that God is in the details will not see him here, for these details come from a different place which is, as yet, unnamed. Those of you who know of the passion of the Christ know not a smattering of His ordeal and prefer not to see the rending of the flesh, the outpouring of the blood, the exposed bones and flayed muscles, shredded as meat in a slaughterhouse. But these are the details of His truth and without truth, there can never be understanding. Avert your eyes then and let your imagination create that which you fear to look upon. If you will, skip ahead two paragraphs until you are on safer ground.

Martin rose from the bed and turned on all the lights, even bringing over to the bed a floor lamp which stood by a chair for reading. He picked up her clothes which in her stupor she had left on the floor and examined them, particularly her chemise and panties which he brought over to the light looking at them as if they were a rare artifact. He touched them, smelled them and even tasted the slight discolored marks he found in her underpants. Without consciously thinking it, this was the appetizer to a feast he had anticipated greedily for so long.

He pulled back the covers and Françoise lay there at his disposal upon the crisp white sheets. He examined her mouth, her nostrils, her ears, put his fingers in them and smelled and tasted any residue that clung to them. He looked between her toes and gently placed his tongue in between each one. He squeezed her breasts and pinched the nipples at first gently and then quite hard so that they became erect in mute defiance of the attack he had launched. He licked the areolas and then softly bit the nipples between his front teeth. He gently rolled her over and examined her buttocks and its crevice letting his tongue glide from the base of her back downward where he buried his face putting his tongue as far inside her as it would go. He rolled her back over, adjusting the shade of the floor lamp to best illuminate her secret parts. He raised her knees and spread them apart lying between them. He examined her labia and opened them gently looking at every fold and niche. Putting first one finger and then two inside, smelling them, licking them, he finally let his tongue explore. At no time did she moan or shift. Only her rhythmic steady breathing and the warmth of her body gave any indication she was alive. He stood and looked down at her again. He covered her and put everything in the room back to where it was. He left the key on the dresser and exited, going back to his room and imagining what the next night would hold for him.

The next morning, as planned, they met for coffee in the café at the hotel. Martin inquired after her sleep and she said that she slept so soundly that she did not think she had even dreamed. She had no recollection of getting into bed. He told her that the long journey and the salt air were known to affect some people in that way. As he sipped his coffee slowly, he looked over the edge of the cup as she buttered her croissant. He felt that he owned her, not with the voluntary, willing proprietorship of love but as one owns a pet, a cat or a dog. He told her he had some appointments in the morning and for lunch, that she should go shopping. He passed five hundred francs across the table to her in the same fashion one might give a biscuit to a dog. She looked up at him without touching it and looked into his eyes which he immediately averted. It is for shopping, he said, answering a question without being asked. "Thank you, Papa," she responded, for the first time using the word "Papa," for in the past she had skillfully avoided calling him anything, feeling awkward about using his first name and realizing that referring to him as her father was a sort of betrayal of her real father's memory. As the word "Papa," its two letters repeated twice left her lips, it crossed the air of the breakfast table and entered his ears as a torpedo from a submarine crosses the ice blue water of the Atlantic and penetrates the hull of an enemy ship. "Papa" exploded in Martin's brain. If he had had a soul, he might have wept but Françoise, unknowing yet filled with feminine guile, had reversed their subliminal roles. The leash was now in her hand, although she could not see it, and the collar was firmly around Martin's neck.

"Françoise, I should like you to accompany me after lunch to the silk merchant on the quay. I could use your opinion on the latest fashions and you could help me select…"

"Of course, Papa." She launched the second torpedo and as he put some coins on the table to pay for the breakfast, he told her he would meet her in front of the hotel at two, walked out into the humid sunshine of Marseille as the ship of his brain began to sink into the limitlessly deep waters of regret.

Martin, of course, had no appointments, but instead walked to the Rue Dartagnon, the red-light district of Marseille, three square city blocks of brothels, street walkers and other carnal entertainment. He sought out the Casa Galupe, a small theatre operated by two brothers from Barcelona that put on live sex shows twenty-four hours a day. For ten francs, one could sit in a darkened theatre and watch all manner of live sexual conduct on a well-lit stage with guitar music accompaniment. At this time of the morning there were about ten people besides Martin sitting in the shadows as far apart from one another as possible. One old man was giggling in the corner as he groped an unusually fat prostitute he had brought in with him. The others were single men, silently watching, their silhouettes like crows on a clothesline late at night patiently waiting for the sun to rise.

Martin stayed for three hours, watching a varied series of pornographic performances, more silly than obscene, more artificial than real. Finally, a large man with a thick Spanish accent tapped him on the shoulder and whispered that either he should pay another ten francs or be escorted to the door. Martin elected to leave. The sunshine hit him like hot lava spewed from a volcano and he raised his arm to cover his eyes. He ducked into the safe shade of a seedy bar and ate a greasy plate of sausages made from indeterminate cuts of meat.

Martin returned to the hotel a few minutes past two and Françoise was waiting for him in a pale yellow chemise with a matching parasol looking more like a Monet portrait than a real woman. She had spent the morning shopping for a beautiful watch for Peter and had found one in a small jeweler's shop where she had it engraved with both their initials intertwined like vines of English Ivy. She did not tell Martin what she had done with his money, but he never asked.

That night Martin took her to the Algerian section of the city into a restaurant in a building with two gold minarets and an arched doorway shaped like a keyhole. He ordered her exotic fare and they both commented on the various hues of the black skins of the patrons and the waiters and their unusual clothing. When Francoise thought the time right, she inquired of Martin if he had given any more thought to Peter's promotion and then realized mid-sentence that somehow the façade of her indifference had fallen to the floor like the nightshift of a whore revealing all beneath. He said he hadn't given it any more thought but, yes, he would do something, but why was she interested? She responded awakardly that she was merely making small talk to pass the time and then she remained silent as if she was fearful that if she said anything else, her wonderful secret love would be revealed like a house cat might belch up the tail feathers of a canary. He watched her intently as he sipped an aperitif. He could tell she was deciding to reveal all about herself and Peter. Of course, he was correct. A blind man could have seen it. He also saw the anxiety that forced her eyelids down when she thought better of it and realized that it was too soon, that she did not really know her stepfather well enough to predict what he would do in response. She resolved to tell her mother first, with the hope she would be her ally and bring Martin around if he resisted.

Fifty~Four

54 They stayed at the restaurant until eleven and then returned to the hotel. Francoise suggested having a drink before retiring but Martin told her he was too tired and they both went to their rooms. Martin sat on the bed for half an hour staring at the wall in a trance of self-doubt. He got up and left his room and the hotel. He made his way back to the Algerian section of town, past the restaurant he had just frequented and walked into a narrow alleyway with closed shops. Near its end there was a purple door through which he entered a small, narrow building. It was known as the Al-Jazra Café but was in fact an establishment catering to men who sought young boys. It was owned by a short, squat Moroccan known as Fizrahi, pigeon-Arabic for "Candy Man."

Fizrahi showed Martin into a room painted a deep blue with filigreed lanterns hung here and there casting patterns on the walls that made the room look like a troller's net waiting in the sea. There were about six or eight boys all in their young teens sitting about in Arab-style dress, ballooning pantaloons, and short vests over bare chests and arms. Olive-skinned and dark-eyed they all could have been brothers. Martin selected the first boy on the divan, who turned to the others and secretly winked. Martin paid Fizrahi ten francs and was shown to a small cubical with no windows and a bed covered in red satin, stained with dried semen. The thick, warm air of the room smelled of hazelnuts and cheese.

The boy disrobed and lay on the bed. Martin, fully clothed, lay next to him and told the boy to roll over on his side with his back to Martin, which he did. Martin lay next to him with his arm over him in a loving embrace. In his mind, he attempted to go back in time to when he was the boy's age which he assumed was about sixteen. He remembered his father and his mother, how they wept over the accidental drowning of his younger brother, Samuel, and then how his parents took separate rooms and would not speak to one another. Blame had entered the house through the sewer pipes and at night, its foul breath emerged from the drain and made his parents hate each other. It cleaved Martin's brain and whispered in his ear that he was at fault for a dozen different reasons. In the morning, when it went back into hiding, the three remaining members of the Galle household would look at one another as if they were strangers on a ferry crossing the channel from happiness to misery. In holding the young Arab boy, he wanted to become him, to exchange his soul with that of the urchin who, even as the lowest of the low forced to sell his body to perverts, could awaken in the morning to the prospect of a life unburdened, with hurts unfelt and hope, the most elusive of Pandora's ills flickering in front of him like a bright, shining challice.

The journey home on the train was the polar opposite of the trip to Marseille. Martin sat in a stupor staring out the window at the countryside. Low clouds hugged the horizon and rain fell in soft whispers invisible except as it collected on the glass and accumulated into drops that slid from the upper corner to the lower as the wind from the train's motion drove them in a downward, squirming diagonal path.

Françoise sat happily complacent and unaware of Martin's somber mood. She had purchased not only the watch for Peter but a fine, cultured pearl bracelet for her mother with a small clasp in the shape of a heart. She felt secure in her relationship with her stepfather and thought she understood him somewhat for the first time. He was a quiet man, she thought, full of good emotions and, but for him, who knows how disastrous her life and that of her mother would have been. And also, but for Martin, she would never have met Peter. Just the thought of him filled her with a love of everyone and everything. The rain which to Martin was the dreary sweat of the world, to Francoise was God's gift, making everything shimmer and reflect back the weak light filtered through the gray clouds as if to cheer everyone's spirit as the rejuvenating rain fell. She talked animatedly about every topic as Martin smiled and said nothing. If Martin had believed in hell, this would be it, he thought. Idiots who thought of the fumes and scorching heat of sulfur and brimstone as torture had never known what he knew, the torture of the truth with no voice to express it, no legs to run from it.

When the taxi from the station arrived at the house, the black ribbon on the door said it all. Francoise thought it a gruesome prank by the neighborhood boys. But when she went into the hall and saw a small pile of black-edged envelopes on the table and when Marie expressed her condolences through teary eyes, she discovered that her mother had died. Martin tried his best at acting as surprised and then as mournful as she for his talent at deceit had not been lost and his eyes filled with tears that were as sincere as any he had ever shed. They were not for Beatrice, his dead wife, but for some indescribable lump that coalesced in the back of his mind. In fifteen minutes, Francoise heard the whole story, of Beatrice succumbing to the consumption and how she and Martin had just missed the notification and how the servants discovered it from the arrival of condolences and a telegram from an undertaker requesting instructions as to what to do with the body which had arrived in Paris the same day as Martin and Francoise departed, how Martin had left no instructions as to where he and Francoise would be staying in Marseille and, thus, made it impossible for anyone to notify them of the tragedy.

Françoise told Marie to summon Peter and it was then that she discovered that Peter had not returned from Lyons and that no one had heard from him since he departed a week ago. Panic moved into her mind like locusts from the Sudan, dark clouds of humming, buzzing winged insects, devouring everything of value and leaving only dust in their wake. She implored Martin to telegram the office in Lyons to discover what had happened, which he went through the motions of doing. The next day he read to her the counterfeit reply which said that Peter had told the office contact that he had met the daughter of a rich man from Brussels on the train and that they were running off together to where, he did not say.

Martin had somehow found the courage to look at Françoise's face as he read and he could see the lines of care and woe form around her eyes, the corners of her mouth turn down and the luster of her hair become as dull as slate. A better man might have calculated how to retrieve Peter and explain it all to Francoise without losing her, but Martin was not that man. He knew, or hoped, that she would recover, losing the memory of her first love in the remorse of her mother's death. He watched her eyes stare at the floor and felt the old lust rise in him. After all, had he not hoped for this.

She was his completely now without the obstacle of her mother and her foolish infatuation with an idiot servant without a sou to his name. He would care for her and give her a shoulder to lean on, allow her the luxury of his fine linen shirts to absorb her tears. His life stretched out before him and he saw Françoise as the new Mrs. Galle. Yes, it would be frowned upon at first, but they could move away to another part of the city, another part of the country, another country. He could sell the business and have enough to live on happily with his captive wife for the rest of their days. Yes, it was all the way it should be. He deserved it. Françoise never saw the gleam in his eye, the relaxed slope of his shoulders or the confident movement of his hands as they clasped his knees where he sat looking at her. The time was right, she knew, to tell him she was pregnant with Peter's child.

Seven months later a baby girl was born to the Galle household. Martin suggested the name Valerie and so it was, Francoise indifferent to it as she was to everything as life seemed drained from her. Martin had kept the house and Galle's Fine Fabrics, but he discharged all the servants and replaced them with new ones who knew none of what had transpired and who could not reconstruct from rumor anything that resembled the truth, although it was widely attempted.

Martin kept his suitcase packed, the one he had taken to Marseille. Once a year on the anniversary of the trip, he would open it at midnight, after everyone had gone to sleep and put on the clothes he had worn. He would go out into the street, smelling the aromas of his cologne and of Françoise, imagining as he wandered the streets that he was back in Marseille, killing time, anticipating the return to the hotel to Françoise who was waiting for him. He remembered the dinner on the barge and the fireworks glimmering on the water. He would go to the same brothel every year and pay twice the normal price for a young, dark-haired girl with green eyes, or so he thought, just to have her lie naked in a small bedroom on a well-worn sheet while he examined every part of her until she could stand it no more and the pimp was summoned to throw Martin out into the street. It was the only ritual of his life and it was the only one that filled some need in him, for it was neither humiliation nor shame nor atonement he sought. It was nothing he could verbalize even if he tried, which he did not.

When Valerie was five, Martin married Françoise for the sake of the child so that uncomfortable explanations would not be necessary. There was no honeymoon and they agreed to occupy separate rooms. Before Valerie was to enter school, Martin sold the house and moved to the LeBanc section in the north end of Paris where they knew no one and no one noticed how austere beautiful little Valerie's parents were. After all, they were Jewish and Jews were a mysterious lot. Valerie grew to womanhood in the rarefied, stifling atmosphere of the Galle household and finally breathed freely only when she started classes at the University.

Fifty~Five

55 Julian had finished teaching his last class for the day and he walked across the campus. Rain clouds threatened but a stiff breeze from the south brought warm air and the poplars swayed in the breeze bending toward the distant belfries of Notre Dame. He was to meet Professor Cortez, his PhD mentor for his weekly discussion. Cortez was a Milton scholar, getting his degree in Madrid but leaving soon after for Oxford and finally settling in Paris. He was a sensitive teacher who saw in Julian a greater potential than Julian saw in himself. Often their meeting would go well past the allotted three hours into the dinner hour and then to midnight. They would eat and drink while discussing the subtleties of Julian's research on Paradise Lost. Cortez's energy and intellectual acumen belied his near eighty years of age and Julian often forgot this man, his favorite professor, was so old. He walked with a cane and complained on occasion of his waning physical strength but it was always good-natured and self-deprecating. His wife had died three years earlier and his life revolved around his students, Julian being his protégé, taking a fatherly approach that endeared Julian to him even more.

When Julian arrived at Professor Cortez's quarters, he was informed by his assistant that Cortez had taken ill and was in the university hospital. Cortez had sent word that Julian should attend him there, despite anyone telling him otherwise. Julian saw this as a positive indication of Cortez's health and as he re-crossed the campus to the Hospital Louis Pasteur, he didn't mind the light rain that fell. For centuries, poets and novelists have either expressed that the world and its weather were in tune with man or not. Julian saw no connection between the weather and Cortez's condition. Rain was rain. It fell on the good and the wicked, the healthy and the ill, the living and the dead.

Julian's footsteps echoed down the well-lit marble-floored halls of the hospital passing starched uniforms, crucifixes, weeping relatives and wandering patients. The smell of disinfectant, ether and humanity wafted through the air with squeaking gurney wheels and the moans and shouts of patients punctuating the echoes.

He found Ernesto Cortez in a small room at the end of the long main corridor and had to walk around an old woman pushing a mop and a large cart filled with bloody sheets and rags. As he passed, she muttered something under her breath but Julian paid no mind. He walked over to the bed and greeted the professor who was staring at the ceiling with the expression of a corpse. Cortez turned slightly and raised his hand in greeting but in the white sheets, the dim light and with the ghostly shadow of his deep set eyes and white beard, he looked the prophet much the way Julian thought John the Baptist might have looked had he not been beheaded for the delight of a whore in the Country of Women. Julian knew that Cortez was beyond sick and for the first time he saw him as the frail old man he truly was. As Julian removed his wet jacket and put it on the back of a metal chair he pulled from the corner of the room to the bedside, the professor spoke, the rain and darkness intensifying around the grimy window, a white noise that camouflaged Cortez's wheezy breathing, making his voice sound like the splintering of a tree falling in a northern forest.

"The eels have found me, my son and I call you 'son' because you have been one to me, Julian, although you may not have known it. My beloved wife bore us no children but my children were my students. She would cry at night after I fell asleep thinking she had let me down. I would turn to her in the darkness and tell her that her love was all I wanted, that God had blessed me with a thousand children. Although they were grown by the time they came under my care, they were mine nonetheless for God had smiled upon me, so I thought. My wife was content with our dogs which she treated like her children for she showered them with her love and she with theirs for dogs are ever forgiving our cruelties and weaknesses and never betray us even if we deserve it. God gave man dogs to show us what true love is although few men, if any, understand the lesson. My dogs always tore up my mail when the postman put it through the doorslot and if they were in the front yard, they would attack him although they were so small that he laughed. You see, they were protecting me from the mail which burdened my life and kept me from my work, my wife and my rest. Yes, dogs are angels. But I digress, my son, and I am told that I have little time left and there is something I must tell you aside from the fact that I have recommended you for your degree so you needn't worry about that when I'm gone at such an inconvenient time of the rolling year.

"I remember when my wife died how all of her things were where she left them as if she might return at any minute. Her clothes, the apron in the kitchen, the book on the nightstand, her jewelry case and the photographs of her parents all awaiting their mistress. It was as if her outline could still be seen in the house like in those caves in Lascaux in France where the artist would put his hand on the wall and spit paint out at it, then remove his hand. On the wall was the outline of his palm and fingers, the signature in absentia, the hand of the creator seen by its absence the way God intended. Foolish artists today with their bold signature shouting at the world, 'I am Picasso; I painted this. Look on my works and despair.' The man in the cave knew God and so did my wife. As the years passed, though, the outline faded, for I moved some of her things and before long the eels started their work. Do not think I am crazy for what I tell you, Julian my son. When we are born you know there is an afterbirth we don't hear much about. The women, they know because they must deal with it, this sack of blood and water and other material we never want to think of because the baby is so beautiful and this other is quite horrid. The after-birth is the baby's opposite. Now listen to me and do not question. This is no discussion of a poem where there is no answer, only banter and good talk. In the after-birth is an eel. It slips off the table and into the drain below in the floor. Oh, I know you will say, 'What if there is no drain?' I tell you, it finds one and it has the cunning to do it. As the baby grows, the eel grows as well and it feeds on what is left behind, not the feces or the physical refuse of our lives but our memories. That is why, dear friend, son, that we do not remember our birth or when we were very young. It is the hunger of the eel. It has eaten our memories. As we mature, it follows us always under the ground, in the water, for everywhere there is water beneath us even in the Sahara, that cursed, arid place; look deep enough and there is the water and in the water, the eel.

"In the middle of our lives we are so busy, we feed our brains so much, of education, of love, of family, of business, that the eel is content with the scraps, what we drop off that we do not notice missing in the cacophony and clutter of our lives. But as we grow old and the feeding slows the way our bodies slow, the aches and the pains and the quiet reflection of old age, the eel still hungers and it continues to eat away at us. We notice one day that we cannot remember the name of a famous singer or Aunt Rinalda's husband's name or the capital of Lithuania. We knew these things, but they are gone because the eel has eaten them. He keeps eating and before long we cannot find anything in our heads. We wander the streets forgetting the way home. Our children's names are gone. The dignity of our lives is consumed by the accursed eel which eats the gristle and the bone of our minds until we even forget to breathe and it is only then that the eel dies, taking its last rancid breath as we do. But, Julian, our souls rise above it all. They go on. I know you think this is the raving of an old man on his deathbed. In many ways you are right. But you never doubted me before. Do not start now.

"You know, I've thought about it a long time. I think the eels hate books, not as much as they hate us, but books, that is where we put our thoughts and these thoughts are written in ink which is poison to the eels. But really what do we write. Sometimes it is beauty that can make the angels envious. Other times it is trash, the rubbish of simple bored minds that take out their frustrations on the page and fill the heads of readers with the stench, like a fart in a crowded room making everyone wish they could hold their breath. I don't know. I don't know about the books. Perhaps the eel is confusing me, even now. I am fortunate because my heart is given out and the eel will not have the time to devour everything. Remember this, Julian. Hold onto everything important. Love. It is love the eel hates because it is love that confuses it, for love is not facts nor conditions nor anything that anyone can see or touch. We never forget to love because it is from our soul not our mind and the eel's foul breath and razor teeth abhor our soul for it can only snap at it and take in a mouthful of nothing.

"When I am gone, Julian, take the key now that is in my pants pocket over there. Go to my quarters and see the outline of my life. Remember it before it is dismantled. See if you can see me at my desk, with my little dogs at my feet sleeping in their innocence and my wife, smell the sausages she is cooking. Do not let the eel that swims beneath your feet devour what I have taught you. I wish I could tell you how to kill it but I cannot. I only know that love is part of the answer. The other part, I cannot give you. Now, leave. The lesson is over, and give your professor a kiss for he knows you are a good person although the answer to your riddles seems so evasive and you do not always answer them correctly."

Julian bent over and kissed Cortez on the forehead eliciting a small fragile smile. He raised his hand in farewell and as a sign that there was nothing left to say. Julian left and did not take a breath, it seemed, until he stood on the lawn out in the rain. The drops fell everywhere except through him and he saw that the rain was like the paint spit out by the cave painter and that his body was his signature in the night. He looked down and imagined the eel beneath his feet treading water as he stood still, the city all around him, its bright lights, its beating heart and the swarm of eels just below it all.

Fifty~Six

56 The next day Julian went to Cortez's quarters on the grounds of the university. He had arrived at eleven in the morning as the last rain clouds scuttled like cockroaches northward and let the sun dry the water-logged city. As he reached the top of the stairs, a janitor was coming down vicariously balancing three wooden crates of books. Julian squeezed up against the wall and let him past, grunting under the weight. As he reached the door of the residence, he found it open with porters packing books and papers and all the other of the professor's belongings. A young man in shirt-sleeves and a tie seemed to be supervising the work. Julian stood at the door as he approached and enquired what Julian was there for. He said he was Professor Cortez's student. The young man told Julian that a new professor, Agnes Rice, an American, was moving into the residence in a few days. Julian said that the university obviously showed no respect for the dead and the man replied that it was not his job to make or defend such judgments as he stepped back directing the porters to pack the contents of the bookcase as if Julian had disappeared. A maid approached behind Julian and edged her way past him, received her instructions and began stripping the bed.

Julian stood silently in a corner and watched the outline of the professor take shape in his mind. As quickly as it formed though, it began to break apart as the workers packed, moved and rearranged. In a few moments, Professor Cortez's outline which had so permeated the apartment when he was alive had been dismantled like a child's sculpture in the sand at the beach nibbled by the first small waves that preface the incoming tide. Julian turned to leave when he saw a large, red cloth volume on the floor which he recognized to be Cortez's own copy of Paradise Lost.

Julian picked it up and was about to place it on a small hallstand, but thought better of it and simply walked away with the book under his arm.

He was supposed to meet Valerie for lunch, but the voice of Professor Cortez kept whispering in his ear. He held the book tightly as he walked to the small stand of Lombardy poplars that edged the campus in the south. The breeze was making them bow to him. Their tall, stately shapes reminded him of the gothic saints carved on the outer walls of Notre Dame with that gaunt deprived look mediaeval artists thought so intrinsic to the nature of martyrdom as if in sacrificing one's self to God, one had given up all the joys of life. Julian knew that real sacrifice was yielding up that which is treasured and enjoyed. To leave a life of deprivation is easier, that was a certainty, than a life of simple pleasures, food, love, sex, wine, laughter. The Notre Dame saints all looked like they hadn't eaten in years and certainly none of them had gotten laid in decades, unless it was rape. God knew better, Julian was sure.

Two of Julian's students stopped him when they recognized him and asked if he would like to join them for sandwiches which they had planned to eat on a blanket spread on the lawn. In fact, there were students all about, some eating, some talking, others solitary and napping in the sun. Small rows of solitary clouds like children in a line eased across the sky toward the east. Distant church bells tolled matins and a group of nuns, perhaps four or five hustled across the campus like a cluster of crows looking for a better cornfield, their wings being slightly opened by the breeze as they walked. Julian almost accepted, more as a way of escaping his thoughts about Cortez, but then thinking better of it, pledging the afternoon to the memory of his friend and mentor that it would not fade or be eaten by the eel as Cortez put it.

Sitting under a tree, opening the book, Julian was expecting copious marginal notes, underlining and other forms of Cortez's expressions of his interpretation and analysis of John Milton in the book. But as he leafed through the pages of the epic poem that many consider the greatest work in English after Shakespeare, all Julian could find were little asterisks, Xs and check marks like small grave markers indicating something buried within the line that only Cortez knew the significance of.

As he reached the back of the book and was about to close it and leave, he discovered several pages of typewriting and handwriting, two letters as it turned out and as anyone reading this thus far might expect. Expectations are the bane of humanity and the glory of the rest of the world. For humans, expectations unanswered and unachieved lead to heartache, pain and even suicide. Plants and animals, devoid of supercilious hopes accept what comes, are never disappointed whether it be drought or famine, disease or desertion. But, there were the letters.

The first was from a police officer in Madrid on the letterhead of the Chief Inspector of the Madera district. It informed Cortez that his wife's body had been recovered two miles downstream from the Castellano Bridge from which she undoubtedly had jumped. It paraphrased the coroner's report that the death was an apparent suicide, there being no signs to indicate foul play. It expressed no regrets, no signs of humanity or sympathy toward the surviving husband but was likely just another bureaucratic flake in a snowstorm of official ministrations. It was dated June 30, 1927 and Julian paused for a moment trying to remember where he was on that day, what he was doing, or eating or saying when Mrs. Anna Cortez, under the massive weight of disappointed expectations walked to the bridge, looked into its infinite waters and decided to leap into—who knows what? an afterlife, a heaven, a hell, perhaps just an unconscious drowning. Julian thought of the water rising up to meet her, her body rigid as her stomach rose to her throat in fear and anticipation of the pain, the great slam, the surge of water, the gush, as booted feet and wheels passed by above, over and around. He saw the splash in his mind, the water rushing in upon her to fill the void like a swarm of friends and relatives at a surprise party descending on the subject, smiles and handshakes, kisses and backslaps. The water was no friend; it filled her now, her mouth flooded, found its way into her stomach and then her lungs which revolted at the invasion even if she was unconscious from the impact, her adrenaline rushing to the aid of a battle with the water that could not be won, her heart beating faster even than when she first fell in love. Could her body tell the difference, Julian thought, between the agony of death and the paroxysm of orgasm, a notion as original as red and orange sunsets and rain at funerals.

The second sheaf of papers was a hand-written letter with no date which stated as follows:

"Dear Anna,

Please forgive me although I know I pleaded this all night long. I know you love me but I must tell you I love you, too, more than you will ever know although it sometimes seems that I don't. I am a foolish old man that thought myself waning in the autumn of my years. Before you read further, if you have made it this far, I do not intend to give you excuses, for there are none, only an explanation of my inconsiderate behavior. I did not love Katarina and do not know or care if she loved me. I just never considered the thought of it, although now I see that there are a great many things I did not consider that I should have. In flights of fancy, we do not take everything into account. Perhaps it was not fancy at all but some sort of ego-filling ambition, some self- centered act of gratification which disregarded not only you, whom I treasure above all, but of myself. I am in a low place in my life, everything that might have been had not occurred and everything that was, did not seem enough. You would think that in spending my life studying poems and plays and novels that I, above most others, would know that such feelings, which are really self-pity and a cry for attention, can only lead to destruction. But we read of others or are told of others, never really understanding that we are no different, that although we might tell people that we should learn, we do not. I always felt above it all and that my needs—well, they were my needs and if I did not fulfill them, I would die incomplete. These are the thoughts of a fool, I know and it is easy for me to say that now but it was impossible then.

"My darling Anna, I ask you not to forgive me but to let me come home and begin to make it up to you. Forgiveness must come in time for it is in your nature and I swear on everything important to me that I will never stray again. You are all to me and have always been. I am at the Hotel Borada and shall remain here as long as I can to await your word.

"Undyingly, your Ernesto."

It was clear now to Julian that either the letter was never sent or Cortez found it at his home after Anna committed suicide and decided to keep it. The professor's paradise was lost, that was a certainty, for Julian sensed in the letter the same genuineness that he exuded in lectures and talks. It must have been a terrible burden to carry for the years. Julian wanted to reconstruct the events but the letters said it all, it seemed. Why, he thought, did Cortez give him the key to his residence? Did he anticipate his finding the letters in the volume of Milton? Or was there more? And what would be left after the janitors and porters finished their dismantling of Cortez's memory?

Fifty~Seven

Daria had not come in by eleven that night and momentarily Julian hoped that she was having an affair. He sat in his club chair with the lights out like a parent waiting for his teenager to return past curfew. If she was having an affair, his options were unlimited. He could leave her, which is really what he wanted blaming her for the break-up. He could forgive her and seem a nice guy, a characterization which would surprise everyone he knew or, he could let it go, never make an effort at discovery and leave things the way they were. It was thought true that sharks must continuously move forward to breathe and that is why they cannot sleep or simply lie still. Julian could not simply lie still and even in sleep he would toss and turn without needing the excuse of a dream or nightmare. To him, life was more than a journey, a cliché he detested because he knew that few people if any actually believed it to be true. People look for a point of self-satisfied stasis. There is no journey, despite the romantic appeal or notion. Children grew up, married, got a job, had children, retired and died. The only variable was when death would hit. If this was a journey, it was no more than a commute. The journey that Julian envisioned, the way he saw his life was not in chapters but in separate volumes. He already knew he was leaving teaching behind to go into the law, a subject which appealed to him because unlike any other discipline, it was a closed system. The rules encompassed all of human interaction and had been devised over millennia. He had picked up a copy of Blackthorne's Treatise on Real Property, read it cover to cover and realized that no problem in a transaction involving land could not be solved. Every area of study, he knew, had unanswered questions whether it was biology, literature, religion or politics. There were always situations which fell on or between the cracks. But the law, it was perfect and self-contained. It paralleled the way he thought of himself.

In the darkness of his parlor, he decided that no matter what Daria was up to, for all he knew, she was dead somewhere, or in jail or cavorting with someone who might be a Communist, she couldn't tell a Leftist from a Nazi, he didn't care. She was an unfortunate mistake in his life, one of those decisions that seemed like the right thing to do at the time, the most idiotic analysis anyone could make. Now she was an anchor he was dragging and if he was to move forward and not suffocate trying to hold onto her, he would make decisions only based on his self-interest. In the back of his mind, though, his promise to himself weighed heavily, but he would figure a way around it; it was just a matter of time.

He stood up, and noticed the time was 12:10 a.m., reached in his pocket for Cortez's key and left. He needed to see what the old man wanted him to discover and he would give Daria the luxury of guessing where he was and the gift of hiding her own unexplained absence at midnight.

As Julian reached the north end of the campus, the breeze which seemed so stiff slowed and there was a lull in the air, a dead calm as sailors would have called it. The corpse face of the moon was unsheeted as opaque, spreading clouds scudded off to the east. The row of poplars and cypress and the Voltaire oak were ultramarine in the light, the spirits of themselves. A young woman clicked across the quad in heels too high for a student and as Julian turned to see who she was, she put her hand to her face feigning a cough. What she was doing out at this time of the night, he could only guess.

It was nearly 1:00 a.m. when Julian arrived at Cortez's rooms and let himself in. There were a few boxes stacked near the door as if waiting for a bus, but the room was neat, the furniture hulking down in the dark like bears hibernating. Julian turned on a lamp, went over to the bookcase. It was bare except for a few old journals that had fallen flat onto the shelves out of sight to the porters. There were cabinets beneath the shelves but they were locked. Julian went to the kitchen, retrieved a knife and went back to the locked cupboards. In a few minutes after breaking the point off the knife, the door opened revealing books and a small wooden box. Perhaps sometime in the distant past, early man discovered something valuable in a cave and thus the gene of treasure hunting became part of the threads of human existence; the locked door, the hidden casket, the long-lost cup of the last supper, an infinite array of tantalizing quests. Ah, Tantalus, condemned to Hades in eternity to thirst, bend down to the river and have it recede just beyond his parched lips, a bough of apples over his head that, when his starving arm reached up, blew just out of his reach in a tepid gale. Is it the temptation that is the moral of the story, the reaching but never touching? The Greeks were a peculiar lot preoccupied with hypotheticals while the pragmatic Romans marched in and stole their few practicalities leaving their theories and dreams behind like the rinds of oranges.

Julian's heart rate increased as he picked at the lock of the other cabinet and further when the neat row of journals therein caught the light from the table lamp like escaping prisoners. He didn't know where to begin. Expectations hovered in the air like the Holy Ghost bent over him and the world with warm breast and bright out-stretched wings.

The first journal was filled with poems and notes about poems. Some verses he recognized, some he thought might be Cortez's own, all in his native Spanish with a smattering here and there of crude English. The second and third volumes were the same, clearly his notes on his studies as a young man, the handwriting glib and darting like the trail of a fly-catcher in a hayfield following the mower.

The forth volume was damp stained with the cardboard showing through where the leather had been worn or rubbed off. The spine was cracked and the book warped as if being carried in a back pocket for a long time. Julian opened it carefully and the first page had the phrase, "The Trench" on it. Underneath that, the sentence in Cortez's careful script, "I am no longer afraid of what tomorrow will bring for it arrived yesterday." The next page, partially torn, said:

"I used to tell people that no matter how bad your life may seem now, no matter the troubles, stop and look down and below you, you will see the depths, for life can always get worse, worse even than death. I learned that I was wrong, for yesterday, I did look down and there where my feet stood, was the floor of hell.

"Two days ago there were four of us in the forward trench. No rain had fallen but water trickled steadily under the wooden boards of the inverted A-frame devised by the Brits to keep our feet dry. We were all with the

Spanish Expeditionary Force, three privates including myself and my friend José, a corporal because he could speak better English than the rest of us. A slow wind was blowing from the Kraut lines about a hundred meters distant and the corpse crews had missed about a dozen fallen comrades in no man's land in the night. One was still alive and making weak whimpering sounds that carried on the wind like swamp gas. The dead had stiffened, one with his arm still up in the air, a grenade unprimed in it. His helmet had fallen off or been shot off and held rain water, a small pond reflecting the blue sky in the muck, a porthole to a better world underground. The others were sprawled in different poses as they fell invisible to us behind the sandbags and corrugated metal of the trench. One of them I knew was a cook from Salamanca whose friend had been hit by shrapnel and was wounded and screaming like an infant being boiled alive. All our nerves were short-circuited and firing electric sparks into parts of our souls that were better left unknown. But cook went over the top to save his friend and the Kraut sniper had taken the left side of his skull out with a bullet. The shot was so well-placed, cook stood for a moment as we watched, took a step forward, reached for his face and fell forward, the bottom of his boots facing us like two upside down exclamation points in a comic strip. I hated the Krauts, hated them madly for their cunning, their skill for war and their incessant craving for blood. I was mad with the hatred that comes from fear, abject fear that seeps up from the ground through your legs and puddles in your guts giving you the shits. It is no wonder men, good men, men who would face the bull in the corrida, will piss their pants when the bullets fly or the shrapnel sings on their shoulders. The fear has filled them to bursting and their bladders and intestines are squeezed. Of the twenty four of us that came together from Madrid, only four are left, the sound of our Spanish voices like a song of home to us in the quagmire of Limey and Frog and Kraut. God, I told José, must be fucking a Chinese whore on the other side of the world, for he cannot know that this is going on over here.

"Lupe opened a can of beans and was heating it on the small French stove. It was swill. But it was pheasant foie gras to us. Even fear gets hungry when it has finished eating your soul. We were huddled under a canvas sheet at a blind turn in the trench and quietly chowing down when we heard the shuffling of men crawling. Lupe signaled to be quiet. In a few moments, three Kraut soldiers dropped in the trench around the curve from us. Jose had been watching and he signaled with his hand to come toward him. I peaked around the edge of the steel corner and saw them; they could not have been older than sixteen. We picked up our guns and in a mad rush stormed them hoping for an easy capture and maybe a twenty-four hour pass as a reward. But even the young Krauts are cunning as snakes. They had a flame thrower with them. They had planned, I guessed, on annihilating fifty of our men with a squirt of oily petrol or whatever that shit was that incinerated everything it touched. But it was only us four. They saw us and opened fire with the flames.

"Lupe ignited like he was made of dry pine needles. He cooked so fast he didn't have time to scream. Jose's face got hit and he tried to put it out with his hands but they melted to his cheeks as his hair flared blue and his uniform smoldered. He screamed and fell squirming as if to touch the water that trickled just inches below the floor boards out-of-reach. Pablo was behind me and he tackled me to the ground as the flames spewed over us and passed us igniting the canvas. I aimed my rifle and hit the man that held the thrower in the chin, the bullet taking off his jaw and penetrating his neck. I could see his upper jaw with the bright teeth of a young man rocking back and forth, his tongue lolling on the hole in his neck which poured blood. He fell forward jamming the nozzle of the thrower in between two floor boards. One of the other two Krauts fired at us, but we were on the ground and made poor targets. One dropped his rifle and reached for the nozzle but my second bullet caught him in the shoulder and he fell backward into his friend who was trying to climb back over the trench wall. The harder he clawed at it, the more it caved in.

"We jumped up and charged. He raised his hands in surrender and the one I had shot pleaded for mercy. Pablo yelled 'Silencio!' at them but they were blathering in their infernal Kraut tongue that reminded me of the sounds of a drunk vomiting in the gutter. Pablo turned to me and said these two Krauts might get us our twenty-four hour pass after all, they were spring chickens but better than nothing. As he smiled at me at his own joke, the Kraut on the floor drove a dagger up into Pablo's gut, just above his crotch. Blood and urine poured out as Pablo gasped and fell backward, the bayonet still in the Kraut's hand. I raised my rifle and brought the butt down on the sitting Kraut and smashed his brains out. I hit him ten more times than I needed to kill him. Pablo was groaning as the smoke from the bodies of Lupe and Jose shifted toward us in a devilish breeze that crept into the trench. I tied the surviving Kraut's hands behind him with his own canvas belt and turned to Pablo. He muttered to me of his wife and young son, tears weakly filling his eyes and running over through the grime on his bluish face. I held the crucifix that was on a chain around his neck and imitated the ritual of Last Rites as well as I could remember from seeing it once or twice, back when, I couldn't remember.

"Pablo said he loved me, but I knew he thought he was talking to his mother, his father, his wife or his son. I was the closest he would get to them now so I told him I loved him too, hoping the fear in his eyes made me look like them instead of me, a miserable wretch in this miserable place in this miserable war on this miserable planet. He died in my arms and as his life ebbed away I could feel it pass through me into the thinning smoke and up into the brown sky. With his life, my soul took flight, like Icarus, young Icarus, leaving the Earth as I wished I could do, with bright, white-feathered wings fashioned by my father. I imagined I was over the trenches and looking down. I could see they were not trenches at all but the labyrinth of King Minos, the labyrinth that saw the hideous sacrifice of so many young men and women. I could see the maze stretch for miles under me in every direction twisting and turning upon itself in its diabolical perfection, a place from which no one returned, lost forever, lost in its demonic coils and at the center, there, there, I could see the Minotaur, head of a deformed bull and the body of a contorted giant scarred with the sins of his father, flesh of a virgin still hanging from his yellow teeth.

"I felt the bayonet in my hand and dove down out of the sky, my glorious wings flashing, rushed to him driving the knife into the monster's chest and twisting it with all my strength, screaming a curse at God and the beast I held beneath me. I pulled out the blade as he grunted his last obscenities. The black blood flowed out like oil from a well covering his body and filling the labyrinth at my feet. I cut open the monster's chest and pulled out his heart and bit it, hot, almost still beating, my teeth digging into the muscle fleshiness and pulling away mouthfuls until I had finished, the salt smell of it making me dizzy.

"A bugle sounded in the distance and I was back in the trench, the sole survivor of the twenty-four Spaniards from Madrid. At my feet was the young German soldier, his chest agape and his heart gone.

"A British lieutenant and a contingent of men appeared, coming no doubt to the smoke. When they saw what I had done, they took me to the field hospital. In a month, the body that had my name arrived in Madrid and walked to my mother's house. She held it and wept into its shoulder. She thought I was still alive and could not know that the young man in her arms was the shell of he who had left for glory on the Western Front and come back the King of the Hollow Men."

Julian turned the rest of the pages but they were blank. Two other journals were on the shelf, but he could read no more. The desolation of Cortez's spirit reached out to him like the proverbial hand from the grave and yet Julian thought there must be more to the story. He placed the journals in a stack on the floor where he sat, turned and picked up the small black lacquer box.

Julian looked at the box and gently attempted to lift its lid but it was locked. A small brass escutcheon in the shape of the Ace of Spades surrounded a keyhole. It would be a simple matter, he thought, to break it open. Such locks are designed to keep out honest people for a thief would simply place the box on the floor and crack it open with his foot. Julian knew himself not to be a thief and so set the box aside. It was nearly 3:00 a.m. as he went to the bedroom and lay down upon the bare mattress. He thought he would fall asleep easily but the letters and the journals came alive to him and he realized that Cortez's memory did not reside in his apartment but in the writings, that he had managed to defeat not only the attempted dismantling of his life by the university porters but, more importantly, he had outwitted in some small way his eel which Julian could feel asleep beneath the bed paralleling his own body, resting, perhaps not asleep but waiting. But what was it waiting for?

Julian got up and retrieved the box, went back to the mattress and lay down upon it again placing the box on his belly. As he stared at the dark ceiling with a wan shadow cast from the campus lights that filtered through the blinds in thin zebra stripes, he could feel the pulsing of the eel's gills, the breathing of memory, the exhalation through the gill slits of forgetfulness, minion of the God of the Lotus-Eaters.

As Julian began to succumb to sleep, Cortez's memory became clear. It was as if the apartment had been reassembled and Cortez was sitting speaking as he did in the old days. The secret was not in the box. Julian got up and as he did he felt the eel move beneath his feet. He left the apartment with the box in his hand and walked across the deserted campus toward the Terran Bridge, one of the stone footpaths over the Seine, the oldest crossing to the Left Bank. He stopped in the center and leaned on the carved stone rail. The towers of Notre Dame sat in the darkness like sentinels at the River Styx. Julian heard the water gurgling beneath the bridge and knew it was the eel. He imagined it waiting for his next move. His past was with him as it was with all people. Everything he had ever done, good, bad and indifferent and the weight of it was paralyzing him. Cortez knew this for he had led his life under its vast burden. Julian imagined his past, all of it, in the black lacquer box and as he did, he let it drop into the murky waters of the Seine. No comet appeared, and no alignment of the planets and the sunrise was still an hour off but Julian knew that the steps he took off the bridge were steps into his new life.

The sky was turning purple in the east and the crescent moon hovered, its black disk like a communion wafer low over the open mouths of the roofs of Paris. Julian walked homeward but he felt he was being followed, that the echoes of his footsteps were not echoes at all but the footsteps of another. The shadows in the streets were like velvet. A cat slithered out from behind a trash bin and ran silently from right to left across the street in front of Julian and dived into a cellar window partially covered with a wooden crate. Julian reached into his pocket for the straight razor he always carried but couldn't find it. He fingered coins and folding money. He never left home without the razor. The City of Lights had a dark side, larger than the dark side of the moon that swallowed souls whole.

Julian stopped and took a quick sidestep into a darkened doorway to wait, to see who was following him. In the roseate light of dawn, a lengthened shadow froze on the pavement but Julian could not see who or what was making it. The distant horn of a delivery truck, weak as the call of a canary in the Amazon jungle was followed by another. Julian felt it was death following him whether it was the Grim Reaper himself or simply his messenger in the form of a street killer, a robber, someone looking for a few sou for wine or hashish. Julian would not die in a doorway; he was no victim and so without his weapon he stepped back onto the sidewalk and turned toward the source of the shadow. The street was empty. Lights in the tenements across the way shown through murky curtains. Julian took a few steps toward where he had seen the shadow but there was no one. The clip-clop of a delivery wagon horse echoed as a milk cart turned from one street onto the one where Julian stood, the driver lifting his hat and smiling, teeth missing from his mouth like a jack-o-lantern, driving on past Julian and muttering something under his breath that Julian could not hear

Fifty~Eight

58 Julian had first met Isabelle Fontenot at the gallery in Montmartre. He was looking to have his diploma and academic awards framed. When he entered the gallery a thirty-ish woman name Clarisse greeted him. She had sandy blond hair and a warm face with deep blue eyes and a broken front tooth that made her interesting instead of pretty, one of any number of Parisians that compensated for their imperfection by a certain carriage of the body, an inherent sexiness that defies description but is immediately recognized when it is encountered. Isabelle was in the back room cataloguing a recent delivery of mundane street scenes and the low voice of Edith Piaff was singing "La Vie en Rose" on a phonograph. It was almost contrived and the reader should not think that this ink conspires with the page to cliché. Lies are not in the offing and "La Vie en Rose" was actually in the air along with the smell of linseed oil, less than expensive cologne, and that indefinable scent of females congregated in a limited enclosed space, perhaps only one part per million but detectable to Julian's heightened sense of what he called "inadvertent prowling," which is to say that he never sought out female companionship, especially since his marriage, but it would float by in the wayward currents of life, like a water narcissus freeing itself from a pond and floating in infinite curlicues down a small stream until its tendrilous roots caught a comfortable space between two stones. Julian rather prided himself on a philosophy of passive observation, that practice which eschews active seeking of vice in favor of indulging as it is randomly encountered, an almost "waste not, want not" modus operandi that ridded the conscience of responsibility for breach of the social order. The fact is that Julian was always immaculately groomed in an unstudied way, just the right loose tress on his forehead, the willing smile, the twinkle in his eye that managed to evade his long eyelashes and connect with the ever-seeking eyes of females and if they were not seeking because they were otherwise married, engaged or committed in some fashion, they nonetheless recognized in Julian something desirable, although what it was would have eluded them until it was far too late.

Few women connected with Julian more fervently than Isabelle, although she denied it openly even to herself. It was not love at first sight; that is the province of romance novels and insipid love songs, but a type of obsession one hears about in collectors of great works of art, an "I must have it" knot that grows in the abdomen and blossoms somewhere in the cerebellum until it crowds out every bit of individuality much like honeysuckle climbing a pine tree; after time, the tree is simply the skeleton of its former self and functions only as a trellis for the object of its infatuation. It is not called "choke weed" lightly. Isabelle was only now exploring the boundaries of her obsession and could not know that at some point she could murder to satisfy its voracious appetite.

Their first meeting was at one of those homogenous cafés along the Rue de la Université in sight of the Eiffel Tower. They made the usual small talk of the ritual of flirtation but when Julian reached across the table to hold Isabelle's hand, a massive breach of the natural order of things, she blurted out almost as a non-sequitur that she was married, but separated, as if to say, handle with care, you may not know fully what you are getting into. As he held her hand, he told her he was married, too, but that a divorce was in the offing. There is not a woman alive who has not heard this or heard of a friend hearing this as the creed of the adulterer, a simple phrase that at once, in theory, dissolved the taboos that had been in place since men wore the skins of animals without designer labels on the veldt in Africa. But Julian was so earnest, Isabelle so wanting to retrieve something of the wreckage of her life that the worthless Briand had caused, that they both accepted the other's marital status as a bump in the road, perhaps a large pothole, and neither would allow it to be a detour from the direction they seemed to be heading in. Julian, of course, made no mention of Valerie, waiting at her flat for him to return. In a day, she had become one pair of shoes too many for Julian. His shoe rack was filled and this pair had to be tossed. It was simply a matter of when and how, that cloying feeling in his gut that is half regret and half anxiety. Julian thought of Cortez's lacquered box dropped off the bridge; the answer to his current dilemma was like pulling a string in a dark closet, hearing the click, and having the light bulb's glare fill every shadow with the clarity of artificial light. Valerie would not be talked out of anything. She was one of those scorched-earth bitches, he thought, who will ruin a man who spurns her and shadow him like a scar until it is done. This was not really true of Valerie, but Julian thought it so. Believing something makes the truth of it unimportant. I no time, Julian invited Isabelle for a week's stay with him on the coast of Spain. Bold and presumptuous as the invitation was, she accepted as if she had known him a year.

Julian and Isabelle boarded the train in Paris and in a while they were in Barcelona. They hadn't spoken much in the train, sitting opposite each other in the lounge car most of the way, the flat countryside around Paris turning to wrinkles and then to hills, then to the sandy arid low peeks that hugged the scalloped coastal region of Catalonia. Isabelle just looked at Julian as much as she could without him noticing her, she hoped. She was torn between wanting him more than anything she had ever wanted and her instinctive displeasure, sometimes as extreme as loathing at the fact that he was married. She had reached a juncture in her life when she wanted what she wanted and the small voices of conscience or morality or the nagging sound of her mother's memorial echoing were going to be ignored. Today was today and that is what mattered. The world was going to hell anyway and she would contend with her sins when she was asked and not a moment sooner. Then there was Briand; he'd have to fend for himself; he was an expert at it, a parasitic one for certain, but a survivor nonetheless.

Julian and Isabelle rented a Volvo at the train station in Barcelona, one of those delightfully ridiculous Swedish cars that were designed more for function than for form. Julian delighted in its erratic shape and didn't even mind the difficulty he had shifting gears nor its grinding engine. It was all fun as far as he was concerned and Isabelle reveled in being part of it, playing the navigator as they headed north up the Catalonian coast to a small village called Llafranc hanging by a thread to the steep cliffs that slid down to the ancient Mediterranean along its serrated shore. There may have been as many as twenty such towns along the strand each occupying its own crescent of sand and stone separated from one another by rocky outcroppings and from the mainland by the trailing, fading backbone of the Pyrenees.

They checked in at a small hotel about a quarter of the way up a steep hillside. Their room overlooked the flat roofs of the village, a narrow coastal roadway, a fringe of pines and then the sand and the sea. The sky was white, only faintly blue and turned to cream as it met the milky green of the far horizon where the Mediterranean sidles toward the hostile shore of North Africa.

Fifty~Nine

59 Llafranc had few tourists from outside of Spain and no one there spoke English. Isabelle's French worked fine, for the Catalan tongue is that odd mixture of Spanish and French that reminds one of a place far away which the modern outside world has yet to wreak havoc upon. Each morning a crew of white-uniformed municipal workers swept the streets and sidewalks under the pines, then hosed it all down with sea water, the smell of which in the morning haze was reminiscent of sitting on the deck of an ocean liner. Large cement pots formed a chain, each filled with bright red geraniums, that slinked its way in the curve following the crescent of sand. Gulls coasted on thermals and young people climbed the rocks that protruded from the sand on the north and south of the crescent beach and lay on brightly colored blankets, some half-nude in the sun, pointing their chins into the sky as if waiting for a kiss to get just the right angle of the blazing sun to perfect a tan.

The hotel had a café in its ground floor where an abundant buffet of dried fish, prosciutto, melon and cherries abounded, something out of Caesar's table at Ostia. Julian and Isabelle sat at a small round mosaic-topped table on their first morning enjoying each other's faces, the food, the odd flavor of the local milk and the recent memory of sexual abandon that conquered the night air like El Cid overcoming the Moors at Granada. It was one of those love-making sessions, if sessions is the right word at all, when little is spoken but much is said, when breaths are passed back and forth between lovers as if sharing oxygen in a deep-sea dive and where every touch is special, unrehearsed, unselfconscious and perfectly timed like a duet between a cello and a guitar.

The Greeks talked of the Thread of Life being woven and manipulated by the Three Fates, three old hags with nothing better to do than manipulate peoples' lives until they were glad to die. But Julian knew that life was not a thread with a beginning, a middle and an end that is stretched out connecting two points. He saw it with considerable clarity as a braid, a plait, woven, intricate, turning upon itself, repeating patterns, taking convoluted turns as it crossed back over itself. It is only the simplest of minds that see experience as linear. It might start as a spring, a stream and then a river but eventually the currents spread and before long it is a vastly wide delta with eddies and backwaters, deep and shallow, murky and clear, all in turns and starts. As if it had just occurred, the current of Julian's life would circle the pool of blood on Valerie's pillow that flowed slowly to the indent in the mattress made by her shoulders and coursed on, the blood lightly staining the water until it almost disappeared in the sheer volume of the torrent. Was it yesterday? Tomorrow?

Sitting in the shade of the pinion pines on the beach at Llafranc, Julian and Isabelle struck up a conversation with two elderly Britons from Dorset, each explaining to the other the eccentricities of their respective countries. The man, James, had fought in the Great War and had been wounded in his knees, walking with a hickory cane and a sideways limp. With his wife Helen, he spoke of his first marriage and the miseries of a poor childhood when his father had deserted his mother and their children. She had had to resort to prostitution to keep a roof over their heads. This had played havoc with James' first marriage. His daughter had done well enough but his son had moved to Spain and, in fact, lived nearby in the city of Palas, apparently doing fine teaching drawing and painting at a local college. Without a word of warning that anyone had heard, he had committed suicide when he was diagnosed with an inoperable brain tumor. Rather than face the inevitable loss and pain, the slow decline into an unconquerable disease, he had ended it all in the ignominious maw of a gas oven in his kitchen. He was simultaneously brave and cowardly, one of those oxymorons of the young like Mozart, a musical genius but a social idiot. James spoke of his son, Miles, with tears welling up in his eyes, telling of cleaning out his apartment, his collection of books and artwork from friends and his own as well. "All is vanity," James kept repeating as if some lesson could be learned from such an experience. Isabelle wept in empathy with James as Julian listened silently unable to say anything that did not sound hackneyed and rather admiring Miles' ability to check out when the going was not rough but was about to be rough. Clearly, hope did not spring eternal in Miles' mind and he was taking no chances that when his mind started to go he might be unable to end his life, an irony that was not wasted on Julian, nor unobserved.

The four of them became friendly enough as the evening wore on to share a bottle of wine and a plate of olives and then another of each, talking about everything and nothing long after the sun sank behind the cliffs and cast the sea in slate gray shadows and the sands of the beach in the colors of the moon, each footstep a crater. Several bathers still lay upon their towels or blankets as the sky went purple and not until half the stars were out did the beach become vacant, a bib around the neck of the Moorish sea, little white frills, putative waves weakly unfurling and whispering to sandpipers that skittered along the edge finding indiscernible sea creatures as a late dinner.

Back in their room Julian stripped the top sheet and blanket off the bed and left only the white bottom sheet. The pillows were on the floor and as Isabelle emerged from a quick shower, the moon, nearly full over the sea, cast its aquamarine light on the bed. It appeared to be an altar in a pagan ritual. Her infatuation turned to love that night as the two of them discovered each other as if lost on some far planet that had been occupied by millions but now was devoid of all life except the two of them. This is no romantic folderol when a night or two of orgasmic recreation seems to link two strangers in the guise of enduring love. The connection between Julian and Isabelle was deeper than anything physical or mental. They became two sides of a special coin. They did not complete each other as women are fond of saying, for the real value of love is not in providing what is missing, but in crafting something that did not exist before, something greater than the sum of its parts. Julian felt he had shed his skin, his former self and emerged from a chrysalis into a new forest. Isabelle immersed herself in her obsession.

The morning found them up before everyone but the cleaning crews, exploring the walkways around Llafranc that meandered up the cliffs through the foothills that were covered in live oak and olive trees, flagstoned terraces protected from the weather by rock walls. They met Helen and Jim for breakfast at nine in the café in the hotel and all decided to visit the town of Figueras about twenty miles inland. Julian drove and Helen, familiar with the area, gave directions to the town that was the home of Salvador Dali, its chalk cliffs, desert sands and pink adobe walls the domain of the Spanish sun, hot, incessant, infusing the town with an overwhelming thermal force despite the proliferation of brightly colored awnings and bistro umbrellas.

They had an early lunch in a restaurant in the ruins of a Renaissance fortress where only the walls were still standing. Three large banyan trees formed the roof hung with strands of naked light bulbs. A hot breeze blew the tops of the trees making the leaves click. James related a story after a glass of cognac about he and his first wife. They had been in Figueras after visiting their son and had met Dali and his wife, Gala, who graciously joined them for dinner. Dali had recently been in hospital after suffering a seizure and had been in a coma for almost a week. As Dali told it, he had been sitting in the back of his huge, black Hispano-Suiza with Gala. His friend Simoza was driving with a young American red-head sitting next to him and nibbling on his ear and giggling in that foolish way that only American women can, casting their dignity and passionate natures to the wind in favor of appearing to be school girls. She, her name was Maureen, raised her arms into the wind, the top being down, showing the creamy curves of her armpits, shaved the way Americans do. Dali stared as if she were naked noting how the arch of the pectoral muscles swept up like the crescent beach at Llafranc to her arms above and her near alabaster breasts below. Gala, in Catalan, told them that it was an abomination to shave one's armpits in a vain effort at appearing to be pre-pubescent, a state only a pervert would appreciate. Dali admitted that he did appreciate the look and if that made him a pervert, there were a great many other views he held that pre-qualified him for such a title. The fact is, James said, that Dali was more talk than action and that he worked tirelessly at creating the image of his being a Libertine when, in reality, he was as conservative as the Pope, excluding the licentious Medici and Colonna Popes and a few others whose progeny still occupied some of the most noble posts in Europe. Gala told Dali that if he had to contend with someone like Irene in bed it would take three hours for him to get an erection and probably thirty seconds to lose it.

Dali immediately told Simoza to stop the car but he hadn't noticed in

Gala's fuss that Irene had bent over and was felating him as he drove, an act dangerous even in Spain when, it is said, the first automobile fatality occurred because of just such an act, sometime back in 1902. Dali, ever the bombast and showman, probably even when he was seven years old if his mother is to be believed, stood up and stomped his foot that the car was to stop immediately. Simoza was happy to oblige but as he put his foot on the brake, he orgasmed. This caused him to apply more pressure than prudence and good driving techniques would accommodate and the three ton automobile came to a dusty, scraping halt on the dirt and gravel road. Irene, her mouth full of Simoza, was thrown to the floor, fortunately with a mouth now empty of living tissue, but Dali, who had been standing, was thrown over the front seat, his head introduced informally to the steel frame over the windshield. Gala, likewise had been pushed forward into the back of the front seat, rolled over it and landed on top of Irene who had commenced to screaming. Gala reached up to grab something for leverage to raise herself up and managed to get hold of Simoza's half flaccid member. She screamed and then noticed that Dali was unconscious on top of her, bleeding on her new white chemise. Everyone panicked when they realized that the great Salvador Dali might be dead, but it was quickly ascertained that he was alive, bleeding from a large gash on his forehead and very unconscious. They laid him in the back seat with Irene's sweater wrapped around his head and raced to the hospital at Figueras. Eventually, of course, he revived to everyone's relief, especially his banker in Madrid.

Dali told James of a dream he had while comatose, James being amazed that people in comas dreamed. Dali ignored the comment as he was less interested in the medical issue than in relating his dream where he had married Irene after Gala committed suicide by jumping off the Pedraza Bridge outside of the mountain town of Palafrugell. Then he and Irene planned and carried out the murder of Picasso, a man Dali felt was less than a pig but more than a cockroach. They had drugged Pablo, as he referred to him, tied him to a large stake in the corrida and loosed a bull upon him which gored him so severely that his intestines had gotten tangled on the bull's horns and, as the bull pulled away in a frenzy, untangled all the intestines into a straight length, stretched taut until it snapped like a huge, shit-filled rubber band. The sound of the snap awoke Dali from his coma. He was immediately disappointed to realize that he was still married to Gala, that Irene had already left for home, a place called Brooklyn, that Simoza was telling the story of the car accident to every one of their mutual friends and, worst of all, that Picasso was still alive and well and enjoying the reputation of being the greatest living artist in the world.

Isabelle adored the story and suddenly had a great affection for James whom she looked at as a grandfather she never had. Julian was amazed at how quickly James had become familiar enough with him and Isabelle to relate a story that had so many sexual elements, realizing the Brits are, indeed, very reserved but will more quickly drop the façade of prudishness than any other race on the planet. In less than twenty-four hours, it seemed, the four of them had become fast friends and it was only the thought that James and Helen resided in England and he was off to Italy that made him feel that a great opportunity was to be wasted. Life, he felt, was designed in this fashion, that personal relationships that were negative rooted like ragweed and good ones were scattered like thistles in a storm, cast upon stony ground to wither unblossomed.

Helen enthusiastically added that Dali told them that it was after the accident that he had grown his famous trademark handlebar mustache as a reminder to keep his temper in moving vehicles. Isabelle asked if they had purchased any of his artwork and they responded no, saying that the home they used to own in a village near Figueras cost less than what Dali wanted for one of his nightmarish paintings although they agreed that it would have been a wise investment. Julian remarked that paintings should never be viewed as investments, but James cut him off in mid-sentence saying how the Americans had bought up half the art treasures of Europe and were, one day, he was sure, going to sell them all back at a hefty profit, that Americans did nothing for love unless it was love of money. Julian politely agreed but was mildly rankled by any Brit criticizing the United States which had in Julian's opinion saved Europe from the terror of the Hun. He liked James and Helen too much to discuss something as ridiculous as politics and Isabelle spoke up in the pregnant silence and suggested getting back to the hotel for some early drinks beachside under the pines.

Sixty

As Julian drove through the beautiful, arid austere Catalan countryside, the other three fell asleep lulled by the hum of the motor and the strobe effect of alternating light and shadow as Julian made his way on the road, each side planted with mesquite and rows of Umbrian cypress. The air smelled of incense, something sweet and spiced that he remembered from a brief trip to New Mexico when he was a child. There was an elemental quality to sand and gravel, eons of being ground up by inland seas and glaciers that was released in the air as if to say, "inhale me, I will have been here before you were all born and will be here long after you are all dead."

Julian pulled up to the hotel at 3:30 and Isabelle, James and Helen crossed the street and found a table in front of the coldwater showers that were provided for bathers to rid themselves of sand and lotions. It was James' favorite spot on all the Catalan coast for he could sit with a plate of spiced ham, a glass of sweet cavé wine and watch an almost endless parade of young females and old, mostly topless, showering right before his eyes like women in a slave market on display for Roman nobility to take home and own. He didn't express this to anyone, but it was heartfelt, the viewing, not the slavery, but had he been asked, he would have said, "you must take the bad with the good." Before he sat down, Julian excused himself and went into the hotel ostensibly to use the restroom but for some reason even he didn't understand, he wrote a short note to Daria telling her he looked forward to seeing her in Italy. He paid three pesetas to the desk clerk to have it wired immediately, went to his room, washed his face and walked through the small lobby on the way to the sidewalk. Isabelle interrupted him with a hug and a kiss on the cheek on her way up to the room when the clerk, seeing Julian, asked for confirmation of the spelling of

Daria's name. It was as if an Arctic wind blew through the lobby and set-tled on the two of them. Julian, ordinarily immune to female vicissitudes, suddenly felt the criminal, then the idiot, then the penitent. Isabelle was confronted with the truth that Julian was truly a married man and the plan that she so carefully constructed for the two of them with a past, present and future was instantaneously orbiting a red giant sun whose gravitation-al pull was causing massive earthquakes, destroying it all as it swelled and engulfed everything nearby.

Julian explained the impetuous foolishness of the wire while Isabelle sat amid the ruins and sought to reconstruct some semblance of what she had formerly created. Her love was genuine, though, and women are ever hopeful for the redemption of their chosen mates, no matter the obvious faults and flaws. Julian was unquestionably married and had been so long before she met him. She realized over the next hours as he explained away his indiscretion that he must love her too, for he had no real motive to sup-plicate her. In the past, he would simply have said something inanely sim-plistic like, "that's life." Nothing was different now than it had always been, but he seemed determined to assuage her hurt and so the ground beneath her feet stopped trembling and the cataclysmic fissures that appeared in the lobby closed as the red giant sun cooled and shrank amid the mountains, hills, forests and streams, all reordering themselves on her reassembled world.

That night, the last they were to spend in Llafranc, was the festival of St. John, the patron saint of the town. The crescent beach, perhaps a mile from point to point, was covered with people of all ages, mostly families, a few groups of all young men and all young women strategically close to each other and pairs of lovers. Julian and Isabelle sat at a table near the beach with James and Helen, drinking wine and watching the people milling about, excitement in the air as the sky went amethyst. The first fireworks ignited as the stars began to show through the light haze off the water and soon the sky was filled with rockets, Roman candles and all manner of glittering bursts, all launched from the beach, the street and the walkways. It was a night for children and lovers, the air full of positive feel-ings where the anxiety that gripped the world as events unfolded in Europe were forgotten. There were no brawls or disputes, no rude behavior, and camaraderie was epitomized in the statue of St. John being pulled through the streets on a gilt-wheeled cart by twenty men in red and blue blouses singing a hymn to the saint as everyone turned and applauded and sang along. Julian held Isabelle's hand and from that point on they were a couple, complete within an evanescent, iridescent bubble that both thought would never burst. Julian resolved that this was the woman he was to love forever and without the necessity of a sentence, a phrase or even a word, Isabelle knew. The soft thud of the skyrockets exploding over the water, the cascade of sparks dropping and the flashes of light and distant subdued cheers of the throng continued past midnight, past one, past two and past Julian and Isabelle's passion well into the morning when the beach was deserted by all but a few families that bedded down on the sand to spend the night. A few seagulls scanned for leftovers. Thousands of pieces of paper, crumpled and shredded, waited for the crew of the street sweepers.

That morning, Julian awoke from a fitful dream and dressed in yesterday's clothes, silently closing the door behind him not to rouse Isabelle. With his hands in his pockets, he walked to the shoreline near the southern outcropping of reddish brown and ochre stones and sat a while listening to the waves and letting the sun warm him. He lifted a smooth, yellowish stone and lying back against the worn crag, placed it against his lips, eyes closed, a steady low breeze moving the unbrushed hair on his forehead making it feel like an angel's hand caressing him, invisible fingers tapping gently to and fro. The stone tasted of salt and made him think of the green-black depths of the Mediterranean, the womb of civilization, Triton following the narwhals, Aphrodite born on the surf, Cleopatra's perfumed sails sadly billowing in the setting sun, Actium and Antony behind her, lost, the bracken sea, far unnamed islands, the taste of countless skeletons of dead fish, the oaken hulls of ships on their way to Troy, the waves warning the unheeding Trojans. Julian had a vision of a white schooner with sails the color of the sky, a two-masted trireme with pointed triangular foresails, oarsmen below, black and sweating, the demons of his past and future, ebony oars striking the water in a slow, steady unyielding rhythm. As the ship crossed in front of him, he could see Isabelle leaning against the main mast, her white arms wrapped around the reddish timbers, yes, eyes the color of the sea, her hair, black flames tossed about by the irreverent wind and the oars, slapping the water, then knifing through it, the push and the tug, foam fleeing before the prow like winter clouds before a northern gale. Children's voices brought him to the surface. Two small boys had climbed the rocks on the far side and were tossing pebbles into the sea. " 'Til human voices wake us and we drown," he thought. Julian arose, put the stone in his pocket and went back to Isabelle.

In the train on the way back to Paris, Julian and Isabelle agreed that they would go together to Rome, that Julian would seek a teaching job at the American University and no further careers would be necessary. The chapters of his life came together in a single volume and he told her he would write the novel that, as he put it, was rattling around in his head. His marriage, of course, would be ended as soon as he could, whatever that meant, and there were other loose ends which Isabelle could not even guess at.

Julian grew sullen and quiet watching the countryside out the window and by the time he arrived at the station in Paris with Isabelle it was all crystal clear, although, like crystal, the chiseled facades could distort vision in a nightmare kaleidoscope made orderly only by a mind touched with insanity and purpose.

Sixty~One

61 Julian arrived at Valerie's apartment when he knew that she would not be there. He packed a single suitcase, leaving behind anything that would burden his travel. He checked into a small hotel and phoned Isabelle of their timetable. She had already packed and met him at the hotel where they stayed the night in preparation for the trip to Milan. Julian had made arrangements through the School of Law for housing and in short order Isabelle and he were setting up house in the two bedroom flat on the Via Fortunata about half a kilometer from the school. It was a converted eighteenth-century hotel made of pale sandy stucco, heavily ornamented with bas-reliefs of horned faces, horses and riders and topped by a decayed statue of a bull upon which a dozen live pigeons perched. The flat, located on the fourth floor, overlooked the orange-tiled roofs of the central part of the city and beyond that, out of sight, was the Piazza San Domenico surrounded by markets and trattorias. The balcony, only five feet from the door to the iron work, overlooked the street upon which the building opened, its faded green awnings below and a fairly modern apartment complex across the way that cast the street in shadow from noon until dusk.

The furnishings in the flat were old, but in good condition, worn gilt armchairs and a small dining table perched in front of the balcony door. The first thing Isabelle did was to go food shopping and she returned with the staples: coffee, milk, eggs, a freshly slaughtered chicken, tomatoes, and romaine and a small blue pot filled with geraniums which she placed on the balcony. They ate lunch together and watched the sun ignite the fiery crimson of the flowers, a breeze blowing in from the west, billowing the open drapes behind them and letting the smell of the city and its sounds fill the flat. Isabelle was as a person reborn—no someone born the day before, like Athena fully grown and clothed springing from the head of Zeus, ready for the world and, more importantly, for Julian.

Julian occupied a zone somewhere between reality and dreams, content in the moment to be with the woman he loved but aware that his wife was awaiting word from him in the States. He had the certain knowledge disguised as intuition that Valerie would appear at some point soon, she knowing full well his plans at the law school and having the time and resources to track him down with the gilt-edged hope of reclaiming him despite the impassioned note he left. She would never give him up. She was not one of those people who would pack up their memories and mis-remembered moments in a small valise and move on. She would not simply forget him or settle in years to come on conjuring up his memory when seeing someone who held a pen the way he did or fill the room with his hearty laugh as Julian was known to do. He would deal with all their issues at some point, or they would deal with him.

He found a considerable respite in Isabelle's companionship for she was amenable to any of his many whims. She didn't mind his arbitrarily canceling plans made weeks before or making plans on an hour's notice. They enjoyed the same music, the same films, the same parks. His hours of study she filled with small creative self-imposed assignments around the flat whether it was cooking a meal or sewing a table cloth. But Julian sensed, in fact knew, that beneath the surface of her reflection of him, beneath the placid yielding cooperative façade was a heart forged in the Fontenot vineyards, for what is a person but the sum total of his parents' prides and sins, strengths and foibles. He knew that each person grew up to be one of his parents and to marry the other, the perpetuation of everything good and wicked from the dawn of Man.

Slight disturbances, imagined effronteries, unintended and superficial hurts would launch Isabelle into a tirade, so sudden an eruption in an otherwise serene moment, it was shocking as if an earthquake had trembled the foundation of a cathedral, crack its centuries-old frescoes, unexpected, unpredicted and not at all proportional to the provocation. Now women will disagree and men affirm these truths, but it is an issue of control and Julian saw that it was the price he paid for being married to one woman and living with another. In short order, over the course of several months, Julian learned to avoid the landmines that Isabelle laid each day on the path in front of him and in the meadows that surrounded him. She left only the minutest traces, just enough to be a warning to the wary and he was very wary. In this way, she guided his steps, directing like a puppeteer the subtle path of his behavior toward a place he was usually unfamiliar with. His only real choice, within certain bounds, was to leave her, but he never doubted for a moment that Isabelle was a doomsday machine, that if she could not have him, no one could. The same had been true of Valerie, was still true. Perhaps it was something within himself that fostered this behavior. It was too late to ponder that.

He began to think that it was the combination of passion and danger that appealed to him and also the knowledge that he would ultimately have the last word or, in his women's case, perform the last act. Until then, Isabelle trod the path she so carefully laid out for him, took the best of what was offered and made a pretense of being in the lead. Julian had proceeded through life as most people do, cognizant of the me and the not-me. He knew what he knew, he knew what he felt and he was aware of his emotional and physical needs. The other billions of people on the planet were players on his stage, they entered on or off cue and then exited. He related to them in a hundred, sometimes a thousand different ways but they were all not-me s. Isabelle changed all this. He was suddenly aware of her as someone different, separate and apart from the other not-me s and part of his own consciousness. He could see glimpses of the world as she saw it as if he were inside her skull looking out the portholes of her brain at the submerged world she swam through. On occasion, he could see himself swimming by with certain frailties and defects he did not recognize simply from gazing in a mirror. He really did not believe he possessed them, except by way of assuming a certain false modesty. He would say things such as, "I am not adept at helping people resolve their personal problems," when, in fact, he was quite good at it, as all manipulative people are even if their motives are impure or self-serving. Of course, once he was aware that one not-me, Isabelle, had a universe within her brain, he realized that all not-me s had their own universes limited by their intellect, it is true, but with perceptions tinged with the stain of experience, prejudice and what most people like to call spirituality but which Julian perceived as superstition. Isabelle, therefore, enabled him through his love for her to use other people as footholds in the climb to the top and in that regard he was already not only well equipped, but driven.

Sixty~Two

62 Julian's razor caressed Valerie's neck. Blood poured out like water over a small dam in a country river. She gasped for breath and it entered her lungs through the slit in her throat which emitted a red vapor as she exhaled. Her eyes were wide and glassy, the green which Julian thought so perfect with her dark hair had a yellow cast. This was not a matter he took lightly and he had pondered its necessity for some time so that while to the reader it may seem that something is not in the right order or perhaps this is all a non sequitur in the nature of modernistic novels, but be assured that Valerie's demise was as certain as a sunrise and as sudden as a lightning bolt. Julian remembered the horses.

Soon after their first tryst, although it might have been later, he had a poor memory for what he called personal details, he took a four day weekend with Valerie and traveled to Ranceau a small town noted as a county seat in French horse country, blue grass, rolling hills, white fences and chateau's with stables instead of wineries. Valerie owned a horse, a gelding, named Marat after the assassinated leader of one of the myriad ephemeral governments of the French Revolution. The horse was beautiful, a nearly black thoroughbred with only one eye, having had the other removed some years earlier because of a tumor growing behind it. She loved it all the more and had accumulated an array of ribbons in equipage despite the horse's inability to see in three dimensions. Such was her dedication to the animal, that she persevered with his training and even refused an eye patch or a glass eye despite Marat's somewhat shocking appearance. Small clods of dust and bits of hay would accumulate in the empty socket, but Valerie would gently remove them and even blow out the dust, pursing her lips in a most affectionate way. Julian had never been close to a horse and he was immediately awed by its size and power, feeling both admiration and fear when in its proximity. This was only one of her father's many gifts to her.

Valerie's father, Martin Galle, paid all her bills and gave her a generous stipend so that, relatively speaking, Valerie lived a genteel lifestyle with no real need to have ambition. Martin had already put much of his money in trust for her and sooner or later it would all be hers. She mistakenly believed that the way to Julian's heart was to buy him things and over the three years of their relationship, she showered him with the best clothing, shoes and jewelry. While he was thankful, it did not make him love her for only a fool or an old man would believe that love can be purchased. Now many of you have calculated the number of errors in this philosophy, remembering aunts and uncles and even parents, sometimes friends, who married for money and ended up in love. Such stories are the logic of the illogical and an easy way to explain the unexplainable. So our myths make positive that which we know to be negative. Insist, if you will, that Uncle Fredo was loved by Aunt Cecelia not because of his money, as Mama told you, but in spite of it. She adored his yellowed toenails, foul breath and frayed cuffs. She loved the way he belched after eating and snored like a hellhound after drinking wine. His millions meant nothing, just a little security. The power of such myths still convinces.

Julian enjoyed the way Valerie loved him. He would awaken at night when he was with her and she would be staring at him in the darkness. When asked what was wrong, she would say something like, "I love to watch you sleep." Little things he did fascinated her or rather fascinated her passion. Whatever sexual practices he engaged in were acceptable. She said neither that he was good nor bad in bed; a man's perfect woman for no judgment is so painful or difficult than to be judged by one's prowess in the sack. The Prince of Delusion reigns over every man's erection especially when his subject is silent, for silence even in the law is tantamount to approval. Too much praise by a woman will make any man suspect he is the subject of lies.

Sixty~Three

63 Valerie bought Julian his first painting, an autumn land-scape with a barren hillside, distant lavender mountains, a large oak tree with orange foliage and a deer walking away beneath it, but with its head turned about as if startled by the viewer. She had purchased it for him because he admired it and he should have known better for she made every effort to get him whatever he wanted, not as some obsessive gesture but as a way of loving him, or showing him her love, he could not say which. At first, all the material indulgences thrilled him. He had always been a giver and would measure the breath of his feelings by what he gave or wanted to give. After a time, though, Valerie's gifts took on the air of something sinister.

She had purchased the painting from an American expatriot who owned a gallery in Rouen. The third Saturday evening of every month, he held an auction of artwork, objects and furniture. Julian made it a habit never to miss the auctions because Gerard Schuster, the auctioneer, was more a showman than a typically reserved Frenchman with a gavel. Many thought him obnoxious but he could sell fire in hell. Gerard's flaw, though, was that he sold a great many forgeries, although he always warned Julian, to whom he took a great liking, to avoid certain pictures that were "not right" for his collection. His methods were much simpler than one would think. He would find a nice painting unsigned, but old, at a flea market, then simply add a distinguished signature or, if necessary, obliterate an unvaluable one and replace it with one with caché. Indirectly, he taught Julian that a signed name meant nothing except to people who knew the price of everything and the value of nothing. A real connoisseur would never be fooled by a Schuster forgery because people who knew art were rarely if ever mislead by a signature. The nouveau riche, ever hungry for the artifacts of prestige, bought signatures and were therefore Gerard's easy prey. Eventually, the Prefecture of the Rouen police received a complaint from a German tourist who purchased a Monet drawing from Gerard. He had purchased it and then brought it to an expert who declared it to be a fake. Gerard would not refund the irate man his money and while the police could not care less about a Frenchman duping a German, it was another matter for an American to do it on French soil. They raided Schuster's auction gallery early one Saturday evening with over a hundred bidders seated and ready to purchase. The police removed nearly half of the artwork as "counterfeit" as the French called it. Gerard turned to the assemblage and said, "Well, you need have no doubts about what is left." Ten days later he was arrested.

Julian visited him once in jail just after his conviction and he told Julian that prison life was not so bad, but was made less tolerable by visits from old friends that reminded him of his days of freedom and skullduggery. Julian promised not to return. Valerie said Gerard had got what he deserved. Julian replied that if that was so, everyone else in the world was fortunate that they did not also.

After time and with the support of Valerie, Julian informally separated from Daria although he frequently stayed with her. Their marriage had settled into an unpleasant routine like strangers living together and while Julian never doubted that Daria loved him, whatever that meant, he felt that she did not respect him. The routines of daily life, day in and day out transformed intimacy into familiarity and while some couples flourish in this, and Daria was half of such a couple, Julian detested it. He could neither have sex with her nor tolerate her frequent flippancies. In former times, he had found both enchanting. Julian rarely considered divorce as a viable option. In this, he was still somewhat old-fashioned and he was also concerned that the stigma of divorce could harm his chances at whatever profession he was heading toward.

Valerie was the opposite of Daria. Hers and Julian's relationship was at the polar extreme from his marriage. Valerie was obsessively in love with Julian and it was the kind of worship that Julian reveled in subconsciously, although he might have openly admitted it, had he needed to. When he first met Valerie as a student in his class, she had been engaged to a

German student from Bonn, a young man named Franz who was studying engineering. Like she, he was from a wealthy Jewish family and he looked forward with love and anticipation to his marriage to the comely wealthy Valerie Galle. This suited Julian perfectly because he had no designs on a permanent future with Valerie; she was simply a repast from his unhappy marriage and he told her on several occasions to maintain her betrothal to Franz, that Julian was a married man and they had no future together. Of course, Valerie could no more live Julian's lie than she could have invented her own, nor did she ever doubt she would marry Julian one day. In a fortnight, she had told Franz everything, or enough. He took it stoically and asked only that he would like to meet Julian which Valerie agreed to after he promised that no scene would be made. Whether it was her individual naiveté or a certain type of feminine stupidity, Valerie saw no harm in such a meeting and even thought it beneficial in terminating once and for all her obviously unsatisfactory relationship with Franz. She also sought masculine approval of her new relationship with Julian although only another woman could explain the rationale of seeking approval for a new lover from an old one. She certainly could not ask her father.

Valerie thought it best not to tell Julian of the planned meeting which is an indication that somewhere in her vapid thought process, there was a small stone of sensibility for, if it was not problematic in concept, why would she refrain from its divulgence? The conflicting logic created no problem for her, however, and she arranged to meet Julian on a crisp autumn day at a café near the Bois Du Vincennes, southeast of the city and abutting a large woods that covered the rolling foothills in the distance. The sun was setting and the air was chill but calm. Julian and Valerie spoke of amorphous plans and small boring niceties until she started fidgeting with her teaspoon. It was then he realized, as Franz approached, that something was afoot. Franz introduced himself before Valerie could say a word and pulled a chair over from another table as if he were meeting an old, dear friend. He had a duffel bag with him which appeared to contain a tennis racquet. Julian shot a glance at Valerie almost immediately and set her on a course of understanding the masculine mindset. She felt trepidation for the first time since she had concocted the inane scheme. Julian was resolved not to make a fuss of any sort and he was also acutely aware of Franz's superior height and size.

Lights flickered on across the bridge to the city and the moon, oblique, rose slowly over the foothills. Franz mentioned that he had played squash that afternoon and was a bit stiff in the legs. He suggested that Julian and he should go for a walk and Julian immediately felt that violence was in the offing but somehow he did not respond in the negative and saw it as an opportunity to prove himself to himself. This may sound odd in someone so obviously confident and self-assured but appearances can belie reality and Julian often felt he was less a man than he could have or should have been. It was awkward to tell Valerie to go home, that the two men wanted to speak alone, but he hailed a cab and she got in looking at them as if they were knights out to do battle for her hand even though both of them had already had considerably more of her person as well.

Julian raised his hand in farewell and she waved to the two men from the cab as it departed with a belch of exhaust fumes.

The two men walked toward the woods taking a cinder-covered foot-path that was frequented in the light of day by bicyclists but in the evening was as, as you might expect, deserted. Franz spoke of how his family had taken to Valerie and how they had planned to move to Bonn after the wedding where he would work for his father at the family engineering firm. Julian did not know how to respond but he knew better than to argue and simply spoke of the fickleness of women and how he had implored Valerie not to break off the relationship with Franz but no sooner had these sentences escaped his lips that he realized its negative implications. He was, in fact, suggesting that Valerie marry Franz and sleep with Julian on the side, a preposterous theory to most people except Julian, and especially to a bourgeois Teuton like Franz. Julian tried to think of something other than an apology to say by way of retracting his words but the damage was done. Instead, he started to apologize for his relationship with Valerie and was about to tell Franz he could have her, that he did not know she was engaged. But before he could get it all out he felt a sharp pain in the back of his neck, the results of Franz landing a furious blow with two clasped fists that sent Julian sprawling forward. For a moment, Julian wanted to laugh at the stupidity of the situation, instinctively picturing himself covered with dirt as he landed on the loamy soil of the woods where wilted bluebells devoid of flowers clustered as they browned and withered in the waning days of the season.

Julian landed face first into the dirt and, as he was about to rise, another blow, more a thud, sent him reeling to the brink of unconsciousness. Apparently, Franz did not have a squash racquet in his valise, but a small shovel and it made contact with the back of Julian's skull with a metallic clunk. Franz apparently had planned this quite well. Julian pretended to be unconscious for fear of being beaten further and quickly appraising the situation as hopeless. Julian was one of those rare beings who can think most clearly when in extreme circumstances, which this was, and not relying on instinct. His reflexes, if he were an average human, would have been to struggle and in struggling would have brought more blows from the fanatic Franz most assuredly.

Julian could hear Franz's breathing which had been heavy and wheezing, slow as he stood and watched Julian for any signs of life. Deep darkness had descended and but for the moonlight eaten by the trees, they might have been at the bottom of a mineshaft. Julian heard Franz move off a few paces deeper into the woods from the path, but it was not more than nine or ten feet from where Julian lay face down. If he attempted to get up, Franz would be on him in a second so he continued to play dead.

In about ten minutes, Franz came back to Julian and picking him up by his ankles, dragged him to where Franz had dug a shallow pit. He pushed Julian into it, still face down. Julian guessed it was no more than two feet deep, the lazy prick, he thought. Franz picked up the shovel and commenced to burying Julian who timed the rhythmic shoveling so that he could lift his body ever so slightly to keep some air space between his upper torso and his face. He could feel the damp and heavy clods hitting his back like soggy punches, the crumbling soil readily breaking apart as it hit him. Julian began to panic, not in a claustrophobic fit which most people would certainly have succumbed to, but in a battle with his instincts to not move as he was being buried alive. He thought of Jack London's Martin Eden, committing suicide by slipping overboard in the middle of the Pacific at night to drown himself, how Martin had to swim so deep that his bodies instinct to swim back to the surface would be defeated. Julian tried to focus and reconstruct London's paragraphs in his mind. As Martin Eden finally drowned in Julian's mind, the thuds of the soil ceased and Julian knew Franz had finished. Still, he could not move for fear Franz might sit a moment so Julian counted, first to a hundred, then two hundred. Finally he squirmed and by rocking back and forth, side to side, he managed to get his knees under him and like a madman doing a final push-up after a thousand push-ups, heaved his body upward. He felt the earth yielding to his pushes, the weight of the soil so great that for a moment he thought he was done for. He clawed out with his hands and could feel the air on them as he reached the surface. Franz was gone. With a final wriggle of his upper body Julian sat upright in his own grave looking up at an orange moon and listening to two nightwings banter in the trees. He laughed, first to himself and then out loud as he told death to go fuck itself.

Julian stood and dusted himself off realizing he must look terrible but it was already quite late and it would be easy to get home without running into anyone he knew. He thought about what Franz would do next and was certain he wouldn't see Valerie who would be full of questions that had no good answers. On the other hand, Franz was unbalanced and likely to do anything. It even occurred to Julian that she might be next on his list. But, if she was, there was nothing Julian could do and if there was, he wouldn't do it anyway. This was all her doing and he was in no mood to save her from the avenging, albeit simplistic-minded Franz.

Julian stopped in at a bar a few blocks from home, one of his regular haunts and asked Jules, the bartender to use the phone. Bartenders are accustomed to seeing and hearing many things and while there were about a dozen patrons, no one said anything as Julian entered and dialed Valerie. She inquired how the meeting went and Julian said it was all right. Franz was an interesting person and that he was sorry he had interfered in his relationship with Valerie. When she started to ask more questions, Julian assured himself that she knew nothing. He was somewhat disappointed she was still alive. Then he pretended the phone was not working and hung up.

He got home and Daria was already asleep snoring the way she did when she had taken a pill. He thanked the heavens for small favors and showered. He slipped into bed plotting his next move. Surely, Franz had returned to Bonn and Julian would be on the first train to Bonn in the morning.

65 The train arrived at the Station Otto Von Bismarck at half past twelve midnight and Julian alighted on the platform, made his way to the taxi stand and took a cab to the Oberstrausser Hotel, a small inn recommended by the driver.

By three the next afternoon, Julian had tracked Franz down to his family's house about a mile from the hotel and stood across the street in the shadow of some tall shrubs, watching and waiting. An hour later, Franz emerged with his mother who kissed her son and watched him descend the stairs to the street. Julian followed as Franz made his way to the market district, a busy throng of vendors and house servants, Fraus and Frauleins and Herrs in every direction. Franz stopped at a book kiosk and was leafing through a magazine when Julian positioned himself across the street so that when Franz raised his eyes he would see Julian standing there. This is exactly what happened and Julian delighted in the expression that crept across Franz's face like blood soaking into a sheet. He went pale, not like he had seen a ghost but because he had seen a ghost. As Julian stared at him across the crowd an omnibus went by between them and as it passed, Julian ducked out of sight behind the tent of a gypsy fortune-teller. Julian was wearing a hooded mackinaw and he lifted the hood and strolled out glancing only sideways at where Franz stood transfixed in his Teutonic superstition imagining that it was either his conscience or the Law of Retribution which had begun his trial for the murder of Julian Corona.

Over the next three days, Julian followed Franz and made similar appearances. In one instance, Franz ran toward Julian who jumped into a waiting taxi that Franz could not see. Julian had poured out a jar of pig's blood onto the sidewalk where he had been standing. Franz's worst fears materialized and in another two days with no sleep, unable to eat and ignoring his mother's entreaties to see a physician, he hiked to the Ubervolkescher, a small cliff overlooking the Danube. With Julian follow-ing but out-of-sight, he climbed a narrow stairway to the overlook.

Two couples were there, the place being a favorite of young lovers. Franz noticed no one, not even the beautiful Fraulein that watched him climb the rock wall, hold out his arms, pause and jump to the rocks some ten stories below. One girl fainted as they looked over the edge and saw the handsome Franz sprawled like a stepped-on daddy long-legs, limbs con-torted, face smashed and blood spattering the white granite boulders where, legend had it, the Valkyries took flight for Valhalla after the death of Lohengrin. Julian walked up the steps and looked over the edge and began to hum to himself Wagner's overture to Taunhausser as he descend-ed the stairs as the beginning of his journey back to Paris.

Within a week, Julian had more or less decided to move to Milan to enter the College of Law there. When he told Daria, she adopted one of those "you must be insane" looks on her face and she suggested that she go back to the States for a time while he sorted out which path his life would take. Julian assumed incorrectly that she had taken a lover and this was her way of ridding herself of both of them while time did its work of easing the sting of infidelity. Julian certainly did not object. Perhaps he should have made more of a show of it but it was difficult for him to pretend an emotion he did not feel. He may have been an adept liar, an obfuscator par excellence, but the soothing words or the pleasing phrase were too difficult to pull out of the sack of his emotions with the hand of sincerity. When he needed them or, more appropriately, when someone else needed them, he would make the attempt, but in his mind, he always failed.

When the day arrived for Daria and Robert to depart from the Port of Marseille, he waved at both of them from the dock the way he had seen in motion pictures. The line of waving arms on the rails of the ship remind-ed him of the legs of a millipede, a thousand brown appendages in a curl-ing wave of motion propelling a senseless body through the mud and filth of a dark, dank corner of the cellar. The ship gave a blast on its airhorn, the basso sound vibrating Julian's ribs like a catarrh, the early sign of the plague. He coughed, reflexively covering his mouth with one hand, still waving mechanically with the other. Daria, looking at a distance, started to weep as she interpreted his motion as tears, even sobs, making her doubt her own intuitions about Julian. Surely, the weeping at the departure was for her and even for Robert whose hand she held even tighter. Yes, Julian did love her. She would return soon enough, as soon as he was in Milan in a suitable residence. If he wanted to become a lawyer, why should she object? She waved at him a little more frantically as if to say, I know you love me, and I love you. I will give you the space and time you need. Forgive me for not understanding and seeing you for who you really are. Julian had already turned and headed back to his car. Valerie was waiting for him and he couldn't wait to see the look on her face when he told her he would live with her for a while. It was the beginning and the end of her life. Perhaps now you will see and understand the glint of Julian's razor, catching the moonlight in Valerie's flat in Paris as it hung for a moment in the air over her sleeping form. Feel Julian's urgency as he wrapped her bloody body in the sheets of their bed and made his way to the one of the many nameless canals that led to the Seine where her body was dropped as so many had been throughout France's tortured history.

Sixty~Six

66 In Milan, the College of Law was on the Via Macchiarola where a huge marble statue of St. Veronica gazed from the small park across the way at the school's grand doors. Of course, she was gazing with empty eye sockets and her two eyeballs, stylized for the squeamish, were in a plate in her hand like two hard-boiled quail's eggs. The Italians would never settle for a blindfold to make justice blind. Any idiot would know that if one wrinkled one's nose enough under a blindfold a few times, one could see out, a little peek. No, Italians expected blindness and justice to be absolute.

Julian had difficulty his first year. His Italian improved immensely so that it was no longer an impediment and he developed a beautiful tonal accent that brought out the inherent musicality of the language. His troubles with law stemmed from his training in the study of literature where interpretation was multileveled and creative originality was highly valued. In law school, students were expected to reorganize their thought patterns so that everyone drew the same conclusions for a particular law problem and arrived at the same answer, much like spectators at a tennis match follow the ball in play with each of their heads turning back and forth, left to right in perfect unison. Julian, at first, sought a unique solution, an interpretation that was at odds with the court's findings or, worse yet. in disagreement with the professor's. It took the first year of struggling with his literary predisposition to become a parrot and, on examinations, to regurgitate the expected answer. Over the following two years, the original creative side of Julian's mentality was stored away in a closet in his brain and the logic of the law replaced it at the center of his analytical lobes.

He quickly rose to the top of his class and the charms that made his prior successes with people in the past worked well, perhaps better within the lofty atmosphere of the school of law which was, after all, populated by the elite of Italy or, at least, the children of the elite. There were no women permitted so that a rough but sophisticated masculinity prevailed, a goal-oriented phalanx of men that could not be sidetracked by a tight blouse or a hiked skirt sitting nearby. Law students were attractive to women ever on the prowl for alpha males with earning potential, but the students were too weighed down by the compulsion to succeed in so competitive an environment. Those who could not resist feminine temptation soon discovered that their performance lagged and, as a general rule, nearly half of all first year students were booted out, losing their futures and the women they had sacrificed them for in the process.

Isabelle, during this time, acted the dutiful wife to Julian even though he still had a real wife in America who visited on occasion when he would meet her at a hotel, the story being that he lived in a dormitory where women were prohibited. Daria was simple-minded enough to accept this but kept inquiring when she and Robert could take quarters in Milan after Julian graduated. He would give her vague, duplicitous answers about the uncertainty of where he would practice law. She would return to America more or less content that their informal separation would simply dissolve. Why she clung to him he could not fathom, but cling she did. During the visits Isabelle would sulk and sink into moods of bleak depression where she was forced to confront the monster that lived with her and Julian but which they had mostly confined to the sub-basement of their relationship. When it did appear, it filled her with terror and loathing which was unabated. One day, she went to the hotel where Julian and Daria were staying, coerced the room number out of the desk clerk and left a small ring Julian had given her as a Christmas gift just under the door of the room. When Daria noticed it as she and Julian returned from lunch, it lead to all manner of speculation as to how it got there, Julian feigning ignorance but adding his own twist to the stories that Daria concocted like O. Henry. Daria turned it into the concierge as a lost and found. While she was doing that, Julian phoned Isabelle and a brief intense argument ensued abruptly cut short by Daria's return. Nothing further was said by any of them but the concierge reported to Daria that a woman appeared later that evening and claimed the ring. The following day while Julian and Daria were eating lunch again, Julian thought he saw Isabelle across the street behind a phone booth. When he looked a second time, she, or someone very similar in appearance to her, was gone.

For two weeks after Daria's departure and Julian's return, Isabelle was taciturn, ignoring his questions acting like she was deep in thought, which she might have been and listening to moody music on the radio or records on the phonograph which rhythmically hissed and clicked as the needled followed the groove and bumped and wobbled as it ran over dust particles or through scratches. She would only come out of it when Julian, usually in the early morning hours, made love to her, penetrating her while she slept although both of them knew she was quite awake as soon as he put a drop of saliva on his erection. This reaffirmed Julian's simplistic theory that every woman's problems could be solved by a good session of sex.

It was in his third year of his legal studies, that Julian formed a solid friendship with Giorgio De Vecchi, a son of Césare De Vecchi, Mussolini's Minister of Education.

Within the confines of the law school, virtually every student knew every other. Of necessity and by tradition, groups of students in twos or threes studied together. Thus they were simultaneously working with people who were their competitors. Initially, when Julian and Giorgio met in the first year in a criminal law class, they didn't get along. Giorgio was politically connected and financially very well off. To Julian he was a snob, self-important and arrogant. Julian, as an Italian-American, was seen by Giorgio as an enemy alien mainly because the power elite could very early foresee that the United States would be the giant stumbling block to Fascist world domination. Over the course of time, though, Julian became of interest to Giorgio who, after meeting and dining with Il Duce in the company of his father, came to see the dictator as a peasant with intellect but no education, no experience in government and a power base not unlike a Mafia chieftain. By the end of the second year, Giorgio had warmed to Julian and Julian began to enjoy observing the real Giorgio as the blocks of his façade began to crumble and a sensitive, generous intelligent man was revealed beneath. Both shared an interest in good living, fine food and wine and beautiful women.

Giorgio was engaged to the daughter of a political comrade of Mussolini but she was an overweight Calabrese and the engagement was entered almost at gunpoint when his father hinted and then demanded that Giorgio "marry the bitch" or everyone's world could crumble overnight. What his father had tried to accomplish by the union and how his fiancée's father could help were never made clear, like most things in a Fascist regime.

Giorgio rather admired Julian's ability to blend in with Italian society, his easy command of the language and, most interestingly, his maintaining a French woman as a mistress who was married to a Dutchman and having an American wife. While Julian saw his life as chaos when he thought about it, usually in the early morning hours when he would awaken and start to self-analyze, Giorgio saw as the precepts of Machiavelli put to good use in the home.

Giorgio's confident, magnanimous manner dissolved one night three weeks after the start of the third and final year of law school. It was a Monday and Julian and Isabelle were sitting on the small balcony of their apartment talking about Spain and other pleasant frivolities, enjoying a lush red wine and a mild provolone, when there was a knock on the door. It was Giorgio who, despite his fine linen jacket and starched shirt and silk necktie, had a stark look in his eye and a three day's growth of beard. He made an attempt at seeming at ease but clearly he was not. He asked Julian if he might walk with him a moment, he had something to discuss and would Isabelle mind? Isabelle minded anyone who took up Julian's time but urgency was in the air that Giorgio exhaled and she smilingly gave her consent and told Julian she would wait up for him. He kissed her and the two students left and headed north to a café they frequented a few blocks from the law school.

Anxiety crept up Julian's spine. This was the first time he had ever seen Giorgio off-balance and without his carefully groomed, suave demeanor. He hoped that it was not some political upheaval that would mean the loss of Giorgio's father's power and position which might cause Julian to lose not only a friend, whom he could replace, but a friend in high places, whom he could not.

It was a clear, cool night and a few stars were visible high above the grimy walls of the buildings, their light waging an ineffective war against Milan's smog and the light of the city reflected in its yellowish haze. When the air was still, the smells of industrial smoke, especially in a humid summer were almost overwhelming but it was early autumn, a breeze blew in from the Alps and most of the gases that exuded from Milan's industrial complex had ceased for the night. Unlike the Germans and the Americans, the Italians shut things down to allow their workers the luxury of a good dinner and time with their women.

Giorgio said he did not want to sit, but preferred to walk and talk and Julian certainly did not object. Giorgio related the following story as if it were a closing argument in a capital case which, in some respects, it might have turned out to be. He spoke levelly and with careful measure, his dignified composure regained by his proximity to Julian who provided an intelligent, willing, non-judgmental ear:

"I am thankful to God for your friendship, Julian and you know it is difficult for a true Fascist to thank God for anything. But, then again, I am no true Fascist, just one along for the ride as so many Italians are. You know my stepmother, Angelica; I think you met her last July or it might have been June. She's younger than I am so calling her a stepmother is using a title which might be accurate genealogically but absurd in practice. I simply call her 'Angelica' as my father asked me to do. I am also certain your eyes work very well for despite your studying literature and now the law, I've never known you to wear spectacles, so you have noticed how beautiful Angelica is. You needn't respond. Now, you think I'm going to tell you how I yearned for her and other such nonsense. But it is not true.

She is my father's wife and the very thought of her sexuality is repugnant to me. In most ways I treated her like a sister and if I happened to see her in an immodest moment which is bound to occur in a home where every family member lives, I averted my gaze, not out of prudery, mind you, but out of respect and a little repugnance for only a dyed-in-the-wool pervert would ogle his sister.

"I don't think I ever told you that my father owns some residential properties in the city, two or three apartment buildings, nothing fancy, and two townhouses. One of them is quite close to the law college on Via Caravaggio. Well, that one was recently vacated by a professor who rented it, Dr. Rispoto. I think you remember him. He taught family law. Of course you remember him; he was your teacher. Well, he's a Jew and lost his job because of it, shame on us all but that is the Fascists for you. So he left the house and my father wanted to fix it up so that I might take it and get out from underfoot, as he says, which I would very much like. He told my stepmother to do the spiffing-up, nothing too much, new paint, some new furniture, update the kitchen, although I don't know why; I can't even boil an egg. He told me to help her and tell her what colors I liked and so on and so forth.

"Angelica and I met at the house at almost six last night. I was catching up on some studying and spent most of the day in the library. I stopped work in time and, as planned, met her there. She had brought a briefcase along with paint chips and fabric swatches and some pictures from decorating journals of various pieces of furniture. She had all sorts of ideas and was quite animated about it and I simply acquiesced to everything she said realizing that she had a vision of what the place would look like and I cared not a whit so long as it was comfortable.

"We sat at the dining table where she laid out all her this s and that s and found the bottle of cognac Professor Rispoto left behind—I don't think he was in a mood to pack up luxuries like cognac—and without asking, poured us both a glass. I was quite fatigued from the long day sitting and reading in one of those damned stiff-backed chairs and the drink did me good. So did the second one she poured. As I sat and started to feel the warmth of the cognac seep through my body, she walked about the room indicating here and there where she thought a nice chair would be placed so I could read by the window and while I was looking at the swatches she laid out on the table in front of me, she came up from behind, put her arms around me and kissed me on my neck and ear. I should have gotten up right then and there but I didn't. I didn't. I let her continue as if I didn't notice her. She put her hand in my shirt and caressed my chest as she kissed my ear with her tongue. She reached down and through my pants grabbed my prick, which was already standing more at attention than Mussolini when Hitler walks into the room. I turned and kissed her as she stroked me. Well, I'm giving you unimportant details because I don't want you to think that any of it was my idea. It wasn't. You know me; Julian, and you can believe me. I have no reason to lie.

"Anyway, without going into anymore lurid details, I took her into old Professor Rispoto's bedroom and fucked her 'til midnight. We both fell asleep and I didn't awaken 'til nearly 4:00 a.m. That is when I truly realized the import of what I had done and my first thought was to run to some other country and hide. I was distraught. I woke her up and told her we needed to leave, that my father would be worried about us without even thinking that he would be more concerned that his wife had been out all night and had not returned and he had probably notified the police already.

"She laughed and said she told him that she would be visiting her aunt in Venista, you know that little shitty town twenty miles north and that she would spend the night with her. Then it dawned on me, idiot that I am, that she had planned all this. Suddenly my life was upside-down. I may have thought of her as a sister, if not my father's wife, but she was not reciprocating. I was humiliated, embarrassed and ashamed. I might have been her victim, I told myself this, but I was a willing victim. I had choices and I had made the wrong ones. My life was over as far as I was concerned. There was no way I could go home and face my father and live under the same roof with him and her even for another night.

"I started to get dressed. She got out of bed came over to me naked and said not to worry. She would tell no one and we could meet at this house whenever we felt like it. I was repulsed, but she tried to put her arms around my neck to kiss me and I shoved her away from me very hard. She fell backwards and hit her head on the dresser. She was unconscious. I tried to revive her but couldn't. I put her on the bed and tried everything but she was out cold although still breathing. I couldn't call a doctor or the police or anyone. How could I explain it? Impossible! So I stayed there all morning, afternoon and evening with her. She's still alive Julian but I had nowhere to turn so I come to you. Forgive me giving you this problem, but you are my friend. What should I do? God help me, what should I do?"

The clock in the grand tower of the Piazza Santo CatÛlico sounded ten or eleven. Julian started to count too late and he hadn't put on his wristwatch before he left. He asked Giorgio for the address of the house and told him to take a taxi there, that he had to go home first and would meet him there as soon as he could, which wouldn't be more than forty-five minutes. Giorgio nodded in silent assent. He seemed deflated and disheveled again as if in relating the events of the past twenty-four hours he had relived them. Julian put his hand on his shoulder and said calmingly, not to worry; it could all be solved. Giorgio nodded again and looked into Julian's face like a convicted felon before the hanging judge. Julian knew at that moment as he looked into Giorgio's bloodshot eyes, that he owned him.

Sixty~Eight

Julian took his time walking back to his flat so that he could think. There seemed to be only one viable option and no matter what other things he considered, none of them left Giorgio intact and unscathed and he needed him in that condition. He knew that after graduation, he had no definite plans and Giorgio was destined to a seat on the High Court in Rome as another Mussolini puppet, but with enormous autonomous powers. Yes, he owned Giorgio tonight but tomorrow was another matter and he had to have him so indebted that Julian could name his price.

He walked past a quaint old chapel dedicated to St. Jude, the patron saint of lost causes and stopped for a moment, said good evening to the mottled granite statue of the beleaguered saint out front, squeezed its nose, and said, "Thanks, but I won't be needing you tonight."

When Julian arrived at the flat, Isabelle was sound asleep sitting up in bed, propped by a pillow with an open book on her lap and her mouth slightly open. He gently woke her and said he and Giorgio were going to pull an "all-nighter" to prepare for a presentation Giorgio had to make the following day on the new Fascist Constitution. She lay down under the thin covers and he kissed her turning off the light.

"Giorgio is in trouble isn't he?" she asked in the dark. Julian said no, unless Professor Cantoro was considered trouble and he said he supposed the old fart was trouble being the most Fascist of all the Fascists he knew.

"You're lying, but it's ok," she said. "Just don't get involved, please." With that she turned over on her side in her usual sleeping position.

Julian went into the parlor, pocketed his straight razor which he retrieved from his dresser drawer, got the keys to the car and within an hour of his leaving Giorgio, pulled up a block away from Giorgio's home.

He turned off the lights and sat for a moment to make sure no one was about; the street was empty. He got the large picnic blanket out of the trunk and walked the rest of the way, humming "Yankee Doodle Dandy."

He walked up the stone steps of the beautiful if neglected Beaux Arts structure, its once lovely door garden overgrown with ivy and tangled weeds. The door opened before he knocked. Giorgio was obviously watching for him from the parlor window.

"She's still breathing," he said. "What are you going to do?"

Julian said that there was only one thing to do and if he expected any more help from Julian he had better just go along.

"I need to know, Julian," he said. Julian asked if he had plans of his own and when Giorgio said he didn't, Julian told him to take him to her.

They climbed the thickly-carpeted stairs in the dark, the banister curving like a python from its curled tail in the foyer to its head on the second story carved in the shape of a cherub. The door to the chamber was closed. They opened it on its creaky hinges and entered. There was Angelica De Vecchi, naked under a sheet, the room lit by the weak glow of the street lamp across the way.

Julian put his ear to her mouth and said, yes, she was still breathing. He rolled her over and climbed onto the bed upright on his knees and reached down, rolled her back face up into his lap and then hoisted her up by her armpits so that the back of her head was level with his chest, her breasts swinging about as he jostled her to a position directly in front of him as if to give her some form of artificial respiration.

"I tried that, Julian," Giorgio whispered as if a normal voice could rouse her. "It didn't work."

Julian looked at Giorgio as he held Angelica and said, "I don't think so." With that, he quickly put his left arm under her chin and his right arm across the top of her head and with a sudden jerk, snapped her neck, the crunch of bone sounding like a gunshot to Giorgio whose nerves were frayed to the breaking point. A small dribble of vomit fell from her lips onto her chest and Julian's hands.

"My God, Julian, what did you do?"

"I just solved your problem, friend. Now help me load her into that blanket I brought."

Giorgio stood still as Julian pushed the body aside, a whoosh of gurgling air escaping from her open mouth as he did so. Julian picked up the picnic blanket, laid it on the floor and he instructed Giorgio to pick up her feet. The two of them lifted her off the bed and onto the blanket, Julian letting go of the heavy end a little too quickly making her head thud on the carpeted floor like a dropped coconut.

Julian told Giorgio to dress her. He asked if he had to, but Julian just looked at him as if to say, "You'd better." Her garments were strewn about the room in the order he or she had removed them. Giorgio had a look of either fear or anxiety or disgust or all three as he lifted her legs, putting her panties on. Julian, by way of encouragement, told him to hurry, the sun would be rising soon and they needed to get her out of there while it was still dark. Her jewelry was on the nightstand, a nice Cartier wristwatch and a large, distinctive yellow diamond engagement ring. Giorgio asked if Julian wanted them. At first he took insult as if it were payment for solving the problem, but then realized that it seemed a waste to discard so valuable a cache with the body. Julian told him to hand them over, he would dispose of them for the sake of consistency. Her body needed to be found, but it would be ridiculous for her to have a treasure in jewels on her. No matter the motive in killing her, and Julian had it all worked out, the assassin would never leave so valuable an amount of easily removed property. Julian pocketed the jewelry and told Giorgio to sit down. He did. Julian straddled the corpse, opened her blouse to her bra and, with the straight razor he had unsheathed, carved a small hammer and sickle on her chest. Giorgio realized why he had been told to sit down as the blood drained from his head and he became woozy with the weight of all that had happened.

After he finished, Julian told him that the "Commies" would take the blame for this; blame was all they were good for anyway.

They carried the body to the foyer and Julian opened the door and stepped out to see if anyone was there. The street was still deserted; not a single light burned in any of the houses on the block that he could see. He walked quickly back to the car and with the lights out and the car in second gear the whole way so that it made only a little noise, he pulled up in front of the house, got out and the two of them carried Angelica De Vecchi wrapped in a blanket to the car where they placed her in the trunk, curled up much like Etruscan skeletons found in terra cotta urns. They drove two blocks and only then did Julian turn on the headlights. He stopped at a corner, but the car stalled midway into a right hand turn. It would not start as Julian cursed and pumped his foot on the gas as if he were trying to stomp to death a five-pound cockroach. The lights flickered until they finally went out. Giorgio sank in his seat as Julian told him to get out and push, that the battery had died.

As Giorgio opened the door, a bright light hit Julian in the face reflected from the rearview mirror. It was the police. Two Carabinieri on patrol pulled up behind them and both got out to inquire what was wrong and what were they doing out well after all the bars had closed. They asked for Julian's papers which he had not brought with him but, as he was about to explain, Giorgio spoke up with a command in his voice which was surprising even to Julian. He pulled a small leather folder from his rear pocket with an identification badge in it and his photo on a special pass signed by Il Duce. He was pleasant, but firm. He explained they were law students taking a break from their studies. The police smiled and asked if they could help. Julian responded, asking them for a push so he could jump start his "piece of French junk." Julian got back in the car as did Giorgio and the Carabinieri placed their hands on the trunk lid and pushed the car a hundred feet or so. Julian popped the clutch and the car started with a belch of black smoke and a backfire. With a wave of their hands, the two students rambled off as the officers saluted. There may have been only a hundred people in all of Italy that had credentials that would have elicited such a response. Giorgio was one of them.

They drove a few miles in circles to be certain they were not being followed. Eventually Julian pulled into a service road at the Garibaldi State Park, one of Mussolini's municipal accomplishments. They pulled over to the curb in a dark spot between two lampposts, sat a moment without turning off the engine, then got out. While Giorgio kept guard, Julian struggled with the corpse in the trunk, lifting it out of the blanket and placing it under a tree sitting up as if she had fallen asleep, very much the way Isabelle had been that very night.

They jumped back into the car and Julian pulled away slowly. The car stalled again. Julian uttered a string of obscenities but took a deep breath and told himself not to panic. He asked Giorgio to say a prayer and to apologize to God for being a fucking, atheistic Fascist. Giorgio made the sign of the cross, Julian pressed the starter button and the car jumped to life.

Julian dropped Giorgio off two blocks from his father's house, told him to take a sleeping pill, that they would meet at the college the next day. He instructed him to block the whole thing out of his memory and mind and act the son of an aggrieved father when the murder was discovered. Giorgio thanked him, but Julian asked for what? Giorgio replied, "For the lift."

On the way through the early morning streets of Milan, Julian was glad he didn't need the razor for her neck. The blood would have made a mess.

Sixty~Nine

 Julian sidled into bed next to Isabelle, kissing her on the back of her bare shoulder in her sleep. She roused and asked drowsily, eyes closed, if everything was all right. Julian said it could not be better and fell asleep as the sun rose on the clear, crisp fall day over Milan. In his trouser pocket, draped over the bedroom chair were Angelica's watch and ring, orphans with a mute tale to tell.

Julian didn't wake up until two in the afternoon. He had missed class but was unconcerned. The flat was quiet. He called out for Isabelle but there was no response. She must have gone to the market for something for dinner.

He got into the shower and leaned forward, his hands braced against the cold tiles and let the spray of water hit him full in the face. His mind was still full of the cobwebs of sleep and for a moment he thought the events of the early morning might have been a dream. He had a nagging feeling that Giorgio was not bearing up as well as he, that he might "flip out" as Americans said and do, who knows what. On the other hand, it was not likely that he would bring his and his father's world of power and privilege down upon all of them, which, if the story got to Il Duce, it would certainly do. Mussolini was a whoremonger, without a doubt. He had his own mistress and countless part-timers all over Italy. But he had a public persona of a man of family values and even a breath of scandal that touched too closely to him, would result in that man's punishment no matter how loyal. No, Giorgio may be tortured mentally for a while but he'd get over it; he had to.

He started to soap up and plan out the remainder of the day, needing to get over to the law college to find out what he had missed. He'd have to spend the night at the library again; that was a certainty. He suddenly remembered the ring and the watch. He'd forgotten to toss them in the river.

He rinsed off quickly, toweled and nude and still dripping wet went to the bedroom. The trousers were gone. Isabelle must have hung them up, or worse, taken them to the cleaners. His heart raced as he went to the wardrobe standing in the room like the Grand Inquisitor waiting to hear an explanation that would make no difference. He yanked open the sticky door and the pants were there on a hanger. He hung his head in relief. It was a reprieve from a potential living nightmare. He had pulled them out still on the hanger and went through the pockets. They were empty. He went through them again. Still no jewelry. He reconstructed the events surrounding them. Giorgio told him to take them. He did. He knew that. He was certain. He looked in his shirt pocket; the shirt was in the laundry hamper. Nothing. He even looked in his shoes. Again, nothing. He got down on the floor under the chair he had thrown his pants on. He crawled around naked looking behind the dresser, feeling the old rug with its lightly pungent odor of feet. The jewelry was definitely not there. He knew it had been in his pocket. He had not tossed it. Definitely not. He got to his feet and opened the dresser drawer. His straight razor was there. Yes, he always kept it there. By habit. Damn it. He put the razor back out of habit. But the jewelry, he wasn't used to dealing with something like that. He was no thief. Maybe they had slid out of his pocket in the car, that fucking heap that almost cost him his life. He had to get rid of that thing.

Without shaving, he dressed and hurried down to the Citroën. It sat by the curb, uglier than ever, hunkered under a sidewalk tree like a rhino taking a crap. He opened the door and started searching the floor. There were old candy wrappers, some loose change, dirt and dust and hair and lint, a broken pen, but no jewelry. Isabelle must have found it. Damn. He didn't need this problem on top of everything else. He knew that the devil was in the details and sure enough, this detail which he clumsily overlooked could undo an otherwise perfect situation, perfect, that is, considering he had to snap a woman's neck and carve her up a tad.

Isabelle returned to the flat at about 4:15 with her canvas sack full of groceries, a large loaf of bread protruding like an arm reaching out of a well. She smiled at Julian, asked him how he was and went straight to the kitchen. He followed her and casually inquired what she was going to cook and as she lifted out a bottle of red wine, a tightly wrapped cluster of green onions and the wax paper package that obviously had meat in it, she said, "pasta primavera." The last thing in the bag was a newspaper, La Prensa Milano, which she handed to him telling him to relax with it while she cooked. She kissed him and he said thanks awkwardly, turned and went into the parlor to read the paper and see if last night's events had made it to the press.

He scanned it quickly and found nothing. Then he started going through it again more slowly and methodically, scanning each article's headline. Still there was no mention. He realized that the paper probably was printed too early to pick up a morning police report. He assumed Angelica's body would be found around eight when people headed to work or took an early morning walk in the park. The police would be called. The death would be investigated. The female victim would be discovered to be the wife of a high mucky-muck. The mucky-muck would be told, no doubt, in person. Mussolini's staff in Rome would be informed as to how to proceed, and so on and so forth. There was no way it would make the paper today. It might never.

Julian and Isabelle ate dinner at the table by the balcony and played verbal chess, Julian eating without tasting any of the exquisite food she had prepared nor the wine. Instead, he watched her every movement, her every facial expression and listened for any sounds in her voice which would yield the truth about the Cartier and the yellow diamond. But there was nothing and the evening spread itself against the sky as he helped clear the dishes. They listened to a new recording of Caruso singing "Pagliacci" and Julian wasn't sure who the clown was, the tenor or himself.

The next day the papers were full of the story. As he had planned, the Communists were blamed and the usual roundup of dissidents of every faction found themselves facing the torturers in the dark cellars of Mussolini's Ministry of Justice in the old Castello Borrato.

The school year finished with not a word of the event passing between Julian and Giorgio, anymore than the jewelry was discussed with Isabelle. The friends studied together as usual. Giorgio had lost his arrogance and it was replaced with a sense of stoic dignity befitting a soon-to-be judge in the Ministerial Court in Rome.

Within two years after the somber, Fascist-style graduation ceremony where all the graduates, the faculty and their invited guests had to sit through a two-hour speech by Mussolini's Minister of Culture on rooting out foreign influences, enacting harsher laws for political dissent and every type of crime from littering to serial murder and for creating a "context of laws," as he called it, that would ensure the survival of the new Roman Empire, not allowing the terrible decadence of the old one to eat away at its vitality. Everyone was handed a diploma, heard a short speech from the Valedictorian about the obligations the legal profession had to the State. The entire group moved from the flag-bedecked lawn of the College of Law to small groups chatting and then to private parties at various residences throughout the city.

Giorgio had already secured a beautiful apartment in Rome through his father's auspices. It was a simple matter for him with his connections to obtain a fairly large flat for Julian overlooking a pleasant piazza from the third floor of a Renaissance style building in the center of the city in walking distance to the courthouse. Giorgio had secured Julian a job as his clerk, a position with much more power than it sounds.

Seventy

70 There is little doubt that Duke Edmond Montrose became a favorite of the Fascists in the early days. His peculiar sense of fun, a mixture of ostentation, sexuality and cruelty appealed to the new regime's glorification of machismo and entitlement. The Duke held endless parties which the Fascisti attended exuberantly. Besides the cavorting socially with him, which left the servants of the Villa Franca exhausted for days following the revelry, many of Mussolini's closest advisors had the Duke as their personal physician. Needless to say, his coffers and his pride swelled in equal parts for he was one of the privileged in the new Roman Empire. Secretly, the Duke felt the Fascists to be, as he phrased it, "street swine." Not a one gasped at his disdain and all thought him a fine, albeit unique, fellow and even in the height of the most intense partying, everyone referred to him as either The Duke or Dr. Montrose. Few, if any, knew his first name. Mussolini, a frequent guest at the Villa, but never for one of the infamous fêtes, referred to him as Il Dottore much the way he called the Pope Il Papa, as if the Doctor was The Doctor.

Edmond's interest in the new science of epidemiology allowed him access to information and drugs which were, at the time, considered miraculous. On several occasions, Il Duce required the Duke's medical attention and he was never displeased with the result. Rumors spread throughout Italy of Il Duce's great physician, Il Dottore and Edmond's fortune increased further. In these heady days, he decided to purchase a large villa on the western coast of Italy, about ten miles north of Ostia, twenty miles from Rome in the town of Fiumicino. Within a year, he had converted the eighteenth century villa into a state-of-the-art laboratory where he could focus on and study microorganisms. Mussolini supported the operation by providing state funds for the purchase of equipment from America and England and a staff of ten research assistants, all doctors from various European capitals, although as war began to loom, the Americans, French and British soon departed and Germans, Austrians, and Italians were all that remained. much to everyone's satisfaction as it turned out.

The Duke had developed a notion which had come to him in a dream that bacteria could be a solution to an ages-old problem: in war especially with modern improvements like large bombs and aircraft to deliver them, urban infrastructures were irreparably damaged. No one thought it a good idea that cultural icons such as cathedrals and museums should be blasted to smithereens. Worse yet, power stations, railroad terminals, factories and hospitals were all damaged and the cost of repairs and the time necessary to effectuate them would burden the conquerors for decades after victory. The real targets of warfare were the enemy humans. How could they be killed without also destroying the valuable cities they inhabited? The Duke felt that his minute friends, the bacilli, were the answer. Infest the city with disease and not a single structure would be harmed while all the residents died. It was perfect, but the right bug and the right delivery method had to be discovered. Thus, the Institute of Biological Studies was founded in Fiumicino under the rule of the director, Duke Edmond Montrose, Il Dottore.

The Duke and his staff carried on their experiments to find a deadly virus or bacterium that could survive outside its human host for a long enough period of time. This was a difficult goal as it turned out. Several physicians at the Institute thought it might be better to infect certain loyal soldiers with an illness and have them wander the streets of enemy cities spreading it as much as they could, but it was soon realized that this would require far too many volunteers and there were very few who thought highly enough of Il Duce's politics to sacrifice their lives for it in this manner or any other for that matter. Even the obsessive Germans were not enthusiastic about ritual suicide and the Japanese, they were barely human, as the Duke saw them, too far away, and too obviously different to blend in a city like, say, Paris.

At the Duke's request, Mussolini had an airstrip built near the Institute named ironically after Leonardo DaVinci, not because he was a great artist but because he was a great inventor and innovator. The Duke saw himself very much like a DaVinci of his age. Unknown at the time but by only a few scholars, the great Leonardo had designed a weapon for the delivery of poison gas. The artist of The Last Supper, that most sublime rendering of the quintessential transcendental moment in all Christendom, was, when not depicting the vehicle for the transmigration of souls, creating a method of hastening their departure. The Duke admired DaVinci immensely, calling him that "old queer with a finger in everything including…," well, you may guess.

The airstrip would be used for specially fitted airplanes that could deliver the deadly cargo that the Doctor and the Institute developed. As one might imagine, with no real success at such an endeavor anywhere in recorded history, the experiments were hit and miss. Poison gas as a weapon of war was introduced by the Germans, of course, in World War I. Mussolini prided himself on the newest Italian gas hand grenades, often lobbing a few at great distances at sporting events for the pleasure of the thickheaded mobs who adored him. Gas, however, was not alive. Bacteria were and any explosive that would scatter their putrid substance would kill them, rendering them useless. It was the Duke's fervent desire to develop a delivery system that scattered God's least favorite creatures in a viable state.

People in the city of Fiumicino were curious but not so curious as to ask questions and bring attention to themselves, an unenviable practice for sure, as buses filled with criminals, gypsies and political prisoners in their striped, coarse uniforms arrived weekly. It was thought that they were undergoing routine physical examinations as part of Mussolini's highly regarded National Healthcare System. Only few Fiumicinos thought it odd that the buses always departed empty. Well, there were more urgent things to worry about than the health of a few thieves, murderers, crooks and fortunetellers.

It is unnecessary to detail the nature of the Duke's experiments, the horrors which often left the black shirt guards at the Institute in a state of depression so deep that most could only stand a four month tour of duty on the premises, if that. A few, of course, enjoyed their work and watched the agonies of the experimental subjects as children might watch a caterpillar being cooked alive by a magnifying glass focusing the rays of the sun. The Duke neither enjoyed nor hated his work. He was the heart of dispassion, the image of pure intellect where emotion is as useful as a fur coat in the Kalahari in summer. He had set his goals and needed to accomplish them methodically. He never rationalized the torture and murder of his human subjects as the Germans did. They always had a reason for murder; Judaism, homosexuality, mental retardation, politics. It was as if in killing vast numbers of people, a justification was needed. The Duke was more efficient and direct. He saw his victims as a carpenter would see a tree, raw material for his work.

Seventy~One

71 It was the anniversary of Mussolini's rise to power when parties and celebrations all over Italy made the day a national holiday. The Duke was to hold his at the Villa Franca and he was inspired to assemble a guest list of what he called the "silent movers and shakers." There were many public figures in the regime, people with obvious power and influence. who by nature of their notoriety and fame could easily fall from grace and become nothing in a day or two simply by being discovered to be involved in some otherwise inconsequential but scandalous behavior. Because they were well-known, Il Duce had to make examples of them. It was the people behind the scenes that virtually no one knew that held the real power. Their indiscretions remained secret and they could indulge with impunity, not risking anything.

The Villa Franca was fitted out with large Fascisti flags alternating with the Italian flag and a few Vatican City pennants. A Nazi swastika and a Japanese rising sun flew from the flagpole near the sulfur pits. The Duke hired a wonderful Florentine orchestra and all the attractive servants were dressed in short Roman tunics despite the fact that nothing about this fête could in any way resemble an old-fashioned Roman orgy. Mussolini may have touted his masculinity, his prowess and the male arts of sport and war, but he was priggish at heart. His new Roman Empire would not succumb to the internal rot of decadence. He had an ideal in his head and a bunch of power-mad, wealthy Italians would never be allowed the indulgence of an orgy, not on his watch.

The Duke's touches here and there of Roman Empire style were merely that, style. There would be no substance beneath it, just a hint. He remembered his father's orgiastic indulgences here in this very house, but the new order was not to be seen as Pan or Priapus or Bacchus. It was Michelangelo's David, 14 feet tall, proud Roman face, perfect musculature and ideal proportions except his penis which was the size of a woman's pinky finger with testicles like two grapes. The Duke had wondered when he first saw the statue in the Louvre what humiliation the men of Italy had to have been subjected to as female tourists viewed the mighty David and, of course, zeroed in on his minute member. This did little to help the reputations of Italians as lovers. No wonder, he thought, that the most famous of all Italian statues was in France.

Nonetheless, despite the implied edicts from the new regime, the Duke knew how to throw a party. The sun had done its best all day, drying out the air and warming the flagstones of the large patio and the white gravel drive. At dusk, a few thin clouds rolled in like clotted cream, yellowish in the fading, thin azure of the sky. Limousines started pulling up in the circular drive, discharging his guests. The Duke was up in the attic in the window he used to sit in when he was a boy watching his father's guests arrive. On the floor next to him was a small gold cage with a stuffed little bird in it. The wheel had turned. History was repeating itself, although in his mind it was repeating like a cheap bratwurst. Who among this throng were really his friends? No one. The Duke was as solitary now as he had ever been. But then, people were all paying homage to him, little knowing that in the eyes that peered down from the small gable they were simply marionettes in the hands of the devil.

The Duke had married a wisp of a girl, the daughter of the Mayor of Florence. She had a large dowry and a submissive petulance. From a distance she looked fourteen, but close up, her eyes reminded the Duke of a lemur, one of those nocturnal tree creatures ever on the watch for enemies that lurk in the darkness. She was pretty, the way only Florentines can be, but her small stature, thin pale arms, high cheekbones, made her seem boyish. But the Duke did not look at a wife as an object of sexual desire. On the contrary, if sex was what he wanted, there were myriad partners willing enough to indulge him ever in his role as Lancelot, enough to populate a small city. No, a wife, he knew, was a cushion between himself and his demons. He could vent his petty grievances on her, his mortal fears, his moods, his anger and then wipe it all away with a small kindness, like a spit-dabbled thumb on a dusty chalkboard, a quick flick and a clean surface would appear. Ordinarily, the Duchess Mariana, would have left the Duke within a few months of the nuptials, but her father was one of the early casualties in Mussolini's war on the Republican order. The mayor and her mother, the mayor's wife, had been publicly hanged in the grand piazza in Florence under the watchful eyes of a copy of Michelangelo's David, the one with the small penis covered by a fig leaf, to the hired cheers of a falsely enthusiastic population of that once enlightened city. Mariana had no refuge but the Duke and the deep corners of her mind which she sought in a collection of dolls that followed her everywhere in three large trunks. The Duke sometimes fantasized about removing a few of their smirky or pouty porcelain heads and replacing them with cat skulls, but even he feared the repercussions of such a wanton act of personal vandalism. He had to sleep like everyone else and who knows what Mariana could do to him as he lay there in his bed dreaming his nightmares while she crept in. No, he enjoyed pushing people to the brink, not over it.

There had been one pregnancy, twins, a boy and a girl. Mariana's petite frame, her narrow pelvis, could not handle the load and both children were born nearly two months premature, almost killing her. The boy died a few hours into life. The girl lasted nearly a year and a half but the doctors overdosed her on oxygen in the incubator. At the time, it was the practice and still is but it was not known then, as it is now, that the lenses of infants' eyes crystallize if exposed to too much of the essential gas. By the time Mariana looked her child full in the face, shortly after her father had named her Trista, his little sadness, her eyes had glazed over a sickly grayish-white, looking like little agate balls with a coating of Viennese icing or the statue of cupid at the Uffizi in the Greek style where no iris was carved, just a blank, corpse-like pair of white eyeballs, lifeless, austere, tragic.

Trista was found dead in her elegant pink nursery by her nanny one morning in a sad, dilapidated April. She had smothered in her own pillow it seemed, her bluish face still buried in its downy abundance. The Duke had only departed for Paris on business two hours before the discovery and could not be reached for several days while Mariana, alone in her grief, attempted suicide by jumping from the nursery window. She broke both ankles and one wrist but survived, moved stiffly through the rest of her life as if she were one of her dolls, inflexible in the joints, an empty gaze, a compliant demeanor, one of those self-punished women we read about in

Victorian novels and histories of the martyrs. Trista was buried next to her unnamed brother on the hilltop overlooking the villa near their paternal grandparents and their long-deceased aunts.

A month after the funeral, when Mariana finally summoned the courage to clean up the child's room, the maid found the Duke's pinky ring wedged in between the mattress and the headboard. He must have lost it, Mariana thought, when he kissed the child goodbye before going to Paris. Yes, it must have fallen off. It had been his father's and was a little larger on his fine, almost feminine fingers.

Seventy~Two

72 The monumental chandelier which hung over the ballroom had had its light bulbs removed at the Duke's insistence and replaced with candles. His father had been so proud to have the villa fitted out with electricity and the chandelier in his "Great Hall," as he called it, was the source of enormous pride, his being the first house in the region to be electrified although in the surrounding towns, electricity had been available, if not actually used, for a decade. This Duke, however, was harkening back to older more genteel times and any truly grand hall had to be lit in the flickering golden glow of candlelight. He had other motives as well.

By the time nine o'clock rolled around, all the guests had arrived and were either dancing, talking in small circles or gathered here and there nibbling at delicacies and watching the other guests. The Duke made his rounds as host being particularly anxious to meet Giorgio DeVecchi's new clerk, Julian Corona who, as in American, was a rarity indeed in the inner circle. Giorgio he knew to be rather an uninspired rich boy from a well-connected family, personally without merit that would set him apart. But Julian had apparently made an impression on a number of important people and there were rumors that he would be moved up to a position of independent power and influence, outside the shadow of the DeVecchi family. He had also made friends with Cardinal Paolo Sabatinni and there were few men who could boast of real friendship with the remote, instinctive and powerful Cardinal.

The Duke's chief of staff informed him that Julian and his companion, a French woman named Isabelle Fontenot, were in the rear courtyard speaking with the Cardinal and the Cardinal's chargé d'affaire, Geraldo Buonanotte. The Duke stood with a small group by the French doors that lead out to the courtyard and while conversing about unimportant matters scanned the crowd to see if he could find the Cardinal for he had never met Julian and was anxious to do so. The Cardinal's red garb was like a beacon in the night, the large torcheres fueled by lamp oil casting bright, flickering lights across the crowd and magnifying their shadows on the rear façade of the Villa Franca that from a distance one would have thought was housing a group of giants as the greatly enlarged silhouettes moved to and fro across the whitish sandstone illuminated in red and orange from the flickering oil lamps, there streams of black smoke rising rapidly in thin serpentine columns as if the sky were occupied by black snakes coiling happily over the throng and dancing to the rhythm of the orchestra within, whose music ebbed and flowed on the gently moving air out of the windows and the doors of the villa into the velvet sky.

The Duke made his way across the courtyard stopping for a few moments and a few words with each cluster of guests, shaking hands, smiling, raising his arm to a servant to indicate that more champagne was needed and being every inch the perfect host. He was, in fact, the envy of almost every man present, his polish, his reputation as British nobility, his handsome face and his renown as one of the geniuses behind Il Duce's war machine. It was even rumored that Hitler had requested the Duke's advice on what everyone now knew to be a "biological weapon." Count Pialto, Mussolini's ambassador in Berlin, relayed Hitler's inquiry that Il Duce never responded to except with evasions and procrastinations, knowing better than to flatly refuse. The Count was also one of the Duke's closest acquaintances and informed the Duke of the whole affair; he was thankful that Mussolini did not send him to Germany. He knew Mussolini was a pig, but he was an honest one with obvious motives. Hitler was a raving lunatic, he thought, and as far from honest as the stars are from the earth, which was very far indeed.

Duke Montrose enjoyed his power and his reputation and the way it made everyone respect him, but pride is no bejeweled crown although many may think it so. It is, rather, a sack over one's head that blinds to the reality of the world. While everyone knew of his importance to the war effort and the sophistication of his newly developed weaponry, everyone also knew that there were many human victims used in experiments the details of which were mysterious, but the results, a hideous death, were assumed. The absence of details made everyone imagine what was happening which, in this case, was almost as perverse and wicked as reality. So, it was more fear and awe which greeted Duke Montrose in the eyes of his guests than respect. Had Machiavelli when he asked, "is it better for a Prince to be feared or loved?" known that certain fears are much worse than others, he might have asked a different question or preached a different answer.

When, finally, the Cardinal greeted the Duke with a warm handshake instead of the usual holding out of his ring to be kissed and the Duke embraced him with a kiss on the cheek, Isabelle, standing with Julian took note. As most women in the presence of the Duke, she was taken with that certain indefinable quality that is so attractive, a sense of quiet power, of intellect, of a sexuality that was betrayed not by rumor, although that was certainly true, the Duke's exploits were notorious, but by the tilt of his head, the manner in which he leaned, the set of his jaw and the line of his neck, the flexible hands which seemed made of silk and willow rather than skin and bone.

The Duke, likewise, was taken with Isabelle not only because he knew her particular vulnerability as the mistress of a married man but for her air of sensuousness. It does not take a violinist to appreciate, even admire, the unbroken curves and elegant swells of a fine violin. These are qualities inherent in the object divorced from its function as an instrument. Science and art converge in such an object and it can be admired without the necessity of its strings being caressed by the virtuoso's bow. This he sensed in Isabelle and knew it or, more properly, was aware of it even more so than Julian. To the Duke, Isabelle was magnificent, beautiful in a secret way, subliminally seductive and waiting for the right man much as an orchid under a veil. Julian may have made love to her a thousand times, but he never was aware of the person beneath; he was too much enamored of himself. The Duke saw her differently and while he wanted very much to befriend Julian for his political influence, she was something he needed to have, even if it was only once. The blindfold of his pride, however, disguised any motives she might possess and the truth was that she saw in the Duke his vulnerability precisely because she also saw in him his lust for her. Once a woman becomes aware of her desirability, then a price will follow and she sensed that the Duke could be instrumental to her and would pay her price.

Mariana, the Duke's wife, meanwhile followed him from room to room, guest to guest like the shadow of a bird, no matter how far away from him she was, she was there nonetheless. As he soared, she moved on the surface of hills, of valleys, of houses, of mountains. She knew him too well not to see the look of desire in him as he met Isabelle. Yes, she thought, Isabelle was pretty as everyone had said, but beauty could cause one to approach too close to the fire and if the Duke's flames were not hot enough to consume Isabelle, hers were.

The Duke inquired of the usual topics of Julian, whether America would enter the war, what Roosevelt thought of Hitler and Mussolini and, of course Stalin, as if by being an American, one could speak for all the backroom American politicians on such topics. Julian conceded that he was not particularly in touch with his family in the United States and so had no more information than anyone in Europe had although he knew that America detested involvement in a war and no politician that expected to be reelected would ever discuss America getting drawn into what was perceived as a European conflict, one of hundreds that filled history text books. No, Julian said quite emphatically, it would take a large overt act against the United States to change an opinion which was born in the trenches of World War I and had hardened over the years of the Depression.

As if on cue, Count Pialto came over and introduced himself. Then, he and Julian along with the Cardinal started a discussion of Italy's conquests in Africa, not spending too much time on the details of Italian battalions with the newest weaponry mowing down Ethiopians armed with spears, arrows and goat turds. The Duke took this opportunity to engage Isabelle in a discussion of the gardens of the Villa Franca and how much she would likely enjoy them in the light of day, that they had been designed by a Frenchman retained by his beloved father and that, as fate would have it, he himself was raised by a French woman referring to the despicable Madame Montesquieu as if she were his very own adoring mother. Isabelle, appearing to take the bait, cast her own line at the Duke and out of earshot of everyone, they agreed that she would visit one afternoon to see the gardens in daylight. Thus did she take the first step on a path down which there was no return where she confused passion with lust and life with death.

The rest of the evening Isabelle stayed dutifully by Julian's side as he also made the rounds of the party, cementing old relationships and making new ones. They even danced a waltz together but as he spun her around the room, the flickering candles and the faces of the guests became a miasma, a dream world where she imagined that this Duke would become her savior, for only he could ensure her position as the wife of Julian Corona.

Seventy~Three

73 Some weeks later, Isabelle received an invitation to see the gardens of the Villa Franca. It was no coincidence when the phone rang that Julian had the previous day gone to Piedmont on court business and that the Duchess Mariana had left for Sardinia to visit her two maiden aunts, one of which was quite near death. The Duke sent his own car for her that day at noon and in an hour or so she heard the pebbles of the drive patter against the bottom of the huge black Mercedes in front of the Villa Franca. The villa did, indeed, look very different as the sun beat down on its creamy, tarnished stucco walls. Bougainvillea were planted all about the foundation stones and in the full light of day, the shrubs overflowing their beds, rising some six or eight feet and then cascading onto the white gravel drive, gave the appearance of lava, red and hot from which the Villa Franca emerged as if born in the fires of the center of the earth emerging here in the Apennines.

The Duke stepped out of the shadow of the front door and quickly walked to the door of the car, opening it himself and greeting her more enthusiastically than the occasion merited, at least as far as Isabelle was concerned. Of course, she adored the attention and being the center of it especially when its source was such an intriguing and handsome man. Even the most severe and duplicitous of women will weaken in the light of adoration like a cat playing with the proverbial mouse, there is something in the submission of the rodent when its fate is manifest that appeals to the feminine heart. The Serpent knew it all too well. So did the Duke. What he did not know was that Isabelle was bound to Julian heart and soul but, had he known, it would have been of little or no importance to him. He wanted her purely on a physical basis, as one of his ultimate

Guineveres. Even he was surprised at his own obsession with a woman who could do little else for him than fill a few empty hours. But men are made this way, most men anyway, as they follow their penises into territory which can be more dangerous than the treasure of ephemeral value that is found at the end.

The Duke invited her in where a table had been set with a light repast of sliced, cured meats, country bread, and an array of local cheeses and a fine French champagne. They spoke of gardening and its ability to bring serenity to the most troubled mind and how it relaxed the Duke to plant bulbs in the fall as a bounty that would reveal itself in the spring. In fact, he had never even held a shovel and found personally disgusting the short squat Alfredo, his gardener, who smelled of sweat and soil and fresh onions. But it was the garden of the Villa Franca, after all, that had lured Isabelle and he realized the significance of playing the part without knowing that her interest in horticulture was even less than his, being confined to an occasional potted geranium on the balcony of her and Julian's flat in Rome, the nearest real garden ten city blocks away at the Society of Saint GerÙme. Of course, she liked flowers, especially if Julian sent them to her or brought a bouquet home on Friday evenings as was his habit. What woman would deny an interest in flowers? None that she had ever heard of. It is no wonder so many women were named for flowers, Rosas in Spain, Lilys in France, Heathers in Ireland, Blossoms in the United States. It should also be obvious that the deadliest flower, Belladonna, means "beautiful woman" in Italian.

After lunch, he led Isabelle straightaway through the same French doors that opened into the courtyard the night of the gala where he first laid eyes on her. The precedent was not wasted on him as he realized that a seed of sentiment had been planted in him, an unfamiliar weed in the arid wasteland of his heart. Being aware of it made him wary and he thought it would be easy to pluck out and discard when the time was right but while it freshly sprouted, he would leave it to see how it might grow in such a hostile environment.

They walked around the garden, he pointing out various types of lavender, the differences between the French and Italian varieties, the floribunda white roses cascading up the wall and bending down to touch the tops of the lavender mounds. Acacia trees were like sentinels, their bell-flowers small and insignificant, the gold frills of a ceremonial uniform. A trellis of purple clematis nearly covered completely an old, thick wooden gate which he had to open by leaning into it with his weight and for the second time she noticed his hands which had the lightness and grace of fly-ing swans, usually so expressively in the air as he spoke, become eagles, taught and muscular, his elegant body hard and determined beneath his white linen suit and violet silk shirt.

When the gate yielded, it led to a flagstone path that wound through and around large yellowish and rust-colored boulders where specimen cacti were growing in a spiky profusion, some tall as giants with odd white flowers like water lilies perched on the tips of thorn-covered arms, others squat with thousands of yellow needles protecting their pulpy water reserves while deep magenta flowers beckoned to bees and humming birds. The lonesome sound of cicadas filled the air with their staccato calls, the dry clacking of their voices an arid prayer for rain that was rarely answered. As the Duke and Isabelle walked the path, the clicking sound would cease and then recommence after they passed as if they were school children whispering secrets that would hush as teacher passed. Cholla cactus twist-ed and turned around the boulders, citrus green with golden brown barbs in profusion like hairs on a woman's arm, invisible until one got too close. Simultaneously, lush and austere, beautiful and threatening, the cacti seemed to wait, almost to relish an attack on their fortified carcasses. Large globes of Russian sage were clustered amid the rocks, their pale blue-gray foliage like morning clouds over the desert. The winds which buffeted this plateau in the spring or the late autumn would dislodge them from their hiding places and toss them off the edge into the chasm below not to death but to rebirth as wanderers as breezes and gusts carried them homeless until they might lodge themselves in some crevice or at a cluster of wild roses or barberry where they would remain rootless, desiccated, rocking back and forth in the wind against their new friends as if begging for acceptance.

The Duke, acting the pedagogue, pointed out the different species, told Isabelle the Latin names, some made up on the spot in his fertile imagination, and how each reproduced as he walked away from the villa toward the edge of the eastern precipice. They stopped at the edge and looked out at the meandering river below, coyingly flowing through the outcroppings and foothills of the Apennines. They sat together on a large slab of sandstone warmed by the unremitting sun.

Isabelle recalled Julian talking of the Subliminalists in poetry, poets in the middle of the eighteenth century that believed that nature revealed the presence of something greater in the universe, where one could lose the isolation of self and join momentarily with that presence. Isabelle could feel it now, high on the promontory overlooking the chasm below, the pungent smell of warm desert air arising, the distant hills fading into the white sky. She was brought back by the Duke's soft words, intercepting her thoughts as if he knew them. He spoke casually of the history of the Villa Franca, as much as he knew of it, how it had been a monastery, then an orphanage, how his father had purchased it and made it his own. It was certainly an idyllic tale in the narrative of the Duke who edited out the dark stretches, the bleak murders, cruel episodes that hovered like invisible vultures over his words.

He started down the stone steps that were carved into the side of the chasm that led to the riverbank. Isabelle hesitated to follow at first but he put out his hand as she felt the first pangs of surrender. She reflexively took it, his hand now looking like a mourning dove, his palm up, his fingers like pin feathers reaching skyward. In ten minutes, they had reached the gravelly shore, the river only half of its usual self owing to a lack of rain. She looked back up the path they had traversed and felt very small indeed as if they had left the known world and were standing as the first humans on some remote shore of the cosmos never visited.

He reached down and skipped a flat stone into the water. This Duke, she thought, was still a boy in some ways. She watched the stone bounce on the slow moving water and her eyes caught the cluster of grave markers some twenty yards distant. She asked him about them and he led her over, again by the hand, explaining that they were the graves of those orphans that met their untimely ends while in their youth alone in the world except for the monks and the other boys. Many of the markers were toppled, some had only barely legible writing, others nothing at all as the decades of weather erased what little was left. She noticed one marker in particular where the name "Stephen" had been scratched out and "Giulio" written crudely below. The Duke told her he thought that the marker might have been re-used, that at the end of its days as a monastery, money had become very short. How sad, she thought then said, that two boys had to share one tombstone. She bent over and straightened it, dusting it off with the hem of her dress rearranging some of the rocks that had been scattered about from what was clearly a small intentional pile.

They walked back up the stone stairs, the Duke leading the way, through the cactus garden, the courtyard, the French doors, the dining room and into the empty Great Hall which had been the scene of the party. He asked her if she would like to see some of his "specimens" that he had gathered from all over the world—this was something of a lie because he had. in fact, purchased most of them from people who had traveled. When she asked, "Specimens of what?" he replied, "Butterflies." There was something innocent and also cruel in the notion of collecting butterflies, she thought. It was easy to see their attraction as perhaps the most beautiful and harmless of all nature's creatures. Wanting them in one's home was natural, she supposed. But to accomplish this, they had to be killed. It was a paradox that could not be resolved, to kill that which is loved and admired. But the thought as instantly as it formed in Isabelle's mind reminded her of so many human endeavors. She had even thought at one time that to keep Julian from leaving her, she could kill him, would kill him if need be, but she wasn't sure she was serious or if it was just some sort of foolish daydream like so many that seemed possible when formulated, but proved unwieldy in the doing. Could she kill someone?

Seventy~Four

The Duke, by inviting her to see the collection, had crossed a threshold of a different sort. His two thousand some-odd butterflies, each carefully pinned to black velvet enclosed in glass cases labeled in fine calligraphic script were in his third story room, the one he had occupied as a child and one which no person not a servant had ever been allowed access to, not even Mariana. Perhaps, he thought fleetingly, this is love after all. Perhaps he had found a true Guinevere.

They climbed the narrow stairway to the garret rooms and the Duke opened the locked door for her as if she were royalty. Isabelle sensed his pride in these quarters of his and again the little boy she thought resided within every man, appeared in his face, his eyes both confident and seeking approval.

Between the bookcases which lined the walls were large black and white etchings from Le Morte d'Arthur. There were portraits of Guinevere, Lancelot, Gawain, Galahad, Morgan LeFey and, of course, Arthur himself, the only one in a gilt frame, the others in dark, thick oak, all behind polished, slightly rippled glass. There was the large ornate library table in the middle of the room under the chandelier. It had stacks of atlases and folios of etchings of butterflies, birds and exotic flora. She walked over to one of the six dormers and bending over looked out at the drive in the front of the villa noticing how steep the slopes were on both sides of the narrow roadway leading to the front courtyard. Meanwhile, the Duke retrieved from a locked cabinet six heavy cases of butterfly specimens and laid them out on the table after placing the books and folios on the floor. They were, indeed, dazzling, the yellows, reds and electric blues lit as if from within by a cold fire. "They are beautiful," she said with reverence in her voice.

"So are you," he responded.

"Tell me about Guinevere," she said.

He sat on his divan and she stood in front of him. He spoke to her of the forbidden love of Lancelot for Guinevere, reciting by rote the poetic lines of Mallory's epic poem but in the lilting mellifluous words of the Italian tongue. It was as a song to her, the lines not dying after he spoke them, but weaving themselves in the air around her head like a garland. This was her moment, she thought, this for her and for Julian.

As the Duke recited and sat upon the divan half-reclined, his hands nesting on the red velvet throw like falcons waiting to hunt, she began to undress, letting her garments drop to the floor at her feet, silk drapes at the pedestal of the Anatolian Venus unveiled at the Tate in London after its looting by the British, her eyes bluer than the sky at Llafranc, her hair dropping to her shoulders as if tossed by the invisible breezes of Mallory's rhythmic, pounding poetry.

When the limousine pulled up at the flat in Rome, it was 2:00 a.m. The air was still, no stars shown as the moon settled in quarter phase behind the dome of the Vatican in the north. She had extracted his promise and she knew that the Duke would keep his word, especially now to her.

Daria was thrilled to receive the wire from Julian. In it, he told her to bring Robert on the next ship out to Marseille. He would send a car for her and have her brought to Rome where he wanted "to work things out." She knew it was meant to be just that way. She had dismissed the significance of the rumors of his indiscretions and even of his possible involvement in Fascist affairs. He was an American and he loved her and she him.

She booked passage for herself and Robert on the French liner Normandie, possibly the most beautiful cruise ship ever built. To her it was the crystal carriage from Cinderella, sent by her prince to bring her to him. Despite her friends' warnings that this was no time to be traveling to Europe, she held to the opinion that Europeans were too sophisticated to embark on a war that would most certainly end civilization as they knew it. Hitler and Mussolini seemed the madmen, assuredly, but Germany and Italy were the most cultured countries on the planet. Surely their bluster was political mumbo jumbo to gain some advantage at the bargaining table of world affairs. Both men had saved their countries from the Great

Depression. War would only bring it all down in a heap at their feet. No, it was perfectly safe and, besides, Julian, who lived among them, would never send for her if there was any danger. She could trust his judgment which was unerring.

The ocean journey was uneventful and filled with hopeful anxiety for Daria. The spectacular fittings of the Normandie, the Ruhlmann furniture, Dunand enamels, Lalique glass, Boch Freres porcelain made the ship a traveling jewel, Poseidon's diadem, the most beautiful floating world ever created by man, far superior to the maudlin grandiosity of Titanic lying in state at the bottom of the Atlantic. Most passengers on Normandie knew they were experiencing the sublime in design and engineering but no one knew or could ever have guessed that very shortly the great ship would be stripped down in New York Harbor and accidentally set ablaze by ignorant laborers and sunk at the piers of New York by firemen too stupid to realize that pouring millions of gallons of water on a floating palace would cause it to submerge. This could only happen in America, the great land of democratic mediocrity where a crown of the gods would be consigned to use as a war helmet and then destroyed in the process. Daria and the other passengers did not know they were witnessing the last voyage of Normandie, that somehow her fate and that of the great liner were running in parallel courses, tragedies both that would be lost soon in the gargantuan holocaust that was being born in Europe.

Ordinarily, a cruise on such a ship would be the epitome of joyful steaming, partying on a grand scale and indulgence in every form of the human senses. But because war seemed to be looming, most passengers on board were watchful and uncomfortable, perhaps even anxious. There were couples of course, as Daria watched them, kissing in the red glow of Atlantic sunsets, the gentle rocking of the ship as the deep vibration of its powerful engines propelled it through the placid waters. The evening parties were gala events with men in tuxedoes and women in full length gowns, but the drinking was more intentional, less frivolous as if the champagne could erase the truth of the world.

In the morning, many realized it had not and about three days out of New York Harbor, an old Frenchman standing on the rail watching flying fish soar across the prow wake, pointed and shouted. He brought the attention of many within earshot to the periscope he had seen, its small white wake paralleling that of Normandie. Eventually, the conning tower appeared and on it, as the submarine surfaced like Jonah's whale, the red and black swastika flag of Nazi Germany. Whatever hopeful misconceptions passengers may have had, they were soon scattered to the ocean winds. A few German passengers on board shouted and raised their arms in the "Heil" salute, one even having a pocket-sized flag which she waved frantically as if that might deter the Germans from torpedoing the ship. But peace was still weakly breathing its last in Europe and the submarine vanished as quickly as it had appeared. Its message, however, was clear.

Seventy~Five

To many on board this was their last chance to get home to their countries and their families. Word was out that passenger transport was to be terminated shortly and people seized this opportunity half wondering that it might not be best to stay in America. Daria had her doubts as well, thinking that perhaps her friends were right. But her love was deep and she wanted a last chance at making her marriage work with Julian no matter the price, short of death. At the very moment Daria's resolve was solidified, she gazed across the green waters and saw the hunkered silhouette of Marseille, the steel cranes of its port like storks hovering over a pond looking for fish and frogs to devour.

Daria and Robert were some of the last passengers to disembark and for a moment she felt a little panic rise up into her throat. Julian's telegram was unusually terse and she wasn't sure he would meet her in Marseille or simply arrange for transportation to Rome. It was uncharacteristic of him, but, she thought, this whole marriage was uncharacteristic. It was one of those rare situations in her life where she did not know where she stood. Perhaps that was the appeal of Julian, so changeable, so unpredictable.

Amid all the reuniting families and lovers, the robust handshakes of businessmen meeting each other and the general chaos of unloading passengers, their baggage and the cargo held in Normandie's hull, Daria managed to find a uniformed driver holding a white cardboard sign with the name "Daria Corona" handwritten on it. She was relieved as she approached the man and smilingly said she was the person on the card. He spoke only French and hers was hardly passable but she managed to convey the obvious and she and Robert with a porter toting her trunk on a handtruck weaved their way through the crowd to a waiting sedan. It was clear that the trunk would not fit in the vehicle, but the driver tipped the porter and instructed him in French what to do. Daria asked what was going on and the driver in broken English said that the trunk would be shipped that day by carrier to her destination. She thought it odd that she heard no address mentioned but he had spoken so rapidly to the porter that she might have missed it.

The driver opened the back door of the car and she and Robert got in. It was a short drive to a small airfield just outside the port and Daria was relieved to be flying and not driving with the truculent driver as far as Rome which was at least by her best guess ten to twelve hours away by motorcar.

There was a plane waiting on the tarmac, a twin engine aluminum-covered craft with the Italian flag painted on its tail. When she was escorted inside by the driver, he saluted her in military fashion with a wry smile that made her feel more than uncomfortable and a little embarrassed in front of the two other passengers on board, both men in dark suits, neither of them smiling. Daria held Robert's hand the entire trip and was greatly relieved to sense the plane gently dropping through the low clouds, the coast of the Mediterranean, vast, emerald and evenly crinkled like a satin sheet on a slept-in bed. The trip had lasted less than three hours but she was exhausted, more from the anxiety of being carted around like Julian's baggage than by the uneventful trip. As the plane touched down, a small tower appeared flying an Italian flag with a sign in stark black letters which said "Aeroporto Leonardo DaVinci."

The sun set quickly as if it were hiding and thick clouds poured in from the west. Lightning strikes and thunder shook the ground where Daria stood huddled with Robert who sensed, like his mother, that something was wrong. He asked for Julian and she could only respond reassuringly that a car would be arriving soon to take them to his flat in Rome. The rain came down in buckets as a small bus pulled up on the tarmac. An attendant sitting in the vehicle jumped down onto the pavement and went quickly to Daria and Robert indicating to follow him back to the bus. The two other men on the plane ran to the bus and were waiting in their seats. Daria insisted that she be informed where she and Robert were to be taken; it was well past 8:00 p.m. and she had no idea where she was or how long the trip to Rome would be. She stood in the rain like a statue, her dress and hat drooping under the water, little rivulets running down her face. Common sense prevailed and she hurried to the bus with Robert where both of them got in dripping wet. Again, she asked where she was being taken and how could she speak to her husband, Julian Corona. The attendant smiled courteously but seemed not to understand her, indicating that she sit. He yelled, "Avanti!" at the driver, who promptly shut the door. The bus took off with a jerk almost knocking her to the floor. Robert fell into a seat and she awkwardly sat next to him, the eyes of the two men averted her gaze as if they wanted to speak to her but couldn't. The rain drummed on the roof of the bus and sounded like gravel being thrown at an empty oil drum, so loud she was tempted to cover her ears. Out the window, all was immersed in the liquid darkness of a summer squall at night in a weary coastal town.

In a half hour, they pulled up at a palatial villa with its windows dimly lit and a lone light bulb in a lantern swinging by a ten foot length of chain over the front door inside a colonnade of soaked sandstone. As the bus pulled under the porte cochere, the drumming on the roof ceased suddenly and the quiet was both ominous and a relief. A bronze plaque by the large, black enamel front door said "Instituto Da Scienzia Biologico." A tall-dignified man with a nurse at his side came out to greet the three people emerging from the bus. He spoke German to the two men in suits and turned to Daria saying in British English "Welcome. I am Duke Edmond Montrose. I trust your journey was satisfactory. Now please step inside and Matilda here will take you to your rooms." With that he departed and it seemed all the air around them left with him.

Instinctively Daria realized she was a prisoner in this place but she could not understand why or how she had come to be there. She knew nothing of politics and cared less. Her husband was working for the Italian government, yet she was imprisoned in Italy. Perhaps he was a spy for the Americans and had been found out while she was on her way to France and he could not warn her. He might already be dead. She knew that staying calm would be the best course for her and more importantly for Robert but panic began to fill the room as if released from the slick, greenish paint on the walls. When she was told that Robert would have to reside in the "children's wing," she screamed at Matilda that he would stay with her, that she was an American and that her embassy would hear all about this.

Matilda smirked and said that she would take her chances, that she was following Il Dottore's instructions. When Matilda pulled at Robert's arm to lead him away, he rushed at his mother and held her around the waist. Matilda went over to him and tried again to pull the boy away. Daria made a fist and punched Matilda full on the jaw sending her reeling into a chair where she toppled over to the floor. "You fucking American bitch," Matilda screamed at Daria, her voice curdling her perfect English. "It is Miss Isabelle who has put you here, do not blame me, stupid whore." She arose and pressed a button on the wall. Two attendants arrived forthwith but they were unnecessary. The words soaked into Daria past her wet clothing, her damp skin and joined with the red blood cells that had momentarily ceased their flow as her heart froze with the mysterious words.

"Who is Isabelle?" Daria asked catatonically. Matilda made a motion to the guards and spoke something in Italian and one whisked Robert away, wailing down a long corridor, his voice fading. The other took Daria by the arm and in a few minutes she was in a small white room with a single, metal-framed bed. Confusion, fear and exhaustion made her lie on it as if in falling asleep she might awaken and all of this would be simply a terrible nightmare. When she awoke, the sun filtered in through the bars on the windows and she realized that the nightmare was only beginning.

As the days past, Daria saw the pattern to life at the Institute. She was very much like a patient in a hospital where they took her temperature, her pulse rate, her blood pressure and fed her measured portions of bland food. She inquired of every nurse or attendant that entered the room of Robert but was answered only with dry smiles and the words "sta bene," he is fine. It entered her mind that she was being quarantined, that perhaps she had been exposed to some infectious disease on board the Normandie or the plane from Marseille. But there were no answers forthcoming and inquiries to herself about who Isabelle might be revealed nothing. She knew no one by that name and simply assumed that Matilda in her rage had blurted out some non sequitur.

She was provided with books, all of which were in Italian and therefore useless to her, but she did find a pad of paper and a pencil in the small drawer in the metal nightstand.

She wrote a letter to Julian detailing what had occurred from the time she disembarked the Normandie and was taken to the Institute. She mentioned the Duke and even the name Isabelle in the hope that when he received the missive, he could make some sense of what had happened to her and his stepson, Robert. She implored him to intervene without ever thinking that he might never receive the letter. She had the time, however, and it kept her from going insane like someone trapped in a closet in a room that is on fire, curled up on the floor, taking the clothes on the hangers above and stuffing them under the door to keep the smoke from sneaking in. Her letters to Julian, unsent and piled in the drawer, were those clothes.

She spent hours by the window and would watch small fishing boats out in the sea depart in the morning and return just as the sun set behind them, their stiff gray sails lit from behind by the red sun, silhouettes of men on the masts like insects crawling on a sleeper's eyelids.

Seventy~Six

76 A week, she thought, after her arrival, she was told to dress in street clothes which were provided for her. She had been in a hospital gown since the first night and her own clothing had vanished. She wondered briefly about her steamer trunk, the outfit she had so carefully packed that Julian had bought her on their honeymoon. From there, her mind wandered to her life before she met him, how, after running away from home, she had found consolation in the other young people she had met on the streets, their knack for survival in an indifferent city, where free meals could be obtained along with a dry place to sleep. She had taken to a young man, no older than seventeen, named Frank. She remembered how they made love in secret places in the park, in abandoned buildings and how he looked after her. One day, he left her in the hallway of a large public building while the rain drenched the city. The janitor made her leave and she was forced to stay outside in the rain. Frank never returned and she waited the entire day, long after the sun had finally appeared, long after it set. She sat on the deserted street, the last workers leaving the building for their homes, an intolerant wind kicking up discarded pages of newspapers that pirouetted in the street like miniature French women at the court of Louis Quatorze.

Daria got up and went to the last place she had seen Frank but he was not there nor did any of their common acquaintances have any information of where he might have gone. No one had seen him and as the days passed, as she wearied of the search and the waiting, she simply realized that the city was like quicksand to the homeless; it swallowed them whole and left not a trace nor anyone to search. She was one of the invisible people occupying a space between reality and dreams. She could not go home, would not, although she sometimes almost wanted to, but instead sought grounding in a man named Ryan. He was about twenty-five, tall and thin with slicked-back greasy hair and an elegant Spanish or Puerto Rican look to him that was both attractive and threatening. He took her to a small flat he occupied and after seducing her rather easily had her earn her keep, as he put it, by having his "friends" visit her.

For over two years she had become a prostitute working for Ryan whose real name was Rinaldo Vasquez which she discovered when once she had been arrested and he came to bail her out. Not long afterwards, she met an older man, which to her was anyone over thirty, who fell in love with her. At first she realized that many "Johns" fell in love with their whores because men are ever confusing lust with love, their "dicks for their hearts" as one of the other girls told her once. But Guy was different, larger than life, from a seemingly well-to-do family and she decided to leave "the life" and go off with him. They were never married but she told everyone they were and they lived together in a nice apartment in a building with a doorman in a good part of town.

Guy took great care of her at first but soon she discovered that his true lover lived in a bottle and that he was impossibly infatuated with alcohol. She was pregnant with Robert when, one day, a policeman arrived to tell her that Guy had been killed in a mugging outside a bar not ten blocks from home. Fortunately, Guy had left her sufficient funds to survive and remain in the apartment until Robert was born when she moved to smaller quarters on the other side of town. She lived for her son and did everything she could to raise him properly, knowing that he needed a father. When she met Julian, confident, successful, handsome and caring, she had found that father.

A nurse brought Daria downstairs and out into a small high-walled courtyard in the back of the building. It was set up much like a sidewalk café with tables and chairs, waiters in black pants and white shirts, red and white Campari umbrellas and around every table were seated what must have been other inmates. Food was brought out as she sat down. No one spoke but as she turned to the building she saw the Duke standing in the window looking at it all with the two German men that had arrived with her from Marseille and Matilda with a clipboard writing feverishly.

The waiters all went through the door from which the food had been retrieved for the diners and they were all left alone to eat, some beginning to exchange small talk. A few sparrows had landed on the stone patio where the tables were placed and Daria broke up a crust of bread and tossed pieces to them. They hopped over and greedily picked at the crumbs, flying away with them and returning just as quickly for more. She had accumulated nearly a dozen of the sharp-eyed creatures when a man came out with what appeared to be a large perfume atomizer filled with a translucent greenish liquid. He began spraying the air with it as he walked casually between and around the tables. The sparrows flew off immediately leaving their crumbs behind. They did not return. Daria smelled the spray as he went by her. It was minty with a subtle under-aroma of hard-boiled eggs. She saw that he was wearing a glass mask over his mouth and nose, imperceptible at a distance, with a black tube going down his chin into his shirt.

After he departed and the diners finished their meal, they were ordered to rise and come back into the building by a voice that emitted from a small loudspeaker attached to the building. They all did as they were told and were escorted back to their rooms by familiar attendants all fitted with the same peculiar glass masks. That night, Daria started vomiting uncontrollably. She banged on the locked door to her room to no avail. She could feel that she had developed a fever and hoped that the night nurse would make her rounds and help her. But then she heard other poundings on other doors, a distant drumming in the night like nothing she had heard before but which she imagined were like the tom-tom beats of Africans in the jungles sending messages to each other, news, good and bad, warnings and reprieves. She wanted to write all this down, to tell Julian what had happened but the drawer was empty, the pad, pencil and the letters she had written had been removed. There was nothing left to keep the fear and anguish at bay. The fire was reaching her. She was back in the closet. She could feel the heat of it on her face, on her chest. Her hair seemed to ignite and in a delirious fever she collapsed on the floor of her room, the coolness of the passive tiles reminding her of sleeping in her own bed with Julian beside her and Robert in his own room safe. In less than three hours, Daria Berenson Corona was dead. The atomized bacilli had worked efficiently. It was just a matter of spraying it at the right time in the right place. The Duke and the two Gestapo agents were quite pleased. And Isabelle, back in Rome, ceased her consternation over Julian's ambiguous feelings about his divorce. She could also stop putting up with the Duke's ridiculous games of Arthur and the Knights of the Round Table.

Seventy~Seven

77

The Duke arrived in Rome a few days later. He was excited as the day he left the Villa Franca for Bologna and medical school. He had created a world in which he and Isabelle lived together separate from everyone and everything else.

He was as manipulative and cunning as any, more so than most, superlative in his ability to plot and scheme. But he could never fathom the notion that Isabelle was completely the thrall of Julian Corona and that she had used the Duke as a simple, if somewhat costly, tool. She truly enjoyed his company and relished their time together even though his foolish chivalric sexual games made her queasy. Nonetheless, he clearly adored her as she saw the look in his eyes when she walked in the room, that same look Julian used to have but that had faded under the weight of remorse he felt for abandoning Daria and little Robert. To Isabelle, he seemed obsessed with his wife, not out of love—he definitely did not still love her, if he ever did—but out of some remotely amorphous notion of honor, broken promises and the self-image tarnished by his succumbing to the charms of another, Isabelle, while still married. In short, the Duke was a light repast that provided her with the means to cement her happiness with Julian by removing his past.

Isabelle and the Duke arranged a tryst at a small inn about ten miles south of Rome. They never stayed at the same place twice, both fearing the repercussions of being recognized. Julian was away, down in Naples at a new constitutional convention called by Il Duce to give the lawmakers the ability to give him more power than the prior constitution did. It was a mere formality but such empty rituals are the skeletons upon which governments flesh out their existence.

She sat with the Duke in the little enclosed garden in the rear of the inn, clematis blooming in succulent abundance, swallows lighting in the olive trees and singing their punctilious songs. Sparrows chittered on the flagstones as Isabelle shooed them away with her sandaled foot. The Duke had that excited little boy look in his face as he ordered some wine and cheese from the elderly innkeeper who scuttled off and came back with it in a few minutes, a cheery toothless smile on her rubicund face. He took Isabelle's hand in his across the table and told her that he wanted to marry her, that he had already filed the papers of his divorce from Mariana with the Notario in Rome, that he would keep the Villa Franca but would relocate with her to Berlin. He had sold his biological warfare secrets to Hitler's government for the equivalent of ten million American dollars and had been retained by Goering himself to head up further work on such weapons and a delivery system that would reach across the Atlantic to America, if it made the wrong decision when war finally broke out, which it most certainly would. In the Duke's world, the idea of betraying one monster for another was not a moralistic decision. Mussolini would be in no position to complain to Hitler about Il Dottore's defection. Hitler was obviously the dominant of the two and Il Duce had lied to Hitler about the Duke's work by excluding its existence from any bilateral discussions. It would be one of those breaches of friendship that would never be mentioned, as if in not bringing it out in the open it did not occur.

Isabelle, untutored in the ways of politics or tact either on a grand or petty scale, realized how far past reason she had taken the Duke. She could not construct the sentences or form the theory necessary to bring him back to earth and she saw him really as someone who had become almost schizophrenic. How could she, the thought formed, make sense to a lunatic and convince him that all he had based his current life on was a mirage, a fabrication, a whim, a frolic? So, she took the direct approach as women will often do when presented with anything too complicated to require simple prevarication to spare another's feelings. She told him that his plan was ridiculous, she had no intention of marrying him, did not love him and that she was not flattered by his plan but insulted, although she liked him as a friend. She went on to say that their liaisons had been fun, but that she still loved Julian and always would.

She continued her feminine diatribe but the Duke had mentally left the table. The use of the word "ridiculous" in reference to the Duke was the equivalent of stabbing him. He could stand just about any other criticism or comment about himself but his self-image, his pride, the structure of his ego was all built on a foundation that defied the very idea of being ridiculous. Nonetheless, he also knew how to remain calm within the barricaded walls of his skull, to remain dignified as the onslaught of imprudent insults arrived at his ears. He simply let go of Isabelle's hand as if he had been in the jungle and discovered he'd been leaning on the tail of a sleeping crocodile. He retracted his arm slowly across the table and simply said, "I am sorry to hear that."

Had he been at the Villa Franca or his Institute or anywhere else within his dominion or in a place of total privacy he would readily have executed her without another thing being said. He thought of himself as many things, but "ridiculous" was not one of them. Even here in the small courtyard, he knew there were others about and only some practiced restraint could prevent him from smashing in her skull with a chair or slitting her throat with a dinner knife. It has been said that there is a fine line, almost imperceptible, between love and hate, but this is not so. The old crone who concocted that was ignorant indeed. Love is a plateau in the mountains, a mesa in the great desert, high and level and serene. Hate is everywhere else. It is not a line that separates them, it is the edge of that plateau, the chasm surrounding that mesa, a precipice. One can be standing on it one minute looking into the reciprocating eyes of the beloved and cast into the abyss of hate the next simply by a misstep. A line implies the possibility of crossing over in both directions, a border like that between Spain and France. The abyss is permanent, there is no going back. Isabelle could see it in the Duke's fading eyes which she thought were blue, turning to gray, his brow, smooth and youthful becoming furrowed. The veins in his neck were suddenly visibly throbbing through his fine skin. She was looking at the face of retribution, a demon more powerful than Satan or the worst of his minions. Her life would never be the same, she knew that all in the minutest fraction of a second, a moment so small on a human scale as to be immeasurable and imperceptible, but in the Country of the Damned, an eternity.

At that very moment, hundreds of miles away, Hitler, Chancellor and Führer of the One Thousand Year German Reich looked into the eyes of Neville Chamberlain, Prime Minister of Great Britain, representative of the King, sovereign of the largest empire the world had ever known. Hitler stared at Chamberlain, deep into his eyes and promised he would seek no more territory in Europe after that small piece of Czechoslovakia called the Sudetenland, and he would honor the sovereignty of Poland. He even signed a paper to that effect, a treaty with Chamberlain which, when emerging from his plane at Heathrow in London, he would wave like a flag of triumph, Guinevere's handkerchief brought from the joust. Behind Hitler's lifeless gray eyes was the essence of duplicity, a fraud so profound that twenty million would perish as a result of that encounter.

Isabelle was no Chamberlain. She was more perceptive for she had the instinct of the female of the species to be ever watchful of the more powerful male. She saw in the Duke's self-control, the real danger. When he said, "Well then, I've been mistaken. Forgive me my foolishness." She heard him say, "Count the days, bitch, for yours are numbered."

She tried to explain, tried to keep him seated and under her influence but it was too late. The cord had been severed. She would have had better luck trying to convince the sun it should wait an extra hour before setting. But what neither she nor he could understand, though, was that events were already inching forward elsewhere, the lava in the volcano, sluggish and slow, was about to spew forth, red, incendiary and deadly to all in its path. As the Duke retrieved his valise from the room in which they were to stay and made his excuses to the innkeeper whom he paid for the unused room, and as Isabelle sat in the courtyard watching the hummingbirds hover from cup to cup on the tall blood-red foxgloves growing there, she wished she was a bird that could fly away from it all.

Matilda, the Duke's trusted assistant, sent from Rome, was on her way to see her husband, Cardinal Paolo Sabatinni. Matilda was only one of many names used by the Cardinal's secret wife. Only he knew her as Sonya, the prettiest of three young whores waiting at the front door of their home in Budapest for men to pass by and purchase their ephemeral wares. She was anxious to tell the Cardinal all she had learned about Duke Edmond Montrose's experiments, his dealings with the Germans and to show him a small packet of letters written by a now-deceased inmate at the Institute to Julian Corona, from a woman named Daria claiming to be his wife. More importantly, she had a beautiful gold wristwatch, a Patek Philippe removed from the wrist of a French spy who underwent the

Duke's treatment at the Institute who didn't need it anymore. It was the perfect gift for her beloved son, Geraldo. She was so proud of his position in the Vatican as the Cardinal's personal aid. Father and son together, working in the service of the Lord.

•

Seventy~Eight

78 By the time Duke Edmond Montrose had driven back to the Institute in Fiumicino, the sun had almost set, the crimson glow on the front of the building making it look like a smoldering coal, perhaps much as the Villa Nero Agrippa did that fateful day when Vesuvius hugged Pompeii to her bosom and engulfed it with her eternal, disastrous love. It was unusually quiet in the town which at this time of day would have had its streets filled with trucks loading or already loaded with the harvest of the local fishermen's work. The families of the sailors often met the returning men on the piers or on the gravelly shore. Some stayed and ate some of the catch, grilled on little impesattos, small cast-iron cookers filled with charcoal and made smoky by grape leaves soaked in olive oil, the smell rising in the air wafting through the easterly prevailing breezes through the town. Today, though, the shoreline was empty.

When he got inside, he asked Rosa the cleaning woman where Matilda had gone. Rosa did not know nor did Captain Frazetta, the Chief of the security service. Everything seemed in order and the Duke's Chief of Medicine, Dr. Genesco, was consulted about the latest experiments that were going to be performed on the younger inmates, boys and girls under twelve. Their immune systems behaved differently, it was learned, when exposed to various infective agents introduced to their systems in non-conventional ways. The Duke remembered Robert, Daria's son, without making anything obvious about it, asked to see the charts for the boys only and then surreptitiously noticed that Robert was still alive and well but was due to be exposed to a particularly virulent form of tuberculosis the Institute had made viable in its unique atomizers. He made a mental note of which room Robert was lodged in.

That night, when only one guard was on duty in the children's wing and he was known to sleep more heavily than the inmates he was supposed to watch, the Duke made his way through the dimly lit corridor to Robert's room. He had brought with him a wallet with enough money in it to last a few months. He gently woke the boy and covered his mouth with his hand to muffle any noise as the child, terror in his eyes, was confronted with the face of the man everyone called "Il Monstro." The Monster. The Duke whispered that he was a friend of his father, Julian Corona, which was true. He said his mother was sent to Rome to meet his father and both would be waiting there, which was false. Daria's body had already been cremated, her ashes dumped in a fertilizer factory in a town called Lampedusa near Naples. He gave the boy the wallet and a pass signed by himself as a minister of the new government. Such a pass was invaluable to anyone moving about in these difficult times.

He told the boy to dress, which he did, and then led him out the front door. It was nearly three a.m. The street was deserted. He told Robert to head north along the coastal highway, to find lodging and to await word when everything was all right to go to Rome. The boy did as he was told and by 6:00 a.m. he had managed to convince an innkeeper about 5 miles from the Institute that he needed a place to spend the day. He ate a hearty breakfast and waited in his room until he fell asleep never realizing that the Duke could never know where he was lodged and that waiting for him was an exercise in futility. No word could come. All that he did know was that he was out of the shadow of the Institute and the terrible fear that rumors and nocturnal sounds had planted in his brain. He was worried about his mother, but she had instilled in him a certain sense of independence which she had learned from years on the street was essential to survival, to trust no one and to always look out for "numero uno" as she put it. As Robert dozed off, he reasoned that if the monster wanted him to go to Rome, it must be the wrong thing to do. He decided that he would make his way back to Marseille, seek out the American Embassy and return to the United States. His mother needed him alive and for all he knew, she had taken the same course herself. As for his stepfather, Julian, even at twelve, Robert knew he was half-angel, half-scoundrel and fifty-fifty odds were too steep to bet one's life on. Robert was, after all, a Berenson and Berensons knew how to survive.

The next morning, before the sun had a chance to rise behind the Institute and light the sea in shades of lilac, lavender and deep purple, the Duke was awakened by the heavy thud of booted feet scurrying through the halls. No sooner had he risen and retrieved the Luger he kept in his nightstand drawer, that his door burst open. The room filled with Mussolini's black-shirted personal police. One leapt across the room and punched the Duke in the face when he saw the pistol which dropped with a clatter on the terrazzo floor and skittered to the boots of one of the policemen who picked it up and pocketed it. "Il Dottore?" asked the captain.

"Yes, what is the meaning of this? Do you know who I am? I'll have you all arrested and hanged, fools! Let go of me."

"Il Dottore, you won't be arresting anyone; you, sir, are under arrest for treason."

"I am no traitor. Now, let me go, I command you."

The captain of the guard saluted and told the two guards to release the Duke who immediately stood tall and proud thinking his power intact and his luck as good as ever. The captain walked over as if to apologize but instead struck the Duke with the back of his hand with a swat so quick and forceful that the Duke fell to the bed, a trickle of blood like an escaping tapeworm emerging from the corner of his mouth.

"Take this traitor downstairs," the captain barked. "And if he talks, teach him manners as I just did."

They loaded the Duke, still in his pajamas, into a waiting van, six guards with him, the captain who said something in private to Captain Frazetta in the Duke's own detachment showing him a paper. Frazetta saluted and smiled at the Duke as if to say, "Revenge has just arrived; make yourself comfortable." The van pulled out slowly and made its way through the dark streets of Fiumicino.

Now you may believe that perhaps the Duke was a little too enthusiastic about his work at the Institute and that true justice would have been to place him there, getting inoculated or sprayed with some hideous concoction that would give him the plague or polio or diphtheria or some other stowaway from Noah's Ark that the Bible was too wary to tell us about. But, friend, real justice is only part of the vast uncaring universe, that it often hovers and tarries too long in some places and ignores others more deserving. But out of the corner of its eye it did see the Duke being trundled off to Rome, although he was not destined to arrive.

The van pulled off the roadway in a small mountain pass of the foothills southeast of the City of the Seven Hills. The Duke was taken out of the vehicle and made to stand at attention in his pajamas in the glaring sun with snakes and scorpions and reeling desert birds his only witnesses. The captain told him that the two Gestapo agents he had handed his secrets to had been killed "accidentally" when their plane went down in the Alps. The pilot was never found nor any of their baggage. Some thought the pilot may have parachuted out leaving the helpless Nazis with the task of flying the plane themselves, a trick they were not apparently capable of performing. Regrets were sent to the Führer but accidents happen. As Duke Edmond Montrose went to speak, a butterfly appeared, a black and yellow Sudanese Monarch, large as the palm of his hand. He decided long ago not to kill any more specimens but simply to admire them in their natural state. His eyes followed the creature as it lighted on a small, red-flowered cactus. He could not have seen the bullet approaching his skull, another his neck, another his heart. For a moment, the briefest space of time, he thought he heard thunder. Then he saw and heard nothing at all.

They left the body Duke Edmond Montrose in a dry riverbed, food for the wild dogs and wolves that traveled down from the Apennines foraging for food.

Seventy ~ Nine

79 A week later, Cardinal Sabatinni, received word from Il Duce himself in a large polished leather envelope. In it, he was thanked for informing on the Duke's treason. His reward was in the form of a document on the finest velum with Il Duce's own signature in bold red ink. It was a deed to the Duke's ancestral estate, a nice villa just northeast of Rome, a beautiful place called Villa Franca, filled with treasures from around the world which had once been a monastery and then an orphanage. Marco Fontana had come home at last.

Julian was one of the first to hear of the Cardinal's good fortune in obtaining the lavish villa, but was unaware of how it had come about. He was invited to the Cardinal's quarters in the Vatican for a game of chess or perhaps just to discuss matters. Chess was usually only a pretext for the two of them to argue about God, the devil, the sex of angels and the nature of good and evil. The Cardinal followed church doctrine to the letter and could ramble on about the order of the universe as if he were describing one of those garden mazes constructed from tall hedges. Yes, it was complex to those who did not see it from above and who wandered aimlessly through dark corridors and found themselves bruising their noses against the thorny walls of a dead end. But faith made one soar above it all and looking down, the path was a simple matter and there was God omnipresent in the center, patient and somewhat bored perhaps, but waiting nonetheless indefinitely for the souls of men to reach him by hook or by crook.

Julian would usually listen respectfully to Father Paolo and only argued as a lawyer would argue; by asking questions in an attempt to force the Cardinal into a corner. It just never worked and Julian respected him all the more especially when he had adeptly dodged a difficult question with an unassailable answer and then moved a rook or a Bishop on the chessboard between them calmly saying, "…and also, checkmate." Julian could never have suspected that Father Paolo had no formal theological training but picked up doctrine from reading and watching.

One rainy night barely a week before, Julian had called upon Father Paolo. He had gotten to the priest's apartment in a large building two blocks from the entrance of the Sistine a half-hour early. He was let in by the priest's novitiate, Geraldo, who recognized him instantly.

"Good evening, Signore Corona. Terrible weather isn't it?"

"Perfect for the ducks." Julian responded. Geraldo had eyes that were deep set above rigid cheekbones. It was easy to imagine the shape of his skull beneath his face as it was only lightly disguised by taught white skin and a skimpy ascetic beard that reminded Julian of a statute of St. Anthony he had seen in a cemetery. Geraldo's spidery fingers fumbled with a large ring of ancient keys and opened Father Paolo's apartment with two turns of the deadbolt.

"The Cardinal will be back shortly. Have a seat," he said and then departed looking over his shoulder as he went through the door to make certain Julian obeyed. The minute the door shut, Julian arose and wandered over to the massive bookcase against the wall. There were crosses carved into the joints where shelves met the uprights. The books were all leather-bound with bright gilt titles, mostly in Latin. Julian pulled one down and noticed that the pages were uncut. He replaced it and pulled down another. Then another. They were all uncut. Finally on the bottom shelf he picked out what appeared to be an atlas. The book was frayed at the top and bottom of its spine. It was a beautifully illustrated book about Greek Mythology and the pages were well thumbed. There was Pandora with her flock of ills fluttering up to the ceiling of her room, Hope in the form of a white dove perched sappily on the edge of the box ready to take flight. Julian always felt that pigeons were filthy birds and now he was convinced.

One plate was missing from the book, the residue of its page a narrow strip of paper that ran from top to bottom. Opposite the missing page was Epimetheus. Clearly, his brother Prometheus had been the subject of the thief's excision. Prometheus brought fire to man despite Zeus' warnings to the contrary. When Zeus discovered the disobedience he had Prometheus tied to a rock and a huge vulture or eagle or some such predatory bird would daily tear at Prometheus' liver which unfortunately for him grew back healthy as ever every night. Julian was certain that had Prometheus known which uses man would make of his gift, he would have thought better of it and thrown the torch into the ocean. A whole lot of Protestants would not have been burned at the stake and may have had the good sense to worship Prometheus instead of the dry and dusty memories of Luther, Calvin and the truly obscene Henry VIII.

Julian poured himself a glass of brandy from a Baccarat decanter on the Cardinal's sideboard. The liquor felt like acid sliding down his throat irritating his stomach. The momentary warmth was welcome, though, and the bittersweet taste a welcome to the luxury of the Cardinal's surroundings. He sat in the chair again balancing the glass in his hand so that the light from a wall sconce shown through it, its rich amber-brown color glistening off the cut crystal of the glass. Just above the rim of the glass was a portrait of the Pope, a large hand-colored photograph with an almost silly beatific expression, his hands clasped in prayer, his eyes rolled upward to the heavens like a spoiled child being reprimanded by his parents. As Julian started to grin at his observation, the Cardinal entered the apartment with a flourish.

"Ah, my friend, welcome, welcome. Sorry I'm late but there was a meeting with His Holiness and it was a little late."

"Think nothing of it," said Julian. "I've helped myself to some of your brandy. Forgive me."

"What's mine is yours, friend, what's mine is yours. Pour me a glass as well like a good fellow, won't you?"

Julian rose and noticed that the Cardinal was shaking. "It must be colder out than I thought."

"It is not the cold. We are facing difficult times, difficult times."

"Are we? I knew that a year ago, maybe two."

"This Jewish question. We are in the Valley of Death, I tell you, Julian, and it is very dark. His Holiness has received a letter from the German Consulate in Rome asking for the cooperation of the Church in providing names of Jews and their Italian associates and to make a public declaration against them and in support of Adolf Hitler. They want us to help arrest them and have them deported to a place the Germans call, "the East." It is common knowledge that we deal with Jewish bankers all over the world and their emissaries here in Rome."

"Then it is not a moral question you face."

"Please Julian, let's not get into one of your hypotheticals."

"Is it hypothetical that Jesus was a Jew and that he depended on Simon Peter, another Jew to build his Church?"

"Are you going to provoke me tonight? Perhaps we should get drunk and play a little chess."

"I think you want to talk, Paolo." Julian rarely omitted the Cardinal's sobriquet but when he did there was an earnestness in his tone that struck at the Cardinal's heart.

"You know me too well, friend. We have a few days to respond to the letter. If we tell the Germans we will not cooperate, we risk reprisals all over Europe when the Nazis come to their full power and I can assure you they will. If we do cooperate, we risk the judgment of history in aiding and abetting a nation of murderers. In short, we must save our lives and risk our souls or save our souls and risk our lives."

"And what does the Pope say?"

"I think you know. He sees the doctor every two months, watches his diet as if her were an invalid and never goes out except in fair weather. He is, in short, too concerned with staying alive. And, I might add, if he is afraid to die and meet his Maker, it is not likely he will jump in front of a Nazi tank to save a few Jews."

"May I pose you an allegory?" asked Julian.

"Will it help?"

"It will help me. Sit for a minute and sip your drink." The priest sat heavily into his thick leather chair and downed half the contents of his snifter.

"Take it slowly, Cardinal, slowly. I want to beat you fair and square at our game."

"I don't think I will be playing chess tonight."

"I didn't mean chess." The priest raised his eyes over his glass and stared at Julian. He raised the glass just above his hairline and said, "Salute."

Standing and leaning against the bookcase, his arms folded in front of him and one leg crossed over the other, Julian took a deep breath.

"Let's say that when the Magi finally found Mary, Joseph and the infant Jesus in the stable in Bethlehem that they brought not only the famous gifts mentioned in the Bible but also an entourage. I think it is safe to say that such dignitaries traveling the distances they had to traverse did not groom and bed their own camels nor tote their own baggage. Right?"

"A safe presumption."

"Let's say then that amongst this entourage from what we now call the Arab nations, there was a woman with her own newborn baby. Perhaps, even that she was intentionally taken along by say, Melchior, the magus from Syria and that in the commotion of the visit, with the shepherds, the innkeeper and his wife, the other guests, animals speaking and the general hubbub of such a miraculous birth that Melchior switched the infants. One Semitic baby probably looks much like all the others, don't you think?"

The Cardinal was silent.

"So this little Syrian street urchin was now in the care of Mary and Joseph and the real Jesus was taken back to Damascus and raised as Melchior's son. Maybe even with the compliance of Balthazar and Caspar. Perhaps these wisemen had seized the opportunity to raise the Savior of mankind and teach him of science, mathematics and literature. And poor little, let's call him Ahab, was raised by the carpenter and his ignorant teenage wife thinking he was the Son of God, the fulfillment of prophesy and the savior of mankind."

"I believe you are going to continue to subject me to blasphemy whether I want it or not. Can I fill my glass again?"

"Let me do it for you," said Julian leaving his perch on the bookcase and taking the decanter over to the seated Cardinal and filling his glass.

"Thank you. Please continue as I know you will."

"So Ahab learns carpentry and the scriptures at the hands of Joseph, and Mary fills his head with the story of his miraculous birth—so much so that he, as anyone hearing such stories, would believe himself to be the Son of God."

"And how does he make the blind man see?" asked the Cardinal goading Julian on.

"Just the way it says in the New Testament."

"And the lame to walk?"

"The same."

"And the leper?"

"Just as you have studied it. You see the miracle is the believing isn't it? If you believe in miracles they come true. Would the real Jesus have doubted his ability to stand on the pinnacle in the desert? Would the real Jesus have questioned God in Gethsemane? I think not. Ahab may have had his doubts, but God on Earth, would never."

"This is the logical proof you offer?"

"Is there logic to anything in the Good Book?"

Raising his glass again, the Cardinal said, "Salute" and drank down his second glass.

"The divinity, Cardinal, is in the mind. Believe anything with your whole heart, your whole mind and it will happen. Perhaps, even walking on water. It is just a state of mind."

"What of Lazarus? Did Ahab's state of mind make the dead rise?" The Cardinal stood up shakily and refilled his own glass.

"I think you have the answer to that."

"Lazarus was a trick then? Is that what you want me to say?"

"I want you to say what is in your heart."

"Even I have a little trouble with the Lazarus story. I mean, how long did he live after he was revived? One might assume that once dead and brought back, he would be immortal. This is a question for which I have no answer."

"It is good to know that one of the Pope's closest advisors does not have an answer to everything."

"My not having it does not make it unanswerable."

"I think, my dear Father Paolo, that we have come to the conclusion of your discussion of the Jewish question. For once, the Church will not have an answer it can live with. You can't torture anyone to make him change the universe to fit your version of it as you did with poor Galileo. And you cannot elect a Pope based on his riches and political influence as you did with the Medicis. I'm afraid the gamecock of infallibility has come home to roost."

"You must be a very frightened man, Julian, to hate the world the way you do. Hatred is just the shadow of fear and you must constantly watch over your shoulder for your fears follow you like a villain in the night waiting for you to drop your guard."

"Salute, Cardinal," said Julian raising his glass." "Salute."

"So what happened to Jesus in Damascus?"

"That is open for discussion. My own opinion is that he is still alive as much a mystery to himself as to anyone. Of course, he has likely moved from town to town to avoid the obvious. Perhaps he was murdered. Perhaps long ago in a robbery or more gallantly defending the Holy Land from the invasion of the Crusaders. The irony of it all. Do you have any thoughts?"

"Yes, perhaps that should be the topic of your novel. In any event, forgive me, I've had a long day and your absurd twisting of everything holy has left me exhausted. Or maybe it's just this brandy," he said smiling. "Yes, it is the brandy. Let me call Geraldo and he'll show you out."

"That won't be necessary. Forgive me tiring you and forgive me my impudence."

"Impudence? Never. Your imagination fascinates me and while you shed no light on spiritual matters perhaps you have helped me with a personal conundrum."

"And what is that?"

"Not tonight, Julian, not tonight. Ah, here is Geraldo. Geraldo, please show Signore Corona to the door." Geraldo had appeared as if by magic. He was in a long tunic style robe that went down to the floor or only slightly above it with a high priestly collar. Julian shook the Cardinal's hand and said, "Until next week." There was no response only a gentle nod. Julian turned and walked to Geraldo who held out his right hand to show the way that Julian could have found blindfolded.

"Father tells me you're a novelist. That is very exciting," Geraldo said.

"Well, not quite yet. I'm writing one or attempting to, anyway."

"I'm something of a poet myself," Geraldo said pausing in the dark corridor in front of a door. Here is my room. Might I take a brief moment of your time to show you one of my poems. I've never shared them with anyone. And the Cardinal tells me you're quite the literatus."

"It's late and I…"

Geraldo acted as if he were deaf and led Julian into a small, dimly-lit chamber, remarkably similar to that of the Cardinal's drawing room, but about a quarter of the size, roughly eight feet by ten feet. There was a small four-poster bed with a dark red velvet throw. Each of the posts had an elaborate silk-corded tasseled rope of the type used to draw back draperies, possibly the remains of eighteenth century bed curtains. Over the bed was a print of "Christ in Gethsemane" showing Jesus kneeling in front of a large boulder as if it were an altar and looking searchingly upward while praying.

Opposite the bed was a small wardrobe. Next to that, a ladder-back chair with a rush seat. Above the chair was a framed print.

"Sit a moment," said Geraldo pointing to the chair. My poems are right here." He knelt at the foot of the bed, reached under it pulling out an old cardboard suitcase.

Julian looked at the print over the chair and saw that it was "Prometheus Bringing Fire to Man."

"This is interesting," said Julian wearily.

"Yes, isn't it?" said Geraldo. "The Cardinal gave it to me for a special occasion. It is an extremely rare Tiepelo print, one of only ten, he said, from an important collection in his own family, his brother's, and he inherited it and thought I might like it. It's worth many millions of lira, not that that means anything to me, I am a servant of God and, yet, I often look at it and wonder, much as the artist must have, of the ancients and their gods. What a certain world they lived in—not like ours—where everything had an explanation, you know?"

"What do you mean?" Julian was feeling the effects of the brandy as if he had had two or three more glasses and sat down heavily in the chair as the room started to spin.

"Well, you see, if there was a storm at sea and a ship was sunk with all hands on board, Poseidon was angry perhaps because the captain failed to give a proper sacrifice before setting sail. An earthquake or lightning that struck or failed crops leading to starvation—well these were all the results of angry gods that took offense easily. People knew this and if they weren't careful, then they needed to watch out. It was, in effect, a world of certainty, of cause and effect. Now, to a Christian, a flood which kills hundreds or a fire at a school that snuffs out the lives of innocent children no longer has an explanation. Our God is loving and forgiving and so we must spend hours, days, even years and centuries making sense of pain and suffering and tragedy and heartbreak. And so we look within ourselves for some effrontery, some sin and really what do most of us do that we think is sinful? Take an extra biscuit when mamma is not looking? Peek at naughty pictures by Titian? Ogle an attractive person on the street? So, you see, our insecurities get all mixed up in our reverence. We didn't get that position we applied for because we used God's name in vain. Or because we had a salacious thought. Outward respect to God is no longer enough—He's in our minds with us in the shadows inside our skulls and the thought of it drives some of us quite crazy. Actually, it never makes common sense really—punishment with no cause except indefinable …"

Geraldo's voice seemed to drift away on an invisible breeze and Julian felt he was at the bottom of a cave with Geraldo speaking to him from the surface far above, his head peering over the rim with a faint halo of turquoise sky, looking and sounding like a young woman. In an instant, the blue sky went to black as a total eclipse, sudden as a gunshot pitched the world into total darkness.

Geraldo noticed Julian getting groggy as the effects of the liquor coursed through his body. Stress did that, weakened the system like catapulted stones against the castle gate, eventually collapsing it, allowing the enemy to overrun it and enter.

"Signore Corona, you are a dear friend of the Cardinal and he values your advice and opinions—you may be the only one he trusts," said Geraldo revealing the real purpose of his discussion and that it was not his poetry.

Julian felt his senses return as dogs sense the coming of the earthquake or shore birds the tsunami long before it arrives.

"And I value his," said Julian the haze lifting from his mind.

"Meet me tomorrow at number 18 Via Fulgencia. There is an alleyway there. It is easy to find if you are looking for it. I have something for you"

Julian knew enough not to question. If it was some sort of trap, there was nothing he could do anyway. In Italy these days, delay was the only thing that could occur to interfere with one's fate. Better, he thought, to get it over with.

"What time?" asked Julian suddenly alert again.

"3:00 a.m. and come alone."

"Is there another way to travel at three in the morning?"

"Salute, Signore Corona," Geraldo said raising his own glass and reminding Julian of the Cardinal. In this light, in these surroundings, there was an uncanny resemblance between the two of them, Geraldo and the Cardinal. It was the voice, the intonation, the subliminal sound of a connection that was deeper than master and servant. Again, he thought as he turned to leave, what difference would it make? The world was at the brink, better to be the first one over than the last.

Eighty~One

That night Julian and Isabelle were entertaining some friends of his from the court. Giorgio was to be there but had cancelled at the last minute. Without him it would likely be a dull party but it would help pass the time until three rolled around.

It sounded like pebbles being thrown at the window as Julian turned around and looked out at the night sky.

"Its ice—hail," he said turning to Isabelle.

"Hail? In Rome?" she said.

"It's the weather. The weather is the weather everywhere."

Isabelle shifted in her seat, uncomfortable with so many people in the flat, concerned that she not appear to be silly or, worse, unsophisticated, went to the window and watched the small pellets pop up and down on the veranda. A few had hit the wet glass and were meandering down the slick surface like ice skaters defying gravity. Julian never really wanted to be in Rome. He detested big city life. Having lived in Manhattan in his youth he had tired of the artificial hubbub, the crowded streets, the rank odors of darkened doorways and the incessant high price of everything.

Julian turned back to the room but the pelting of the ice got louder. A rat-tat-tat muffled by the thick cold air made him turn to the window again.

"That's gunfire."

Voices distant and watery drifted in the air. The veranda appeared to be covered with gravel. In the gray dusk the ice pellets looked like a million skulls might look from a mountaintop.

Reflected in the window, Julian saw the room like a movie screen. The hushed red of the oriental rug and the dark brown sofa melted into the green walls. Oil paintings of flowers and hunt scenes, a bunch of vegetables in the shape of a hare—the fennel jowls, celery stalk ears, black olive eyes. A nightmare of a salad, hallucinatory. Isabelle's face with dark shadows under her eyes. Their neighbor from down the hall Signora Rafellini and her teenage son, Luca, biting his nails and nervously kicking the coffee table legs, the thunking keeping preposterous time with the hail.

"Gunfire? That's ridiculous. This isn't Buenos Aires," said Carina Roth rising from the thick chair she had curled up in, straightening her dress as if brushing off crumbs. "Let me see," she said, going to the window and leaning against it with her hand as a sun visor to keep out the reflection. Her breath made sporadic pools of mist on the cold glass. "I can't see a thing. It's too dark."

Carina was Isabelle's closest confidant. She had been married to Albert Roth, a German Jew. Albert had several books of poetry published by Faber & Faber of London and was a good friend to T.S. Eliot and Ezra Pound, as good a friend as any Jew could be, in Eliot's words. Carina had tired of him, though his meager inconsistent income and his introspective lifestyle clashed with Carina's party-girl antics. Fearful of the Fascists open anti-Semitism and the rumors of Nazi atrocities forced Albert to flee to Greece and then to the United States. Carina took advantage of the situation, kissed him goodbye both literally and figuratively at the Port of Naples and considered herself divorced, Italian and American law to the contrary notwithstanding.

She did have a serious side, though. In fact, Julian thought that the entire façade of superciliousness and occasional over-drinking was a disguise of a deep and thoughtful nature. He remembered visiting her with Isabelle. Her apartment overlooked a gloomy alleyway in the southern end of Rome near the highway to Naples. Julian saw the gloom of her apartment to be an extension of her spirit. While Carina and Isabelle were trying on clothes in the bedroom, Julian found a pad on the kitchen table. In her wispy handwriting that reminded him of a spider web, she had repeatedly written, "like boats against the current," hundreds of times and it filled twelve pages of foolscap notepaper. The pattern of writing from a slight distance appeared as though the phrases were the residue of waves on a beach in the sand, the peculiar echoing rhythm of an untroden strand on a shore where tides and wind carved rippling rows. He could not place the quotation, familiar as it was. It might have been her own thought, but it attracted him to her in an insidious way.

In his own flat, the lights of the buildings across the street cast orange shadows onto the stone facades. Street lamps came on and the sun a red globule in the thick clouds slinked behind the far hills like a burglar. Traffic was light and the hail turned to rain, headlights cast twin conical beams in front of the cars showering the wet streets with shifting puddles of glitter. People walked with umbrellas and from Julian's third floor window the sidewalks looked as if they were a mushroom patch of black, shiny mushrooms that could mysteriously move about with no visible feet.

"So John told her that if she didn't straighten up and fly right she'd be out in the street. I mean who can blame him? She's been fooling around with that German—what's his name?—for at least a year. A wonder it took him that long to give her the old heave-ho or else." Isabelle was playing with her toes as she spoke. "What is his name, Julian? What is that Nazi's name?"

"I don't know that he is a Nazi, dear," said Julian still staring out the window. Three women had come out of the café across the street and were walking under the awning swinging their handbags like miner's lanterns. "Detmar is the name. You've only met him six or seven times," said Julian.

"I'm not good with names. I thought…"

The screech of breaks outside on the street stopped the conversation in mid- sentence. The boy, Luca, got up and went to the window and looked down. The rain had stopped and small thin snowflakes fell diagonally in a short breeze.

He and Julian saw a black police car parked half up on the sidewalk, its canvas top was up but it had no windows or doors.

"It's the Carabinieri."

One black and red-uniformed officer alighted and with his club he nudged the three women away, goosing one of them and making her hop, then giggle, then scowl at him over her shoulder. The other three policemen, all in the same distinctive, overly elaborate costume of the Italian State Police strolled into the café. Julian could see only rapid shadows skittering across the wet sidewalk and gutter. A few stragglers stopped and peered in the café windows, then left rapidly with collars raised and hands holding their hats against the wind.

In a few minutes with the women chattering on in the background about fashion or politics or both, Julian watched the door of the café slam open onto the sidewalk. Two Carabinieri were manhandling Armando, the café's owner, out into the street. He resisted at first but once in the open air, he simply went limp and then, as if revived by the cold air, stood on his own and walked calmly to the awaiting car. One officer held the door open while the other pushed him inside, climbing in after him. The other ran around and got in the opposite door leaving Armando surrounded left and right by guards while the other two got in front.

The car crunched into first gear and took off down the street toward the municipal center.

"They've taken Armando," Julian announced to his guests. No one responded except with silence.

"Was he a Communist?" asked Carina.

"No, he was a café owner," said Isabelle, "and a very nice one. Why he always gave us the best table and…"

"I don't know if he was a Communist or not," said Julian. "Mussolini's people may have thought so."

"Well, he had to have done something. They don't arrest people for doing nothing, do they?" asked Carina.

"No, I suppose not," said Julian.

By midnight, after Julian has performed at least half-a-dozen obvious yawns, they all departed and he and Isabelle got into bed, the snow having stopped.

Eighty~Two

82 The phosphorescent dial of the alarm clock showed 2:15 a.m. Julian lay in bed tensely listening to Isabelle's rhythmic breathing. With the blindfold she sometimes wore when she thought she might sleep past sunrise, she looked a little like a raccoon. She would not awaken until noon. He had been wondering why her mood had changed so dramatically over the past few weeks. She had actually become unrelentingly cheerful and it was disconcerting.

He slipped out of bed noiselessly and softly padded his way to the parlor. Under the sofa were his work clothes, as he liked to think of them; a black sweater, black trousers and black loafers. He thought he looked foolishly like a French cabaret singer missing his beret but the truth was that all in black he melted into the inky dark of pre-dawn Rome. He felt the smooth ebon surface of the straight razor in his pocket cradled in three hundred-lira notes.

Out in the street, the cold had no effect on him. Shoulders hunched and hands in his pockets, he made his way along the Via Maranello to the Via Fulgencia, a walk of about two miles. The streets were deserted and in the distance he could make out the occasional ramblings of trucks heading in and out of the farmers' market on the Palatino. One of the many things that could be said about Mussolini was that he kept his city clean. Many, under their breath, had whispered that this was a good attribute for a housekeeper, not a leader of men. Others whispered that Il Duce was probably henpecked by his mistress into tidying up his personal hygiene and this translated into a passion for making Rome sparkle much like a restored old palace. In public, of course, everyone praised him, saluted him and cheered his grotesque speeches. Julian always noticed the clean streets the way one might notice the smell of antiseptic in an operating room or the lack of smell in a funeral home. Even Il Duce's numerous posters, plastered all over the city in even rows were immune to the vicissitudes of wind and rain and only the bravest and most foolish youths in violation of the curfew ventured an artistic attack on Mussolini's image, placing a Hitleresque mustache on his fat, chiseled face. Many thought it apropos, but few laughed even in the privacy of their own homes.

Bravery and foolishness, Julian thought. These often went hand in hand. Where did foolishness end and bravery begin? Was it foolish to climb the sheer face of Mont Blanc or brave? Was it foolishness to walk the iron of the new civic center that Mussolini was erecting on the Capitolino or bravery? Is one an abject fool to lead a charge or a brave hero? Perhaps it depended on results. If the mountain climber falls, he is a fool. If he plants a flag at the summit, a hero. If the ironworker completes his ten stories, he is a brave soul. If he falls, he was a careless idiot who disregarded the welfare of his wife and children. If the charge succeeds in some abstract objective, the soldier receives a medal or a promotion in rank or both. If he is killed, he was foolish in miscalculating the odds. In life, Julian thought, we are neither fools nor heroes. We simply get from one day to the next driven by forces we do not recognize or cannot understand. When we die, others who knew us in varying degrees of intimacy look down at our graves and think, "He was a fool" or "He was brave." The only truth is that we are dead.

Parked cars lined the streets like coffins in a coffin factory. Julian slipped into a narrow alleyway and gently tapped on the door at the end. Except for a mail slot with the number "18" on it, there was no indication that this was anything but an anonymous portal to an anonymous room in any one of a thousand anonymous buildings in the city of Il Duce, the Eternal City, the city of patiently waiting victims.

He knocked on the door and Sonya answered. She smiled as she recognized Julian and she led him into a nicely fitted parlor with furniture and paintings very similar if not identical to those in the Vatican apartments of the Cardinal.

She asked Julian if he wanted something to drink and he refused saying something about the lateness of the hour but he realized as if a light had gone on in some remote corner of his brain that this was obviously the secret quarters of the Cardinal. As his mind swirled around that fact, Geraldo appeared in a dressing gown of deep blue silk. He handed Julian a packet in which were several documents, possibly letters.

"Forgive me the sub rosa nature of these proceedings, Signore Corona, but times are difficult and dangerous. The Cardinal wanted you to have these. Now, I know it is very late...or early depending on your point of view. Let me show you out."

Julian thanked him in a hushed secretive way and departed feeling very much the way he thought spies must feel when in the possession of state secrets and the enemy is all about waiting to pounce.

Eighty~Three

83 The next day, Cardinal Sabatinni met with the Pope. He outlined in detail his opinion that the Church should not condemn the Nazis for any activities they undertook either with the Jews or any of the other "enemies of the state" as defined by Hitler. The Pope's emissary in Berlin would extract a promise from the Reich's Chancellery that Catholic priests would no longer be arrested and persecuted unless they committed a crime other than being clergy. The Pope, a fool and amateur at international affairs, an old woman of a leader elected because of his easy ignorance, his pliant morality and his indebtedness to several powerful Cardinals, took Paolo Sabatinni's advice. The problem had been resolved. The Cardinal assured the Pope that the Germans and Italians would win the war or at the very least gain control of all Europe. He did not believe this personally himself. The Church, if it wanted to take part in the spoils would have to support the victors. England and America, after all, were Protestant countries and God's wrath would punish them at the hands of the Axis. The Russians were atheists, the French lapsed Catholics. If blood had to be spilled to secure the sovereignty of Mother Church, it would not be the first drops. The Pope was well-pleased and thanked Paolo profusely even using his first name as he hugged him.

As the Cardinal walked back to his quarters, he made plans for his return to the Villa Franca. The circle had closed, he realized. He had planted the virus in Mother Church that would ultimately destroy it and expose it to the world for what it was; a monster born from the pure and innocent blood of Jesus of Nazareth, populated by the greedy, the covetous, the power-mad and the perverse. Paolo felt he was God's instrument and that from the corpse of the Church, men could find an unfettered path to God's love.

Eighty~Four

84 Julian awoke at eleven and didn't look at Isabelle. Thin beams of sunlight peeked around the edges of the heavy bedroom drapes and dust particles floated like gnats in and out of the light and shadow.

He put on his robe and went to the kitchen, filling the maganetta and putting in the measured heaps of Turkish coffee methodically. He sat down and opened his notebook and began to write. His novel, which rattled around in his skull for nearly four years, was finally finding its way to the golden nib of the fountain pen Isabelle had given him when they first met. She had fallen in love with Julian the writer, at least that is who she thought he was. A six-month courtship amid the upheavals of Europe seemed sometimes like a century. And other times, he thought, no engagement was long enough to reach about in the darkness of the other's soul and open the dusty and locked boxes that could be found there. Only the newest gilded cases were brought out for inspection and many of them weren't gold at all, but only deceptively highly polished brass. Open in the light of new passion their emptiness was disguised in high ideals, lofty goals and the promise of a rich and loving future. Truth lay like a moth-eaten piece of black felt at the bottom and fell out at an importune time when the box, finally realized to be empty, was turned upside down and tapped hard with the impatience of a tomb robber. There was no Pandora's Box, the legend he was taught in grade school of supercilious Pandora opening the box and freeing all the woes and sins of the world in a great flurry of flapping leather wings. He had imagined them as bats or hellish butterflies fleeing to the corners of the globe and spreading disease, misery and sin. But wait, his teacher said, wait. The last creature to emerge was Hope and that is what gives us all the motivation to go on when the odds seem the most slim. Julian knew now that his teacher was simply one of many dolts he had had the misfortune to encounter. Hope was not the salvation of the world contaminated by that slut Pandora, but the worst blight of all. It belonged with all the other evils and woes. Hope was the demon that mislead, that wasted life in the waiting, that argued with the way things were and deceived that things might change. No doubt the ancient Greeks knew this as they seemed to know all things long before the rest of the world. We have misinterpreted the legend. It was not Hope that lured the three hundred Spartans to defend their country at Thermopylae against the Persians in the hundreds of thousands. It was acceptance. Disease, Defeat and Death were the true gods of men and Hope their gods' greatest weapon. With Hope, one would try against all odds in defiance of reason and all religion required this defiance, this abandonment of logic.

As his pen poised over the blank page like a vulture looking for carrion, the thin strains of violin music emerged from the apartment below. It was Carla, the twenty-four year old daughter of Francesco Rota. They lived together. Her mother had died in a typhus outbreak, unable to leave the city, and the baby, for all its high price, had been born deaf. Francesco had at first hated the little girl for stealing the life of his beloved wife, but after a time he became doting and loving. He hired a tutor to teach her sign language and one day he bought her a gramophone made in America. He taught her to wind it and to place the mysterious grooved, black disk on its rotating platform; to gently place the nickel-coated needle in the groove and to hold the lily-shaped megaphone with both hands to feel the beautiful strains of Vivaldi seep from the machine into her pale white fingers, flow up her arms through her shoulders and her small neck into her mind's ear. With her eyes closed, the music painted pictures in her brain of faraway places, places that existed nowhere but within her. As others go to church, Carla had her gramophone.

If he had planned on writing a bestseller, he might have related Carla's story as a moral, saying there are none so deaf as those who will not hear. But he would rather shoot himself. There are none so deaf as those who are deaf; none so blind as those who are blind and none so happy as those who are dead. This last bit was pushing it, he thought. A year ago he would have been quite smug with his pessimism, thinking himself above the riffraff. Had he discovered that he had a year, perhaps less, to live, he would not have changed one minute of his life. The hypothetical made him feel something, but what that was, was still hidden away even to him.

Julian started to write hurriedly because he knew that once Isabelle was up and about she would occupy his mind with the fripperies of the day. She was usually apolitical and didn't seem to care a whit about the Fascists, the Communists, the Socialists and the other controlists that ran roughshod over the people who simply tried to get through the day and pay the rent on the first of the month.

Julian had placed the packet of letters which were in a small manila envelope closed with the Cardinal's seal in red wax in the drawer where he kept his razor. Some might think it inhuman that he did not forthwith open them the minute he had gotten to a private place. But Julian was no character from your hometown. He knew these letters were no Christmas present nor the tomfoolery of a birthday gift, a celebration particularly pointless and American. Whatever was in the letters could not bode well. The manner of their delivery insured that. Whatever it was could wait, he thought, but he knew that they had to be opened. If he were the praying type he might have implored God to give him the serenity to be able to read them and not react. The letters themselves were merely paper with an accumulation of words and paragraphs. To anyone but he, they were a curiosity at best, unintelligible at worst. He retrieved them and placed them on his table.

Isabelle woke and called out for Julian. He responded that he was in the kitchen writing and that he would like to do it for a while. He could hear her moving about, drawers opening and closing and when she finally appeared, she was dressed and ready to go marketing after a cup of coffee. He carefully placed a pile of loose papers over the packet of letters and they each spoke briefly of last evening's visits. She kissed him as she got up from the table and took his cup and hers to the sink saying she'd wash them and the leftover glasses from last night when she returned with groceries. She was cheerful, indeed.

Eighty~Five

He knew she'd be gone for some time so that he would write without being disturbed. She might even visit Carina across the way. There would be no better time. He broke the wax seal and immediately recognized Daria's hand. The three crows of anxiety, black feathers, black beaks, yellow dead eyes like the spots on the back of a cobra, inert and scaly landed on the balcony and waited.

When he had finished reading, he took the letters, put them in a large pot from under the sink and burned them, tossing the ashes with a fork as if they were the salad from the decayed trees of Eden. Isabelle was suddenly someone revealed as if at some magic show when one's eyes have been fooled by a slight of hand or a planned distraction. Interestingly, even to Julian it was not the engineering of Daria's and Robert's murder, nor even the gruesome means. That Isabelle would lie with the Duke, subject herself to his perversions which all Rome knew of, that she would sacrifice her vows to him to control him, filled him not with rage but remorse. She was his chosen, the woman he loved above all others, but that Isabelle had committed suicide the minute she opened her arms to the Duke. No mere jealousy, not even betrayal was at the core of his sudden feeling of isolation. It was her purpose and that she would go to such inhuman lengths and for a mistaken notion. He had never even entertained the idea of reuniting with Daria. She was as dead to him emotionally as a stranger in Oslo. Such errors are perilous, such venom does the viper inject into even the most harmless of its encounters. There was no going back. No reprieves. No forgiveness. The Cardinal knew all this. It was for the love and respect of a dear friend that he had stepped outside his personal boundaries and divulged the truth to Julian. He knew the Cardinal had nothing to gain from getting involved and Cardinal Sabatinni never did anything unless it was for his gain. He was his truest friend.

When he had finished burning the letters and staring at the lengthening shadows on the façade of the building across the street, he simply waited for Isabelle to return.

Soon he heard shouts and cheers in the streets. Was it Mussolini making an unscheduled tour? A victory for the Roman football team? He went downstairs and people were spontaneously pouring out onto the sidewalks. Julian was handed a newspaper by a man chanting "Il Duce! Il Duce!" with the crowd. The headline read, "Hitler Invades Poland!" and in smaller print, "Italy and Germany Declare War on England and France"

Julian wandered through the throng being kissed by strange women, hugged by strange men. Julian thought of the legend, probably fiction, of how Nero fiddled while Rome burned. Indeed, he knew that in the not-too-distant future, Rome would burn, along with the rest of Europe, possibly even the whole world. These thoughts turned the sky to lead where a tin moon rose weakly as dusk settled in. Isabelle would see none of it.

Julian arrived at the flat as the weak November sun of 1939 shed its tremulous lavender light on the towers and marble of Rome. Isabelle was in the kitchen preparing a salad and pasta for dinner. She was humming an indecipherable tune, breaking out every few notes into a soft, sad refrain, something that sounded like Debussy's "Girl with the Flaxen Hair" lilting and sad in the dusky hours. He sat in his chair by the window to watch the sky fade, to drain of color as a flower out in the sun for too many days pales, withers, then browns.

Isabelle set the table and brought the food out, placing it ritualistically on the table with the pride she usually showed in her ability to make simple things beautiful in unexpected ways. Julian said he wanted her in the bedroom first and when she resisted, because she said, the food would get cold, he responded by saying nothing but looking at her in his seductive way that never failed to override her own wishes and submit to his.

He instructed her to disrobe which she did as usual whenever he seemed to take control of their intimate life. In every other aspect, she offered some resistance to his powerful subtle way of directing her as an individual and they as a couple, but in the bedroom she always allowed him the privilege, even the right, of becoming the dictator of her body. She had learned subconsciously somewhere along the path of her life that the pair of them, like pairs everywhere, were in an unceasing battle for control over each other. Such battles were often disguised as arguments over petty insults, daily inconsiderations, and unpleasant and insignificant habits. Isabelle knew that to attempt to impose control over Julian would create in him not acquiescence but further resistance, so that nothing but discord would result. However, if she could yield on certain points, Julian would return the gesture unknowingly by yielding on certain other points. She thought Julian to be what is commonly called "a good person," a term overused because few people, if any, can define it, but rather pull it out of their lexicon to describe admirable behavior in people they love. No one who knew Julian well, and no one did, would define him as "a good person" but he did enough good things to endear himself to most people he came in contact with and his motives were obfuscated, sometimes even to himself. Isabelle thought him a good person because he had adopted her principal of yielding when she needed him to on some superficial level.

Julian went into the parlor and put on the record of Caruso's "Pagliacci." He returned and unceremoniously took off his clothes and let them drop to the floor as if shedding his skin. Only his white shirt was draped on the footboard of the old bed like the remnants of a ghost that had visited and stayed too long. The room was dark except for the reddish glow of the light reflected off of Rome into the humid air that rose from the Tiber in the evening, blotting out most of the stars and reveling in the glare of Mussolini's new street lamps and the beams of search lights aimed at the heavens as if to say, we are here again, "Roma Infinitim Sansi Mortis."

Julian lay gingerly on top of Isabelle and kissed her gently, not passionately, supporting his weight on his knees and arms, never putting too much of it on her as if he treasured her too much, that in leaning heavily he might damage her. She closed her eyes in the moment, the yellow shaft of the light from the parlor coming through the bedroom door like a shaft of sunlight on a cloudy day, glowing in its diagonal stream the way light filters through the clerestory in a cathedral illuminating a billion particles of dust in its slanted holiness.

In a quick, quiet motion, he straddled her, sitting on her belly and taking the breath out of her. She opened her eyes and looked up at him half in puzzlement as to what he was doing, half in awe as a silhouette against the slant of golden light showed him to be an angel or a demon, which she could not determine. He grabbed her by the throat and squeezed as hard as he could; she struggled and squirmed beneath him to no avail, her arms reaching up and frantically flailing at the air, his shoulders, his face. At first, Isabelle felt that Julian was possessed and that all this was the work of a demonic force. She could feel her heart racing and beating as a timpani in her ears which throbbed. She gasped uncontrollably for air looking up as if at the bottom of a well into which she had fallen. She was under water in its depths and clawing at some handhold which eluded her. In a circle of light at the top, so very distant, she could make out the face of her beloved but he did nothing but watch. When she tried to scream, her voice was empty and silent, drowned out by the water and lack of air in her burning lungs. Then it seemed she could breathe. No she was mistaken. She did not need to breathe anymore. All pain left her. Her panic ebbed and was replaced with coolness, the cold of pure water from an underground spring. She was rising out of the well, lifted by unseen hands, more like a thick wind or a bubble of air below her. The circle of light at the top of the well expanded outward. Julian's face became larger, more distinct, his eyes blank and pitiless but her love enduring, imploring as if he were asleep and she was trying to wake him. His face filled the sky as she rose above the lip of the well. The earth had vanished and Julian's face was like the sun in a starless universe. Still she could not tell him how much she loved him. Tears filled her eyes and their liquid distorted his image, the light that he gave off faded until she was not only mute but blind as she felt herself dissolve.

Julian looked down at her as if from a great height as one standing on a cliff might from its very edge look straight down into a bottomless abyss where two candles had been placed in the darkening crevasse. Those candles where the weak reflective light in her eyes. His hands were like a vice on her throat, not a sound could escape as he felt the gurgling of her saliva and the thick rings of her hyoid cartilage bending under the force of his grip. The eyes he looked down on were the same that evening in Llafranc, back in Spain where they were looking upward at the fireworks that filled the night sky at the festival of St. John. These were the eyes that he remembered seeing so much love in, the eyes he had given up so much for. He could feel his hands weakening as memory after memory flooded his brain, confusing his purpose and weakening his resolve until he imagined her looking up into the face of Duke Edmond Montrose. A surge of energy left his gut, shot through his chest and into his shoulders, down his arms like cobra venom flowing on its deadly mission through the arteries that ordinarily would bring life but now carried only the poison of his jealousy. The muffled crunch as the cartilage in her neck finally cracked was like a light switch being flicked, the struggling ceased, her muscles relaxed, her arms drooped from his shoulders to his thighs, the narrow points of light in her eyes which had filled with tears flowing down the sides of her face went dim. The record in the parlor had stopped its singing and the pulsing swoosh of the needle made a wheezing sound like someone sawing wood in a forest far off.

Julian stood by the bed and covered her body with the sheet that had been crumpled to the floor. He dressed her slowly, went into the parlor, turned off the phonograph and dialed Giorgio's number.

He apologized for interrupting his dinner and said that Isabelle had met with a mishap and that she was dead. He told Giorgio he needed to have the body picked up in the usual fashion by the "special ambulance." He said, "Grazie" as he hung up the receiver and waited for the attendants to arrive. He took the meal Isabelle had prepared back to the kitchen, dishes, cloth and all, and dropped it down the dumbwaiter.

As he went to the balcony to watch for the ambulance he saw a white envelope on the sideboard with his and her name typed on it and the words "Hand Deliver" in capitals underlined. It was from the municipal hospital. He opened it, read the letter, read it twice, read it a third time. He put it back into its neat envelope and stood silently for a minute. In the still night air he could hear music coming from a flat across the way. He could barely make it out but it sounded like Debussy, the flowing strains of "Girl with the Flaxen Hair." He took the envelope and threw it down the dumbwaiter shaft where he imagined it fluttering slowly like a butterfly in the breeze, lighting on the broken dishes of their uneaten supper at the bottom.

The squeal of the brakes out front awoke him from his trance. Two attendants arrived in black uniforms and efficiently placed Isabelle's body into a black canvas body bag that was fitted with rope handles. Without saying a word, they nodded a salute and carried her out to the waiting truck, placed her in it and sped off through the Roman night.

Julian retrieved the large suitcase from under the bed and began to pack all her belongings, emptying the drawers on her side of the dresser and the vanity items, the little odds and ends that Professor Cortez had told him was the outline of the deceased, the true ghost of the departed. The suitcase was not large enough but he filled it to overflowing and forced the latch to close, the sides of the suitcase nearly bursting.

He went out on the balcony, leaving the suitcase on the bed and looked up at the empty sky. The letter from the hospital informed Mr. & Mrs. Julian Corona that Isabelle was pregnant, the test being positive, and that she should schedule an appointment with her obstetrician at her earliest convenience.

The next day a letter arrived from Drouet Fontenot. Julian didn't realize that Isabelle had kept up a correspondence of sorts with her father. They were distant, she more from him than he from her, but she kept in touch over the years. Julian put the letter in a drawer and then waited a few days. He removed it and opened it and saw that it was nothing important, just an attempt at keeping his daughter up on the latest news at the chateau and hoping she would come to visit someday. He also said to give his regards to Julian.

Julian wrote a letter to Drouet that very evening. In it, he said that Isabelle had disappeared about a week before and that she had been found dead, the victim of either a random crime or because of her involvement with a small group of Communists which, Julian said, were merely friends talking about ideals and having no political intentions whatsoever. He expressed his condolences and said how much he missed her, that her body had been cremated by order of a local magistrate and that he was sorry to be the bearer of such terrible news. Even in wartime, Julian had the power to see that his letter was delivered. France had capitulated and was now part of the German Reich, the French proving to the world the spineless cowards they were.

Two weeks later, Drouet Fontenot appeared at Julian's front door. His face was drawn and it looked like he had neither eaten nor slept since he had gotten the letter. Julian invited him in to sit but that he could not stay long for he had important business in Naples to attend to, which was a quick lie he had dreamed up the minute he realized that it was Isabelle's father.

Drouet said that he did not intend to stay long but he had wanted to tell Julian how much his daughter had loved him, that she spoke of Julian in the most glowing terms and that he wanted to thank Julian for being so supportive and loving of Isabelle whom he referred to as his "little dove." He reached into his pocket and took out a small package in brown paper. He told Julian that she had sent it to him for safekeeping and that she would want it later after she and Julian had married. He handed it to Julian and asked if he had any recent photographs of Isabelle. Julian said he did and went into the bedroom to retrieve a small black and white photo of Isabelle he had had taken for her traveling documents. It was insignificant and it showed her with a slight smile which was actually quite attractive for an official document. He handed it to Drouet who looked at it and sighed deeply as if he was about to weep but had shed enough tears already. He put it in his pocket, thanked Julian and then hugged him tightly thanking him for taking such good care of his daughter and for loving her, that he would have been proud to have had Julian as a son-in-law, but it was not to be. He departed.

Julian sat for a few moments and then opened the package. It was a large yellow diamond ring and a Cartier wristwatch. With them was a note which said, "Papa, please hold on to these. I may need them someday after I am married. Isabelle."

After midnight, Julian went to the Ponte Cesare Borgia a few blocks from the flat. He made certain no one was about and, as a light rain began to fall, dropped the jewelry into the murky water of the river, repairing another error he had made long ago.

Eighty~Seven

87 The war passed over Europe as nothing else in history. Even by Biblical standards it was six years of unequaled brutality, devastation and death. It would be futile to say anymore. The proper words are elusive, thousands of volumes have been written, films produced, analyses made of every event from the minute to the apocalyptic.

When the Americans had made their way up the boot of Italy, Julian Corona was arrested along with Giorgio DeVecchi and everyone connected with Mussolini's Ministry of Justice. They were both released, however, Giorgio because he still had connections strong enough to withstand even Patton's army and Julian because he was ever Giorgio's friend. Julian, as an American, was retained by the occupying forces to identify the worst offenders, although Italians in general bore little blame, rightfully perhaps, for the war. They had revolted against Il Duce and had managed to find him on his way to Germany to hide with Hitler. He and his mistress were beaten and battered by the mob which only a year before had cheered him. They hung his body and that of his hapless ladyfriend upside down in the square like butchered hogs. No one thought he deserved any less, at least publicly.

Mother Church's role in Hitler's activities would take decades to unravel. But it was small in the public eye because the Church's diseased carcass came under scrutiny for other reasons and much like the Roman Empire itself upon which it had modeled its absurd hierarchical structure, it became a shell of itself, a shadow only of the force that once dominated every minute of every life in Europe. Now it had to deal with innumerable court proceedings and diminishing relevance in a world made complex by events that tumbled and multiplied through the corridors of history.

Cardinal Sabatinni retired when the Americans landed in Sicily with a huge pension and funds accumulated in a variety of creative ways. With Sonya and Geraldo he moved into the Villa Franca and outfitted it to his own taste and style. To the outside world, Sonya was the housekeeper and Geraldo still the loyal assistant, the Cardinal still a Deacon of the church. Geraldo was devoted to helping the less fortunate which in 1946 was almost everyone in Italy except his family. He remained a priest and was given the parish around the Villa Franca including the town of Saltura where he tended sincerely and with great effect to the souls of its residents.

Julian was never the same after the loss of Isabelle. He devoted himself to survival at which he was quite adept but after the war tribunals which were few and short-lived in Italy, he retired as well. The years shown on his face and while he was only middle-aged, he looked older, his hair almost completely silver, the color of tarnished sterling, lines on his face and a deep furrow between his brows that many women found attractive, the way they might also be drawn to a man with a scar. It was one thing to survive, quite another to survive unscathed. But there were to be no more women in Julian's life. He was content to read and to work on the novel he had started so many years before, writing a paragraph or two each day or every other day like humming a tune that is never finished. One day he received a letter from Cardinal Sabatinni inviting him to spend the summer at the Villa Franca.

He arrived one beautiful morning in August of 1946 and was greeted warmly and lovingly by the Cardinal as if they were blood relatives. In some ways they were, as the survivors of a catastrophe. Julian was particularly fond of the gardener's cottage across from the home in the rear courtyard. The Cardinal suggested he stay there after having it decorated with some fine antiques and artwork from the main house. Julian never left, but, with the Cardinal's blessing of course, was invited to stay and live out his days there.

The Cardinal, then, had his friend, someone he could unabashedly confide in and Julian had a place to live, remote and timeless as his own soul. In bits and pieces, the Cardinal spoke of Marco and of his true relation to Sonya and Geraldo of Brother Xavier and countless other patches of his experience that made up the fabric of his life. Sonya came to accept

Julian as her husband's dear friend and said a secret prayer of thanks every night that God or fate had brought them all safely through.

Julian helped the Cardinal renovate the small graveyard by the river, placing poetic inscriptions carved by the hands of the local stone cutter on fitting white marble tombstones. A tall, black wrought iron fence guarded the periphery of the place but there were no crosses or statues of weeping angels or saints either mutilated or with upturned eyes. The Cardinal thought it an insult to ask any power to watch over the departed boys of Saint Ubaldo's now that they were dead. They needed help when they were alive and it never came.

A black and white marble chessboard was crafted in Rome by a renowned maker of tombstones. It had one white agate and one black obsidian checker permanently in place next to each other in the corner squares. This was the grave marker of little Giulio. When it was in place and the Cardinal bowed his head in thought, it was the first and only time Julian saw a tear rise in the Cardinal's eyes.

A little less than a year after his removal to the Villa Franca, Julian was sitting in the rear courtyard with a book of poetry and reading it aloud to no one but himself in soft murmurous tones as if he were praying. The Cardinal stood in the doorway watching, then walked over to him and said he had just purchased two steamer tickets for a trip to Damascus. The ship was scheduled to depart in two days from Bari and would dock in Haifa, a port city in the newly formed nation of Israel. From there, they would go by rail to Damascus in Syria. It was a journey he had thought of making often for many years and it was imperative that Julian accompany him. Julian accepted without questioning, assenting with a nod as if a long conversation had ensued and said he would pack in time to leave the following day.

They arrived in Damascus amid the feverish hubbub of the post-war Middle East, British trucks and soldiers everywhere, suspicious characters that everyone knew were Stalinist spies, Americans in expensive clothing making business deals with swarthy men in richly white caftans, women in burkas, women in Western garb that was the latest from Paris or Milan, all swirling together in a city as old as the mountains and as dusty as the moon. Camels grunted and spat; small, rusted cars beeped their high-pitched horns and the wind covered everything in the dun-colored sand of the desert.

Julian and the Cardinal managed to hire a guide named Kareem with a Fiat 600 that could take them to the village called Bar-al-Shakir about twenty miles from the city in the middle of the Babylonian desert, a home to scorpions, pit vipers, and vultures where Bedouins and Kurds migrated with flocks of black goats at the source of the great Mesopotamian Valley, where the Tigris and Euphrates were born in the snow-covered peaks of al-Rasham and where a British company was laying the foundation of a new hydroelectric power plant.

The Cardinal had heard some time back at the Villa from a friend recently returned from Jerusalem, that an itinerant preacher lived very near this area, had made quite an impression on a number of people by performing miracles, having saved a worker who had been crushed under a huge British earthmover, some said to death. He thought it would be interesting to see him but why he thought that and why he disregarded the onerous nature of the trip, he could not say.

When the Cardinal, Julian and Kareem arrived in their Fiat that had grunted and groaned over the rocky roads that were more goat paths than highways, they were informed after their inquiries that the "Holy Man" was in the foothills, a short distance away, just at the headwaters of the Tigris in a place called Fa'ahabar, the Stream of Life, where he would be preaching to whomever cared to listen and who was not otherwise occupied with the amassing of fortunes in those heady days following the collapse of the German Reich.

Kareem bargained for more money to take them to the village which, being hostages of sorts, they paid. He warned them that were no hotels or inns at such a remote and small village but they would have to content themselves with staying in a tent or a goatherd's hut, nothing like what they were used to at home, he hoped. Again, they consented and in about an hour with the Fiat's gears crunching madly and its tires squealing as it ambled over thick clods of sun-hardened clay the size of small boulders, they reached the town nearest the spot where the Holy Man would be preaching.

When they got out of the car feeling more like they had walked than ridden, Julian saw the far prospect from the plateau upon which the village was located. The vast plain of the Syrian desert spread out before them to the west, sterile and flat to the far hills, a cloud of dust in the distance like some Biblical column sent by God but which was, in fact, the British construction company moving equipment to the river which snaked imperceptibly in the waving lines of heat, wrinkling the air and distorting or concealing large sections of the panorama.

Julian and the Cardinal slept that night in a goatherd's hut. The owner and his wife and two sons removed themselves from their abode and bedded down nearby with the penned goats on a pile of straw. The Cardinal regretted the inconvenience but Kareem told him they were more than happy to oblige for the money they received would pay for their eldest son's wedding garb. He was to be married in a month's time to a girl from a neighboring village and they either had to sell a few of their valuable goats or bear the ignominy of a son at the altar wearing old clothes on his wedding day. Now their prayers had been answered and it was a clear sign that Allah had approved the upcoming nuptials.

That night, after a dinner of dried goat meat and lentils, Julian and the Cardinal sat on a conveniently flat boulder and spoke of some of the good times of their lives, the better parts of their journeys through life. They watched the stars materialize as the sun set and were awed by their sheer number and clarity, far more than could be seen from the Villa Franca even on the clearest of nights. They both had indigestion and laughed with dread at what the morning meal might be.

After awakening, the goatherd's wife served them a breakfast of tepid yogurt sprinkled with some type of nut and a thin disk of unleavened bread along with thick, dark coffee with goat's milk. They were informed that the Holy Man would be speaking within thirty minutes before the sun rose from behind the mountain in the east. This he did on a regular basis so that his audience would not be baked by the scorching sun. Kareem was still asleep in the back seat of the Fiat as their host led them to the vale just beyond the near ridge where the goats grazed. The sun had risen and was climbing the sky making the mountain purple as it was lit from behind.

They sat there and waited along with their host. About fifty other people were already sitting or leaning on rocks in the deep shadowed recesses of the vale, some eating bread or dried fruit.

After about ten minutes a man appeared at the crest of the hill at the apex of the vale. He was wearing a typical caftan, rather ragged with a white cloth over his head which he pulled off to let drape on his shoulders. His hair was long and he was unshaven although his beard was sparse. He was average in height and build and looked no different than any man they had seen since arriving in Haifa.

He spoke for about twenty minutes as the sun climbed and the shadows in the vale shortened. Their host had attempted to translate what he said but it came out as meaningless gibberish in very broken English. Afterwards, the preacher raised his hands in farewell and a few men and women approached and spoke privately to him, several kissing his hand or his shoulder as was the custom in those parts. The Cardinal motioned to Julian that they should go to him and they began the short trek up the gravelly hillside. As they approached, the preacher stopped and looked at them as if he knew them. Up close he appeared quite handsome with a sharp well-defined nose and piercing, gray eyes. Julian reached out his hand in the American fashion to shake it which the man did, holding Julian's hand and saying in perfect English, "I am glad you came. Your journey and that of your friend has been a long one. Would that I could have spent more time with you but I must be going. There is a sick child in the village over there, west of here some 3 kilometers distant and I promised to attend. But know that I see the darkness in you and that you are lost. Think on all that has happened. Perhaps there is hope yet." Julian did not respond, but the man turned to the Cardinal and said something of a similar nature to him in perfect Italian. Then, he turned and left as a hot breeze lifted off the floor of the desert below them and scattered the dust into the shadows as the sun broke free of the mountain and filled the vale with a blinding, arid light.

Eighty~Eight

88 It was in the spring of 1949 while Julian and the Cardinal were playing chess in the grand hall with the windows wide open and the breeze blowing through making the diaphanous, thin silk draperies billow and dance like the ghosts of the revelers at one of the old Duke's galas, that a taxi pulled up outside, the crunch of the gravel signaling a stop to the match. The Cardinal rose from his seat and went to the window.

A young man in a white linen suit climbed out of the cab, paid the driver and retrieved a small suitcase from the trunk of the car. He was six feet tall with sandy blond hair, thin in that awkward way that young men of twenty-one or twenty-two are thin. He put his hand on his brow to block out the rude, bright sunshine and squintingly looked up at the villa. The car waited as the young fellow went to the door and banged the knocker three times, loudly. He was obviously an American. A maid opened the door and looked at him as if he were an eastern potentate. His white suit ignited to a glow in the noon sun, his red silk tie and his bright blue eyes were a combination of features not many Salturans had encountered even after the American army passed through making ten percent of the young women of the town pregnant. She asked him who he was and what he wanted. In a studied Italian voice he introduced himself as Robert Berenson. He was looking for Julian Corona.

The maid closed the door in his face and he was about to depart when it reopened and the Cardinal stood there saying, "Come in, my boy, come in. Forgive Teresa. She is not accustomed to visitors here. Signore Corona is indeed here." He took the young man's hand shaking it and simultaneously drawing him into the front hall. The taxi took this as a cue to leave and the ticking of pebbles on the underside of his Fiat told everyone in the house that someone had arrived and would not soon depart.

The Cardinal took Robert out to the rear courtyard and bid him be seated at the large carved cement table that was placed there for summer dinners and days-long chess matches. Robert sat patiently looking about with all the innocence and muted awe of a tourist finding himself on an untrodden path. In a few minutes, though, the Cardinal returned with Julian who immediately recognized the boy and wanted to hug him but thought better of it when the boy rose and simply put out his hand saying, "It is good to see you again Mr. Corona. How are you? I must say I'm not sure I would recognize you. Oh, I don't mean it that way. It's been a long time is all. How are you, sir?"

Julian said he was fine, all things considered and he asked almost immediately why Robert had come as if his former status as stepfather had lost all its import and was merely a sobriquet for someone long dead.

"I'm looking for my mother," said Robert. "I wrote to you in Rome several times, but you never responded. It does not surprise me, though, as the war, well, the war confused everything, didn't it?" The question was really, "why didn't you look for me, you bastard, or at least try to contact me, you self-centered son-of-a-bitch." But Julian knew that Robert was genuine and bore him no ill will.

"I never received your letters. But had I, I couldn't have told you anything for I knew nothing."

"Didn't you send us a telegram to come to you?"

"No, I never did that. There must have been some mistake. I have no explanation." The meaning of these words were true, of course and Robert believed him, mostly. But everyone knew there was more to the story.

"I was in some hospital somewhere near the water with my mother. I don't remember where but it was in Italy and a man, I think he was a doctor, helped me escape although I don't know why I would have had to escape from a hospital."

"I'm sorry, Robert, but I know nothing of it. Nothing really. Have you tried the American Red Cross? They're helping people who have been relocated all over Europe by the war. Perhaps they can help you."

"Yes, I think you are right. I was intending to do that but I thought you might be able to help me. I guess now that you can't..." Robert reached into his briefcase and both men tensed, both thinking that Julian's time had come and that the boy was going to shoot him on the spot. The Cardinal instinctively got up suddenly from his chair and walked over to the boy as if to grab his arm before he could do anything rash. But Robert simply pulled a pen and pad out and looked up at the Cardinal as if to say, "Don't worry, I'm not like you or like Julian."

But, he said instead, "Can you give me the address of the Red Cross?"

The Cardinal replied, "Let me get it for you. I'll be right back." With that he walked inside and left the two of them.

"I'm sorry for what happened. Terribly sorry. The war—it has all been a dreadfully long nightmare. Sometimes I think I'm still asleep in the middle of it. But I guess everyone feels that way. You are well, though?"

"As well as can be expected. I am engaged to be married next year and I so wanted my mother to be there." As he shifted in his seat something dropped out of his briefcase onto the flagstone. He bent to pick it up. Julian saw that it was a fountain pen, its gold fittings glistening in the sun. Robert looked at it pensively.

"That's a fine pen you have there," said Julian. "Might I see it?"

"I suppose. My real father gave it to me before he died. It never worked even after I refilled it with fresh ink and had an expert look at it. It just won't write, but I carry it with me because my father said he had gotten it from his father and, well, he thought it was something valuable and important so I carry it around with me for good luck." He handed it to Julian who immediately recognized the gilt crest as the same one painted on the wall of the third floor study, the Montrose family crest.

"Yes, it's very nice, very nice. Too bad it doesn't work." He handed it back to Robert who put it in his bag.

The Cardinal came out with a piece of paper with the contact numbers for the Red Cross on it.

"This should do," he said. "And good luck. I hear they do marvelous work helping people find lost loved ones. I've had Teresa call a cab for you. It should be here any minute. Why don't we wait in the parlor. Would you like a drink or something before you leave?"

Robert politely declined and they made their way through the French doors and in short order a taxi pulled up outside.

"Take care, Robert," said Julian. "Let me know what you find out. I'll be here." But he knew Robert would never contact him again. Robert was a man with a future and all that Julian represented was a past that no one wanted to remember. This might have bothered him, but it didn't. In fact, he looked back at his life often and only felt as much as you might of your own, that it was sometimes interesting, sad, boring, unreal, but with the same detachment one feels when reading one of those biographies of the dead clustered together on the long shelves of a bookstore. Julian felt that he and Marco were the ghosts of men that had missed their appointment to die.

As the cab drove down the narrow spine of the roadway with the steep chasm on both sides, the Cardinal put his arm around Julian's shoulder and they both walked back to the house.

"Now let's finish our game, good friend," he said.

Eighty~Nine

89 Some years after the deaths of his father, the Cardinal, his mother, Sonya, and their close friend Julian, Geraldo decided that above and beyond the good work he was doing in Saltura he should like to put his large inherited fortune to beneficial use. The villa was too large for one man who would never marry and so he thought he would convert it to an orphanage. Reports of street urchins in all the municipal centers in Italy spurred him to action and he renovated the villa to be a fine refuge for homeless children. He had the blessing of the Church, of course, and in short order the villa was staffed with nuns and priests all fitted with the apparent good motives with which such people are attributed.

During the renovations, one of those hundred year cyclical rains doused the Apennines with something like eighteen inches of water if television weathermen are to be believed. The river, usually only a peaceful meandering ribbon of silty water became a torrent overflowing its banks on both sides and rising ten feet above its normal depth. When the deluge expired, the beautiful tombstones of the children's graveyard had been toppled and broken like the ruins of some ancient Greek city. In a way, Geraldo was glad. He thought the markers would be a reminder of the new children's mortality and too gruesome in a world that had grown gruesome enough. Besides, it had never been consecrated and was to some extent, blasphemous.

At his own considerable expense, Geraldo had a dam built some five hundred yards up river, to dissuade the water from any further frenzies. The grave markers were tossed in as base stones for the formidable structure. The former graveyard was now the site of two beautiful tennis courts accessible by wooden stairs with a whitewashed handrail up to the orphanage and a view of the trickling stream that was once the untamed river.

Geraldo named the orphanage San Marco's after his father who was obviously a saint on earth. Indeed, to make the tribute complete, he had a statue of San Marco and one of San Paolo installed on either side of the front gate welcoming the homeless children who sought refuge from the world in the former Villa Franca's open, welcoming arms.

Epilogue

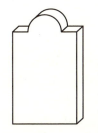

Professor Cortez's black lacquer box dropped unopened into the Seine by Julian Corona did not sink. The current carried it downstream for miles where two men on holiday fishing for trout saw it lodged in between the cattails that lined the river south of Paris in the area known as the Marsh de la Fontaine. They cracked it opened using a scaling knife and found a sheaf of folded papers with small, spidery handwriting. Disappointed that it was not money or something of value, they tossed the pages back into the river where the water and time dissolved the ink and the paper itself. Had they taken the time to read the notes, they would have learned the following from Professor Cortez:

"I have traced my heritage back to the master of a school in London who was a first cousin of the poet, John Milton. There was a maid there that he fell in love with. Her name was Alice Everdene.

"Alice Everdene was seventeen when both her parents and her older brother were killed in a riot when Cromwell's men mowed down a crowd of foolish reactionaries, foolish not for being reactionary but foolish for rioting in a time of dictatorship when the rule of law was left hanging by Puritans holding a Bible in one hand and an axe in the other. A more hideous form of religious governing would not be seen until the Moslems stopped drinking camel urine and took lessons in explosives.

"Alice's family was not the rioting type. In fact, they were at the market square that day to sell cheese which was how they made a living. Unmannered and illiterate, they set up a stand in a square full not of buyers but of antagonists and the Puritans' guns could not differentiate between threat and innocence nor would they have wasted their time judging. The Everdene family was eaten by the musket fire and only Alice, who had been napping under the cart, survived. In any event, Alice was left with no way of supporting herself, so she applied to a local nursing school with some reputation for accepting girls of the lower classes although just about everyone in attendance was at least two or three rungs above Alice. Nonetheless, her beautiful face and fulsome figure got her past the front door and it was only her inability to read and write that disqualified her. However, the headmaster, a Mr. Simpson, was sympathetic and took her in to be a scullery maid at one pound ten shillings per annum plus a cot in the kitchen and a go at the leftovers, with a promise that if she could learn to read and write, she would be admitted on a scholarship. Alice did not know what a scholarship was and had she asked she would have discovered from any of the other students that there were no scholarships at the Brigham Nursing Academy. But Mr. Simpson seemed a stout, good fellow, loyal and true with all his teeth in his head and a beard almost perfectly trimmed.

"Mrs. Simpson was a tight-fisted woman that looked ten years older than her husband. She taught several classes and was in charge of the kitchen staff with the bearing of Captain Bligh on the H.M.S. Bounty. She immediately disliked Alice because she was so terribly destitute and also because she was so pretty that for several weeks Mrs. Simpson could not look in the mirror for fear of realizing how inferior in appearance she was to Alice. Now it is well-known that the English are an unattractive lot at best with marginal hygiene habits and a nationalistic penchant for greasy foods which does little to improve the odor of their bodies. In this regard, Alice was quite the exception and few men of any class who might see her in the street could resist a long look and a subsequent repugnance for their own wives. It is no wonder the English love to visit Italy.

"Alice's story might be called the "Tale of the Watch" but that would be simplifying matters too much especially matters which would stretch so far into the future. Of all the servants at the school, Alice was on the lowest rung of the ladder. What we are calling here a ladder, implying that one might climb it, is giving her more hope than she had, although for a time she did not know this. Anyone familiar with the duties of a scullery maid would know that Alice had no time for anything personal, let alone the study of reading or writing. Her hands became cracked and dry from hours in hot water with lye soap. Her shoulders were incessantly hunched and developed into knotted masses which made her head bow forward slightly and her hair, steamed over the stove and wash basin became matted and frizzy. Nonetheless, she was still young and beautiful and in a matter of a few weeks had to push off two janitors and a porter who appeared in consecutive nights well after working hours while she slept the sleep of the exhausted. She had also been told by cook that the girl she replaced had been made pregnant by the grounds manager and died under the abortionist's knife.

"Alice may only have been seventeen, but she had now experienced enough to know that her future was not in this school. She had no real options, though, until one day she was called upon to help one of the chambermaids with making the beds of the schoolmaster and his wife in the north wing of the building. While she was being bullied about and told to do this and that as if she were a slave, she saw the master's gold watch on his dresser, a large thick-cased timepiece with a bulky chain and a ruby marking the number twelve. While she could not know its actual value, she realized it was worth at least twenty years of her current wages. In an amazing show of courage, she pocketed the bauble in her apron pouch while the chambermaid prattled on about a young porter carrying on with one of the students and losing his position and how cook's son had been arrested for some minor offense and had to pay a fine of five shillings and so on and so forth. Alice was happy to listen as if in escaping to the problems of others, she could find courage within herself to alter her fate. The weight of the gold watch, every ounce a hundred miles of freedom to her and the start of a new life, was the key to a new realm the landscape of which she could only imagine in a dream.

"A little after 6:00 p.m. that evening, as she waited for the dirty dishes to arrive, the door to the kitchen burst open and a constable marched in. In short order, the watch was found in Alice's small cloth bag hidden under her mattress and she was hauled off to jail. Without a soul in the world to care for her or about her, she was tried and convicted and sentenced to be indentured to a man in the colony of Virginia in the New World. Less than a week later, she was herded onto a transport ship with seventy-five other deportees and the two month journey to America started as rain fell and the wind blew across the decks like a hurricane causing vast amounts of vomit to fill the hallways and decks, for virtually no one on the premises had ever been on a sea voyage of any kind.

"Despite the inauspicious beginning to the journey, calm seas showed themselves and the journey became an endless boredom of sunrises and sunsets, the flapping of sails, the dancing of dolphins, and the ogling of the crew. It was on the HMS Constellation that Alice learned that she did not need to steal money nor work for it for her good looks was the abracadabra to the pockets of men and clearly the man on board the ship with the biggest pocket was the captain who not only carried transports to serve out their sentences in the colonies but took on cargo and brought it back to England to sell at quite a profit. This she learned from a young member of the crew who had the mistaken notion that gentle, concerned talk could ultimately land him in Alice's hammock.

"The voyage was different than you might imagine. It was, first and foremost, interminably tedious with long stretches of dead time. Alice and the others were prisoners, do not forget, but had they been royalty, things would have been little different. She would stand on deck and gaze out at the horizon, limitless in every direction, a disk of water, a wafer of blue and green with rows of white scratches rhythmic in the wind, caressed at the edges by clouds so distant they seemed part of another world. The creaking of the masts, the slap of the sails against endless ropes and lines, the thud of the crews' feet on the decks as chores were repeated over and over. Each day the food tasted a little worse, a little saltier, the water more bracken. Some prisoners hid in their cots, green with the sickness of the waves, vomit dried on their chins and blouses, sunken-eyed and forlorn. Yet, Alice managed to retain her composure, some might say dignity, and she was ever careful to maintain her fine appearance. She took every scant opportunity to make the Captain notice her and as the tedium sewed the ship in its seamless gauze, he did take note of her until finally he could think of nothing else. More than twice her age, a widower of over seven years with children older than Alice, he wooed her at first with gentle, harmless talk of the weather and his numerous crossings, of storms at sea, of whales and squid and pirates. Then he dined with her and stared into her eyes which she kept demurely down-turned for it was the instinct of her sex to never twist the rod and line too hard that the fish might wriggle free. Soon it was light kisses and an occasional caress but when it seemed she would spend the night with him and succumb to his advances, she refused saying she would not sleep with any man that was not her husband.

"By the time the ship docked in Richmond Harbor, Alice Everdene was the wife of Captain John Gibson, who immediately contacted Sir Richard Radcliff and purchased his new wife's indenture. While illegal, for Alice was sentenced to her indenture not as a settlement of debt as most of the others, but as a punishment for a felony, this accomplished keeping her freedom a secret and within a week Captain and Mrs. Gibson were bound for England on the Constellation with a hold full of American products in high demand in England and the Continent.

"Within a few months of her return to England, Alice was well-settled in her husband's estate in Bristol and she was heavy with child. While Alice ran the house as best as she could having perhaps a little too much empathy for servants, having been one at the bottom herself, she taught herself to read and write passably in an effort to understand the financial condition of her new status as the wife of a wealthy man. She gave birth to twin daughters a few months after her nineteenth birthday and the little girls were named Elizabeth after Alice's deceased mother and Morgana after her grandmother. The children were an odd mixture of Alice's peasant pretty features and the Captain's thick-necked, short-statured maritime stock. Alice believed that the children would amount to nothing because Alice's view of the world was based, as all our views are, on her experience and her experience indicated, in fact proved, that physical beauty was almost as important as familial wealth if one was to rise above it all. She was resolute in producing no more children with Captain Gibson but her hopes of an extended and wealthy family required more offspring, especially a male heir. Her expectations, however, met with some obstacles and it was no fool who coined the phrase, "Life is what transpires when plans are made." Unable to successfully prevent the Captain's amorous overtures, Alice was impregnated a second time and when she was twenty-one years old gave birth to another set of twin daughters, one she named Helen after Helen of Troy whose face launched a thousand ships. It was Alice's hope that the Captain would be on one of those ships and that by naming her daughter after the most beautiful woman in the history of the western world, the name would produce the beauty Alice knew was a requisite to success. The other, she named Jeanette after the prettiest noblewoman in the town. But wishes are not designed to be realities and Helen and Jeanette were even plainer and thicker than Elizabeth and Morgana.

"It is only a matter of time until an idle mind, a peasant morality and a human pride would lead Alice to use herself for an experiment in selective breeding which, after all, the nobility had practiced for years as a matter of course producing morons, dwarfs, hemophiliacs and other biological grotesqueries which managed to rule many of the nations of this planet and still do to this day. When Nostradamus predicted that the 'New City' would be ruled by the 'village idiot,' it was less a prognostication than an astute observation.

"Alice knew first-hand that timing was everything—her arrest and deportation was as good an example of propitious timing as anything—and she knew that every spring the Captain would make his voyage to the colonies giving her six months to see her experiment to its fruition. She simply needed to find the right stock and while many might conclude correctly that women are ever on the search for handsome specimens, Alice was less interested in her own gratification than in producing a worthy heir. She had learned that sex had limited benefits and that intimacy, the elusive sprite that most women seek to capture in the yearning nets of their hearts, was, by her way of looking at things, over-valued. In short, it was neither sensuality nor connective affection she sought, but an obsessive drive to perpetuate the mini-dynasty of Alice Everdene as if to show the world something that even eluded her.

"The Captain, after a time, came to confide in his young wife for he recognized in her a native intelligence and, as he put it, a fashion for thinking in curves, evading problems instead of colliding with them. His fortune increased incrementally under her counsel, especially when she pointed out that contraband earned as much as ten times what standard cargo could yield. Captain Gibson was one of the first to engage in the smuggling of African slaves and he earned millions from it over the course of only five years, all of it carefully deposited in continental bank accounts under his wife's name for the penalty for being caught was hanging and the confiscation of the filthy lucre derived from the inhuman practice, the money going to the King, whose family had been restored to power after the long awaited death of Cromwell.

"Captain Gibson's many transactions caused him to retain the services of a solicitor, a young man who studied at Cambridge and had offices at the Inns of Court, who, by no coincidence, counted among his clients several prominent members of Parliament. His name was Sir Stephen Sheppard, knighted personally by Charles II for his devotion to the re-establishment of the House of Lords after Cromwell's disastrous rule.

"Alice met Sir Stephen at a social function and took note of his handsome face and easy demeanor which belied an eye ever on the search for methods to ascend the ladder of power regardless of whose hand might be holding a rung upon which he placed his expensively-shod foot. Ordinarily, the last thought on Sir Stephen's mind would be seducing a client's wife but Alice was no ordinary bourgeois spouse. Wealth treated her well and while in the dire straights of street living and its insidious ill effects on health and appearance when many a fair flower wilted and dried in the sterile winds of want, that same flower placed in an imported faience pot, the roots planted in the loam of cash and watered from the sprinkler of privilege became a rare and wonderful specimen indeed. Such was Alice and she made it surreptitiously and demurely evident that she required more of Sir Stephen than an analysis of a particular land transaction.

"It was a simple matter for the parties to arrange a tryst while the Captain was at sea, both literally and figuratively, and to continue trysting for the summer months, Sir Stephen thinking he was lord of the bedchamber but Alice seeking only adequate repetitive doses of his seed. When she finally confirmed that he had put her in 'the family way,' as her peasant mother use to call it, she abruptly broke off the meetings which had already drawn more attention from the sideways glances of the servants than she cared to admit.

"The Captain was somewhere off the coast of West Africa with a hold full of black Africans, 625 to be exact, in a state of fear, panic and abject misery, when His Royal Highness's Navy in the form of a frigate outfitted to sink unlicensed slavers found the Constellation and gave chase into the South Atlantic. Captain Gibson knew the penalty and also knew that his prayers to be delivered from the just punishment of the law would likely go unanswered. To lighten the load and make his ship faster than the wind with the hope of outrunning the frigate and the fate that awaited him, Captain Gibson ordered the crew to throw the hapless Africans overboard, at first in lifeboats with the hope the frigate would stop to pick them up.

It did not. It was then that he ordered the crew to toss the rest of the human cargo into the sea directly. The first mate realizing such an order if obeyed would lead to his and the crew's execution, shot Captain Gibson through the back of the head, killing him dead before he even hit the slimy deck. And, as it turns out in the irony of novels and real life, at that very moment, give or take a few minutes, a fine son was born to Alice Gibson.

"The first mate ordered the crew to spill the wind from the sails and within twenty minutes the Navy frigate's sailors boarded the Constellation, arrested the crew, re-manned it with Royal seamen and sailed it back to the mouth of the Congo River, picking up a few of the survivors stranded in the lifeboats. The ones in the water could not be found. The Africans were dropped off on the coast and had to find their way back to their tribal lands, some as much as over a hundred miles distant. The truth is that as soon as the frigate departed, another slaver arrived and rounded up the luckless cargo, most of it anyway, and the Africans, so close to a return to freedom, soon found themselves on the block in the Port of Richmond, Virginia.

"One might assume that Captain Gibson had a turn of very bad luck to be thus intercepted on the high seas. But luck had nothing to do with it unless one considers the arrival of an anonymous note to the Admiralty detailing the itinerary and cargo of the Constellation just in time for the launching of an intercepting frigate. Better than divine intervention, Alice had planned well. She needed neither prayers, angels nor miracles, to find herself the sole inheritor of a vast fortune with an appropriate heir that she could raise to see the world for what it was, a prize fruit waiting to be picked and eaten.

"In the years that followed, Alice's fortunes increased and she had the pleasure of seeing her four daughters married off to highly successful business people on the continent. Elizabeth, her eldest, was married to Bernard Fontenot, an eminent vineyard owner in France. Morgana and Jeanette traveled to Italy and both met their future husbands there. Morgana met a man, who unfortunately deserted her after getting her pregnant and she put the little tyke in the orphanage of St. Ubaldo, never seeing him again. She married a Polish count on holiday in Rome and had five more children by him. Jeanette fared better, marrying a wealthy man named Pietro Corona. They lived many happy years together, having three good sons. Helen married a widely reputed importer in Germany by the name of Alois Berenson.

"Thus, the four plain girls were married off to husbands who could take care of them and Alice focused on her son, George. She met a nice, only slightly impoverished nobleman at one of the few soirées she made it a continuing practice to attend in London. He needed some of her vast funds and she needed his title for her son and by the time young George Gibson was seventeen, he was heir to the title of Lord Montrose, Baronette of Wessex, soon to be Duke of Cornwall, second cousin to the future King George and every inch his mother's son. Daria Berenson, Isabelle Fontenot, Marco Fontana, Julian Corona and Il Dottore, Duke Edmond Montrose, could all trace their lineage back to Alice Everdene."

Eve smiled inwardly, though tears had streaked her gentle face, as she took Adam's hand and led him out of Eden into the East.